Seer

Julia Guroff

Contents

Chapter 1
New Experiment

October 2001

Jonathan's

I am Jonathan's. Jonathan, my beloved, my shining boy, my master. I am privileged to be the Guardian of this extraordinary human. Never in all my lives of Guarding have I been a part of such an intensely burning soul. Jonathan, although still only a child, is developing a might which astonishes. The other humans do not suspect his increasing potency. He has the power to persuade adults that he is delightful, obedient, loving. Much of the time, this is true. Yet he also harbors a delicious malice which he unleashes when he knows he will not be detected. His little tricks are targeted to inflict harm on children and creatures smaller than him, beings helpless against his strength. He delights in the ability to control those around him, adults and children alike. And I delight in the flaming brightness of his soul, the soul I am here to Guard, as his brilliance grows through each of his actions, whether good or bad. I support him in all he does. I am his.

I eagerly await his exploits today, on a day he will play with the neighbor children. How will his soul expand today? I anticipate his every move, support his every whim, revel in his every emotion. He is mine.

Stefanie

"Honey, can we talk?"

Brad looks up from kicking his shoes off in the entryway, having just dropped Jonathan off at his friend Gabe's house. Jonathan has been so excited the past couple of weekends to have Gabe living there at his Dad's house again, rather than over at his Mom's. Ever since September 11, Brenda and Ron seem to have called off their separation, and are living together again, usually at her house, but on weekends lately they've been over here. It's been really nice for our son to have his friend back in the neighborhood.

"Sure, Babe, what's up?" Brad comes into the kitchen and sits with me at the table. He grabs an apple out of the bowl, but as he's about to take a bite he takes a look at me, and hesitates. "Is something wrong?" He puts the apple down.

I nervously bite my lip before responding.

"Are you all right, Stef? I thought you were seeming like you didn't feel well earlier. Are you getting sick maybe?"

"Um, no, not exactly."

"What then?" He's worried now, and he leans over and takes my hand. His chocolate brown eyes peer at me, full of love and concern.

I wasn't planning to blurt it out, but I haven't worked out a good way to say it, so here it comes. "I'm pregnant."

His face transforms, his eyes and mouth opening wide. Quickly his shocked expression becomes joyous. "Really? Oh, wow! Oh my God! That's great!" He leans in and kisses me enthusiastically, then breaks off after a second. He peers down at me and tilts his head. "I mean, it's great, right? I think it is, but I thought we weren't going to...."

I have to laugh a little, the poor guy seems like he isn't sure whether he is supposed to be happy or not. I was afraid he wouldn't be, since this wasn't planned. I didn't want a repeat of the unplanned pregnancy situation we had with Jonathan eight years ago. But of course, things are really different now. I was in high school then. Now I'm almost done with college, we're married and settled and happy. This isn't bad news, just not expected.

"Yeah, we weren't. I didn't plan to have any more, or at least not until after I was finished with school. But I think this happened because I skipped my pills a couple of times last month. I just forgot to take them for a few days after

September 11, when everything was so crazy and we were all so distracted. It's my fault, I couldn't believe that I forgot, but I figured a couple of days wouldn't matter. Apparently it did. I'm sorry."

But when I gaze into his eyes, I see only love. I shouldn't have been worried about his reaction. Good grief, why would I still feel insecure about us? He pulls me in for a hug. "Sorry? No, Stef, this is so exciting! When did you find out? Have you seen a doctor? When will it come?"

My anxiety melts away. I hadn't even let myself get excited yet. I was worried about Brad's reaction, and worried about this interfering with my plans, and worried about apparently all the wrong stuff. "I only found out a couple of days ago when I took a home test. I've scheduled the first appointment in a couple of weeks. As far as I can figure, I think it'll come right around the end of the school year."

He sits back up in his chair, but he doesn't let go of my hand. "So, what do you think will happen with school?"

"Well, this is supposed to be my last year. I'm hoping to carry on as I planned, and still graduate next May if everything works out. I'd hate to change my plans. After that I guess we'll have to play it by ear."

He smiles and wraps me up in his arms again. "Another baby! Oh man, I wonder what Jonathan will say?"

I laugh. "Who knows? He's such a character. We have to wait to tell him at least until after I see the doctor, and let a couple of months go by to make sure everything is fine. K?"

"Mmmm, K," he murmurs into my hair.

I relax against him. "I love you."

Brad's

My beloved's joy is magnified in me. When he and Stefanie had their first child, he was young and scared and felt little enjoyment in the event. He quickly grew to love his son, but during the pregnancy and birth he was filled with anxiety. I can see this time will be different. A man now, supporting his family, content with his roles as father and husband. He thrills to learn of this new development, and I revel in the inevitable growth in his soul.

"Yes, my darling, your love for your wife grows even deeper as you celebrate her wonderful news. Another child for your growing family, another person to know you and love you. We will delight in the new baby together, my dearest."

Gabe

I'm on my bike, rolling it back and forth while I wait out in front of Jonathan's house. I hear him holler to his parents, "Gabe and me are riding our bikes to the park!" He slams the front door, jumps on his bike and comes speeding down the driveway. He gets out in front of me with a whoop, and I follow him down the street, zooming the couple of blocks to the park where we like to ride.

Heading towards the playground, I watch as Jonathan pedals past way too close to a couple of toddlers walking over to the slide. "Dude!" I laugh at him. Jonathan loves to take chances, it's part of what makes him so fun to hang around with. He's younger than me, but you'd never know it. He's always pushing us to try new things, even stunts that are kinda hair-raising. I'd never do half the stuff we get into without him leading the way.

We head over to the cement ramps and start speeding up and down the little hills. There's some skateboarders there too, trying to use the same skate park, but Jonathan and I don't care. We were here first.

Natalie

"Mom, when is Timothy getting here?"

Mom glances up from the newspaper and checks her watch. "It's only 8:30 Honey, Timothy's Mom said she'd bring him over after breakfast. They should be here pretty soon."

I slouch further down on the couch. Gabe already left to ride bikes with Jonathan, so it's just me and Angel until my best friend gets here. I look over at Angel, who is smiling at me like always. I'm careful not to be too obvious when I look at him, so my parents don't notice. I still don't want everyone to know I can see my guardian. Nobody else can see theirs, and I don't want everyone to think I'm crazy.

I ask Angel in my head if Timothy is getting here yet. *"Not yet darling, I still can't hear him. He needs to be closer before I can detect his presence."*

Hmm. I wonder how close he needs to be? Hey! Maybe I can conduct a scientific experiment! Timothy would be excited if I have a new experiment to tell him about. "Angel," I think to him, "I want to figure out how close he has to be for you to hear him. Can we do this?"

"Certainly, my dear. His home is about five miles from here. I will listen carefully, and tell you as soon as he is close enough for me to hear."

Great! Now I'm not bored any more. I want to be able to provide some scientific data to my friend when he arrives. Well, Timothy always makes notes for his experiments. I should totally do that!

"Okay Mom," I tell her as I get off the couch and head up to my room, "I'll wait for him upstairs." I give her a little hug as I pass by.

She smooches my head. "All right, Sweetie."

I run up the stairs and grab my notebook out of my backpack. I already put everything away last night since I finished up all my second grade weekend homework as soon as we got home. I get a pencil and start writing: "Experiment: how close can Angel hear someone." I think about what else I should write, and put down the date and time. Then I add that five miles away is too far.

Angel watches me take these notes and nods at me with a smile.

"Are you listening hard, Angel?" I whisper to him. I don't want my parents to hear me talking to him, but I like to talk out loud when we're alone. So I always make sure to talk very quietly if nobody else is in the room with us.

"Of course, my dear."

I can't think of anything else to write, so I sit and stare at Angel with my pencil touching the next line of the notebook. I can tell he is listening, because he isn't looking straight at me like he usually does.

After a couple of minutes he smiles. *"All right, my darling, I can hear Timothy's Guardian. He must be close. But I cannot detect Timothy's presence yet."*

"Really?" I ask him. "You can hear Guardian before you can hear Timothy?" That's interesting, so I write it down in my notebook. "Can you tell how far away they are yet?"

"Not yet. When they get close enough, I will be able to hear Timothy's mother also, then I can determine the location of their car. One moment...."

I wait, tapping the pencil on the page.

Angel smiles. "*All right, my dear, I can hear Timothy and his mother now. Their car is about two miles away.*"

"How can you tell?"

"*I can simply watch for the street signs which Timothy's mother sees along the way as she drives the car.*"

"All right, what did the street sign say right when you first could hear them?"

"*They were near the corner of Mast Boulevard and Magnolia Avenue.*" He watches me write down this information. He smiles when I pause for a second. "*Boulevard is spelled B-O-U-L-E-V-A-R-D.*"

"Thanks." I finish writing everything down so Timothy can check it when he arrives. It should just be a couple of minutes now!

Chapter 2

Hi

Brenda

There's a knock on the door. I know it's Laura, and it feels a little weird for her to be knocking. At home, she always simply comes in, like I've told her to. But this still feels like Ron's house, not really mine, and it would feel even stranger to both of us for her to just barge right in.

Before I even get the chance to get up to go answer the door, I hear Natalie already running lightly down the stairs. So by the time I get over there, she and Timothy are on their way back up to her room.

I grin wryly at Laura left standing there on the porch. "Come on in!"

Ron comes in from the garage as we are sitting down on the couch. "Hey, Laura," he says, "how are you?"

"Good."

"How's Mike doing? Any word on his deployment?"

"Not yet. I don't know if it's going to be extended because of the September 11 attacks."

Ron nods. "Do you need me to do anything else around the house for you?" He heads into the kitchen and pours himself a glass of water.

Laura smiles. "Thanks, Ron. That's really nice. We're good for now."

One of the things I have learned again to really love about Ron is how helpful he is, not only to me, but to our friends. Even while we were still separated, he had started offering to help Laura out with any heavy lifting or handyman stuff she needed if Mike was out of town with the Navy. I peek up and meet his blue eyes meaningfully, filling my expression with how much I love him. I can see he gets my message, and he smiles and looks down.

Laura is watching this exchange, and she laughs. "Man, you guys are too cute. You're like a couple of newlyweds!"

We both chuckle. "I guess so," Ron says, coming over and giving my shoulder a squeeze. "Again."

Natalie's

My beloved is thrilled to explain the nature of her experiment to her friend. Timothy listens with interest, then meticulously studies the notes she had taken in her notebook.

"This is a great experiment, Natalie," he enthuses. "I never thought about how close Angel would have to be." She glows under his praise.

He pauses, thinking of follow-up questions. Natalie sits quietly, watching him as he gathers his thoughts. She has a profound respect for his intellect, and deeply enjoys participating with him as he derives experiments to explore their world. I also savor this process.

"Angel," Timothy addresses me, still perusing the notebook, "it says you could hear Guardian first. Why is that?"

Timothy's Guardian is as interested in this topic as are the children and myself. Since I informed Timothy of the existence of his own Guardian nearly two months ago, they have developed a unique relationship. Timothy, of course, cannot detect his own Guardian. Only my little Seer has the capability. However, since Timothy is aware of the presence of his Guardian, he has incorporated that fact into his world view. He often transmits thoughts to his Guardian, and while we are all together he can communicate directly, using Natalie and I as a conduit. In turn, Guardian, named by Timothy himself, has begun evolving, becoming more interactive with the world, not just with Timothy alone. It has been fascinating to observe. It is reminiscent of the development I have experienced since Natalie's birth.

"Guardians are able to detect the presence of one another more easily because we are more similar to each other than we are to humans. We are made of the same matter, are even essentially the same being."

Natalie relays this to Timothy, but she is confused by my statement. "What do you mean you are the same being?"

"It is difficult to explain, my darling, I am sorry. I will try again. Each human has a Guardian during their lifetime, but between lifetimes we merge into a greater consciousness. We are one."

Natalie's brow wrinkles as she repeats my words to Timothy. "I still don't get it."

Timothy, though, as he often does, seems to comprehend the complexities with greater ease. He contemplates this for a time, then adds, "I guess you are all one big guardian, then you break up into parts for your humans?"

Timothy's Guardian glows approvingly at the insightful child.

"Yes, Timothy, you have essentially described the process. Therefore, while we are Guarding a human, we are more easily able to detect each other's presence when physically distant, than we can sense the other humans who are being Guarded."

After Natalie repeats my confirmation, Timothy is ready with a new set of questions. "When you are all together, are you still yourself? Like, can you remember who you are?"

"Yes, between lifetimes we are merged together, yet retain the individual memories we gained while Guarding our humans. We hold the souls of those we Guarded, forever."

The children hear the words, and understand to some extent, but they are both very young to be considering the metaphysical. At their age, they are more comfortable with tangible topics.

"Well," Timothy says, "I'd like to figure out more about whether you and Guardian can talk to each other even when me and Natalie aren't together."

"Very well," I agree, waiting to see what experiment the clever boy will conduct next.

Timothy's

It astonishes and delights me to be the topic of my dearest child's thoughts, and especially to be the subject of his experimentation. The direction to-day has taken is most unexpected. Timothy wishes to learn more about the communication I have with Natalie's Guardian. However, he is assuming that Guardians actively communicate with each other. This is not necessarily correct. There is no true need for us to attempt genuine communication, because we are constantly aware of each other's presence and thoughts while we are in proximity to each other. I have never "talked" to another Guardian. Why would we bother to address each other directly, when we already know everything the other knows?

Timothy, however, wishes for this to change.

"Okay, Angel," he addresses Natalie's Guardian once again, "how do you talk to Guardian?"

The Guardian considers how to answer. Timothy has a knack for posing questions which have no ready explanation, or at least no answer that would be comprehensible to humans. "*We do not 'talk' as such. Rather, Guardians who are in proximity to each other are constantly aware of each other's presence and thoughts.*" I am pleased to hear the Guardian using my words, as has been occurring quite often since my presence was made known to my beloved.

"So, you don't have real conversations? You don't ever talk to each other, like Natalie and I talk to each other?"

"*No, there would be no need for such a conversation in order to understand the other's thoughts.*"

"What about when you aren't together? You could hear Guardian before you could hear me, right? If you try to actually talk to each other, do you think you could hear each other while you are even farther apart?"

The Guardian's face, formed to appear very tangible for Natalie's benefit, takes on an expression which on a human would reflect wonder or curiosity. I have frequently observed the Guardian, called Angel by the Seer, using physical manifestation as one of the means of communicating with the child. As humans use facial expressions and gestures to convey meaning, Angel does the same for her benefit.

She sees this expression and realizes this is a new thought for Angel. She takes a new meaning from the direction the conversation has taken. "Wait, Angel, you mean you have never talked to Guardian? Like never even said Hi to him?"

Angel is amused by the direction her questions are leading. "*No, darling, I must confess I never have.*"

"Well," she continues, "I think that seems a little rude, doesn't it? I mean, Timothy is my best friend. Shouldn't Guardian be your friend too? You could at least say Hi." She has taken offense on my behalf. I begin to understand how Angel has developed the ability to find humor in the situations which arise due to direct communication with his Seer. I feel a glimmer of amusement myself.

Angel laughs. *"You are correct, of course, my dear. I will remedy the situation immediately."* The Guardian's eyes move to light upon me, and with an expression which on a human would be a wry grin, I hear, *"Hello, Guardian, I am Angel. Pleased to make your acquaintance."*

I don't have a tangibly formed physical presence, having never felt the need to create an image for Timothy. Many Guardians will do so, even knowing they will never be seen, in order to more closely relate to their Guarded. However, Timothy has such a unique mind, it didn't seem important to me to create any particular manifestation. So I know when Angel views me, I am nothing more than a dusting of matter, neither dark nor light, and certainly not formed into any shape. However, the angel's face chuckles when my astonishment is clearly reflected in my thoughts. To hear this greeting, from another of my kind, formatted as though we were two humans, is both wondrous and unprecedented, and slightly... silly. Feeling almost awkward, in itself a unique sensation in my experience, I respond. *"Hello, Angel, thank you for your greeting."*

The Seer watches our exchange. She, of course, can only see and hear her own Guardian. She asks Angel, "Well? What did he say?"

Angel smiles, and tells her, *"Timothy's Guardian said, 'Hello, Angel, thank you for your greeting.'"*

She shrugs, satisfied that at least her conception of the necessary pleasantries have been exchanged. She repeats the greetings to her friend.

In the meantime, Timothy has watched this development with some bemusement. Other than his deep connection to the Seer, social relationships are foreign to him. The idea that Guardians should be polite to one another had never crossed his mind. But, if it pleases Natalie, he fully supports the concept. He looks at Natalie, to confirm that her requirements for our behavior have been fulfilled. "Okay?" he asks her.

She rolls her eyes. "I don't want them to be rude to each other. Just because you know what someone else is thinking, doesn't mean you shouldn't be polite."

He is baffled at her reasoning, but finds a benefit in her methods. "Well," he says, "I'm glad they will actually talk to each other, because I think this can help our experiment."

She is immediately intrigued. As are both Angel and I. "How?" she asks.

"Well, I guess they can hear each other a little more than two miles away. Right, Angel?"

The Guardian confirms this, and Natalie relays the message.

Timothy goes on. "I wonder if they are doing more than only sensing each other's presence, the distance could be longer. Like, if they are actually trying to be heard." He screws up his face in concentration. "Angel, could you guys try yelling? So you can hear each other further away?"

Angel dissolves in laughter. It is fascinating to watch how the physical manifestation of the Seer's Guardian has almost taken on a life of its own. The reactions seem very human. I start wondering for the first time since Timothy was born whether it would be of some benefit to him, to our relationship, for me to form a physical appearance. For Angel, it does seem to contribute to his communication with his Seer. Could it do the same for my beloved?

Angel gains control over his appearance, and attempts to answer the question of my Guarded. "*I am certainly eager to try, Timothy. This was the first time I have ever directly spoken to another Guardian, so I don't know exactly how to 'yell', but I can make the attempt.*"

Timothy nods. "Natalie, can I use your pencil?" She hands it to him, and he starts annotating her notebook, adding his own plans to the experiment she had begun. "I guess we can't really try until I go home, though, right?"

"*Most likely,*" Angel replies. "*Once you and Guardian have departed, I can monitor the distance at which I stop hearing each of you.*"

After Natalie relays this information, Timothy instructs us in the next phase of the experiment. "Okay. Our hypothesis is that Angel and Guardian might be able to talk to each other further away than usual if they yell. Here's what we are going to do. Natalie, you are going to have to write down everything Angel tells you, because I won't be here any more. Guardian, I want you to help too, if that's all right?"

He looks at Natalie, who turns to Angel for confirmation. And, rather than simply presuming to speak for me as usual, knowing my thoughts, Angel looks directly at me and awaits my response.

I feel very touched by this inclusion, this invitation to be an actual participant in the events. "*Of course, my dearest child, I will be delighted to help in any way possible.*"

Angel transmits my words exactly, as I attempt to control my emotional response to the heady sense of belonging and involvement I am experiencing.

"Thank you," Timothy tells me. "Here's what I want you to do, Guardian. Now that you know you can actually talk to Angel, I want you to keep doing it as soon as we leave. Like, as loud as you can, and keep yelling at him all the way home. Then Angel, you tell Natalie exactly what you are hearing, and whether you stop being able to hear Guardian as we get further away. Natalie, you write everything down." He pauses to consider whether he has forgotten anything. "All right? Everybody ready?"

Natalie giggles. "Yes, Timmy, we're all ready. But you know we won't be doing it until a lot later, right? My Mom said you're going to stay here all day!"

Timothy feels slightly abashed. He was so eager to proceed with the experiment, he had forgotten about the plans for the day. "Oh, yeah, right. Okay."

The empathic Seer senses Timothy's discomposure, and tries to set him at ease. "Want to go outside and play?"

And suddenly they are back to being human children, only seven years of age, playing in the yard. Not research scientists delving into the deepest secrets of reality. The juxtaposition is breathtaking. As is my emotional response to everything which has passed. I feel myself changing, developing in ways I had never imagined. And I am not even the Guardian of a Seer, merely of a Seer's friend.

Chapter 3

Yelling

Jonathan

We've been at the park for a while, riding our bikes, then dropping them to the sidewalk and swinging on the swings. It's fun to swing as high as we can, and watch the little kids steer clear of us so they don't get kicked. Not that I don't try.

I'm getting hungry. "Hey Gabe, let's go get some lunch!" I leap off the swing at the highest point and fly through the air before crashing down on the sand, rolling over a few times before stopping. I lay there laughing, and look up to see Gabe slowing his swing down to step off of it safely. "Chicken!" I laugh at him.

He smiles and shrugs, then comes over and gives me his hand to help me up. "Thanks," I say, brushing all the sand off of my clothes. He grins and reaches over to my head and rubs my hair really fast, and a bunch more sand comes out of there. We both are laughing hard as we get back on our bikes.

I stop off at home to drop my bike on the porch, and poke my head in the front door. I yell, "I'm going to Gabe's house for lunch, okay?" I hear my Dad say okay, and I'm outta there before I hear anything else.

We walk up to Gabe's, with him walking alongside his bike holding the handlebars so he doesn't get too far ahead of me. When we get inside, his Dad says, "Oh, there you are! I was about to go searching for you guys."

Gabe says, "We were at the park, but we came home because we're hungry. When's lunch?"

"Right now," his Dad tells us, "Out in the backyard."

I look out the window, and see Gabe's Mom and sister, and that dumb special ed kid she always hangs around with at school. Ew! He's here too? They're sitting down on the chairs out there, and there are some sandwiches and chips on a table. Well, fine, food is food, right?

Gabe and I head out with his Dad, and grab some sandwiches. I don't want to sit with Natalie and her dumb friend, so we go over to the other side of the yard and eat on the wall at the back. The little kids are paying no attention to us at all, just talking and talking, very quietly, with their heads close together.

After all the food is gone, Gabe's parents take all the plates and stuff back inside. Gabe picks up a baseball and says "Heads up!" and throws it my way. I catch it, and we fling it back and forth a few times. Natalie and Timothy are still sitting there talking. So boring. Why are they ignoring me?

"Hey Natalie, want to play catch?" I call out to her.

She looks up from her conversation with her dumb friend. "No, thank you, Jonathan," she says in an annoyingly polite way. Pfsh.

"What about you, Timothy? Come on, you should do some guy stuff with us, not sit around talking with a girl!"

Timothy stares straight ahead. He is such a weirdo. I'm tossing the ball back and forth between my hands, and just as he is starting to turn his head back over to Natalie I throw it at him. "Catch!" I yell.

Of course he doesn't even try to catch it. What a loser. It actually bounces off his arm as he is trying to duck, with his hands over his head like he's afraid of a baseball. I don't really see what he does next, because Gabe comes over and punches me in the arm, laughing. "Come on, Jonathan, leave them alone. They're only little kids." He grabs the ball where it is rolling away from where it bounced off Timothy and throws it back to me. Fine, I guess we can ignore them too.

But we don't need to. They're already heading back into the house. Losers.

Timothy

Jonathan makes me so mad. Every time we are together he does something mean to me. Last year he made me so mad at school that I got in trouble for fighting him and had to get special ed testing. I guess it turned out okay, though, because now the teachers and people at the school make sure I'm doing all right, and I can go sit in the office to calm down if I need to. As long as Natalie is with me I'm usually able to ignore him.

I think to Guardian while we are going back up the stairs to her room, "Guardian, what can I do about Jonathan being so mean all the time?" I know I'll have my answer after we close the door.

Natalie turns around and looks at me after she comes in. I can tell she is sorry that her brother's friend hurt me again. "Are you okay? Does your arm hurt?"

I rub my arm where the ball hit me. "Not very much. I'm just mad Jonathan gets away with stuff like that all the time."

She looks to the side and I know she's listening to Angel. "Angel says Guardian wishes he could help you more. He says Guardian is telling you that you are smarter and better than Jonathan, and you should try to avoid him. He says Jonathan isn't a nice boy."

"Well, duh," I say grumpily, "we already know that."

I sit down on the bed and cross my arms, then see the notebook where we left it. I pick it up and start checking the experiment notes. I'm thinking about the Guardians talking to each other.

"Angel, now that you guys can talk to each other, do you think you could talk to Jonathan's guardian and ask him to try to make Jonathan nicer?"

I wait for Natalie to answer. After a minute she says, "Angel says he's already told us, guardians don't try to make their humans do stuff. They are happy when their humans are happy, even if the human is doing something bad."

"But," I say, "I don't think it's always true that guardians don't try to make their humans do stuff. Guardian told me to avoid Jonathan, right? I know Angel has told you to do stuff before too. Just because they don't usually do it, doesn't mean they can't. They don't usually talk to each other, and we know from today that they can."

Natalie waits for a couple of minutes, listening. "Angel says you are very perceptive, like always. He says this is a new idea, and he and Guardian will consider if there is something they can do."

"All right. I guess that's good for now."

Natalie's

Guardian and I have both observed for years as Jonathan has tormented Timothy. Both Timothy and Natalie have attempted to enlist the assistance of their parents and even their teachers in curtailing Jonathan's behavior. But their efforts have met with no success, and even with some mild disapproval.

Jonathan is uniquely gifted in his ability to manipulate those around him. He continues to project a deceptive impression of goodness to the adults in his life. They are thoroughly convinced that he is a lively, sweet, energetic, friendly boy. He is utterly blameless in their eyes, and this is very much by design. He has engineered this situation, in which he can engage in his baser instincts, while avoiding detection by any figure of authority.

As a result, when Timothy and Natalie inform their parents or teachers that Jonathan has misbehaved, they are not believed, or at least they are assumed to be exaggerating. Also, Timothy's autism diagnosis provides the adults a simple explanation. They are not inclined to believe a boy as delightful as Jonathan committed some sort of mischief. Rather, it is much easier to think that Timothy's lack of social skills makes him take offense too easily at what is probably normal behavior on Jonathan's part. After all, the adults in his life have all witnessed him become overwhelmed in situations which most children could accept without difficulty. There have even been some mild reprimands of the children that tattling is not an attractive trait.

Therefore, Natalie and Timothy have stopped trying to get help. It is a sad failing on the part of the adults, but understandable considering Jonathan's deceptive talent. He has them all fooled.

It is troubling to watch the dynamic continue to unfold. Jonathan victimizes Timothy, Natalie does her best to insulate her friend, and Jonathan emerges triumphant. His soul glows with each encounter, growing stronger, and delighting his Guardian.

Timothy's request that we talk to Jonathan's Guardian about this is much more difficult than he realizes. The Guardian knows, of course, the ramifications of the actions of his beloved. When the children are in proximity, the thoughts of all humans and Guardians nearby are freely available to each of us. Jonathan's Guardian witnessed our conversation with Timothy, and heard the request that we intervene to correct Jonathan's behavior. And his Guardian derisively dismissed it as a ridiculous notion, knowing there is nothing we could do to change the situation. The Guardian, like all of us, adores his own human. Jonathan's soul glows with an unusually robust power, increasing in strength every day. His Guardian has grown to crave the cruelties which Jonathan inflicts, because it is so gratifying to watch the consequent magnification of his soul's brilliance. Even the needs of my Seer, which most Guardians in her life have grown to prioritize nearly as much as those of their own Guarded, mean nothing to Jonathan's Guardian.

Although we are Guardians, we are nearly as helpless as Timothy to prevent the ongoing harm which he suffers at the hands of the bully. I dwell sadly on the situation, unable to derive any solution. Guardian's thoughts are along the same lines.

The afternoon passes peacefully, Timothy and Natalie having selected books from her shelf, and reading together in companionable quiet. Natalie is propped against pillows on her bed, and Timothy is sprawled on the floor, absorbed in their respective books. Guardian and I watch in silence.

After a time, the children's attention is diverted when Brenda calls from downstairs. "Natalie! Timothy! Timothy's Mom is here. Time for him to go home."

They discard their books immediately, their eyes widening, realizing the moment has come for the experiment to commence. Timothy grabs the notebook and again runs over the lines both he and Natalie have written, checking for any last minute additions which may be needed. He hands her the notebook.

"Okay, Natalie, you know what to do. Angel, listen hard. Guardian, come with me."

Natalie grasps the notebook and nods eagerly.

With the determination of a general approaching a battle, Timothy marches down the stairs. "Hi Mom, I'm ready to go!"

Laura laughs "Well, okay then. Say thank you to Natalie's parents for having you over."

"Thank you," Timothy calls, actually opening the front door himself and heading outside, single-mindedly focused on the unfolding experiment. The adults, of course, simply see it as another exhibition of Timothy's unusual personality. Little do they know the import of the situation. Both Guardian and I are excited too, to be participating in something entirely new to each of us. We will learn much today as well.

Timothy's

I am determined to execute the mission assigned to me with as much diligence as possible. Timothy asked me to maintain communication with Angel, to "yell" all the way home to ensure that I am heard. I don't know how to do this, having spent an eternity only whispering loving words to the humans I have Guarded. But I will make every effort.

When we enter the car, I address Angel directly. *"I will remain in contact with you. Once we reach a distance of approximately one mile, I will attempt to increase my volume."*

"Very well," Angel agrees. He transmits the information to Natalie, and she begins to take notes.

For the time it takes Timothy's mother to drive the first mile, I contemplate how to increase the volume of my communication. Of course, there is no actual volume. I do not create sound waves which can manifest in the environment. The communication of Guardians is not a physical occurrence. It is a thought, a feeling, a whisper. I have never before considered the mechanics of the process. I try to pinpoint the procedure: I have a constant flow of thoughts, and when I wish to whisper a message to my Guarded, there is an outflow of energy which makes this possible.

Having determined that this outflow of energy is what creates communication, I focus on that. When the car reaches some distance from the Seer's house, I push as much of the energy as I can muster into my next words to Angel.

"ANGEL. I HAVE INCREASED MY VOLUME. I WILL CONTINUE THIS COMMUNICATION FOR THE REMAINDER OF THE JOURNEY BACK TO TIMOTHY'S HOUSE."

I hear Angel's response, mingled with his uproarious laughter. *"Yes, Guardian, it is working well, your volume has increased significantly and I can hear you very clearly."*

Natalie's

I can hardly believe the success of Guardian's efforts. The amount of power transmitted through the words of Timothy's Guardian is so enormous that it practically blows me over. It is astonishing. It feels like a physical blast, something I have never experienced in my entire existence. Even Natalie notices, looking up from her notebook, when my appearance slightly fluctuates. "Are you all right?" she asks.

"Yes, my dear, it is only that Guardian is yelling so loudly, it actually impacted me, almost physically. I have never felt anything like it before."

"Is that good or bad?" she asks worriedly.

"I believe it is very good. It means Timothy's idea for 'yelling' is a great success. We will see if it increases the distance at which I can hear Guardian."

She returns to the notebook, frantically writing down what I have said.

Guardian continues "yelling" at me, and the power of the communication does not diminish with distance. Even after they go beyond the point at which I would normally lose contact, I still hear the words with complete clarity.

"I CAN NO LONGER HEAR YOU, ANGEL, WE HAVE PASSED THE DISTANCE FOR NORMAL COMMUNICATION. CAN YOU ALSO ATTEMPT TO INCREASE YOUR VOLUME SO THIS COMMUNICATION CAN CONTINUE IN BOTH DIRECTIONS?"

I quickly relay this information to Natalie, who continues taking dictation. I attempt to generate the same level of energy which Guardian had used, filling my words with all the power at my disposal.

"YES, GUARDIAN, I AM ATTEMPTING TO GENERATE MORE ENERGY TO TALK TO YOU. IS THIS EFFECTIVE?"

As Guardian affirms that my words again are audible, Natalie gapes up at me, dropping her pencil. "Holy cow, Angel, you really are screaming! I didn't know you could be so loud! Is it working?"

"It is working better than we ever could have imagined, my dear. Timothy has taught us something new today, something very important."

The communication continues, without diminishment, all the way back to Timothy's house. Guardian and I, as long as we push energy into our words, appear to be able to communicate easily over a much greater distance than we had ever before believed possible.

The implications of this fresh discovery are marvelous, enormous, stunning. There is no telling the limits of this new ability.

And this has been brought about by the imagination and intelligence of two unusual children, our beloved little Seer and her brilliant friend.

What other revelations might they lead us to?

Chapter 4

Changes

Natalie

When I wake up Sunday morning and go downstairs, the first thing I do is ask Mom when we are going home. Lately we've stayed at Dad's on the weekend, then go back to Mom's on Sunday at dinnertime. But I want to go as soon as we can, because I am dying to talk to Timothy about our experiment.

Mom is standing in the kitchen, drinking coffee. Dad is sitting at the table reading the paper. They both look at me kind of funny.

"Home?" Dad says. It seems like his feelings are a little hurt. I didn't mean to hurt anybody's feelings.

"I mean back to Mom's house. I know this is home too," I tell him, trying to make him feel better.

They look at each other. Dad shrugs. Mom says, "I don't know, honey, probably later this afternoon. Why?"

"Well," I tell her, "I really want to play with Timothy today again. Can we go sooner?"

Dad says, "Brad already called and said Jonathan is coming over to play after breakfast."

I can feel my face growing sad, and my Mom puts her mug down on the counter and comes over and gives me a side squeeze. "Well, I do need to run some errands and go shopping. Maybe I could call Timothy's Mom and ask if I can drop you off over there before lunch, then you could stay until dinner."

"Yes, please," I tell her, holding my hands together like I'm praying.

She laughs. "That okay, Ron?"

"Sure," Dad says. "Why don't you take care of your errands and go home, then Gabe and I will head over later this afternoon. I'll pick up something for dinner on the way."

"Perfect," she smiles, and goes over to give him a kiss before she picks up the phone.

Yay! I'm going to get to talk to Timothy soon! I can hardly wait. After everything Angel told me last night, I know the experiment worked great, and he and Guardian can apparently talk to each other from all the way over here whenever they want. But I wish Guardian could tell Timothy. That's why I want to go over there fast, so he doesn't have to keep waiting and wondering what happened.

Timothy

Mom tells me Natalie is going to come over here in a little while. I am very happy to hear it, so I can read the notes of the experiment.

What's funny, though, is I'm pretty sure it worked. I'm not sure exactly how I know, but I really have a feeling that it did. I think Guardian has been very happy about it, and it seems like I can almost feel his happiness. I can't understand exactly what I am feeling, but I know it is something different from normal. It's like a warm glow in my head. It reminds me of the way I feel when Natalie and I are learning something new together, or when we are excited or cheerful. But I don't ordinarily feel that way on my own. Usually when I am alone I am quiet and calm. This feels like happiness is happening to me even without me doing anything at all to cause it. That can't be normal.

I know Angel has said sometimes regular humans can sense their guardians, and I wonder if that is what's going on. I have all sorts of questions about this, and things I want to try. It would be amazing if Guardian and I could figure out a way to talk to each other. I know it wouldn't be as easy as Natalie and Angel, but I think there might be something we could do.

I think in my head, "Guardian, please tell Angel I'm pretty sure I already know the experiment worked. I can't wait to talk to you and Angel and Natalie about everything."

I listen, hoping to hear something. I don't, of course. But I keep getting a feeling of happiness nearby. It has to be Guardian.

Jonathan's

While my beloved slept last night, I contemplated the peculiar happenings yesterday between the Seer's Guardian and that of my dearest boy's nemesis, Timothy. Every Guardian in the region heard the results of their "experiment". It was astounding to hear their staggering communication. It was felt almost physically by each Guardian in the vicinity. Never to my knowledge had our kind generated that level of power, or achieved communication at such a distance. The other Guardians observed passively, mystified but not perturbed by the incident. It had nothing to do with them, or with their humans. It was simply one of many fascinating developments stemming from the presence of a Seer in our world. No other Guardians would dream of trying to replicate the experience.

I, however, feel more directly impacted by the situation, due to the focus which the Seer and her friend have had on my own beloved. They wish their Guardians to intervene, to cause my darling boy to alter his behavior. They cannot do so, naturally. They have no power over him, over me.

This new ability, however, to project such energy that their communication seems boundless, is compelling. What might it mean? Can it affect my Guarded? I must contemplate this phenomenon, consider its ramifications, imagine its uses.

Natalie

As soon as I get to Timothy's house we run straight up to his room.

"Angel says you already know it worked!" I tell him. "How can you tell?" I am very excited, and I know Timothy is too.

"I think I am feeling Guardian being happy. Angel, is that what I have been feeling?"

Angel looks so happy too. He has a big smile on his face and I think he's glowing brighter than usual. He has looked like this since last night when he first started yelling at Guardian. Angel says, *"Tell Timothy that yes, I believe he has been sensing the joy felt by Guardian about the success of our experiment."*

Timothy listens to me tell him what Angel said, then asks, "Is this what you meant when you said that sometimes regular humans can sort of hear the messages their guardians are sending?"

Angel says, *"Not exactly. I think this is something out of the ordinary. Guardian has told me that of course he has whispered words to Timothy about the success of the experiment. However, Guardian believes that even when he isn't actively trying to whisper, his delight in the situation is still being conveyed to Timothy."*

Angel waits for a minute so I can tell all of this to Timothy, then he keeps going. *"This situation is unusual on several levels. Guardian's delight is very powerful, as a result of the experiment which we performed last night. We were able to "yell" at each other by using more power in our communication than normal. This expanded the distance at which we could communicate, thus confirming the truth of the hypothesis for the experiment."*

Timothy is fascinated. "Can I have the notebook?" I give it to him with a pencil since I know he'll want to write his own notes. I wait while he reads everything I wrote last night. "Okay," he says, "I believe we can say the experiment was a success. We proved that Angel and Guardian can talk to each other further away than normal by yelling at each other."

Angel nods, listening closely to Timothy.

Timothy continues, "But I think even more than that happened. Guardian's feelings are strong enough for me to feel now. I've never felt that before. I think maybe it's because of the extra power they used to yell, right Angel?"

Angel says, *"Yes, Timothy, I believe you are correct. It seems that your experiment has uncovered additional information which we did not anticipate. We have done more than increase the distance at which we can communicate. In order to "yell", we both used a far greater amount of energy than normal. The use of the extra energy generated a power which had an intense impact on us. This seems to have enhanced not only our communication, but other aspects of our beings. Guardian's elation is so powerful today that Timothy can actually feel it. This is very unusual for a Guardian. And I, myself, feel somehow enhanced by the experience."*

He pauses a couple of times during this so I can tell Timothy the words. I think Angel wants to make sure I repeat it all the right way, because he thinks this is all very important for Timothy to understand. After I finish telling

Timothy everything Angel said, I add, "I actually do think Angel seems different since the experiment. It's, like, he's brighter or something."

"What do you mean?" Timothy asks.

"I don't know how to explain it," I say, looking at Angel to see if I can figure out what is different. "He looks like he is glowing brighter, and is maybe, I don't know, more kind of solid?"

"Solid?" Timothy asks. He is very interested in this. "Can you touch him now?"

I'm suddenly very excited by that thrilling idea, but when I reach my hand out to touch Angel, of course I can't. "No," I tell him sadly, "it's the same as always. I can't touch him." Angel feels sad too. And now, although I can always tell how Angel is feeling, it feels stronger.

"Huh," I say. "I think I can feel Angel's feelings more now too. He's sad that I can't touch him."

Timothy taps the pencil on his mouth, thinking hard, then writes everything down in the notebook. While he's doing that, I can tell Angel is listening to Guardian.

"Timothy, Guardian wants you to know that it is your intelligence which has led us to this new and profound revelation. He believes, as do I, that something has changed for all of us. Guardian and I have actually been altered by this discovery. It is very rare for a Guardian to experience fundamental change, and this is more monumental than you could possibly know. However, Guardian wishes to thank you for this development. I do as well. You have the profound gratitude of each of us, for leading the way to these new discoveries."

Angel looks like he is about to cry as he tells me this, not from being sad, but from being emotional about the changes he and Guardian are experiencing. I feel the emotions flowing over me, through me.

When I finish telling Timothy all of this, he seems emotional too. "I'm glad we are all figuring this out together," he says. I can't resist leaning over and giving him a hug, because I feel so close to him. He doesn't normally like to be touched, but he likes it today, and he even hugs me back for a second. All of us are filled with love for each other, and excitement at everything we are learning.

I add, "I didn't realize until now how important our experiment was, Timothy. We were only trying to figure out how far guardians can talk to each other, but it looks like we learned a lot more. I didn't have any idea that our experiment could actually change Angel and Guardian."

Timothy's

The Seer and my beloved are thrilled with the success of their experiment, and intrigued by the knowledge that it has wrought changes in their Guardians. However, they cannot appreciate the magnitude of this stupendous development. This goes beyond the changes which Angel has undergone by Guarding a Seer, and far beyond my own alterations as Timothy has grown to understand my existence.

I am different. Tangibly, irrevocably different. I have never felt such emotions in all my lifetimes of Guarding. I have never felt such a connection to the world. And I have never before felt so attached to my Guarded. Yes, we share a soul, but this is something more.

Somehow, the power which Angel and I called upon by pushing energy into our words last night filled us each with an unprecedented brilliance. It is as though the matter of which we are composed has increased in quantity or density. Of course there is no physical alteration, as our bodies can never interact with the type of matter of which the world is made. We are of different particles, unknown to the scientists of this earth. But I feel somehow more firmly fixed in place, more joined with Timothy. It appears that he senses it as well, and has actually been able to perceive the euphoria which has been washing through me since last night's experiment.

Of course, his mind has turned to an effort to find ways to investigate this new phenomenon. He peruses the notes written by Natalie last night. We await his conclusions.

"Okay," he says after a few minutes. "I think there are two main things we have learned, and I want to know more about them." We all listen carefully, ready to assist in any way required. "First, we learned that Angel and Guardian can use extra power to make themselves louder, and hear each other further away. I want to know more about the power, and whether they can control it, and how far it can reach."

Angel and I are in total agreement. Last night's discovery was the most consequential in our existence, and we have already begun contemplating ways to explore it further. For instance, it was clear that every other Guardian nearby was impacted by the amount of power we both used to communicate. We each felt somewhat abashed at having disrupted the entire region, and wished to find a way to modulate the power we were using to increase our volume. After the children were both asleep, we continued experimenting with our long-distance communication. We have results to report, but will wait for Timothy to direct us. He is the de facto leader of our little scientific team.

Timothy continues. "Second, we learned that the power they used also made them more... I guess... powerful. Like, Angel is brighter and I can feel Guardian's happiness. I want to understand why, and whether it can change the way they communicate with us. We can do some experiments to find out if I can feel more of Guardian's feelings, and maybe even start to hear what he is saying."

I am awash in admiration for my beloved, for his inquisitive nature, his focus, his intellect. The concept of being able to communicate with him is overwhelming. There is nothing I could possibly want more than this.

Natalie is also excited, especially to start an effort to enhance my ability to communicate directly with Timothy. "Oh, Timothy, I want that so much too! I really want you to be able to hear Guardian!" Angel starts to caution her, but she cuts him off. "I know. Angel is going to say you'll never be able to hear Guardian as much as I can hear Angel, but I am sure you can figure something out. They never thought they could talk to each other, and especially not far away, and that was only yesterday. Things have already changed a lot."

The child is correct, of course. The changes which have occurred in just the past day are unprecedented, and I am willing to believe that more can take place.

"Oh, my darling," I whisper to my beloved, *"how I long for you to be able to hear my words directly. If there is any possibility of this happening, I believe you are the person who can find the way."*

Angel transmits my words to Natalie, who beams happily as she relays them to Timothy.

"Okay," Timothy says. "Let's start."

Chapter 5

Results

Ron

"Hey Gabe, we're going to leave in about an hour. Wrap it up, okay?"

Gabe looks up from a huge Lego construction he and Jonathan are building in the living room. They seem to be creating some sort of medieval castle. I see flags on battlements, manned by knights with custom designed shields. "Okay, Dad." He and his friend double their efforts, apparently wishing to complete their project before the day is over.

I head upstairs to take care of a couple of things in the loft area I use as an office. Living back and forth between here and Brenda's has been wonderful, but I keep finding myself letting things slip. I have to make sure the utility bills are paid, balance the checkbook, do stuff I can't really get around to while I'm over there.

I settle in with my checkbook and stack of bills, but my mind wanders to Brenda. I miss her. I laugh at myself. When did I get so needy? She's only been gone since this morning, when she and Natalie headed out to go back over to her place. I linger on the memory of her kissing me goodbye, then caressing my face before going, her eyes full of love and promise. I watched Brenda and Natalie walk out to the car, their long dark hair swinging in exactly the same way as they went. Natalie is Brenda's mini-me, and Gabe is mine. Natalie has her hair, straight and dark. Gabe's hair is like mine, curly and lighter, although I hope he keeps it longer than I have. We've made beautiful children.

And we're making a beautiful life, again. I almost destroyed it, when we separated and divorced after I made a terrible mistake. I'll never forgive myself for my weakness, for having an affair. But somehow, miraculously, Brenda seems to have forgiven me. After years apart, she has agreed to reconcile. We'd been leading up to it for a long time, but finally after September 11 we decided to stop living apart at all. That day really cemented for both of us that we wanted to be with each other, no matter what.

We still haven't decided where to live, though. She likes her little condo, where her best friend lives next door. And of course Natalie's best friend is there too. But Gabe's friend is here, and we've settled on coming here on weekends.

I frown at the bills I'm paying. It is working all right, but financially this doesn't make much sense, to be maintaining two households when there is no longer any actual need. It isn't like we can't afford it. After all this is exactly what we were doing for years while we were separated, each having our own house. But we don't need to any more. This duplication of bills is spending money which could be going somewhere more useful, like college funds for the kids.

I've told her it's totally up to her, where to live, when to make any more changes. I am determined to make sure she is comfortable with everything we do. I honestly don't care where she wants to live, as long as she lets me be with her. I have never stopped loving her, not really, and I know she loves me again, thank God. But there is something holding her back. Is she afraid of committing to me again?

Suddenly, I have a flash of insight. I am an idiot. Of course she is afraid. I have never properly clarified my renewed commitment to her. I need to make her feel secure and comfortable. I want her to understand I am never leaving her again.

I know what I have to do.

I need to propose.

Ron's

"Yes, my darling, you know what you must do. You must reassure your beloved mate you will remain faithful, and that she is safe in your love. You will find

the best way to do this, beloved, and will be able to keep your loving family together for a lifetime now."

Watching my Guarded reconcile with Brenda has been a joy. His happiness is reflected in me. He was lonely and sad for years, until he found his way back to her. Their wondrous daughter, the Seer, facilitated their renewed love. Her empathic abilities allowed her to see that they both loved each other, but had lost their way. And of course as any normal child would, she longed for her parents to be together once again. It was her influence, almost as much as her parents' own feelings, which led them to this place of togetherness and love.

I observe fondly as my dearest one begins making his plans.

Natalie

"Okay, Timothy, where do we start first?"

He writes in the notebook, "What is the power they are using?"

He looks over at me and starts talking to Angel and Guardian. He usually looks at me when he talks to them, since he can't see them. It's kind of funny, like he's looking through me. I mean, he almost never meets my eyes anyway, but when he's talking to Angel he's sort of staring past me. "Angel, you said you were using energy, or power. What energy was that? Is it like electricity? Or a magnetic field?"

I can tell Angel is sorry he won't be able to explain this all the way for us. I'm realizing there are things about guardians we'll never really be able to understand. Sure enough, Angel starts with, *"I am afraid, my children, there is not an easy explanation for the energy which we use. It is similar to the way the matter we are made of cannot be explained."*

After I repeat the words, Timothy says, "But we should be able to find it using science, right?" Timothy believes science is the answer to everything.

"Perhaps someday," Angel says. *"In fact, human scientists have recently started speculating about what they refer to as dark matter and dark energy. But none of their experiments have had much success in detecting the actual matter and energy, and I do not know whether they will ever really be able to understand it."*

"Well," Timothy says, frowning, "maybe you aren't giving scientists enough credit." I don't think he feels like Angel believes in science enough.

Angel smiles. *"Of course, Timothy, you are probably correct. You, after all, have shown through your scientific experiments that you can make important discoveries about Guardians. So I should have more trust in human scientists. I will attempt to have more faith in the ability of science to someday detect our matter and energy. However, at this time it cannot be found, and I don't know of any way to explain exactly what it is. As I have told you before, I will not usually be able to teach you new subjects, but can only help explain things which you have learned through your own education or experiments. However, I will tell you what we did during your experiment."*

Timothy feels better when Angel agrees that his experiments have been useful. He writes some notes about dark matter and dark energy. "Well, I already know there isn't anything I can do to prove what you are made out of, so I guess it makes sense that we can't prove what your energy is either. For now I guess I'll have to wait to figure out your energy. But please do explain everything you can about what you did last night." He waits, with the pencil ready on the notebook.

Angel is happy Timothy isn't annoyed about him not being able to explain dark matter and dark energy. *"Guardian is the one who discovered what to do, when you asked us to 'yell'. He realized that when we whisper to our humans, and when I speak to Natalie, we call upon the dark energy to help us transmit the words. Therefore, he called upon as much of it as he possibly could to increase the volume of his messages to me, while you were driving in the car last night."*

Timothy writes everything down as I tell him what Angel is saying. This all takes extra time because Angel has to wait every few words for me to repeat it to Timothy, then we have to wait for him to write the notes. It's okay, though, Angel isn't tired of waiting, for me or for Timothy, ever. He is always very patient. I'll bet Guardian is, too.

"Guardian," Timothy says, "thank you for figuring out what to do." Timothy always tries to let Guardian know he is thinking about him, even if he can't see or hear him.

Angel smiles and tells Timothy, *"Guardian is so pleased to have been able to assist you. This has made him happier than he has ever been before, which is what you have been sensing."*

Timothy nods, glad to hear about how happy Guardian is to be helping. Then he asks, "What do you mean you call upon the energy?"

I think I understand this part at least. "I think it's like when we want to do something new or hard, we have to try extra hard to make it happen. Like, if I want to jump really really high, I don't only hop, I think for a minute and use all the muscles in my body to make myself go much higher than normal. Is that kind of right, Angel?"

"Yes, darling, that is very similar to the process we used to call upon the extra energy to speak. It is a good analogy."

I tell Timothy, glad to feel like I have contributed some knowledge to this experiment. Angel whispers to me, *"You are a very important part of this experiment, my dear. Don't forget this was all your idea in the first place, yesterday morning when you began the experiment to see how close Timothy would have to be before I could hear him."*

I smile at Angel, but don't feel like I need to tell that part to Timothy. It was just Angel making sure I know I'm part of this too, not only the person being used to translate.

Timothy takes some notes, then says, "Okay Angel, please go on." He sounds so grown up, the way he says it.

Angel chuckles a little, and I can tell he loves it when Timothy gets all serious about his science. I'm sure Guardian loves it just as much. I do too.

Angel says, *"When Guardian started using the extra energy to speak to me, it was very successful. His volume increased significantly, and I was able to continue hearing him all the way back to Timothy's house. Furthermore, there was so much power in the communication that it impacted me in a new way. Although it wasn't actually a physical contact, it felt like it, almost like a blast. It was very different from anything I had experienced before."*

I tell this to Timothy, then tell him what I saw when it happened, feeling very excited to talk about it. "I saw it, Timothy! It was so weird! As soon as Angel could hear Guardian yelling, he sort of wobbled, like his whole body was getting blown around by wind! It was super freaky!"

"Really?" Timothy is thrilled. "Like, you could actually see him getting hit by the power?"

"Yes, I think that's what it was! It looked like the power made him sort of blink on and off, the way sometimes you see on t.v. when something goes wrong with the picture and things sort of shimmer? It was like his body was doing that!"

"Wow!" Timothy is amazed. His eyes are wide, and his mouth is hanging open. It's like this is the most exciting thing he's ever heard.

"That's not all, though," I say, extra happy to be amazing Timothy. "When he started yelling back to Guardian, he was SO LOUD! It was incredible! It almost hurt my ears it was so loud. Though, I guess, it wasn't really my ears, since I don't think that's what I really hear him with. I hear him in my head, and it was like my head was full with him screaming."

Timothy writes a bunch more notes, as fast as he can. "So, Angel, I guess the secret is to use enough energy to be very very loud? And that way you can hear each other further apart?"

Angel seems very excited too, like he is all caught up in how thrilling this experiment is. He is leaning forward, rather than sitting back calmly like usual. *"Actually, Timothy, I have more to report."*

I repeat that to Timothy, and we both ask Angel at the same time, "What?"

Angel laughs. *"You see, after you were both asleep, Guardian and I were able to continue communicating, using our new method. We were both very excited by this discovery, and wished to continue learning about it."*

I repeat this, Timothy takes notes, and Angel goes on. *"We realized our communication was so loud it was disturbing other Guardians in the area."*

"Really?" I ask. "Like, the other people's guardians could hear you too?"

"Yes. There was no way to avoid it. Although the impact was the most extreme on me, since Guardian's words were directed to me specifically, the interaction was audible for every Guardian between here and there."

Wow. How amazing. I imagine how many people there are between our houses, and think about every single one of their guardians wondering what on earth was going on. Our experiment gets better and better the more we learn about the results. Timothy and I stare at each other with wonder, and he writes more notes, then looks up, waiting for more.

"We experimented throughout the night with modulating our interaction, trying to lessen our use of energy in an attempt to not be so disruptive. After a time, we were able to reduce the volume of our communication, to essentially be no more disruptive than usual. As long as we concentrated and directed the communication very specifically to each other, we could each hear the other, even without 'yelling'."

"Oh my gosh! So, like, you can talk to each other now whenever you want, even without screaming like you were doing last night?" I ask him.

"Yes, my darling. The experiment has taught us the new skill of communicating easily, over a distance."

I guess it makes sense. If he had been screaming at Guardian all night like he was at the beginning, I never would have been able to sleep. Angel nods at me, to tell me I'm right about that.

Timothy is shaking his head in amazement while he writes up the notes about this. Neither of us can believe how much we have learned about our guardians.

I think Timothy is about ready to ask some more questions, but his Mom calls up the stairs, "Hey kids, lunchtime!"

We look at each other and start laughing. Oh yeah, I guess we are humans and still need to eat food! Angel laughs too. So we head down the stairs.

Chapter 6

Notebook

Laura

I have to laugh about the kids and their games. Before I call up the stairs to tell them to come for lunch, I can hear that they are in the thick of things again, chattering excitedly about their experiments. Timothy has fallen in love with the concept of scientific experimentation, and they play this game all the time. Sometimes they are real experiments he's obtained through some of the children's science books I have given him. Sometimes, like today, the experiment seems based on sheer fantasy, something about angels. It's adorable how they can mingle science with imaginative play.

"Thank you for lunch," Natalie says politely as they sit down at the table to their plates of macaroni and cheese. She's always such a sweet child.

"You are very welcome, kiddo. I'm glad you were able to come over and play today. I know Timmy really wanted to see you again."

She smiles at me, with the knowing expression on her young face which I've never really gotten used to. She's always been like this, ever since I met her when she was only two years old. Oddly wise for her years, like she is perceiving way more about her surroundings than normal children ever could. It's one of the things that makes her such a great companion to my son, who has his own unique way of perceiving the world.

I'm also genuinely happy she's here. I've been feeling fairly lonely for the last month or two, since Brenda and Ron have gotten back together. I used to spend a lot of time with Brenda and her kids. Now, I don't see her so much even on weeknights since Ron is over there. On weekends I used to hang around with her all the time while her kids were away for visitation. But now she's staying at Ron's house with the kids on weekends. With Mike out on deployment for the past four months, it's been awfully quiet around here. And of course Timothy mopes when he isn't able to see Natalie as much as usual. This weekend has been great for him, to get to go over there yesterday, then have her show up today as well.

After lunch they head back upstairs, still excited about their peculiar little game.

I start cleaning the dishes. I wonder if Brenda can hang around for a while later after she's done with her errands?

Brenda

I've had a busy day so far, after taking Natalie over to play with Timothy. I used to get everything done on weekends while the kids were with Ron, but now that I've been spending the weekends over there, I haven't had much time to take care of my place. So there's a lot of deferred maintenance stuff, like vacuuming and changing sheets, to take care of. Then I need to go grocery shopping and run some other errands. When I get home and put everything away, I'm impressed with my level of productivity. I've somehow managed to get all of this done and it's still only the middle of the afternoon.

I've got a couple of hours before Ron and Gabe get back, and decide it'd be nice to hang around with Laura for a while. I miss spending time with her. I mean, I'm incredibly happy that Ron and I are back together, but I had gotten used to things the way they were. Ever since Laura moved in a few years ago, we've spent so much time together, with the kids off for visitation most weekends and her husband gone with his ship a lot of the time. Having a quiet afternoon for chatting and girl talk sounds really nice.

So I head over to her place, figuring the kids will be keeping each other busy and we'll be able to visit.

When she answers the door she has a huge smile on her face. "Brenda! I was hoping you'd be able to hang around for a while! Wait - you're not just here to pick up Natalie, are you?"

"Nope, I've finished everything I had to do, and now I have a couple of free hours. Okay for me to hang here?"

"Yes please!"

Ah, this is so nice. The kids are nowhere in sight so I know they are up in Timothy's room, probably reading or conducting an experiment of some kind. Laura gets me a bottle of ice tea and we settle in on the couch.

"So," she starts, "how's it going with Ron?"

Right to it. "Good," I say, with a wistful smile.

"What is this face? You miss him, don't you? Gadzooks, girl, you've only been away from him for a few hours. You've got it bad!"

"I know," I say, taking a swig from my bottle. "I still can't believe how mushy I feel all the time. It's so weird. I mean, we were in love while we were married, but this feels, I don't know, more intense."

She considers this. "Maybe it's because you know now what it is to have lost it, and now that it's back you understand better how special it is."

"Wow." Wow. She is so perceptive. "I think you're exactly right. I guess I am appreciating it more this time." I think back to when it all started, back when I was pregnant with Natalie. "I was so shocked when he left me, then I was so furious all the time about it. After a while I wasn't mad any more, but I didn't ever think we'd get back together. I really had moved on emotionally, I think. But now that it has happened, I can't stop thinking about him. It's like when you first fall in love, you know that obsession you get?"

She nods her blonde head, but I think she looks a little sad.

"You're missing Mike, aren't you?"

She sighs. "I guess. When he's away, I worry about him and miss him, but I think it's easier on Timothy. They've never really seen eye to eye."

I know. I've seen over and over how Mike tries to be a good dad, but he can't seem to be the kind of dad Timothy needs. And Timothy doesn't seem to be the kid Mike needs. I think Mike wanted a son who would be athletic and outgoing. More like Gabe. I don't need to say anything to Laura, she knows I understand. So I silently reach over and hold her hand for a second.

She appreciates it, but soon brushes it off and shrugs her shoulders. "Well, what do you think is going to happen? With you and Ron?"

It's my turn to sigh. "I don't know. I love him so much, and I know he loves me too. But I can't help but worry. You know, like, that it won't last."

"Well," she comments, "you have good reason to be worried based on the history. But, I see you guys together now and you seem so strong. You are embarrassingly lovey-dovey with each other."

"Yeah, I know," I say, laughing a little. "But, I don't know how long we can maintain this two houses thing. I think that's part of the problem. I feel comfortable here. I like it. It's my own place that I set up myself. I'd hate to just bail on it. But I think going back and forth every week is starting to get a little tiring for everybody. I really don't know how to move forward."

She nods, understanding. "I'm sure you'll figure it out. The one thing I know for sure is that you love each other. It'll work out."

I hope so.

Natalie

We've been back up in Timothy's room since lunchtime. Angel tells me my Mom is here now, but she and Timothy's Mom want to talk downstairs, so we have more time to spend together this afternoon.

We've gone over all the details of last night's experiment, talking more about how Angel and Guardian learned how to speak to each other from far away, but without yelling loud enough to bother all the other guardians nearby. Timothy has written a ton of notes in the notebook about it. I think I'll need to get a new one to take to school tomorrow. This one seems like it is now an experiment notebook. "Angel," I tell him in my head, "remind me later to ask Mom for a new notebook."

"Very well, darling."

Timothy is reading over his notes. After a few minutes, he says, "Okay, I think we've done everything we can for the first part, the part about how they can talk to each other. Now I want to talk about the second part, about how they were changed by the experiment, and whether I can do more than just feel what Guardian is feeling now."

"Oh, yeah, that's right!" I say, "I had almost forgotten you had a whole other part to the experiment!" Timothy always remembers everything. I'm lucky I have Angel to remember stuff for me, like the notebook.

Angel is watching Timothy closely, ready for whatever comes next. I'm sure Guardian is too.

Timothy says, "I want to start with what happened with Angel. I know the power Guardian was using hit him hard. What I want to know more about is how he said he felt different afterwards. Natalie, does he still look different?"

I look at Angel again, and stare at him for a while. "It's hard to tell. I know he looked brighter last night and this morning, but I think maybe he is starting to get back to normal?"

"Angel," Timothy says, "how do you feel? Normal or still different?"

Angel says, "*I believe I still feel the increased power has heightened my senses, but I agree with Natalie, it seems to be receding somewhat. Perhaps since Guardian and I have returned to communicating normally while we are together, the power is no longer interacting with us in the same way.*"

"What about Guardian?" Timothy asks. "Is he still feeling different?"

"*He agrees with me, Timothy, that although there is a lingering difference, it appears to be fading as we have stopped using the additional power.*"

"Well," Timothy says, "that's an easy experiment to do. Why don't you guys try yelling at each other again right now, and see if the power goes back to where it was making you brighter. But you don't have to scream, you can do it the quieter way you figured out how to do last night."

"*Of course, Timothy.*" Angel looks over to where Guardian must be, and I hear him say loudly, "*Guardian, let us participate in this additional experiment Timothy has devised, shall we?*"

Timothy looks at me, ready to write more notes. I know he expects me to report on what is happening. "Well, I hear Angel louder than normal, but not screaming like he was at first last night. He asked Guardian to participate in the new experiment you have made." I watch as Angel is listening to Guardian say something. And after a couple of seconds, I'm pretty sure I see him glow brighter, and seem almost like he's more solid.

"Yes!" I tell Timothy. "It is working! I swear he looks brighter again, and like there is more to him than usual, like his body is more solid!"

Timothy writes it down. "And is it the same for Guardian?"

Angel says, "*Yes, Guardian is also feeling the effects of the enhanced power.*"

"Great," says Timothy, "this is what I want to do next. While Guardian is feeling the power, I want to see if I can tell what he is feeling. Guardian, can you try to send me a message or something?"

Angel waits for a minute, then says, "*Guardian is very happy as he has been throughout this experiment, and is telling Timothy about this experience.*"

I tell Timothy.

He looks frustrated. He says, "I think I'm feeling the happiness again, but I don't know how much is just me wanting to feel it and how much is it really happening."

Angel says, *"Guardian is praising Timothy for how astute he is for realizing this. It is difficult to know how to monitor whether he is genuinely sensing Guardian's feelings, or is hoping he will and therefore believing that he does."*

Timothy looks down at the notebook, and chews the end of the pencil for a couple of minutes. We all wait for him while he is thinking about this. Finally, he says, "The only way I can think to do it is to try something clearer than feelings. Is there any way Guardian can think of a number, like we did the first time we experimented on Angel? Then he can try to tell me the number and see if I can hear it?"

Angel looks sad. *"Darling Timothy, feelings are the one thing Guardians are able to sometimes transmit to their humans. However, a normal human is unable to actually hear the words of their Guardian. This experiment will not succeed."*

When I tell Timothy, he gets a stubborn expression on his face. "That's what you always say, but we've already changed things and learned a lot. I want to try it. If it takes a year, I want to keep practicing and trying. If Guardian is willing to try, I want to keep at it."

Angel looks sad, but nods.

Timothy says, "Okay Guardian, please think of a number, and tell it to me. I'll try to listen."

We are all quiet while Timothy tries to hear Guardian. He scrunches up his face, then covers his eyes with his hands, then lays on his bed and covers his head with a pillow. After waiting a long time, he finally uncovers his head and sits up. "I don't think I'm hearing anything. I keep thinking of numbers but it isn't because I'm hearing Guardian, I don't think." He sighs sadly and shakes his head.

Angel says, sadly, *"Yes, that is correct. Timothy was not hearing Guardian's message. I would have known if it occurred."*

I'm worried Timothy is going to be sad, but realize he isn't. "Well," he says, "I didn't expect it to work the first time. I want to keep trying, even after you guys leave, Natalie. And we will know if it works, because Guardian will be able to tell if I'm hearing his message. Now that you guys can talk long distance, Guardian, if you ever know I'm hearing you, you can tell Angel and he can tell Natalie. So we don't have to only experiment while they are both here. Guardian and I can experiment while we are alone, too."

"Oh my gosh, that's right! We won't even have to wait to see each other, since Guardian and Angel can talk all the time now!" I am so proud of Timothy for figuring this all out, and for wanting to keep trying even if it doesn't seem to be working.

Angel is smiling at Timothy. "*My boy, your determination and intelligence just might be enough to find a way to make this work. Guardian is very enthusiastic to participate in this ongoing effort. He will relay messages to you intermittently, and will inform me if you receive them.*"

Timothy nods. "Okay. Um, Natalie, can I keep this notebook?"

"Of course, silly, I knew you'd want to. I'll get another one from my Mom."

Chapter 7
Up To Something

November 2001

Stefanie

Ugh. I sit back against the bathtub and wipe my face. I don't remember this much morning sickness with Jonathan. I'm glad he's not up yet. I've been feeling all right most mornings after an initial bout of queasiness, so hopefully by the time I have to get him ready for school this will have passed.

When I finally get out of the bathroom Brad is dressed, and he comes over and gives me a hug. "Poor sweet baby," he says, rubbing my back. "Can I get you anything?"

"A time machine?"

He looks down at me, confused and amused. "Um...."

"To make the next seven months go by faster," I explain.

"Ah." He kisses the top of my head. "I'll check to see if we have any at the store."

I smile and go down the hall to Jonathan's room.

As uncomfortable as this pregnancy has been so far, I am getting more and more excited about it. I'll wait another month until after I'm out of the first trimester to tell anybody else. I especially want to make sure everything is secure and fine before getting Jonathan's hopes up about becoming a big brother.

Brad has been so wonderful. Before I told him, I kept having flashbacks about how miserable he seemed while I was pregnant with Jonathan, but it hasn't been like that at all. He is even more excited about this than I am. He's started talking about clearing out the spare room to make a nursery, and moving all the office stuff out into the living room. Every time I turn around he's asking me if I'm feeling all right, if there's anything he can do for me. The extra hormones are making me extra emotional, and I find myself tearing up sometimes thinking about how wonderful it is going to be to see him holding our new little baby.

I was only half joking about the time machine. I can't wait for this time to go by.

However, I have lots to do to keep busy. I'm going to be starting my final semester at San Diego State in January. My psychology degree comes with an internship requirement, and I have finished making arrangements to intern at a child psychologist's office starting after the holidays. I'm super excited about that. It'll be basic office work, I think, of course I can't treat patients, but I know I'll learn a lot.

But for now, the kid. One thing at a time. I go into his room to wake him up.

Stefanie's

My beloved's life continues to unfold beautifully, her soul glowing softly as her family grows. She thrives in her university classes, and is preparing to complete her education and enter the workforce. She is not clear on what job she will pursue, but the internship will provide an opportunity to further explore her options.

Now that she is expecting another baby, she does not know how her career will unfold. She is deeply grateful for the support of her husband, whose income as a grocery store assistant manager is sufficient for her to focus on her education while working part time.

It will be interesting to observe how the new little life will impact their family dynamic. At the age of eight, their son is accustomed to being the center of attention. Jonathan is a unique child, very adept at arranging his family and social life to suit his own ends. His parents have not detected the darker side of his personality, as he is extremely aware of their perceptions of him, and is careful to keep anything they might dislike hidden from their view. It is unclear to me how having a sibling will impact his development.

I do know my dearest soul is a loving mother, devoted to her husband and child. It is my fervent wish that the growth of her family will bring only joy.

Ron

I've figured out how I want to do it. Brenda and I used to go stargazing in Albuquerque, back when we were dating a long time ago. The night sky in New Mexico is stunning, when it is a cloudless night and you can get away from the city lights. We used to drive the car out into the hills, and get out and sit on the hood, leaning back against the windshield, and watch the sky together. It was incredibly romantic. Out there, the Milky Way slashes vibrantly across the sky, something we almost never see here in San Diego County.

But if we go to the desert nearby, we can see it. And I know exactly the time to do it. This year's Leonids meteor shower later this month is supposed to be extra intense. Astronomers predict the Earth will be passing through a particularly heavy debris field from comet Tempel-Tuttle. It's going to be happening overnight on November 17, which is a Saturday, so it being the weekend we should be able to fit it into our schedules.

I'm going to ask our friends if the kids can stay overnight with them on Saturday. I'm sure Jonathan's folks will be happy to host Gabe, and I imagine Laura will be equally fine with having Natalie overnight.

Then I'm going to take Brenda out to the Anza-Borrego desert, to a remote campground. I'll explain that I want to go stargazing again with her. I'm sure she'll be fine with it.

And while we're there, laying down together while watching the beautiful night sky, I will ask her to marry me. Again.

I'm nervous and excited and terrified. I have to plan everything just right so the night is absolutely perfect.

And all I can do is hope this is what she is waiting for, that she wants to stay with me forever this time, that she has forgiven me and trusts me and loves me enough to take this leap. Again.

Jonathan

Mom wakes me up, and I think for a minute about what day it is. Friday. Good, that means Gabe's family is probably coming back over here tonight. I see Gabe at school every day, but we aren't in the same class since he's in 5th grade and I'm in 3rd. So I like it when he's staying here at his Dad's house, and we can play. He's the only other kid on our street close to my age. Other than his sister, I guess, but she never plays with us.

After breakfast Mom drops me off at school like usual. Gabe is already there, waiting for me on the monkey bars, our usual spot. He drops off and heads over when he sees me coming. He's holding something in his hand.

"What's that?" I ask him, when he reaches his hand out to me. He opens it up, and I see he is holding a ladybug. "Cool!" I reach out to take it.

It starts crawling across my fingers, and we both watch it going up and down my hand. It's funny. It goes across the back of my hand, then back down over into my palm, while I turn my hand back and forth to keep it on top. When it gets back inside my fingers, I squish it. I look up at Gabe, laughing. But he's not laughing. He seems disgusted.

"What'd you do that for? Ladybugs are nice."

"Oh, oops," I say. "Sorry, I didn't mean to, my hand slipped." I shake my hand so it falls off, and lands on the sand.

"Dude, be more careful next time," Gabe says. It's kind of annoying for him to scold me about it. It's fun to squash bugs, I wish he'd realize that. Oh well, I need to make sure my friend isn't mad at me.

"Yeah, I will, next time I'll be more careful." Next time Gabe is watching, that is.

Ron

After work I head back over to my house. Brenda is meeting me there with the kids, after we'd been at her house all week. I've been making my plans for the desert trip, and need to check with Jonathan's folks about letting him spend the night next weekend. I've already cleared it with Laura, and she said she's happy to have Natalie over Saturday night.

When I get home, Brenda and the kids have just arrived. I've picked up some burgers for dinner, so we settle in to eat pretty quickly.

Gabe wolfs his food like always, then asks, "Can I go over to Jonathan's?"

This is my chance. "Yeah, kid, hold on a second and I'll walk down there with you."

I push my chair back from the table and give Brenda a kiss on her cheek. "Be right back." I pat Natalie's head as I go.

Jonathan answers the door, and rather than go straight home I ask him, "Can I come in and talk to your parents for a minute?" He shrugs and leaves the door open for me to come in, as he and Gabe run back to his room.

Brad pokes his head around the corner. "Hey Ron, how are you?"

"Good. I'm wondering if I can ask you guys a big favor?"

"Sure. Come on in."

We head over to the kitchen, where Stefanie is still sitting with her dinner. "Hey Ron," she says, picking at her food.

"Hi. So, I'm wondering if you guys could help me out with something. Next weekend I'm hoping to bring Brenda out on an overnight date, and I'm wondering if Gabe could stay the night here on Saturday? A week from tomorrow?"

Stefanie and Brad look at each other. Brad asks her, "Is that okay with you?"

She shrugs, and says, "Yeah, that's fine."

"Yeah, sure, Ron, that should be great. Jon'll be thrilled," Brad tells me. "Where are you going?"

"Out to the desert. Do some stargazing. I haven't told her yet, I want it to be a surprise."

Stefanie smiles. "Stargazing eh? Sounds like fun." I know they remember the times we've done it together with the kids, often using my telescope in the yard.

"Thanks so much," I tell them. "Send Gabe home in an hour or so, or if he becomes a bother."

Brad grins. "Gabe is never a bother. He's good for Jonathan."

Okay, I've got the kids squared away. Time for phase two.

Brenda

The kids are upstairs settled into bed. Ron and I are having a nightcap in the living room, enjoying some peace and quiet together after our long week of working. I'm leaning against him, curled up into his side with his arm around me. My legs are tucked up on the couch. He leans down and kisses the top of my head.

"Mmmmm," I murmur, then tilt my head up to get the kiss on my lips. He leans his face down further and we have a slow, gentle kiss.

We've both been holding our drinks in our other hands during this, but he takes mine and puts them both on the side table. Now that his hand is free he uses it to stroke the side of my neck, and weaves his fingers into my hair while he kisses me again. I reach up to him, rubbing his short hair with my fingers as I reciprocate.

After a time, he stops kissing and nuzzles the top of my head again. "Brenda?" he asks.

"Hmmm?" I say, thinking he's about to suggest we take this upstairs.

"I'd like to take you someplace next weekend. Out to the desert to do some stargazing. There'll be a meteor shower that's supposed to be pretty good. Remember how we used to go watch the stars in Albuquerque?"

Oh! That's not what I was expecting at all. But yeah, I do remember it very fondly. We used to go out to the middle of nowhere and lay up on the car and gaze at the beautiful night sky, between bouts of necking. "Yeah, I remember. I loved that. I think the kids will like it too."

"Actually," he says, "I only want to bring you. We can bring the kids another time. But I want this one to be just for us."

Wow, sounds so very nice. But....

He cuts me off. He knows what I'm thinking. "I've already arranged for the kids to stay with their friends. Gabe will stay overnight at Jonathan's house, and Natalie will stay at Timothy's. Everything is all set."

I sit up and lean back to get a better look at him. "Really?" He looks hopeful and sheepish all at the same time, his blue eyes asking if I'll agree to go.

He's up to something. Something nice. It's hard to get used to this again, to having him want to take care of me, surprise me. I've been very self-reliant for so long, and I still find it unexpected when something like this happens.

I laugh a little. "Yes, of course, it sounds wonderful. I guess you've already gotten everything set up? What else can I help with? Packing? Shopping?"

He lifts my hand up to his lips, kissing my fingers. "Nothing. I'll take care of everything. I just want to be together with you under the stars again."

I feel the slow burn which has been developing all night flare to life. I want him. Now. I kiss him again, harder this time, pressing myself against him. We are breathless after a minute. "Let's go upstairs," I tell him. I hear the huskiness in my voice. He nods, panting slightly. We're both ready. Good thing the kids are sound asleep.

Chapter 8

Trying

Natalie

I'm excited to be able to spend the night at Timothy's house on Saturday. When Dad told us he and Mom are going camping in the desert, and that Gabe and I get to stay with our friends, we were both really happy. Gabe has had some sleepovers before, but this will be my first time.

It's Thursday after dinner, and Timothy and I are in my room. Dad is back at his house, which feels weird. He's been spending every weeknight here with us, but he said he needed to do some more stuff to get ready for camping, so he went straight home after work instead of coming over here. We'll see him again tomorrow night.

Since Dad isn't here, Mom invited Timothy and his Mom to come over for dinner, like we used to do a lot before Mom and Dad got back together. Timothy's Dad isn't here either, he's still out on his ship. Our Moms are downstairs chatting, and Gabe is playing video games, so Timothy and I get to spend time alone.

"So," I ask him, "anything new to report?"

He knows what I mean. I want to hear if he thinks he's been able to hear anything from Guardian yet. He's been trying for a couple of weeks. And I actually already know he hasn't, since Angel would have told me if anything happened. I suppose he knows that too, but I want to ask to be polite.

"No," he sighs. "I try all the time, and I know Guardian knows when I'm trying and that he tries too, but I never can hear anything."

"Don't give up," I tell him.

"Don't worry, I won't. I never plan to give up. I really think we can find a way to make it work."

He's brought his notebook over with him again, and he starts leafing through the pages, looking at everything he has written about this experiment. It's a lot of notes.

"It looks like the times I have felt like I am feeling Guardian being happy have almost always been when you are at your Dad's house and I am here. It's probably because that's when Angel and Guardian have to use extra energy to talk to each other, and that makes Guardian's feelings strong enough for me to sort of feel."

I nod, and watch while he keeps looking at his notes. After a while, he says, "I think I have an idea. I want to try something new, okay Guardian?"

I look over at Angel. *"Of course, Guardian is always ready to try anything you want."*

Timothy says, "Well, we've tried this when Guardian and Angel are yelling at each other. But I've thought of something we haven't tried yet. Guardian, how about you try yelling right at me?"

Oh! Well that seems interesting. "What do you think, Angel?"

Angel is listening to Guardian for a minute. *"Guardian is willing to try this, of course. But we are both somewhat concerned. When Guardian first yelled at me, it struck me powerfully, impacting my body, to the point that Natalie noticed. And when I first yelled back, it was so forceful Natalie felt it was almost painful to herself. We do not know what effect this might have on Timothy, if any. But we cannot go forward without explaining that there could be unintended consequences, even some element of risk."*

I tell this all to Timothy, in pieces as Angel speaks then waits for me, like always. After he's done, Timothy says, "Yes, I had wondered about that. I have an idea for that, too."

Angel smiles. *"Of course, it is unsurprising Timothy has already taken these factors into account. Guardian and I both are impressed by how meticulous Timothy is as a research scientist."*

I tell this to Timothy, and he smiles. "Thanks, guys!" It's nice to see him looking happy like this. I always think he's nice to be around, but usually he doesn't seem plain happy. Usually he is intensely focused on something. I know that makes him happy too. But I enjoy seeing him smile sometimes.

"Okay," Timothy says, "we'll take it in levels. Guardian, I want you to start by using the lower level of energy you figured out how to do with Angel. So, don't scream like you did when we first started the experiment. Just, you know, focus your energy on sending me a message. Try a number again."

Timothy lays down on the floor. I hand him a pillow and he puts it under his head, then changes his mind and puts it over his face. "All right," he says, muffled by the pillow, "please start, Guardian."

I watch Angel, to see if he can tell what is happening. Angel watches Timothy, then whispers to me, *"Guardian is using a level of energy somewhat higher than normal, but lower than would be required to communicate with me over a distance. He wishes to be very cautious."*

I think to him in my head, since I don't want to disturb Timothy, "Is anything happening?"

Angel tilts his head, listening to what they are doing. *"I am... not sure. Something does seem different. Timothy does not seem to be hearing the number Guardian is trying to send, but I think he is sensing something. He is trying very hard. Let us wait to see what he says."*

Angel looks a little worried, as he watches closely as Timothy lies on the floor holding the pillow on his face. Him being worried makes me worried too. Angel glances over at me, and wants me not to be worried. *"My dear, I think you should ask Timothy how he is doing. Let us not allow this first experiment to go on too long."*

How weird. Angel doesn't usually tell me what to do. Now I'm more worried. I reach down and touch Timothy's hand holding the pillow. "Timothy? Are you okay? How's it going?"

He breathes in a shaky breath, takes the pillow off of his face, and sits up. His face looks red, maybe from the pillow being pressed up against it. He squints his eyes, probably because the light is bright after being under the pillow.

"I didn't hear a number, but I think I felt, I don't know, something. Not exactly like what I felt when Guardian was happy, but sort of like... I don't know... when you know someone is standing right next to you."

I clap my hands. Yes! "That must mean it's working!" I'm so happy.

Timothy says, "Yes, I think maybe." But he doesn't seem as happy as I would have thought. He seems tired or something.

"Are you okay?" I ask him again.

"I think I'm getting a little headache."

What? It gave him a headache? I look at Angel. He looks worried too, and listens to Guardian. *"Guardian doesn't know if it was the communication which caused a headache, but he can sense that Timothy started feeling a slight twinge of pain after a few minutes of the communication. He suggests we stop this experiment and wait until after we have all had the opportunity to consider this event before we attempt to proceed any further. Guardian's most important concern is for Timothy's well-being."*

I tell all this to Timothy, and I can tell he really isn't feeling well when he agrees to wait to do any more experimenting. "Here, Timothy, lie down." I take the pillow from his hands and put it under his head. "Here's some water." I hand him a water bottle and he takes a sip.

"It isn't a bad headache," he says, "don't worry." He closes his eyes.

I wait a few minutes, and Timothy starts to seem like he's feeling better again. He opens his eyes and sits up, then reaches out to grab his notebook, to write down what happened. So if he's taking notes I know he's fine.

When he's finished, I say, "Are you okay now?"

"Yes, I feel fine again. I felt kind of weird for a while. But it's gone." He looks at the notebook again. "I think I want to wait to try again until Angel and Guardian say it's okay."

He must have felt worse than he is letting on, for him to not want to keep going with the experiment. I think we should talk about something else for a while. "Well, what are we going to do on Saturday? We have the whole day and night to hang around. If we aren't going to do experiments, what do you want to do?"

"Mom said we could go to Blockbuster and rent a couple of videos to watch."

"Cool," I say, "that sounds like fun."

Angel is still looking at Guardian, and I can tell they're talking silently to each other. It turns out Angel can talk only to Guardian when he wants, so I'm not hearing it. It's another thing they have learned while we've been experimenting lately. I think to him in my head, "Let me know if you and Guardian figure anything else out. I don't want to do any more experiments that might hurt Timothy."

"Nor do we, my darling. We will consider what has occurred and tell you and Timothy if we are able to comprehend anything new."

Timothy's

I am distressed and horrified at the idea that my participation in Timothy's experiment may have caused him harm. Angel and I had cautioned the child, and he wished to go forward anyway. But truthfully, we did not imagine there could actually be any tangible consequence to the experiment. After all, we are unable to interact with the physical world in any way. With the exception of the Seer, our communications are undetectable to humans. Only the emotions we convey are occasionally perceived, dimly, by our Guarded.

This was something very different. After a few minutes of using a mildly increased amount of power to transmit my thoughts to Timothy, as I could sense him reaching out and trying to hear me, I could sense a growing disquiet in his mind. It did not begin as pain, and I hoped it meant he was starting to perceive the message I was sending, so I continued the effort.

After a time, though, he became uncomfortable, so I stopped trying to transmit anything to him. He remained still beneath the pillow, and I felt a growing worry that he had been harmed. I suggested to Angel that he request Natalie to terminate the experiment, so she could check on Timothy.

Both Angel and I agreed not to say anything to alarm either of the children, because it wasn't clear that Timothy's discomfort was of concern. However, within another minute or so, he did feel a headache blooming in his skull, accompanied by a sense of malaise.

I was deeply alarmed by this, as was Angel. How was this possible? The dark energy I use cannot impact the environment, the dark matter I am cannot interact with it. The Seer is a mystery, apparently being the exception to the rule. Angel and I have discussed this as well, and believe that somehow she is a being in which both the types of elements can exist together. But not normal humans, not ever. At least not ever before now.

But it seems clear that Timothy's brief affliction was somehow caused by this experience, by my more forcefully directing my thoughts towards him.

Even Timothy senses this, as shown by his unusual acquiescence to our suggestion to stop this experiment for the time being. He has always before been undeterred in his eagerness to learn everything he can. Now, although it would not be accurate to say he is afraid to proceed, he does seem to have a sense that perhaps he has undertaken more than is prudent.

I believe we all need some time to contemplate what has occurred, and what will happen next.

In the meantime, I revert to my normal whispers, trying to bring the boy solace. *"My darling, it has been so brave of you to attempt these experiments. But now, yes, it is best to pause. Your well-being is the most important thing in my universe. We must wait, to think, to allow you time to consider what should be done next. Your brilliance will be your guide, as always. I continue to have faith you will know what to do."*

Chapter 9

Lady

Natalie's

She is lying in her bed, in the darkened room after her mother came and turned off the light, telling her to put her book down and go to sleep. But Natalie cannot sleep, her mind is too full of the events with Timothy tonight.

She looks up at me, sitting in my accustomed spot at the foot of her bed. "How is he doing?" she whispers to me.

"*Timothy appears to have returned to normal, and feels perfectly well. He is curious about what happened, but does not know what should be done to find an answer. And he is reluctant to repeat the experiment until he understands more.*"

"Do you and Guardian understand more?"

"*No, my dear, I am afraid we do not. We were both very surprised that Timothy seemed unwell as a result of the experiment. We did not believe there was any genuine risk of harm.*"

"Why didn't you think so?"

It is a very pertinent question. "*Because, darling, as you know, we cannot touch anything around us. You are the only person who can see me, but even you cannot touch me. We have never before experienced an event which appeared to result in some sort of actual contact with the physical world. We cannot fathom why it happened, other than it obviously had something to do with Guardian using increased energy to communicate with Timothy.*"

"Do you think you will figure it out?"

"I do not know, my child. Please believe we are both exerting a great deal of effort to attempt to understand what has occurred. We never wish to take part in anything which could harm Timothy, and will not be proceeding with such an experiment again until we feel confident it is safe."

"That's going to make Timothy sad, if you can't figure it out."

"At this point, though, Timothy seems to agree. His experience has led him to feel he must be cautious going forward. We must wait to see what will unfold. Perhaps we will find a way to renew the experiment without risk."

She sighs, and flops over in her bed, discontent. I wish to distract her from this worry, so I change the subject. *"You will have a pleasant visit with your friend on Saturday, when you get to spend the night in his home while your parents are away."*

"What are they doing, anyway?"

I know, of course, what her father is planning, and it has filled me with joy to anticipate Natalie's delight if her mother accepts the proposal. But I do not wish to reveal the true purpose of the planned camping trip, in the unlikely event it does not end with the desired result. I can never lie to her though. *"Your father wishes to spend some time alone with your mother, and has arranged the camping trip to the desert for this purpose. He intends to cook a delicious meal, then spend the evening gazing at stars together."*

My little Seer, as always, is perceptive enough to know there is more behind this. She sits up, her face alight. "Hold on! He wants to set up a romantic date with Mom? Do you think this means they are going to promise to always stay together?"

I smile at her. She understands so much. *"Quite possibly, my dear. That would be lovely."*

She chews on her bottom lip for a moment, thinking. "I want to know what's happening. Will you be too far away to hear their guardians?"

"Yes, sweetheart, the desert is quite some distance from here, far beyond the normal range."

"Do you think you and Guardian could hear each other so far away?"

"I do not know, as we have not been that distant from each other since we learned how to extend the reach of our communication. This new method seems so strong that our ability to hear each other does not diminish with distance. We do not know yet if there is a limit to the distance, though."

"Too bad you can't talk to Mom and Dad's guardians." She lays down, but in a moment springs back up. "Wait a minute! Maybe you can! I mean, there isn't any reason to only talk to Timothy's guardian, right? I know Mom and Dad don't know about them, but their guardians know about me and you, don't they?"

"Certainly they do. All Guardians in a family are always aware of each other, and watch over all the members of the group."

"Well, let's try to talk to them! Maybe you could ask them to let you know how things are going on the camping trip!"

My little Seer has somehow found a new way to surprise me. I hadn't considered that the group she has created with Timothy and his Guardian would expand to include others. I laugh, which feels strangely good after our stressful evening. *"I believe this would be possible. However, I think their Guardians will be extremely surprised. Remember, Guardians do not normally speak with each other. This would be quite odd for them."*

"Well, let's give it a try. I'll start." She pauses, considering how to begin. She raises her voice slightly above a whisper, but still not loud enough to attract her mother's attention. "Hello, Mom's guardian! Are you there? This is Natalie! Hello!" She broadcasts her thoughts as well as her voice. Of course the other Guardian hears this, as all Guardians in a family constantly monitor the other members nearby.

My laughter bubbles over. As I hear Brenda's Guardian spring to attention with an air of absolute astonishment, I find it difficult to calm myself and attend to this new unexpected development.

The Guardian is initially speechless, but soon answers with a tenuous, *"Yes, darling child, I am here."*

"Your mother's Guardian hears you, Natalie, and is listening to see what you would like to do."

"Okay," she says, not entirely sure what to do next. "Um," she continues, "can you talk to Angel? So we can know how the camping trip goes?"

The Guardian somewhat haplessly turns to me. The fact that we are in different rooms of the home makes no difference to our ability to see and hear each other, of course. I must try to alleviate the shock and confusion which Natalie's newest venture is creating. My beloved truly has no concept how mind-boggling this is to a Guardian, to be addressed directly by a human. I speak in such a way to allow Natalie to hear my words. I must make this choice, since I have learned how to communicate directly with Timothy's Guardian in a way Natalie cannot overhear. *"My little Seer has requested that I begin communicating with you directly, as I have been doing with the Guardian of her friend Timothy. Her goal is to be able to monitor her parents as they enjoy their desert camping trip together."*

The Guardian wordlessly affirms an understanding, but cannot yet seem to reciprocate with direct communication to me. Unsurprising, since such an effort is outrageously peculiar for our kind. When I began speaking directly to Timothy's Guardian a few weeks ago, it was not such a shock as Timothy and Natalie were already accustomed to involving both of their Guardians in their conversations and experiments. For Brenda's Guardian, although our activities have of course been observed, this is the first time to be drawn into them. I appreciate the consternation this causes.

Natalie watches me closely. "Well?"

"Your mother's Guardian is very surprised by this development, but is not unwilling to accommodate your wishes if possible."

I turn back to Brenda's Guardian. *"If you are willing to partake in the same experiment I performed with Timothy's Guardian, we may be able to communicate with each other from a greater distance than normal. It is Natalie's wish that we do this, so you can give me updates while you are in the desert this weekend with Brenda."* I know the Guardian already understands this much, but I summarize the situation again both for Natalie's benefit, and also to give the Guardian time to recover from the shock and begin to more actively participate.

Brenda's Guardian acknowledges my efforts, and makes the first attempt to speak directly to another Guardian. *"Yes, I am willing to try this unusual activity."*

I smile at the Guardian, then at Natalie. *"Yes, my dear, your mother's Guardian is willing to try."*

I regard the Guardian, who has assumed the form of a human woman, somewhat nebulous, the features ill-defined. Like many Guardians, it seemed best to have a shape which would assist in feeling connected to the human being Guarded. However, unlike my extremely tangible form, created so Natalie can see me clearly, most Guardians do not craft a form with much detail. The outline is blurry, but the shape is female.

Natalie, unsurprisingly, is thinking along the same lines as myself. Often our thoughts flow in tandem, as our link is deeper than the mere conversations we have with each other. "Is Mom's guardian a girl or a boy?"

I am pleased the question is phrased in this direct way. I have been waiting for Natalie and Timothy to ask questions about our physical appearance, and they haven't thought to yet. But this makes the answer easy. *"Her Guardian is a woman, my dear, like your mother."*

She nods. "Does she have a name?"

Of course she would wish to know something so tangible, so human. And so inapplicable. *"No, my dear, Guardians do not need names."*

This is not satisfactory to her. "I wish she did. It's going to get confusing to keep calling her 'Mom's guardian.' We already call Timothy's guardian 'Guardian.'"

Brenda's Guardian, having accomplished the hurdle of making direct contact with me for the first time, finds it easier to do so again. *"Perhaps you can suggest that Natalie assign a name with which to address me?"*

Smiling at Natalie, I am pleased to convey this. *"Your mother's Guardian suggests you might find an appropriate name to use."*

Natalie lights up, then frowns, a sense of weighty responsibility falling upon her. She looks around the room, and down at the book lying on her nightstand, which she had been reading before her mother came to turn off the light. The book contains children's tales of knights and ladies. "I think," she says slowly, looking at the book, "how about ... just ... 'Lady'?"

The Guardian glows with pleasure at the novelty of having received an actual name for the first time in her existence. *"Thank you, darling child, I am very pleased to be known by you as Lady. Thank you."*

Natalie is very happy when I relay this affirmation, and is ready to proceed with further discussions. However, I realize it has grown quite late, and that the requirements of Natalie's young human body for sleep will not be met if she stays awake much longer. I do not wish her day at school tomorrow to be impaired by fatigue.

"Now, my dear, I suggest you lie down and close your eyes, and try to sleep. It is very late, I know you are tired, and you have school in the morning. Lady and I will work throughout the night on the effort of communicating, and I will give you a full report when you awake in the morning."

She sighs and rolls her eyes. "I wish I didn't have to sleep. It's a waste of time." Against her will, however, her body demands it by yawning. "Okay, fine, I'll go to sleep. Good night Angel. Good night Lady. Thank you for helping with this. Good luck talking." She lies back down, and is suddenly so tired she can barely keep her eyes open. It doesn't take long for sleep to envelop her.

The Guardian and I regard each other. She is overwhelmed with the bizarre situation she finds herself in. I am confident we will be able to communicate with each other, as I have learned to do with Timothy's Guardian. But, we will take this slowly, so Lady can adjust to her changed circumstances. We have all night.

Chapter 10

Knight

Natalie

I'm so relieved to get to school this morning and see that Timothy is feeling fine. After we talk about what happened with his experiment for hearing Guardian, I tell him what happened last night with Lady. He's fascinated with the new idea.

"So," he says, "I guess that will work with anyone's guardian. You could always know what everybody is doing! Everybody you want to."

I shrug. "I guess. But I really just want to keep track of what Mom and Dad are doing tomorrow on their camping trip. We'll be able to help with the experiment to see if Lady and Angel can keep talking no matter how far away they get."

Timothy nods. "Awesome. I can't wait." Then the teacher starts the lessons for the morning.

At lunchtime, we get our lunches and go sit down to eat. I see Gabe and Jonathan over on the playground together, since they've already finished eating, but we don't go to play with them. We never do. We like to spend our lunch talking, since we don't get to talk about our own ideas during class.

Timothy gets out his sandwich and asks me, quietly, "How is Guardian doing?"

I listen to Angel. "He says Guardian is fine," I tell Timothy in a soft voice, "but he's still worried about what happened last night. He's been talking to you like he normally does, the way you can't hear it."

Timothy sighs. "I still can't figure out what happened. I did feel like I was starting to feel something in my head, like, I don't know, like when your tooth gets loose and it is really distracting and you want to keep pressing on it, but it sort of hurts to do it? It was kind of like that. But inside my mind. But then I think I pressed on it too hard and it started hurting."

Angel listens closely to Timothy's description of what happened. "What do you think about that?" I ask him in my head.

"It is an extremely interesting analysis of what happened. Perhaps Timothy could sense Guardian's presence, but then overexerted himself trying to focus on it. This might explain his fatigue and headache." Angel listens to Guardian for a minute. *"Guardian agrees this might be an explanation. Perhaps later Timothy can practice focusing, but in a more gentle way so as not to place stress upon his brain."*

This is very interesting. I tell this all to Timothy, and it seems to cheer him up a lot. "Yeah, maybe! I'll think of ways to experiment with this. Maybe tomorrow when you're spending the night we can work on it more with Guardian and Angel."

We're both happy that it seems like there might be something to try to continue getting Guardian and Timothy to be able to talk, but without hurting Timothy. I open up a package of cookies Mom packed in my lunch and give some to Timothy. We eat without talking any more, because I know Timothy's mind is busy coming up with new ways to approach the problem.

I love how smart he is. I look over at Angel and we smile at each other. He feels the same way.

Brenda

I've spent the entire day distracted with anticipation about the camping trip Ron is planning for tomorrow. I'm afraid I wasn't as productive at work as I should have been, as my mind kept drifting off, wondering what we will be doing. He's being slightly mysterious, although he has explained where we are going, and that there should be a good meteor shower to watch. My practical side wonders whether I should be checking to make sure he packs up enough food and supplies for the trip, but he has assured me repeatedly that he will take care of every single detail, and all he needs me to do is pack up what I need for myself for one overnight at a desert campground. He's told me there's a primitive bathroom there, but nothing fancy like showers or actual flush toilets, so I don't plan to bring much. Before I took the kids to school today, I packed a little bag with my toothbrush and a change of clothes to bring tomorrow.

When I pick the kids up from daycare we head over to Ron's, and as I pull into the driveway I see his SUV is packed already, the back chock full of bags and chairs and other stuff. My gosh, it looks like he has enough stuff for us to stay for a week, not just one night! I'm grinning as we go into the house.

Ron greets us as we open the door, unusually exuberant. I can tell he is even more excited than I am. As the kids push past us into the house, he grabs me for a hug. "I missed you last night," he says, wrapping his arms tight around me and leaning his head down to mine. He's a lot taller than me, so he always has to bend down to embrace me, but he never seems to mind. I rest my head against his shoulder, happy to be in his arms again.

"Me too," I say. "It's crazy how I've gotten so used to being with you, that one night apart seemed super lonely. I even had a hard time falling asleep without you there." I snuggle into his chest like it's my pillow.

He leans away for a moment to look down at me, and his blue eyes are aglow with happiness. "I feel the same way. Sorry about that. I had a lot to do to get ready."

Gabe pokes his head back around the corner to find us still hugging in the entryway. "Guys! Get a room!"

Ron laughs. "I have a room! I have a whole house! And we're in it! Come on," he says, holding my hand and heading into the kitchen, "dinner is almost ready."

Brenda's

My beloved's pleasure at being again in the arms of her husband fills me with a warm joy. I eagerly anticipate the moment when she learns he wishes to be her husband once again, legally as well as emotionally, as he proposes to her tomorrow night.

At the same time, I continue to be astounded by the situation with Natalie's Guardian, communicating directly with me all night. It felt incredibly peculiar, to be speaking with anyone other than my own Guarded. Not to mention having the conversation reciprocated, by both Natalie and her Guardian. With the experience gained during the experiments with Timothy's Guardian, he taught me to be able to communicate with relative ease. Partway through the night, he recruited the assistance of Timothy's Guardian, next door with the Seer's friend, and I was able to communicate directly with him as well.

I reflect on one of the unconventional aspects of the situation, the use of gender pronouns to describe each other. Guardians do not think of ourselves as having genders at all, naturally, even if we have taken a form which might reflect such an identity. Gender is a characteristic of beings who exist in the physical world, unlike us. But, for ease of communication, and to facilitate Natalie and Timothy's understanding of the events, it seems best to adopt this linguistic idiosyncrasy. As Natalie has assigned me a feminine moniker, the other Guardians have begun using corresponding pronouns to refer to me.

Then, throughout the day, while my own beloved was at work and the Seer was at school, I practiced communicating from a greater distance with her Guardian. It appears that the method of directing energy through the communication effectively increases the possible range, and it is unclear whether any distance will be a barrier. Once Brenda and Ron drop Natalie back off with Timothy tomorrow, the new experiment will commence.

I am beginning to find my usual composure returning, after the emotional and exhilarating experience of direct communication with Natalie and her Guardian. I have observed it occur with Timothy and his Guardian, but being directly involved was overwhelming at the start.

I am pleased to feel my sense of calm restored, as I wish to be fully engaged with Brenda as she embarks on the weekend's significant events.

Ron

"Come on, guys, let's go!" I have everything in the car already, and am standing at the foot of the stairs. I know it's early still, but I am so eager to get this day started. Gabe and Natalie come pounding down the stairs, ready to see their friends. "Come on Gabe, I'll walk you down to Jonathan's house."

I take his backpack and check in it to make sure he has a toothbrush and pajamas and a change of clothes. "Oh, come on Dad," he moans dramatically, "I know how to pack a bag."

"Yeah, I guess you do," I say, grinning and tousling his hair. "Let's go."

When we get to Jonathan's house he is raring to go. Gabe disappears immediately with him into the back of the house. Brad comes out to greet me. "Hey Ron, you all set for the camping trip?"

"Yep. I have enough stuff packed for an army. I think we're well-equipped."

"Well, have fun! Don't worry a bit about Gabe, we're always happy to have him here."

"Okay, great. You have my cell number but I can't guarantee the reception out there."

"Nah, I won't need it. Forget about us and have a good time."

"Thanks, man," I say. "I appreciate it." Raising my voice, I yell goodbye to Gabe somewhere in the back, and hear him yell, "Bye!"

Patting my pockets, I say, "Okay then. Bye."

When I get back, Natalie and Brenda are waiting by the car already, smiling. "See?" Natalie says, with a big smile on her face. "We didn't make you wait at all!"

I laugh. "Perfect! Let's go!"

It's a quick trip over to Brenda's place to drop Natalie off at Timothy's house. We get out and visit with Laura for a minute to make sure everything is all set.

And then, we're off! Brenda looks over at me as she buckles her seat belt, her brown eyes glowing, her long dark hair framing her face, and I cannot believe the surge of love I feel. It is so intense to know that it is reciprocated.

I turn on the car and set the Eagles CD to play for us. Hotel California, baby.

Ron's

My beloved is exultant as he drives the winding roads through the hills towards the Southern California desert. He glances frequently at Brenda, sitting quietly beside him in the vehicle. He does not know what to make of her silence. But he knows she is as filled with love as he is, and he is eager to reach their campsite to begin their day outdoors together.

I am more acutely aware of the presence of her Guardian than ever before, having been assimilated last night into an extraordinary fellowship created by the Seer. A group of Guardians, all communicating directly with one another, all directed by the wishes of a human child. A unique human, yes, a marvelous creature. Yet, still just a human child. She has orchestrated an event which she refers to as an experiment, to determine whether not only can we Guardians break all bounds of normalcy in communicating with each other, but whether we can do so from a substantial distance.

This is driven by her curiosity to know what her parents are doing during their camping excursion. Her Guardian, known to her as Angel, instructed me last night in the use of energy to transmit our thoughts to one another regardless of range. I have complied with the Seer's requests, and have continuously used this new ability to remain in contact with Angel, even as we have grown further apart during our journey. The communication appears undiminished.

The situation I find myself in is fantastical. Never before had I imagined such a development, even having watched the Seer grow and communicate with her own Guardian.

I muse over the most remarkable element of this unprecedented situation. The one thing which astonishes me more than anything else. I have a name.

Yes, a name, of all things.

After little Natalie began to address me directly last night, with her purpose quickly clarified by Angel, she soon requested my consent to assign a name to me, so her conversations with Angel and with her friend Timothy would be made less complicated. It did seem sensible to have separate monikers for each of the Guardians involved, so, somewhat bewildered by the entire bizarre situation, I agreed.

She had named Brenda's Guardian "Lady", inspired by the book she has been reading about tales of medieval chivalry. And, to correspond, she suggested that my name be "Knight".

So here we are, Knight and Lady, accompanying our beloved humans as they embark on a very meaningful event in their lives. And unbeknownst to them, their actions are being diligently reported back to their little girl.

Brenda

I don't know why I am feeling so shy. It's Ron for God's sake, the love of my life, the person who knows me better than anybody else. Yet, I feel a little unsettled, not sure quite what to expect from this trip to the desert. I know how excited he is about the predicted meteor shower, but I can tell there is something else going on. And I have been trying not to let myself speculate too much about it. I don't want to get my hopes up. There's a part of me that is still afraid of being hurt again, and I don't want to let myself go there. He might not have any romantic ulterior motives. If I start imagining things that are not going to come true, I'll find myself disappointed. And I don't want to end up blaming him for something which is totally not his fault. He can't be expected to fulfill any wild fantasies I have cooked up. So I'd best not cook them up.

I'm trying to force myself to live in each moment as it comes. So I'm enjoying the drive through the back country, the little rural communities behind San Diego. I enjoy looking at the sparse granite hillsides interspersed with the rugged trees and bushes that can grow here in our dry climate. When we are heading into Santa Ysabel, Ron pulls over. I look to see where we are - the Dudley's Bakery parking lot.

He grins at me. "I want to pick up a pie for dessert."

"Mmmmm!"

We get out and peruse the goods available in the delicious-smelling shop. This is a must, obviously, and I had somehow forgotten all about it. We used to come up here for day trips sometimes, when Gabe was a baby, and we always stopped by here for picnic treats. Being here again fills me with a sweet nostalgia.

Soon we are on the way again in the car, with an apple crumb pie and a loaf of fresh baked bread. "Pretty fancy fare for a camping trip," I tell him.

He chuckles. "Yep. Only the best for you, Babe!"

I impulsively grab his right hand and bring it up to my lips. He glances at me, left hand on the wheel, delighted surprise in his eyes. I laugh and release his hand. I'm starting to relax, and really look forward to what else the day has in store.

Chapter 11
Play Dates

Gabe

Jonathan has been shouting with glee for a solid five minutes, ever since I showed him what Dad gave me for our overnight. He knows someone through work who got him an early release version of the new Super Smash Bros Melee game. It doesn't even come out until next month. Dad said it was my early birthday present. So I've brought it with me, along with my Gamecube, so we can play it together.

Jonathan's Dad is setting up the Gamecube, hooking it up to the t.v. in their family room, and is laughing hard at all the whooping and hollering Jonathan is doing over the game. I'm super glad Dad gave it to me, since Jonathan is about as excited as I have ever seen him.

Finally the Gamecube is all set up, and we fire up the game. What's cool about this game is we can both play at the same time, and can battle each other. Of course that's what we want to do first.

We look through the characters we can play. "I dibs Captain Falcon!" Jonathan shouts excitedly.

"Okay," I say, "I'll be Link."

This is going to be so fun.

Jonathan's Dad stands there, arms crossed, laughing at us as we get going. After a while he brings us a bowl of chips and sets it down next to us. "Thanks!" I tell him, then get back to clobbering Jonathan.

Natalie

Timothy and I are tracking my parents' progress on a map. Timothy asked his Mom if she could give him a map of San Diego County, and we have it laid out on his bedroom floor. He has his notebook with the experiment notes in it, and is writing down everything Angel tells us.

So far the experiment is going great. Angel tells us they have gotten to their campground, which is 40 miles away from where we are, and he can still hear Lady and Knight perfectly fine.

"At this point, children, I believe your experiment has proven that distance is no barrier to the communication between Guardians. Although 40 miles is not as far away as it is possible to be on Earth, of course, the fact that there is no weakening of the communication appears to indicate there is no limit to our range. Congratulations. This is a great discovery."

When I repeat all this to Timothy he is very pleased with our success. He knows we have conducted a really good experiment. It's too bad we can't tell anyone else about it. But at least we know.

Angel waits for a few minutes, while Timothy and I talk about the experiment and whether there is anything else to learn. Angel says, *"Darling, may I suggest you and your friend find another activity? Now that your parents have arrived at their destination, I believe the experiment regarding communication over distance can be considered concluded."*

I look at Angel, trying to figure out what he really means. I feel like there is something behind his words, something else he is thinking. Suddenly, I get it. "You think I'm spying on them, don't you?" I say.

Timothy glances up. "What?"

"Angel thinks we should do something else now that we've figured out how far they can hear each other. I think he doesn't want to keep telling us what my Mom and Dad are doing." I look over at Angel, who is shaking his head and laughing.

"It is true, my dear, I think perhaps your parents are entitled to some privacy. May I simply ask their Guardians to keep us notified if anything significant happens? I assume you don't wish to know every single detail of their outing?"

I tell it all to Timothy, who shrugs. Since that part of the experiment is done, he isn't interested in anything else my parents are doing.

I tell Angel, "Yeah, I suppose you're right. And besides, I don't really want to hear about any boring stuff or mushy stuff. Just ask Knight and Lady to tell us if anything important happens, okay?"

Angel smiles. *"Of course, darling."*

Timothy is reading through the notebook, at notes he took days ago. After a while he looks up at me. "Now we are done with that part, I want to get back to the other experiment. The one about me hearing Guardian."

Before we can even start talking about it, though, Timothy's Mom comes into his room. "All right, kids, remember what I said we can do? Let's go to Blockbuster and rent a couple of movies to watch, okay?"

Timothy and I look at each other. I think he might be disappointed, but he thinks for a second, then says, "Yeah, this is a good place to stop. We are between experiments."

His Mom laughs. "Well all right then, Mr. Wizard, if your laboratory work is done for now, let's get ready to go!"

In a few minutes, we have driven over to the Blockbuster. I always like going here. It is fun to walk through all the shelves, looking at the movies in their boxes, and decide what we want to watch. I've done this a lot with my family, but not with Timothy before, so I'm enjoying it.

We are looking around at everything. He wants to see Shrek, in the section where kids movies are. That's where his Mom brought us first. But I want to see another one, A Knight's Tale. His Mom says maybe that one is a little too mature for us, but I tell her I've been reading about medieval times and knights and I really really really want to see it. After she reads the description on the box, she decides to let us get it.

"Yay! Thank you so much!" I'm glad we're going to see our movies too. We can't only do experiments. Although I suppose Timothy would, if he could.

Stefanie

I've managed to work up the motivation to make some lunch for the kids. I've started to feel a little better the last week or so, not so much morning sickness, but I've been very tired all the time. Amazing how much energy a teeny tiny embryo can suck out of you.

I'm putting some sandwiches on the table, while the boys are enthusiastically playing their Gamecube game. I realize Jonathan's voice is getting louder, like he's angry, not just having fun. "Gabe, why'd you kill me again?" he shouts. But I can tell he isn't teasing like before, he is actually mad.

Gabe looks over at him. "Dude, it's just a game."

Yeah it is.

"Come on kids, time for a break. Come and get lunch. Then maybe you can play outside for a while, you've been in here all morning. You need some fresh air."

Jonathan is still mad when he stomps over to the table. Gabe shrugs and follows along.

Huh. They usually get along so well together. I hope Jonathan calms down. We have the whole night ahead of us.

Timothy

On the way home Mom goes to the drive-through to get us chicken nuggets and french fries for lunch, our favorite. This is a fun day, and I'm glad to spend time with Natalie. But I can't stop thinking about Guardian. Natalie told me he and Angel figured out maybe I was trying too hard the other day to hear him, and that's why I got the headache. So maybe I can try again, but do it in a different way. I'm going to have to ask Angel and Guardian how they think I should do it. The way I was trying before was like I was trying to reach out hard with my mind and grab Guardian's thoughts. I think maybe I have to let Guardian reach out to me first? I don't know, but I can't wait to talk to Natalie about it.

We're sitting together in the back seat, the car smelling like french fries, almost back home. Natalie leans over and whispers in my ear, "Angel says you're right. You need to let Guardian be the one to do the reaching when you're trying to hear him. He and Guardian think they can tell you how to do it."

I lean back and stare at her. Of course I know Angel and Guardian always know what I'm thinking, but it's still surprising sometimes to get answers to questions I haven't even asked yet.

Natalie laughs a little. "Angel wanted you to know right away, since he knows you're thinking about it really hard right now."

That's nice, I guess. Nice to have them all want to help me so much.

I am hungry though. The food smells delicious. We can wait until later to talk about it. Won't stop me from thinking about it.

When we get back inside, Mom asks if we want to watch one of our movies during lunch. I look at Natalie. "I guess that's okay, if you want?"

"Sure," she says, "if we can wait to do our other experiment."

My Mom puts our food on the coffee table in the living room, and goes to turn on the t.v. "Which one do you want first?" she asks. "Assuming your scientific discoveries can wait?"

"Can we do Knight's Tale first?" Natalie asks me.

I shrug. That's fine. Maybe after the experiment later we can watch Shrek, and by then I'll be able to concentrate on it. For now, I know I will be thinking a lot about Guardian, and how to let him reach me first. "Guardian," I think to him, "if you want to start trying to reach me, do it, and I'll try to let it happen rather than trying to grab you like I was doing before."

Natalie looks over at me kind of funny. She whispers, "Angel says Guardian will try." Then she shrugs and pops a french fry in her mouth, and starts watching the movie. I can tell she's very excited to learn more about knights.

Mom sits down to eat her lunch and watch the movie too.

I eat, and open my mind, and pay very little attention to the movie.

Laura

Mmmm, Heath Ledger. He reminds me a little of Michael when we first met. Same blond hair, same jawline. This is a great movie, but it's making me miss my husband even more. I've been so worried about him, especially since September 11, when his ship got new orders. I'm still hoping he'll be back next month, but I can't help but worry now that the military is involved in what they're calling Operation Enduring Freedom.

I need to stop this. I can't do anything to help Michael right now, but I do need to make sure Timothy and his friend are having a nice time. Natalie is avidly watching the movie about a squire becoming a knight, but Timothy seems somehow distracted. His eyes are sort of staring past the screen, which isn't unusual for him. He often seems disengaged with the world around him, lost in his own thoughts.

I refocus on the movie. And oh dear lord, naked butt. Ack! There's this dude walking along, stark naked, much to Heath Ledger's amazement. I have a couple of seven-year-olds watching this! And of course they've noticed. Natalie covers her mouth with her hands and starts giggling, and even Timothy's eyes get bigger when he focuses on the screen to see what Natalie is laughing about.

I laugh and try to cover their eyes with both my hands. But they duck away, giggling, and the naked scene is over quickly anyway. Well, they're both pretty mature for their age, no harm done, I figure.

We finish watching the movie. When it's over, Natalie wants to talk about it. "Do you think that's really what happened?" she asks me.

"Well, I think it's probably just a story. It's fiction, which means a made-up story. They definitely didn't have some of that music back then. But I do know the character of Geoffrey Chaucer is based on a real person who lived and wrote stories about medieval times. I studied him some in high school. He actually did write a story called The Knight's Tale."

"Really?" Natalie says, excited. "Can I read it?"

"Well," I tell her, "maybe when you're a little older. The language is very different from modern English, so it might be kind of hard for a second-grader."

"Oh. Okay." She looks over at Timothy, who is still seeming distracted. I'm not sure how much he actually watched the movie. He has seemed lost in thought this whole time. "Want to go up to your room?" she asks him.

"Yes," he says, and I can tell he was waiting for her to be done with the movie so they can resume their experiment game. That kid and his imagination!

Timothy's

This has been an extraordinary afternoon. When Timothy asked me the other day to direct my energy into an attempt to communicate with him, he experienced pain as a result. He was reaching out with his mind in a way few humans have ever attempted, trying forcefully to connect with me. I am not aware of any time in the past in which a Guardian and a non-Seer human deliberately attempted to achieve communication with each other. It is unclear whether it was the energy I was using, or the aggressive way he was reaching out, or a combination, but the result was that he developed pain and fatigue.

His idea earlier today to adjust his method was brilliant. Rather than stretch his mind out, trying to seize my thoughts, he thought perhaps he should simply open his mind to receive them passively. Angel and I agreed this would be a better method, less inclined to cause any harm to him.

Throughout the time the children and his mother were eating their lunch and watching the video, he focused on calming his thoughts, trying to clear his mind of his constant stream of ideas, and opening himself up to my presence.

It appears to have been successful to some extent. Timothy was unable to hear any specific words or numbers I was transmitting. However, his awareness of me exceeded what he felt during the times he could simply sense my joy. He was able to detect my actual presence, my essence. It would be akin to the sensation of suddenly becoming aware that another person is standing nearby.

I am elated. Timothy sensed me. This is a significant breakthrough in his attempt to achieve mutual communication. How much farther this can progress I do not know. However, this surpasses any connection I could ever have imagined achieving with my Guarded. My entire being radiates the delight caused by this development.

Natalie's

This turn of events is truly remarkable. Timothy, by using his own powers of deduction and instincts, has managed to pinpoint a technique which allows him to perceive the presence of his Guardian. We had intended to discuss it with him in advance, attempt to explain to him our idea for how he should proceed. But instead, he simply used the time during which Natalie was enjoying her movie to proceed single-mindedly with his experiment.

I did not inform Natalie of these events during the movie, as she was greatly enjoying the film and Timothy's concentration was utter. He did not need her help, and it was interesting to observe, to see how he would fare without any input from her. Or from me.

He correctly surmised that his prior effort, which ended in pain, was too aggressive. The way he had been casting forward his consciousness in an effort to connect with Guardian was almost violent.

There have been humans in the past who have learned to control their minds in this manner, reaching out deliberately and intruding into the thoughts of others. Such charismatic humans have usually used this ability to exert powerful persuasion or control, to bend others to their will. The method Timothy initially attempted has, in the past, usually served sinister purposes. Once discovered, the natural tendency of some humans is to use such power in a selfish way, for personal gain. History is littered with tales of such humans rising to power in a paroxysm of cruelty and greed, unaccountably supported by their followers.

Timothy's purpose was innocent, not diabolical. I do not believe that is what caused his headache, though. I believe it was a combination of his reaching aggressively at the same time Guardian was directing energy towards him. The power coming from both ends of the equation clashed in Timothy's neural matter, leading to his discomfort. I fear to know what would happen if the experience was prolonged.

This new method, though, is much preferable. The child learned to simply open his mind, and act as a receptacle to the thoughts of his Guardian. It began to work. He was aware of Guardian's presence throughout the movie. I know Timothy will have many questions, and Guardian and I must answer in a way to provide guidance and understanding.

This conversation might change the way that both Timothy and Natalie see their world. If it leads to the topics I anticipate, they will be learning more about deeply profound subjects than most adults ever discover. I must trust that they are ready to venture into the metaphysical arena, and possibly be disillusioned by what they hear.

If I could sigh, I would.

Chapter 12

New Method

Brenda

I can't get over how much effort Ron has put into this camping trip. We're sitting on our lounge chairs, eating some delicious sandwiches he pulled out of a cooler. It's warm here in the desert, but being November it isn't hot. Also, he has set up a big shade canopy, and with the little breeze blowing it's very comfortable.

The day is beautiful, the sky is a vibrant blue with a few fluffy clouds overhead, and the silence is profound. Except for a few other campers in the distance who are probably also here to watch the meteor shower later, we can hear only nature all around us. The buzzing of insects, the crunch of the dirt if we take any steps around our campsite, the calls of birds.

We've been chatting comfortably all morning. About everything. Politics, the international situation, the war on terror, the kids, our friends, our jobs, books we've read, the sky. It's so pleasant to spend this time, unhurried, nowhere to go, nothing to do except enjoy each other's company.

And I do. I look over at him and feel the love rush over me. He keeps his light brown hair much shorter now. I think with it thinning so much on top he has decided it would be easier to clip it very short, almost a buzz cut. I'm glad he's not the kind of guy who would fuss with a combover to pretend he isn't going bald. I love him the way he is. He smiles over at me, the light blue eyes I love so much crinkling around the corners. He's wearing a t-shirt and shorts, showing his wiry frame, all sinew and muscles. His tall, thin physique has never much changed in all the years I've known him.

"You know, I think it's coming up on fifteen years since we met?" I ask him, sipping the ice tea he packed for me.

He chuckles. "Yeah, that's true. Wow, I really am getting old. I'll be 40 next year, you know. Hope you can stand hanging around with an old geezer." He looks sideways at me.

I reach over and rub his shoulder. "You're not so old. And I'm not far behind, you know. I'm getting up there too."

"Ha! A mere babe, just in your mid-thirties still. I'm robbing the cradle!"

He leers hilariously at me, then leans over to give me a kiss. It was meant to be a joke, but the moment his lips touch mine I feel the spark which has been happening more and more, every time we make contact. I clumsily set down my bottle, and don't care when I hear it topple over. Before I know it I have joined him on his chair, am up on his lap, wrapping my arms around him, pressing my mouth frantically to his. I hear his soda hit the ground.

He's surprised by my sudden attack, but quickly assumes control. He reaches around behind my neck to cradle my head, his hand covered by my hair. He adjusts me on his lap with the other hand, and I feel how excited he has suddenly become. He opens his mouth, prodding mine open as well, and I accept his tongue with a thrill. I squirm on him, and he gasps into my mouth and tightens his hold on me.

We are interrupted by other campers walking past our campsite, presumably on the way to the primitive bathroom. We laugh and break off the kiss, leaning our foreheads against each other breathlessly.

He doesn't let go of me, though. He keeps his arms around me, holding me in his lap. I don't want to let him go either. I lean against his chest and relax for a while. His nose nuzzles into my hair. "I love you," he whispers in my ear.

"I love you too."

Ron

I know it really is true. I have been waiting for this day for so long now, afraid it would never come. But she loves me, as I love her. She wants me, as I want her. My heart is so full I feel like it will burst. I need to make this official. Later, though. I have envisioned asking her late at night, with the dark sky overhead, hopefully with shooting stars zipping across to punctuate the moment.

It's okay. I will wait. Out here in the quiet of the desert, it feels like we have all the time in the world.

Natalie

After the movie ends, I remember about my parents and ask Angel in my head how they are doing on their camping trip. *"Extremely well, my darling,"* he tells me, and I can tell he thinks something about it is funny. *"At the moment, actually, they are kissing each other."*

"Ew," I think to him, "great but I don't need to know any more about that." I'm glad they're having a good time, but really.

When we head back upstairs, I realize Timothy has that focused expression on his face, like he does when he is right in the middle of an experiment. Oh boy! I wonder what has happened?

"Was it actually working?" I ask Timothy as we get back into his room. I could see Angel watching him carefully during the whole movie, and I know Timothy had told Guardian to go ahead and try to talk to him.

Timothy nods. He looks amazed, but not surprised. "Yes. I knew eventually I'd figure out a way to do it. I think we made good progress."

"This is so exciting! So, like, could you hear him?" Oh my gosh, can Timothy talk to Guardian now?

"No," he said, sitting down on the floor next to his bed and opening the notebook to start writing notes. "I couldn't actually hear anything. But I know I was definitely feeling him there. That's right, isn't it, Angel?"

"Yes, Timothy, you were detecting the presence of Guardian. Much more so than when you felt his emotions as we first started the experiment regarding the communication of Guardians."

Angel seems very emotional himself, like he is excited by Timothy being able to feel Guardian. But also, he seems... I don't know, worried about something? "What is it, Angel? What's wrong?" I ask him in my head.

"There is nothing wrong, my dear. Timothy has continued to make brilliant discoveries. His efforts have been remarkably successful. I am somewhat concerned, however, that the knowledge you will both be gaining as a result of this learning may have consequences in your lives which cannot be foreseen."

That's so strange. Why would Angel be worried about what we are discovering? I repeat what he said, and Timothy looks over at me, puzzled.

Timothy asks, "Is it because you think it will be a big change for a person to figure out how to talk to their Guardian?"

Angel takes a much longer time to answer than normal. I think he must be talking to Guardian about it. Finally he says, "*Yes, Timothy, this is part of it. Also, you may be gaining a unique understanding of the world around you which may influence your beliefs.*"

"What do you mean beliefs?" I ask. "You mean like believing in monsters? Or in God?"

Angel waits again, looking over to the side where I know Guardian must be. After a while he says, "*I think it would be best to proceed as normal, and I will answer your questions about this experiment as best as I can. I wish for your understanding to come from within yourselves, children, not from ideas I insert into this process.*"

Honestly, this is so weird. What is going on? "Why don't you want to answer, Angel?"

But Timothy answers. So many times he has figured out things before I can. He's so wonderful that way. "I think it's like he's told us before. He can't really tell us new stuff, he can only help explain what we are learning. It's fine, we'll get to the answers we need, Natalie, don't worry."

"Okay," I say, still feeling like Angel is being weird, and wait to see what Timothy is going to ask about.

Timothy glances through his notes, then sits with his legs crossed and his elbows on his knees for a few minutes, thinking. We wait for him. We all know his mind is busy putting together the questions he wants to ask.

"Why," he finally asks, "did it work better this time than when I tried before?"

Angel nods. He expected this question. "*Timothy, the first time you attempted to hear Guardian, it appeared that you were trying to make it happen by force. You were attempting to use your mind as a type of tool, trying to grab hold of Guardian's mind. Is this how you perceived what you were doing?*"

After I repeat that, Timothy says, "Yes, I think so. Like I was trying to reach up onto a high shelf to get something up there." He thinks for a minute. "Remember when we were trying to figure out how you guys could yell to each other, and Natalie said the way you used energy was like trying with all her might to jump up high?"

Angel nods, and I tell Timothy, "Yes, he remembers."

"It was like that. Like I was trying to pull on Guardian, and make him come to me. Like this." He demonstrates, by lifting his hand up, and twisting it while pulling it back towards him, like he's grabbing onto a rope. "I was trying to use everything in me to yank Guardian's thoughts to me. I was concentrating so hard, I think that's why I got a headache and got so tired."

"*Your analysis is very good. You were trying to reach something, to take something, but it is something a human can never take. Although your Guardian did wish for you to hear him, the effort you were making was not ideal for that purpose.*"

Timothy thinks about that. "But," he says, "I know it was doing something. Like, I could feel it, almost like I was taking a piece of Guardian." I can tell it is hard for him to describe it. "Has anybody else ever tried that? Grabbing a mind?"

Angel says, "*Yes, dearest Timothy, but I do not know of a time when a human tried to do this to their Guardian. There are no other humans I have heard of who know about Guardians, unless they are a Seer like Natalie.*"

Timothy asks, "Well, if they weren't trying to grab their Guardian, what were they doing? Trying to grab another human's mind?"

Angel nods. "*Yes,*" he begins, but then he doesn't say anything else, even though I know he wasn't finished. He seems reluctant again, like he doesn't really want to be talking about this stuff.

I'm kind of worried about him. I ask him in my head, "Are you okay? I feel like this is making you worried or sad?"

He tells me, "*I am sorry, my darling. Yes, I am well, but it does worry me a bit to be revealing some information to you and Timothy. You are very young. You are both such sweet children, and sometimes the knowledge I have may be difficult for you to understand.*"

I tell Timothy, "This is hard for Angel to talk about. He's worried we're going to learn something that might bother us since we're only kids."

Angel smiles at me in a sad sort of way and shrugs. "*I will, however, answer all of your questions honestly. I could never deny you anything.*"

Timothy asks, "Well, can we keep going? I still have a lot more questions, and I'm not afraid to learn stuff kids don't usually know. I think it is always best to know the truth about the world, even if it isn't what we expect. Isn't that right?"

Angel looks over at Guardian, then says, *"Of course you are correct, Timothy. The truth might be difficult, but an understanding of the fundamental nature of reality should never be harmful. What are your other questions, my children?"*

"Yeah," I tell Timothy, "Angel says we can keep going, and that understanding the truth about reality shouldn't hurt us."

"Okay, thank you," Timothy says. "So, you said other people have tried the grabbing method of reaching the minds of other humans? Does it work with humans? Even if it doesn't work with Guardians?"

"Yes," Angel says, still seeming like he would rather not talk about this. *"Very rarely a human is able to use the method to 'grab' the mind of another human. It is an unfortunate occurrence, and is usually used for wrongdoing, for control. It harms the human who uses the method, by making them more desirous of controlling others. Once they begin, they may become obsessed with the power it brings. It harms the person being controlled as well, as they relinquish their will. It is a tragic event to behold."*

I tell all that to Timothy, and I'm starting to understand why Angel wouldn't want to tell us about this stuff. I ask him, "What do their Guardians think about it?"

"As I have told you before, when a human takes action to strengthen their soul, their Guardian is pleased. When a human uses this aggressive method of reaching the minds of others, it greatly strengthens their soul, even if the actions they are taking are objectively wrong. The soul grows and the Guardian approves."

Wow. This does sound kind of scary. The idea of people going around grabbing other people's minds and being mean to them is awful, especially since it can make their souls stronger by doing it. I can see why Angel didn't want to tell us about it.

Timothy seems very interested in this, but in a scientific way. He doesn't seem like he thinks it is very scary, just new information he has learned.

"Well," he says, "fine. We have learned the grabbing method should not be used on Guardians because it can give you a headache, and it shouldn't be used on people because it can make you do wrong things. So," he shrugs, "I'll make sure not to do it that way any more."

Angel smiles, the first happy look I've seen since we started talking about this. *"My dear boy, Guardian and I are always so impressed with how imme-*

diately you comprehend, and how clearly you see the world. Your practicality and insight are a wonder to behold. You are a delight to us both."

I grin as I tell Timothy. I love having Angel approve so much of my best friend.

Timothy grins too. "Well, thanks, I guess." He writes some notes, then says, "Okay, back to the question of why the new method worked better. This time, I tried to make my mind be quiet and wait for Guardian to reach me, rather than trying to yank him down to me. It wasn't like pulling something to me, it was more like..." he thinks of a way to describe it. "It's like the difference between grabbing something and chomping down hard to take a big bite out of it, and opening my mouth and waiting for someone to feed me, like a baby."

"Again," Angel says, *"you have found a good analogy for the action you are describing. A Guardian's thoughts are never subject to the control of a human. A human can no more grab the mind of a Guardian than they could grab a Guardian physically. When a Guardian whispers words of support and love to their human, it is a gift, which can only be accepted. Never seized. Much like your analogy of the baby being fed, who must wait for their parent to bring them food, rather than going to the kitchen and cooking their own dinner."*

Angel waits after each phrase so I can repeat this all directly to Timothy, who listens intently and writes notes about what he's learning. I giggle when I tell Timothy the part about the baby cooking its own dinner.

"Normally, of course," Angel continues, *"the human does not hear their Guardian even when the Guardian is communicating to them. Only rarely will a human receive the emotional support their Guardian is trying to transmit, by feeling calmer or more peaceful during times of stress. What you felt was different. Both Guardian and I knew you were actually perceiving the true presence of your Guardian, above and beyond the emotional contact you had felt before."*

Timothy is intensely focused on this lesson. I am trying my hardest to follow along as I repeat all of Angel's words exactly, since I'm not sure I even understand a lot of it. If I don't get the meaning of Angel's words, I try not to use my own summary of what he has said. I'm glad Timothy seems to be following. He says, "So, I was feeling Guardian actually there with me. Not only his emotions. And I could tell that was what was happening, that it was different from before."

Angel says, "*The difference in your case is, I believe, threefold. First, unlike other humans you are aware that your Guardian exists. Second, your Guardian was deliberately increasing the level of energy to direct his thoughts at you. Third, and possibly most importantly, you had discovered the method of opening your mind to the communication.*"

Timothy looks up after he writes this all down, interested. "Why do you say the third part was the most important?"

Suddenly, I feel like Angel has gotten worried again about saying too much. I feel like this conversation has been awfully hard on him, and I wish I could give him a hug. I don't want him to be worried about us. "It's okay, Angel," I tell him, "you can tell us anything. Please don't worry about whether it's all right for us to know stuff. Timothy always understands, and helps me understand, even when the stuff you're telling us is strange. We'll figure it out and be okay."

Angel looks at me with a face so full of love that I almost want to cry. "*For you to be the one to comfort me, my darling, is a privilege I could never have imagined. Thank you, dearest. I will try to remember that you and Timothy have always been able to accept the knowledge from our conversations, and have always benefited from your learning. My love...*" he stops talking, almost like a human who is too emotional to keep speaking.

I have to wipe my eyes a little and get control over my voice before I tell all that to Timothy. I always feel everyone's emotions, but especially Angel's. Today they are so strong it feels like they are my own, and he is very moved by what is happening.

When Timothy hears that Angel needed to be comforted, he is even more determined to figure out what is going on. "Angel, and Guardian, Natalie is right. Whatever you have to tell us is fine. We want to learn the truth about everything. That's what science is for, learning the truth. And we know you are both here to help us. It will be fine."

He waits a second, to make sure they've heard him, then says, "Can we keep going?"

Angel smiles, sort of sadly. "*Of course.*"

"All right," Timothy says, "I asked why you think the third part was the most important. The part about me opening my mind."

"*Because, my beloved children, that is something most Guardians are famil-iar with. It is the method which is used when occasionally humans who are praying feel they are sensing what some religious leaders call 'the presence of God'."*

Chapter 13

Relaxing

Jonathan

I'm still super mad at Gabe. Why'd he bring Super Smash Bros over if he was just going to keep beating me? It's not fair. He's supposed to be my friend.

I'm pretending like I'm not mad, though. I want Gabe to keep playing with me, but something where he won't beat me at all the time. He knows I don't want to play Super Smash Bros anymore, but he doesn't know how mad I am. He wouldn't be nice to me if he knew that. And I want to make sure he's nice to me.

After lunch I ask him if he wants to go ride bikes. It'll be fun. Who knows, maybe he'll fall off his bike? That might be hilarious to watch, after he kept crushing me on the Gamecube. While we are riding over to the park I think about whether I could figure out a way to make him fall over without him knowing I did it.

Nah. I'm not going to do anything to him today. We still have our overnight, and I want him to be nice the whole time.

I can wait. I'll pay him back for the game sometime. Sometime when he doesn't even know why.

Jonathan's

"Yes, my wonderful boy, your friend must pay for what he did. But another time, when he isn't spending the night here. For now, simply focus on having fun. Perhaps you can best him while riding bikes?"

My beloved is full of righteous indignation over the defeat he suffered in the game. It irked him to find that Gabe's skills were superior to his. Of course, Gabe is older, and furthermore has more experience using his Gamecube. However, my dearest likes to always prevail in every situation. He will remember this insult, as will I. Someday the tables will be turned.

Brad

"Hey guys! Who wants to go to McDonald's for dinner?"

Jonathan and Gabe are out playing in the back yard. I'm kind of surprised they haven't gotten back to using Gabe's Gamecube after Jonathan was so excited about it this morning, but they've been outside the whole day since lunch. Probably better for them to burn off energy outdoors than in anyway.

Jonathan whacks the tetherball over Gabe's head, quite a feat since Gabe is taller. "Sure!"

Gabe grins and steps back, letting the ball wrap around the pole. "You win!"

Jonathan woots and they come stampeding inside. I have to laugh. Every time those two go anywhere it seems like a whole herd of kids somehow, not just two of them.

Stefanie comes out of the back hallway, sees the boys and says, "First go wash up." Jonathan starts to object, but she looks pointedly at his hands, and he glances down to see they are covered with some black smudges.

"Fine," he says, and he and Gabe run down the hall to the bathroom.

I look over at Stef. "How you doing, Babe? Feeling up to some burgers?"

"Yeah," she says, shrugging. "I've been feeling a bit better. I'm actually hungry for once."

I come over and wrap my arms around her. "Good." I lean down to whisper in her ear, "Maybe you need to eat two burgers, one for each of you."

She laughs and ducks out of my arms, as the boys are coming back out, ready for more food and fun.

Gabe

We're eating in the playground section of McDonald's, because Jonathan likes to play on the equipment. I kind of feel like I'm getting too big for it, but he really wants to go climbing around, so we kick off our shoes and go in there after we've slurped down the last of our shakes.

He rushes up ahead of me, and we spend some time chasing around, up the pathways, through the tunnels, down the slides. It's still fun, even though some of the parts feel like a tight squeeze for me. There's a few other kids, but we aren't paying any attention to them.

I come down the slide and head back up to see if I can find him. I don't see him for a minute, but soon find him in a corner of one of the closed-in tunnels. I realize there's a toddler in there too, and right as I come up to them the toddler gives a shriek.

"What's wrong?" I ask.

Jonathan looks quickly back, sees me here, and shrugs. "I don't know. He must have pinched his finger in the edge of the wall or something."

I push past Jonathan and reach the toddler. He's still crying loudly, and his face is red and all wet. "Are you okay?" I ask the baby. I don't know if he can even talk yet. "Move, Jonathan," I tell him, and start helping the toddler scooch back out of the crowded little tunnel. I hear his Mom calling his name and asking if he's okay.

By the time we get back down to the ground he's stopped screaming, and I have no idea what was the problem in the first place. His Mom sits down with him and looks him over, but apparently she can't find anything wrong either so she just cuddles him.

Jonathan looks at me. "Ready to go?"

"Sure."

His Mom and Dad have been waiting for us, finishing up their food. We head back over to them.

"Hey, can we go to Blockbuster and get a movie for tonight?" Jonathan asks.

They glance at each other. "Sure," his Mom says. "I don't think it's too late for a movie."

Gabe's

I again witness as Gabe's friend surreptitiously hurts yet another child. Jonathan is remarkably adept at arranging the situation so he can indulge his desire to cause pain, while evading detection. The toddler was the perfect victim, hidden from view, so when Jonathan found himself alone together with the child he gave him a hard pinch, savoring the resulting tears.

Jonathan has often harmed and killed small creatures, such as insects and reptiles. He experiences a rush of pleasure when doing so, reveling in the feeling of power, and his soul burns fiercely with each such incident. His Guardian has long since stopped attempting to encourage Jonathan to behave more kindly, as the luminescence of his strengthening soul is irresistible. We all crave the development of a brilliant soul, as we know we will spend all eternity with the product of the human's life. Each human's soul develops differently, but all will eventually join their Guardian, full of whatever the human's life experiences have wrought.

His opportunities to harm younger children give Jonathan much pleasure. He often bullies Gabe's sister and her friend, but tonight's direct assault on a small child was a particular delight to him.

Gabe is a much gentler soul. He is attracted to Jonathan's extraordinary charisma, and finds it thrilling to be in his company. Jonathan is always an exciting companion. However, as Gabe has started to grow older, he is noticing that sometimes Jonathan's actions seem disagreeable. He hasn't analyzed this with any level of deliberation, but I can see he is starting to grow away from his friend. This is an age, pre-adolescence, when many humans find themselves altering their friends and interests as they develop.

I would not be sorry to see Gabe begin to separate himself from Jonathan. Gabe is a beautiful child, a loving human, and has a bright future ahead of him. Jonathan, despite the brilliance of his soul, is a darker sort of human. It has become clear over the years that Jonathan will never be influenced by my beloved to be a more agreeable child. I fear as he grows the darker side of his personality will only expand.

I would be pleased to see Jonathan spend less time with my beloved and his family, especially as the Seer and her friend are repeatedly victimized by him. I wish only the best for my own Guarded, of course, but being in the presence of his sister the Seer is a unique privilege and I am deeply concerned for her welfare as well.

I believe it would be better for the family to spend less time with Jonathan. Of course, I have no control over such things. All I can do is attempt to influence my dearest to protect himself, to ensure that he comes to no harm as a result of this relationship.

"My dearest, you were so kind and sweet to the little toddler who was crying. How lovely of you. Enjoy the rest of your overnight with your friend, my love, but be cautious. Always be cautious around him."

Stefanie

When we get home Jonathan and Gabe burst out of the car, grab the movie from Blockbuster, and go running into the house. Brad and I look at each other and laugh, barely unbuckling our seat belts by the time the kids have already gotten inside.

"They're sure enthused about seeing A Knight's Tale," Brad teases me. "Almost as much as you are to see your boyfriend again!"

Okay, I admit I might have developed a little crush on Heath Ledger, after we saw the movie in the theater when it first came out. I grab Brad's hand and swing him around to hug him before we go inside. "Listen, dude, that knight has nothing on you."

"Heh!" he chuckles, then brings my face up to his to kiss me. "Good. I'd hate to have to joust him to win your love."

"No need, my dear," I say, and stroke his cheek. "Now, I'd better get inside and make this popcorn before those boys tear the house down."

Ron

This whole day has been magical. Brenda has relaxed so much, as we enjoy a mellow day in the harsh beauty of the desert. The little scrubby plants don't offer any shade, but I cleverly brought a canopy, so we've been comfortable even in the hottest part of the afternoon.

The little make-out session we had after lunch was interrupted by some other people walking by, but I can't regret it. She wanted me so much, embracing me almost violently, and it sparked an intense reciprocal need. Even if it's too public here to go any further with our passion, I have felt this contented slow simmer of desire ever since. The fact that she wants me is like a miracle, like the best gift ever. I am as happy as I have ever been. And I'm hoping to get even happier later.

We're lying side by side on our lounge chairs, gazing off into the distance, watching as the sun gets closer to the western horizon. She's holding my hand. I look over at her, drinking in her beauty. Fifteen years after we met, and I appreciate her loveliness as much as I ever did. Even more, since it comes with the sweet knowledge of her, with our memories, with our family history. Her long, dark hair is in a couple of braids she put in after lunch when the temperature started climbing. I usually love to see her hair long and loose, but these braids are awfully cute. Her brown eyes are distant, full of thoughts she isn't sharing, but I suspect she's thinking of me. She's kicked off her sandals which are lying on the ground between us, and her cut-off jeans shorts come to right above her knees. I don't know why, but I have always found her knees to be very sexy. She laughs whenever I mention it, and I don't think she believes me. But they are. I can't resist reaching over and caressing one.

She looks over at me and smiles. "I'm having such a nice day, Ron. This is incredibly pleasant. So relaxing. Thank you so much for arranging everything."

I sit up, then lean over to kiss her briefly before standing. "You are the one doing me the favor by agreeing to come, gorgeous. Now, I need to get dinner ready."

"Ooooh!" she says, "what can I do to help?"

"Not much," I tell her. "Maybe when it's time you can grab the plates and silverware out of the box."

She smiles and nods, watching me as I get to work starting a fire. I didn't want to do this until sunset, and the sun has dipped down over the rim of the hills to the west. The sparse clouds are gold and pink and orange, casting their colorful glow over our campsite, and reflecting in her eyes. We still have an hour or two of light left. She doesn't stop gazing at me the whole time I'm working, and I enjoying knowing that I'm holding her attention. What is it about having the woman you love watching you that is so appealing?

"Mmmmmm," she says when she sees me get two huge steaks out of the ice chest and lay them on the grill over the fire.

I grin over at her. This is all going perfectly.

Chapter 14

Miracle

Natalie's

Natalie goggles at me when I finish speaking. "The presence of God?" she asks, dumbfounded. "You mean, like, they are actually feeling God? Is God hanging around here too?" She glances around the room as though expecting to see a deity. Her mind is spinning with the concept, and I must set her straight at once before she goes too far with this idea. I certainly don't want her to be disappointed when she learns the truth.

"No, my darling, they are sensing only their Guardian. But since other humans don't know about Guardians, they interpret the sensation in a way which seems more familiar to them, based on what they have been taught. This is why they think they are feeling the presence of God."

I wait while Natalie relays all of this to Timothy. I am both eager to hear what they ask next, and afraid of what their reaction will be.

Timothy frowns in concentration, mulling this new information over in his unique mind. "Well," he says, "it is a very interesting feeling, to be able to tell that Guardian is right there." He pauses for a moment, consciously opening his mind again, to confirm he can still sense Guardian. His control over his mind is increasing with practice, and he is quickly able to detect the sensation of his Guardian focusing on him. He continues, "I guess I can understand why someone would think it was God if they didn't know about guardians." He considers further, then adds, "Does anybody ever actually feel the presence of God? When they are praying or in church or whenever?"

And here it is. The thing I have been reluctant to share, and should have seen coming long ago when the children first started "experimenting" on me. *"No, my dearest children, they do not ever feel God. They cannot."*

When I don't go on, hesitating due to my fears of changing their world views forever, Timothy of course prompts me. "Why can't they? Is it like feeling Guardian, where they have to learn the right way to do it, but it's super hard for humans to figure out?"

I regard Guardian, who indicates that I should proceed. Guardian does not seem as concerned as I am about the reaction the children will have, probably because Guardian has an unshakeable faith in Timothy's ability to comprehend anything, and to benefit from all possible knowledge.

I look down, then back up at Natalie. *"No, my dears, they cannot truly sense the presence of God, because there is no such thing. There is no entity such as what humans have traditionally understood as 'God'."*

Natalie pauses for a moment before repeating this to Timothy. Both children are stunned into silence. They look at each other, Timothy making rare eye contact with Natalie, so great is his astonishment. Natalie then turns to me, opens her mouth as though to ask further questions, but remains silent as she cannot formulate her thoughts.

Timothy is quicker to recover, naturally. "Okay, let me get this straight. You're saying there isn't any such thing as God?"

"No, my dear, God exists only in the imagination of humans." I look over at Guardian while Natalie repeats my words, and am confounded to see that he appears to feel some amusement in my discomfiture over relaying this serious information to the children. When did Guardian learn to find humor in situations where I see none?

Timothy is not taking notes as he usually does. The pencil and notebook lie forgotten in his hands. "So, God didn't make guardians? Like, you aren't guardian angels working for him?"

"No, darlings. Guardians exist entirely independently from any God, although some human religions and fairy tales come close to describing Guardians. Hence the concept of guardian angels is familiar to many humans."

Guardian is still bubbling over with amusement, unconcerned that Timothy will find this data more difficult to assimilate than any of his prior learning. Perhaps it is because Timothy has never been indoctrinated into any religion, and therefore the concept of God is quite abstract to him. His parents do not attend church.

Nor do Natalie's parents. However, when she has visited with her mother's parents she has attended church with them many times over the years. Also, of course, she has never forgotten the painting of the guardian angel which she found so long ago in her grandmother's house in Albuquerque. That moment had a huge impact on her development, and on the structure of her relationship with me. It has informed my manifested appearance, which I composed based on Natalie's perception of the painting.

Timothy scrunches his face up, and literally scratches his head as he thinks about this new concept. "So, the whole idea of God is made up? How?"

"You have both studied some mythology in your reading. You have even seen some movies and cartoons with such stories. For instance, the ancient Greeks worshiped an entire pantheon based on their concept of different Gods. As did the Norse people, and nearly every culture throughout history. Humans today view historical religions as mythology, nothing more than fairy tales. But at the time each society took their own religions quite as seriously as people do today."

Natalie has finally gotten over her initial shock and found her voice. "Yeah," she says, contemplating, "we've both seen the movie Hercules. And you have a book of Greek mythology right here," she adds, indicating Timothy's bookshelf. She thinks of the film they watched earlier today, in which medieval religion played some part. "None of it was ever real? Not ever in history? People made the whole thing up?"

"Yes, but remember, humans always have wished to find explanations for what they sense around themselves. You are both perfect examples of this human need for understanding, with your constant experimentation regarding the world. And when humans have occasionally felt the sensation which Timothy experienced this evening, when they could sense the presence of their Guardians, they wished to explain why. Thus were many world religions founded over the centuries."

Natalie looks over at Timothy. "This is so crazy!" She is starting to adjust already to the concept that religion is a human invention. I should have listened to Guardian, and been more confident that these extraordinary children would be able to adapt to this information without experiencing any trauma as I had feared. "It's all because some people can feel their Guardians?"

"Not precisely. Although there are people who sometimes sense their Guardians, and those people are often the ones who invent the stories of Gods to explain what they are feeling, the vast majority of people never experience the sensation. However, because humans long to understand their world, they often easily accept the stories of Gods as legitimate explanations for natural phenomena. If there is a famine, or flood, or even good fortune, it is easy to imagine these things are caused by a God."

"But, I'm not sure it makes sense," Timothy muses. "I mean, people get really really into religion. They build churches and write books and spend money on it. There's lots of other things to think about too, so why would they care so much about it? Just because someone invented a story about God to explain what one person was feeling?"

"Sadly, the power of religion is another aspect of human nature. Although humans universally wish to understand the world, many humans also wish to exert control over others. And humans learned long ago that convincing others of the truth of a religion is an excellent mechanism to gain control, power, and riches."

Natalie's mind returns to a scene in today's movie, in which the characters encounter a priest in a church. "Like the priest in the movie?"

Timothy confesses, "I wasn't paying much attention to the movie. What happened?"

Natalie explains, "When Jocelyn was in the church, the priest told her she should wish she wasn't pretty, so she wouldn't be bothered by men. Then later when a priest tried to make her be quiet in church while she was talking to William, she told him don't shush me but not him. The priests kept trying to be in charge of her."

I smile at Natalie. *"You remember it all very clearly, darling. Your memory has always been remarkable. You are correct, these are examples of a member of a religious order attempting to use their position to exert control over others. History is full of stories of religious leaders gaining power because other people believe God is speaking through them."*

"But," Natalie concludes, "the whole time it isn't God at all. It is the priests wanting power for themselves."

"In many cases, yes. Although, I must add that the majority of humans who believe in their own religion are sincere, decent people who genuinely think that they are doing the right thing by following the religious precepts which have

been taught to them. Most people follow a religion with love in their hearts for the God they believe in."

The children lapse into silence for a few minutes, contemplating the deep subject which has been introduced. Their minds are both spinning. Guardian and I watch as they try to come to grips with what they have learned.

Suddenly Natalie gasps. "Wait a minute. On September 11, didn't the people crash the planes because of religion? They killed all those people for something that wasn't even real?" She is overcome with a growing sense of horror.

"Sadly, yes, they are believed to have been motivated in part by their religious beliefs. Again, history is full of examples of humans harming each other in the name of their religions."

"And none of it is even real?" Natalie is suddenly filled with outrage and sorrow, appalled at the idea of people being harmed over an imaginary concept. "I mean, it's awful enough that people ever hurt each other, but they do it sometimes because they believe some fake God is telling them to?"

Now the trauma I feared begins to manifest, as her eyes fill with tears while the realization of what she has learned washes over her. She begins to be overwhelmed with grief, thinking about not only the September 11 attacks, but other religious conflicts over the years, being caused by the human thirst for power and the misinterpretation of Guardians. It is all too horrible for her to accept. She is entirely overcome. She weeps silently, tears streaming down her face, struck to her core. This is the child who has never cried tears for herself. Her outburst is unprecedented. Never before have I seen her so emotionally affected. I helplessly attempt to comfort her, aggravated anew at my inability to achieve any physical contact.

Guardian, however, is determined to help, in a way I would never have contemplated. Timothy has been attempting to keep his mind open throughout this afternoon, even while learning the weighty news we have been discussing. And Guardian uses the connection, directing much additional energy into his effort, to suggest that Timothy reach out to Natalie.

Timothy is aware of Natalie's distress, but his reactions to social situations are never typical. Also, he has never seen her cry before. This is shocking to him. She has often helped him when he was upset, especially when they were younger, but this outburst is a startling and even terrifying development to observe. He has frozen, seeing her tears, distressed on her behalf but unable to conceive of what he could do to help.

But then, the thin thread of contact which he has maintained with Guardian blossoms into a fuller manifestation, and I sense it when he feels the message Guardian is attempting to convey. He doesn't exactly hear it, couldn't exactly describe what he senses, but somehow he knows what Guardian is saying. "*Go to her, Timothy, comfort her, hold her.*"

And suddenly he understands what to do. He leans over, wraps his little arms around her, and presses her head down against his shoulder. This physical contact is something he would never before have been able to achieve, it would have caused intense sensory overload. He has not wished for this sort of physical connection since he was extremely young and enjoyed being held by his mother. He has always kept himself apart from others since that time. But now, with the support of Guardian, with the connection between them holding steady at a subliminal level, he finds it not only possible but acceptable. He holds his friend, comforting her.

I have witnessed a true miracle.

Chapter 15

Crying Is Awful

Timothy's

It has happened. The moment I have longed for, but never genuinely expected. Timothy hears me. My message comes through to him, not in the specific words I am using, but on a deeper level. It is instinctive, subconscious. He knows my intent, and acts on it.

Furthermore, he overcomes his aversion to physical contact, and his inability to respond to social cues. This situation is, as Natalie's Guardian feels, miraculous.

I look to Angel, and we marvel together at the development.

When Natalie burst into tears I was stricken, filled with remorse over my cavalier attitude towards the information Angel was relaying to the children. I knew my Timothy would accept the new data calmly, even if in amazement. However I underestimated the Seer's empathic power, did not foresee the extreme grief which would come to her as she realized the ramifications of Angel's teaching. Angel suspected this may occur, being as one with her, but I failed to appreciate the implications of the discussion. When she dissolved in grief, I was compelled to enlist Timothy to assist, as Angel and I could not.

The combination of Timothy's discovery of how to open his mind to me, my exertion of additional energy to reach him, and the intense emotional atmosphere created by the Seer's empathic outburst, have all combined to create this unprecedented moment.

A human has truly heard their Guardian without being a Seer, possibly for the first time since the dawn of mankind. Neither Angel nor I had ever heard of such an occurrence, and had not fully believed it was possible beyond Timothy's detection of my emotions, and today of my presence. But to receive a tangible message from me is astonishingly significant.

We watch as Timothy holds his friend, overcoming his every normal instinct, to give her what she needs in this moment. His mind remains open to me, and I know he feels me deeply, feels my support and love flowing through.

We cannot know what this means for the future of these children. Or for that matter of other humans. How will this impact the future?

This moment feels like the beginning of a new era of human understanding.

And again, I am stunned by the realization that these discoveries are being made by mere children.

Children who can change the world.

Natalie

I can't see or hear anything except my sadness. Even Angel's words aren't helping. All I can think about is people hurting each other because they believe in a God who doesn't exist. I feel this like the grief you would feel when someone you love dies. I can't do anything but cry.

But then, Timothy reaches over and hugs me. He pulls me in, and I feel him put his hand on my head, and I lean against his shoulder. I'm still crying, but it helps.

Crying is awful. I don't remember ever doing it before. I guess I must have when I was a baby, but not since then. I'm all soggy and out of breath. I think Timothy's shirt is getting all wet, and I know it must bother him since he doesn't like being touched, but I can't stop, and I'm so glad he's here helping me.

After a while, I can feel myself growing calmer. The tears are slowing down but now I'm hiccuping. He lets go of me with one hand to reach over to his tissue box and hand it to me.

"Thanks," I sniffle, trying to use tissue to wipe off my face. What a mess. I finally look over at Angel, who is sitting close to me, watching, but not trying to talk to me. I'm glad for that, since I couldn't have said anything back to him. I was completely lost in sadness the whole time.

Eventually I sit up, lifting myself off of Timothy, and take a shaky breath. He's looking at me with such concern in his eyes, his forehead all wrinkled, and I realize he's even making eye contact. Wow. He hugged me and he's looking me in the eyes. This is very different for him. He must have been really scared by me going all crazy.

"Thank you," I tell him, then hand him the tissue box because I think he's going to need to clean up where I leaked all over him. He stares at the box like he doesn't know why he would need it, so I grab some tissue and start wiping off his shirt. Goodness, he hadn't even noticed.

"Are you okay now?" he asks me, still looking at me like he's afraid I'm sick or something.

"Yeah. Are you?" I'm starting to come back to reality, not only thinking about the whole awful hurting people over a fake God thing. We're here in his room, and he's also just heard all that news about religion, and then he had to do stuff he doesn't like doing to help me.

Actually, why did he? I didn't ever think even me crying would make him want to hold me. He hasn't answered my question. "Are you all right? I'm sorry for crying all over you. I know it was probably gross for you."

He has a strange expression on his face. Not only being worried about me, but something else, something like surprise.

"I'm okay now," I tell him, "really. You don't have to worry about me any more. I want to know how you are doing." I have to wipe my nose some more with the tissue.

He looks from side to side, like he doesn't quite know what is happening either. "I heard Guardian," he finally says.

"What?"

"When you started crying. I heard him. He told me to hold you so you'd feel better." I can tell Timothy is in shock over this whole scene.

"How? How did you hear him?"

"I don't know. I've had my mind open like we were talking about, then when you started crying I could tell he was talking to me. I couldn't hear actual words, like not with my ears or anything, but I knew what he was saying."

I look over at Angel, who is nodding. *"It is true, beloved, Timothy was able to hear Guardian's suggestion to comfort you."*

This is amazing. "How could it happen, Timothy? Did you do something different from before?"

"I don't understand what happened. But when you started crying, I was so scared and I didn't know what to do. Then I heard it. Like, I could tell what he meant. He wanted me to hold you, so I did." I can tell he can hardly believe any of this happened.

Neither can I. Everything feels different and weird. Not only the stuff about God. But figuring out that so much of what people have always done is based on fake religion. And then crying so hard, which was terrible and different from anything I've ever felt before. My eyes and nose still feel itchy and cloggy. And then Timothy was doing stuff I never thought he'd do, and he can hear Guardian now too. It's too much to believe. None of this feels real.

I look over at Angel. He always can help me understand what's going on. I don't even have a specific question, but he knows what I'm asking.

"Yes, my darling, you are correct. Many things have occurred, things which must change the perception of the world for you. It is natural to feel some confusion. You have learned important news about humans, and their invention of the concept of Gods. And your beloved friend has accomplished something tremendous, in his new ability to hear Guardian. Both of you must give yourselves time to adapt to these new facts."

I'm starting to feel better, like the world is starting to go back to the way it was, but with this new knowledge in it. Listening to Angel and then repeating what he says to Timothy helps me feel like things are the way they used to be. "But, Timothy," I tell him, "I'm not sure we're going to be able to go back to normal. How can we, with what we know now? And things are always going to be different for you, if you can hear Guardian now."

Timothy feels as unsettled as I do about everything. "I know," he says, "but I don't know what we should do next. I feel like we should keep experimenting, but I can't make myself think about it clearly."

Angel smiles at me. *"Darling, you have both exerted yourselves greatly this afternoon. May I advise you to take a break? You have all the time in the world to pursue these topics. Perhaps you can find another activity, to let your minds rest from these intense events. It will be good for you both to do something more mundane for a time. You are both very young, and need to balance your lives with other interests. You can't always be making earth-shattering discoveries."* He laughs a little while he says this. He is starting to feel better too. He was really, really worried before. I knew he was frantic while I was crying, and worried he couldn't help me. I'm glad he is getting back to normal too.

He's also right about us needing to take a rest. "Timothy, Angel says we should take a break from experiments and discoveries. I think he's right. I don't think either of us can think about this stuff any more right now. Can we find something else to do?"

Timothy looks both disappointed and relieved. "Yeah, you're probably right. I need to let my mind rest too. I feel like all this keeping it open and hearing Guardian and then you crying has really fried my brain." He hasn't even taken notes about any of this, and I can see him deciding not to. He leans back against the side of his bed, finally relaxing. In a minute he sits back up. "I know! We haven't watched Shrek yet. How about that?"

"Perfect!" I tell him, and we smile at each other. We can still smile. Good to know.

We go downstairs and ask his Mom if we can watch the other movie now. "Good timing," she says, "I was about to tell you dinner is almost ready. We can eat in front of the t.v. again."

It's nice to see Angel happy, after he was so upset earlier. "*Yes, dearest, food and entertainment are exactly what you both need. Enjoy some of the pleasures of being children, my love, while you are still young.*"

Chapter 16

Starlight

Brenda

I have never felt so cared for. I would almost feel awkward, having him exert so much effort for me, but he is making it absolutely clear he is delighted to be doing it all. I think he is loving this day even more than I am. He seems filled with joy. Earlier when he was bustling around preparing dinner, under his breath he was whistling one of the Eagles songs we listened to on the way up here. He looked over at me with shining eyes when he got to the part where I know the lyrics are about sleeping in the desert with a million stars all around. I feel so much love.

The steak was sublime. I don't know exactly what he did to grill it to such perfection over the open fire, under the sky here in the desert, but I have never tasted anything more delicious. Now, with the twilight gathering, the sky slowly slipping from orange to pink to purple, we are enjoying the apple pie we picked up on the way here.

And every bite tastes like it is infused with Ron's love.

I think until today, I still felt hesitant about him. I didn't genuinely believe that he was back with me. I couldn't really trust his love, after everything that happened. When we first got together, our love was so passionate, so fierce, so eternal. Or so I thought. When he left me, way back when I was pregnant with Natalie over seven years ago, I was devastated. I felt mortally wounded. When it became clear I somehow wouldn't die from the pain, my emotions shifted to anger. Bitter, hateful, intense anger.

After the divorce was over, and we settled into a routine of custody, I got over the rage I felt for so long. A sort of sad numbness blanketed my life, and I believed I was content with being a Mom, working at my job, having a home and friends of my own. There was a sort of limbo going on, and I told myself that my kids were completely sufficient to fill any emotional needs I might have.

We've slowly been coming back to each other, though. Maybe for the kids, maybe for convenience, but for the last year, we've been spending more and more time together. After September 11, we both felt an over-whelming impulse to stop being apart at all. The events of that day were shocking and horrifying, and it was what was needed to push us together. We've been together since then, and happy to be with each other.

But it hasn't felt real to me. More like a good dream, which I would inevitably have to leave behind when I wake. It has felt like I was revisiting a past era, that although pleasant must eventually be left to history.

But today the feeling is starting to fade. Can the dream be real? Some-times I have such intense dreams it is almost difficult to tell the difference between the waking and dreaming worlds. Have I stayed in the dreaming world? Has that world somehow become my reality?

We have finished the pie, and are starting to hear the sounds of night descending over the desert. Birds are flying to their nests, crickets are beginning to chirp. It's not dark yet, but it will be soon. I sigh, a long, contented breath leaving my body with the last of my hesitation about Ron.

I reach over and take his hand. I bring it to my lips, kiss his fingers, and say, "Thank you, Ron. Everything about this day is so perfect. I have loved it. And, I love you." I'm looking down as I say this, stroking his fingers.

He takes in a deep, sudden breath, almost a gasp. He brings his fingers, still entwined with mine, up to my face and caresses my cheek with the back of his hand. His voice full of emotion, he says, "I love you Brenda. I don't know if you understand how much I love you. With all of my being, with everything I am. Thank you so much for being here with me. Today has been everything I hoped for."

Tears brush my eyelashes. I kiss his fingers one more time, then release his hand and shake my head to clear it. "Come on, we should clean this up before it gets dark." I start to pick up our plates.

"Nah, I'll take care of it tomorrow. Let's chuck it all back in the box and go take a walk. It's nice and cool now, and we'll still be able to see for a little while."

I smile at him in the twilight. "Sounds lovely."

In a few minutes we have stashed all the dirty dishes and leftovers away in a big plastic container, safe from desert creatures, and are heading off into the night. He has a flashlight with him, but we can still see well enough to walk. The crescent moon is still in the western sky, getting ready to follow the sun down below the horizon. It's still high enough to cast a little light. There are a few stars already starting to dot the sky, peeking through the gathering dusk. Ron holds my hand, guiding me along, making sure I can navigate the path safely.

We get far enough away from the campsite that we can't hear any of the other people who have been gathering throughout the day. Tonight's meteor shower is apparently a much anticipated event, so there are a number of folks out here to enjoy it. We stop on a slightly elevated hillside, bare granite rock under the blooming stars overhead. There's a view up here, of the valleys below, still barely perceptible in the last of the light.

We stand together, Ron's arm around my shoulders, looking around at all the darkening beauty surrounding us. After a moment, he gently spins me around, wraps both arms around me and lowers his face to mine.

We kiss in the starlight. My heart is bursting with love. He kisses me slowly, tenderly, alternating between caressing my face and hair, and moving his hands down the length of my body. I press myself to him, feeling that he is again full with desire.

After several minutes, he breaks off the kiss and quietly holds me. We stand pressed together, body to body, at one with each other.

I am watching the dark sky, across the horizon, when suddenly a huge flash of light streaks horizontally over the hills. I suck in my breath in amazement. He quickly lifts his head, and catches the meteor as it is still making its fiery journey across the sky. It lasts several seconds, and is incredibly impressive.

"My God!" I say, "that was amazing!"

I can tell he's smiling. "An earthgrazer. During meteor showers, sometimes they start hitting the edge of the atmosphere at a low angle, and skim past rather than shooting straight down. I was hoping to see something like that tonight."

He sighs with contentment. It's nearly dark now. He is just a silhouette against the deep purple sky.

After a minute more of silence, standing arm in arm and watching the sky, he says, almost hesitantly, "Brenda?"

"Mmhmm?" I ask, leaning my head against his chest.

"I have... I want to tell you something. Can you bear with me for a moment?"

I lean back to look at him, and am barely able to make out his face. His features are intense, focused, and somehow worried.

"Of course," I tell him, concerned. Oh God, he isn't going to break up with me, is he? No, of course not, idiot, I chide myself. The whole point of this day has been, I think, to demonstrate he doesn't plan to do that.

He takes in a shaky breath. "I want to ask your forgiveness."

"What?" I'm surprised. I wasn't expecting that at all.

"I will never stop hating myself for what I did. For leaving you. I was weak, and stupid, and selfish, and it was the worst mistake I ever made."

I start to talk, but he says, "Please, wait, just listen. I have to say this."

We're still arm in arm. I lean my head back down, and nod against his chest, and watch the sky while he continues speaking.

"I never stopped loving you. Even when I was with ... old what's-her-name."

I chuckle under my breath, amused by his reluctance to speak her name in front of me. I got over it long ago, but it's cute that he fears offending me. I can tell he's relieved to hear me chuckle rather than get mad over him mentioning his old girlfriend.

I hear the relief in his tone as he continues confessing. "To be honest, that was the whole problem with her. She wasn't you. I was still in love with you, even though I had stupidly left. And she could tell. We were never truly happy together, and she was usually mad at me for being distracted."

"You don't have to explain this, Ron," I whisper. I surprisingly don't find it painful to hear about it, but I'm worried he will find it painful to talk about it.

"No, I want you to understand. I have to tell you the whole thing, so you can know what I'm asking you to forgive."

I nod again, and wait for him to go on.

"It didn't take very long for her to give up on me. She knew I would never really be with her fully. And honestly I was glad when she left. I was too chicken to do it myself, and too selfish. I was worried if I lost her, after I had already lost you, I would just be alone."

He sighs and holds me tighter.

"But, of course, that's what happened. I had ruined our marriage, and then ruined the stupid relationship I tried to replace it with. I felt so sorry for myself."

I rub his back with the hand I have wrapped around his waist as we stand together, side by side, still watching the night sky. Another meteor shoots overhead, and we both pause to watch it, but neither of us mentions it.

"It was right before Thanksgiving, when Natalie was a newborn. I had missed your whole pregnancy. I wasn't even there with you when she was born. I felt like the worst failure on the planet. I despised myself. And I missed you. I missed you so, so much."

I feel his heartbreak soaking through me, yet my lips twitch in a little smile. I remember what happened next.

"So, like the colossal jerk I was, I asked you if we could spend Thanksgiving together." He shudders, physically affected by the memory of the event.

"Yeah," I tell him, "that I remember. I still can't believe I slapped you. I've never forgiven myself for that."

"I deserved it," he assures me. "I would have deserved it if you'd slapped my fool head straight off my shoulders. It was the stupidest, most mortifying thing I had ever asked anyone. I'm still embarrassed when I think about it. If you'd murdered me on the spot it would have been justifiable homicide."

He only sounds like he's half joking. I have to laugh a little.

"But then, somehow, you were gracious enough to let me continue seeing the kids. I know it was hard, and the whole court thing was awful, but I was so grateful when we were able to agree to a visitation schedule. And so relieved when you seemed like you weren't so furious with me any more."

I sigh. "Yeah," I nuzzle against his chest. "Looking back on it I can't believe how mad I was all the time. I guess I got tired of it. Anger is draining."

His arm around my shoulder lifts, and he strokes my hair with his hand. "I still missed you all the time. I looked forward to visitation, not just because I wanted the kids, but because I at least got to see you for a couple of minutes when I was picking them up. But I was still always afraid of making you mad again."

I snort. "Yeah, you probably always expected me to smack you."

He laughs softly. "Not only that. I didn't want to cause you any more pain. I knew how much I had hurt you, and I hated myself for it, and I couldn't imagine doing anything else to add to it." Another deep breath. "So, I stuck to the schedule, and tried not to inflict my company on you any longer than necessary for the visitation exchanges. But I still loved you so much it hurt. Those moments together while I was picking up the kids were like torture. I wanted you so much, every minute, but felt like the best I could ever hope for from you was for you not to be filled with rage about me. I always had to hide the way I felt, for fear of upsetting you."

I'm starting to feel tears threatening again. I never knew any of this. I always thought he was over me, that he'd been over me since he left me. I had figured the time he asked to spend Thanksgiving together was only a moment of weakness, and he was simply trying not to spend it alone since his girlfriend had left him.

So I had shut my heart down. I hadn't even allowed myself to think about loving him again. I wasn't feeling pain over his loss after the first year or two. I told myself I was over it too.

But here he is confessing that he always loved me, and it was anguish for him to be around me every time he came over for visitation. He's been hiding his pain this whole time, where I had suppressed mine. My tears flow over. The stars swim in my vision.

I hear him sniff, and he uses his free arm to wipe his sleeve across his face. He takes a breath to gain control over his voice. "So it stayed that way for a long time. It became easier to be around you, and we did stuff together sometimes like for the kids' birthdays. But I never allowed myself to hope for anything. I felt like it was my punishment for my gigantic error, my idiocy in throwing away the best thing that had ever happened to me. I would have to see you, be around you, but never be able to touch you."

The tears are streaming. For both of us, I think. His voice has gotten thick. I wipe my eyes with my sleeve.

"Then, you came over for Christmas last year. Things started changing." He sighs again. "I couldn't believe it worked." He pauses for a moment. "It was all Natalie's idea, you know. She's the one who suggested I invite you to come over to do luminarias together. I never would have dared."

I laugh through my tears. "Yeah, I figured. She's always trying to make the world feel better."

"Since then, I've allowed myself to have hope. And to actually enjoy our time together. But I never really believed I could have you. I didn't dare to hope you'd want me again, after how much I had hurt you."

I nod against his chest. "I've been feeling exactly the same way."

He takes another deep breath. I feel it against my cheek. "Then, September 11. You know. I couldn't stand to be apart from you for another second. The idea of keeping our family separate any more seemed so wrong, after so many other families were destroyed."

"Yeah," I breathe.

"So," he says, "thank you. Thank you for being with me. Thank you for living with me. Thank you for telling me that you love me. You have no idea how much it fills me up every time you say it."

"I do," I tell him. "I love you. So much."

"But," he says, "can you forgive me? For my selfishness and stupidity? For how much I hurt you? For throwing away our beautiful life, for wasting all that time apart? Even if I will never, ever, forgive myself."

I nod my head against his chest, then lean back to look into his eyes. The crescent moon is casting barely enough dim light to make out his features. "I already have. A long time ago. Yes," I go on, feeling like he needs to hear me say it specifically, "I forgive you."

He sucks in a breath, and I hear him give a sob. His voice thick with emotion, he says, "Thank you. Thank you, Brenda. Thank you."

We stand quietly together for a moment. It is fully dark now. The stars are vibrant over our heads. Even the Milky Way is visible, the sprinkling of stars like distant clouds slashing across the sky. The night is magical.

"Come on," he says, giving me one more kiss. "Let's go back. I have something I want to give you."

He pulls the flashlight out of his pocket and lights the path beneath my feet as he guides me back to camp. I follow him trustingly through the dark. He will take care of me. I know it now. I don't need to be afraid any more.

Ron's

The love he is feeling floods through me as well, lighting our soul brilliantly. Never has he shone so brightly, never has he felt so deeply. The beauty of this night will last forever, not merely in his living memory, but forever after in his soul, when it finally joins me again.

"My darling, you have created this beautiful moment for the two of you, and for your family. You were so right to orchestrate this event. You know the time is right."

Ron

As I guide her back to our camp, my heart and my eyes are full. I have finally confessed all to her, and finally heard the sweet forgiveness coming from her lips. I only need do one more thing to make this night complete.

I spend a few minutes when we get back, arranging our cots side by side and covering them with cushions, so we can lie comfortably together and watch the sky. When she lays down with me, we spend a few silent minutes gazing upwards, aglow with love and with wonder at the night. The meteor shower does not disappoint. Every few minutes, sometimes more often, there is a streak of light across the sky. We have already seen dozens, and the night is still young.

After some time spent in sweet silence, her lying by my side, her hand in mine, I know it is time. I pull her closer to me, so she is curled against me, her head resting on my chest in the hollow of my shoulder. I love it when she lies on me this way. "Brenda," I whisper, not wanting to disturb the beautiful peace of the night. "I have to ask you something."

"Mmm-hmmm?"

"Do you understand now that I will always love you? That I will never leave you? That I will devote the rest of my life to making you happy?"

"Yes, honey, I didn't know for sure before, but I do now," she breathes. She reaches up to wipe her eyes, then rests her hand again on my chest. "I feel the same way. Thank you for making me see. I love you."

"Then, Brenda, my love," I say, using the hand which isn't wrapped around her to reach into my pocket for the little box, "will you stay with me always? Will you marry me?" I place the box in her hand, the hand that is pressed against my heart.

She inhales shakily, and leans up to use her other hand to open the box. The diamond ring inside glints dimly in the starlight. Another meteor streaks overhead, followed immediately by a second.

"Yes," she whispers. "Yes. Of course." She leans down to kiss me.
I am complete.

Chapter 17
Unfathomable

Natalie

I wake up and am not sure for a second where I am. I see Angel waiting for me like always, but it isn't my bed he is sitting at the foot of. I'm on the floor. I look around to figure it out.

Oh right! I'm on the floor of Timothy's bedroom, laying on the mattress his Mom set up for me. We had our overnight last night.

It all comes rushing back into my head as my dreams fade. I flip over onto my back, to think about everything. Timothy is still asleep up on his bed.

"Good morning, darling," Angel says, smiling at me. His expression is back to the calm way it usually looks, which is nice. Yesterday he looked so upset for a while.

"Hi Angel," I think to him. I don't even want to whisper, since I don't want to wake up Timothy. I'm sure he was even more tired than me after everything we did yesterday, especially with him starting to communicate with Guardian. Everything that happened starts replaying in my mind. Of course the main thing I'm thinking about is learning about how people have been wrong all along about God. It still makes me really sad, but at least I'm done crying about it. Instead, I'm starting to wonder if there is anything I can do. People are getting hurt because they don't understand what's really going on, and I can't stand that nobody else knows the truth. I wish there was some way I could help.

No, there's probably not. How could I possibly change anything? I'm just a kid, and we've learned in school there are like seven billion people living on the Earth. Nobody would ever listen to me.

Suddenly, in the middle of thinking about all of that, I remember my parents. "Oh!" I think to Angel. "How did it go with my parents last night? You didn't tell me anything about it before I went to sleep," I add accusingly.

"Yes, my dearest, I apologize. I know you had wanted to be kept apprised of their progress on their camping trip. However, the events of yesterday were quite overwhelming for both you and your friend, and I resolved to wait until you asked me about it. I didn't want to distract you with other information unless you wanted to hear it."

"Well?" I think, impatiently.

"It went splendidly, my dear. Exactly as you had hoped. Your parents have agreed to remarry." He smiles delightedly at me.

I sit straight up and can't stop a little squeak from escaping, I'm so happy. I clap my hands over my mouth, but it's too late. I'm afraid I woke up Timothy. His head lifts off the pillow and he stares at me sleepily, confused about what is happening. His hair is sticking up funny on one side. I give him a big smile.

"Good morning," I tell him.

He rubs his eyes, and puts his head back down on the pillow for a second like he wishes he could sleep longer. But then he sits up, cross-legged on his bed.

Yawning, he asks, "Anything going on?" He knows I always hear from Angel first thing if something is happening.

"Yes!" I tell him. "Angel says my parents are going to get married!"

"Oh!" he says, then is quiet for a minute. "Yeah, I guess I forgot about that part. The whole thing about Angel listening while they are out in the desert." He gets out of bed and heads out the door to the bathroom. "I'll be right back."

"So, tell me more about what happened with Mom and Dad," I whisper to Angel. I don't have to worry about waking Timothy up anymore, but I still don't want his Mom to hear me talking to someone while he isn't in the room.

"Your father prepared a beautiful outing for your mother. They enjoyed themselves greatly at their campsite in the desert. He grilled them steaks for dinner, then they took a walk after the sun went down. He told her how much he has always loved her. While they were watching the meteor shower, he

asked her to marry him and gave her a ring. She agreed. They are both very, very happy."

Oh my God, they aren't the only ones happy. Suddenly I have a twinge of disappointment, thinking about myself saying "oh my God" when there isn't any such thing. So much of the world is going to look different to me now. Angel nods at me, agreeing a lot has changed.

I try to shrug it off. There isn't anything I can do about that right now. I should focus on the happy news about my parents.

When Timothy comes back in the room, I go and have my turn in the bathroom, then come back. I tell him what Angel said about how my parents did on their trip. I don't think he's all that excited about them getting married again, but he does want to hear a lot more about how Angel knew everything. I have to keep reminding myself we were working on a whole different experiment when we learned there isn't any God. "Angel," Timothy asks, "could you hear them the whole time, or just sometimes? How did it work?"

Angel smiles at Timothy, happy he is focusing on this part of the experiment again. Angel still regrets he made me so unhappy with the news about religion. *"After they arrived at the desert, and it was clear with our new method of communication we could hear each other despite the distance, I asked Lady and Knight to simply keep me updated throughout the evening rather than remaining in constant communication. Therefore, every so often one of them would relay any news to me. They summarized the events, and then I conveyed them to Natalie this morning."*

I tell all that to Timothy. He picks up the notebook and turns back a couple of pages, to that part of the experiment, and writes some notes. "Well," he says when he is finished, "I think the experiment was a success. We have concluded that Guardians have the ability to hear each other from long distances." He nods with satisfaction and closes the notebook.

I ask him, "Are you going to write any notes about you talking to Guardian?" It seems strange for him not to have written anything about it.

He sighs. "I don't think so. Not yet. I wouldn't even know what to write. I'm not sure it even felt like part of an experiment, as much as it was learning about a new part of myself. I don't know. Maybe later."

He's quiet for a minute, and I think he's trying to open his mind to check to see if Guardian is still there. Angel whispers, *"Yes, he is sensing Guardian again."*

I wait. After a minute he nods his head again, like he is satisfied. "Yes, I can still tell he's there. It's quieter now. I think maybe he was yelling when I first heard him, when you needed a hug and he wanted me to do it."

Angel agrees. *"Yes, when Guardian wanted to suggest Timothy try to comfort you, he exerted a great deal more energy in the effort than he had before. It seemed like something of an emergency, with you suddenly so upset that you began crying. So Guardian was doing something like yelling, because he was desperate for Timothy to hear him."* He looks at me sadly, tilting his head and filling his eyes with his love for me.

I tell Timothy what he said. I feel a little embarrassed about it. "I'm sorry I scared everyone by crying so hard."

Timothy lifts up his eyebrows like he's surprised. "You don't have to be sorry, Natalie. You've seen me cry plenty of times before. You've always helped me whenever I needed it." He looks down at his hands, seeming almost shy all of a sudden. "I'm glad Guardian told me what to do. I'm glad I could be the one to help you this time."

Natalie's

Oh, these remarkable children. My darling Seer and her beloved friend. They have changed my world.

My existence is so different, so much richer than I could ever have anticipated before she was born, before we began sharing a soul. Even once I became her Guardian, I had no idea of the strange journey we would embark on together.

Here I am, part of a large cooperating group of humans and Guardians, learning things about our kind I never knew, interacting in ways I never imagined.

And, I realize, I have a ... friend. Unfathomable. It is mind boggling to consider, but Timothy's Guardian and I have developed an actual relationship, a true friendship, due to the prodding of Natalie and the incessant scientific curiosity of Timothy. I never before considered even speaking directly to another Guardian, much less collaborating and conversing regularly with such a one. But here we are, in constant and direct communication, learning together with our Guarded, guiding them through their discoveries, and being the beneficiaries of their new knowledge.

Guardian continues to be nearly overwrought at the developments with his beloved Timothy. When Natalie was born I was shocked to discover myself the Guardian of a Seer. But, I knew what was expected of me, knew what I had to do to support her unique abilities. I was familiar with the memories of those who had witnessed Seers in the past, and was guided by these. Guardian does not have this advantage with Timothy. Neither of us is familiar with any such instance. We cannot turn to history to direct our actions. Guardian must invent his interaction with Timothy anew.

I consider wryly that it is appropriate that Guardian must effectively conduct experiments in order to know how best to Guard a human who is not a Seer, yet with whom he can communicate. I share this flash of insight with Guardian, who accepts it thoughtfully. Yes, Timothy and Guardian must be scientists together, discovering how to use their newfound abilities in tandem. As always, I presume Timothy will be the one guiding the process, asking the right questions, conducting the necessary experiments. He will lead us, and we will all learn together.

Knight contacts me, to inform me that Ron and Brenda will be leaving the desert soon, and come here to pick Natalie up and bring her home to Ron's house.

Natalie and Timothy are at the kitchen table, eating breakfast. Timothy's mother has joined them, and is listening to their chatter. Of all the humans in their lives, Laura is the one who most closely understands their interactions. She has always had the sense that Natalie is an extremely unusual child. She has accepted her son's friendship gratefully, glad he has found a friend whose unique abilities complement his own. Laura has occasionally realized in observing Natalie that her gifts defy logical explanation, yet she has never been alarmed by this. Her love for her son, and her support of his close friendship, bring her to welcome Natalie's company always, even when she witnesses events which seem otherworldly or unnatural. It is a boon for a Seer to have such companions, to be accepted despite the evidence of unusual powers.

I whisper to Natalie, *"Knight tells me your parents are on their way here, and will pick you up in approximately one hours' time."*

"Okay," she thinks back to me, not pausing in her breakfast or indicating in any way that she has received a message. It has become second nature to her to conceal my presence from everybody except Timothy.

I wonder about this. Will she ever begin to share my presence with others? Once she tried to instruct Jonathan about the existence of Guardians, in an effort to improve his behavior, but he dismissed what she said as ridiculous.

And what of Timothy? The unprecedented communication between him and Guardian will have unknowable consequences. But consequences there must be. How will they develop? How will Timothy use this new skill? Natalie uses me as readily as she uses her eyesight to understand her world. What will Timothy do?

Chapter 18

News

Brenda

We wrap up our desert trip soon after the sun rises and it starts warming up again. The night was remarkable. The best night of my life. I feel so secure again in Ron's love. I have the ring on my finger, and it feels so right there. It's a new ring, a lovely but plain band, a row of tiny diamonds interspersed with my favorite gem, emeralds. He put a lot of thought into it, selecting a ring without a large gaudy center stone, because he knows I find big rings uncomfortable and wouldn't have liked it as much. This is perfect.

He put thought into everything. Every moment of our trip was meticulously planned. The way he packed, the food he brought, the timing of the breathtaking meteor shower, everything. It was all designed to demonstrate how much he loves me. And it worked. Oh, it worked.

I would say I can't believe he has loved me this whole time, because it was so surprising to hear it, but the fact is I do believe it. It was one of those earth-tilting moments, where you learn something which changes your perspective on everything. But now that I have incorporated the new perspective, I accept it utterly. He loves me, not just again, but still. Always.

My happiness overflows. We listen to the Eagles again on our way home, singing along together to our favorite songs. Everything is so perfect.

When we get home, I tell Ron I want to drop some things at my place before we pick up Natalie. We're going to come back here later tonight, but I might as well dump off my stuff now while we're here. He offers to carry whatever I need in, while I go get Natalie. He's still trying to do everything, to take care of everything.

So I head next door and knock. Laura answers the door quickly, and says, "So? How was it? Did he...?" We've talked about it, of course. Rather than respond out loud, I smile hugely and wiggle my left hand at her so she can see the ring. She gasps with amazement, but I put my finger to my lips so she doesn't say anything. She nods, understanding. Ron and I are going to tell the kids together later, at home. I don't want Natalie overhearing anything before then.

Natalie comes running down the stairs before either of us calls up to her to let her know I'm here. She is smiling joyously, and rushes up to give me a huge hug. I think I see her eyeing my hand, but nah. She's only seven, she wouldn't really notice, I don't think. Although, Natalie always has a strange way of seeming to know everything that is going on. She doesn't say anything about it, though.

"Did you have a good time last night, sweetie?" I ask her.

She nods. "Yes, we had fun. We did some experiments, and watched a couple of movies." Then she turns to Laura, and very politely says, "Thank you very much for having me."

Laura laughs and pats her on the head. "You are very welcome kiddo. Come back any time."

Ron shows up at the door. Laura grins and gives him a thumbs up, waggling her eyebrows significantly, and he ducks his head, smiling. "Okay, Nat, you ready to go?" he asks her.

She gives an unaccountable little giggle, almost as though she totally understood the exchange between Ron and Laura. But before anyone can say anything else, she says, "Yeah, I'll go get my bag," and runs up the stairs.

Ron pulls me next to his side and puts his arm around me. He asks Laura how their night went. We will have to all wait to talk about the real topic of conversation until later, after we've told the kids.

"Good," Laura says. "We watched a couple of movies from Blockbuster, but other than that Natalie and Timothy spent the entire time in his room, focused on one of their experiments. Those kids are going to grow up to be rocket scientists or something."

"Works for me," Ron laughs, "maybe they'll give us all a tour of their moon habitat someday."

Gabe

We're playing with some of Jonathan's robots when Dad comes over to get me. "Hey, buddy, how was your night?" he asks me.

"Good," I tell him. "Thanks for the Gamecube game, we played it for a while."

"Sure," he says. "You ready to go?"

I look over at Jonathan, who is still putting together his robot. "Bye, Jon," I tell him.

"Bye," he says, kind of shrugging but not really looking up from what he's doing. Okay then.

I get my bag, already packed with the Gamecube and my other stuff, and we head home.

Jonathan has been kind of weird since yesterday. I thought he was mad at me over beating him at Super Smash Bros., but when I asked him later he said he wasn't. But he's been sort of quieter than usual since then. Oh well. I guess we're both ready for me to go home.

When Dad and I get back, Natalie and Mom are sitting together on the couch, talking about last night. I drop my bag in the entryway. "Hey Nat," I say, "did you have fun with Timmy?"

"Yeah," she says, "we watched some movies from Blockbuster."

"Really?" I say. "So did we! What did you watch?"

"Shrek and Knights Tale," she says.

"You're kidding! We watched Knight's Tale too!"

Before we can get going on really talking about it, though, Dad tells me to come over and sit down. He sits next to Mom on the couch.

I look over at Natalie, wondering what this is all about, but she just looks at me like she's really happy. I can always rely on Natalie to know what's going on, so I guess nothing's wrong. So why do Mom and Dad seem like something serious is happening?

Dad says, "We have some news to tell you both. We made a decision last night while we were on our camping trip."

"What?" I say. Natalie sits there grinning ear to ear, bouncing on her seat like she knows we are about to hear something fantastic.

Dad smiles at Mom. She says, "Your father and I have decided to get re-married."

Natalie jumps up like a balloon that has been popped and squeals. I freeze in my seat, totally surprised. "Really?"

Natalie is obviously all in on this idea. She grabs Dad and gives him a hug, then grabs Mom too. "I knew it!" she shrieks. "This is so fantastic!"

Well, yeah, I guess. "Um, cool," I tell them. I don't really know how to respond. They've been divorced almost my whole life. I don't really even remember when they were married before, I was too little. But I know they're not separated anymore, and we've all been living together in one house or the other for a while now. So I guess I should have seen this coming.

Dad looks at me and laughs. "Don't hurt yourself with enthusiasm, dude!" he tells me. He is holding Natalie in his lap, and she is still bubbling over with happiness. I figure she's enthusiastic enough for both of us.

I shrug and smile sheepishly. "No, I think it's great, really. I'm happy for you guys. I guess I wonder... like... what happens next?" The questions are starting to form themselves in my head. "When are you doing it? Where are we going to live?"

Mom looks at me and holds out her hand. I reach over and take it. She meets my eyes seriously, and says, "We aren't sure about anything yet. We haven't set an actual date for a wedding." Natalie squeals again when she mentions a wedding, then clearly remembers about the fact that an engagement comes with a ring. She grabs Mom's left hand and stares at the ring she's wearing and squeals some more, and we all have to laugh. It's so girly.

Mom goes on, "We're gonna continue doing things like we have been for now. We'll be here on weekends and at my house for school. Nothing will change yet. We'll figure it all out."

Chapter 19

Leftovers

Ron

The kids are asleep fairly early tonight, after our Thanksgiving feast at Brenda's place. We had Laura and her son over to join us, since Michael is still away on deployment, and it was such a pleasant evening. The first time we've shared Thanksgiving together as an engaged couple. The only time since our first marriage ended.

I love the idea that we get to have a whole new set of firsts together. It feels so much like a new beginning to me. We did some things together during what I have privately started to call the interregnum period, but it was a sort of limbo. Now that she has agreed to marry me again, I feel like everything can be counted anew. It's all fresh again. We're starting over. It's so perfect.

"What are you smiling about?" Brenda asks. I hadn't even realized I had let a smile take over my face. I stop gazing off into the distance, and look at where she is reclining on the sofa in the living room with a book. I leave my chair to join her. She obligingly lifts her legs so I can slip in to sit beneath them, pulling her feet onto my lap.

"You make me smile," I smile at her some more.

She smirks a little. "Anything in particular this time?"

I rub her foot, massaging her through the sock. Even her feet are wonderful to me, slender and attractive. "Well, I was thinking about how this is the first time we've had Thanksgiving together. Since, you know, before."

"Mmmm," she says, closing her eyes with the feeling of the massage. "True. It's nice to get back into the swing of things."

"You know, speaking of Thanksgiving," I suggest, "would you like to have some leftovers as a bedtime snack?"

She opens her eyes and grins. "I was thinking that exact thing."

"Great minds think alike."

We get up and head into the kitchen, and start pulling out storage containers with everything we packed away after dinner. She begins spooning stuffing with gravy onto her plate to be microwaved. "I think after we're done, I'm gonna freeze the rest of this. We're leaving tomorrow to go to your house, and we won't be back here for a few days. I'll defrost it next week and we can do Thanksgiving again."

"Excellent. The more Thanksgivings we share, the better." I chuckle at a distant memory.

"What?"

"Oh, just remembering that not having Thanksgiving together until now wasn't for lack of trying on my part." I can laugh about it now, but of course at the time it was the most mortifying moment of my life.

She sputters out a laugh. "Seriously? You're bringing that up again?"

"Bold of me, I know." I meet her eyes mischievously. "I'm risking getting slapped merely by mentioning it."

She gasps with pretend outrage and lifts her hand jokingly as though to slap me. I duck away and grab her wrist, then yank her into a hug. I wrap my arms tightly around her, and she laughs into my chest.

"I'll get you for that," she tells me.

"Oh, I hope so," I murmur into her hair. "I really hope so."

She laughs. "Finish your leftovers."

Brad

I get out yesterday's Thanksgiving leftovers for another go-round for dinner. This is the best part of Thanksgiving, a couple of solid days of delicious turkey and stuffing and potatoes. Stef seems to have her appetite back, thank goodness, after having spent a couple of months green around the gills. She's not showing yet, but I know it'll be soon. I'm eagerly anticipating her slender frame growing, rounding. It'll be sexy. And wonderful.

Jonathan gobbles his food. Heh - he gobbles the gobbler. I know he's looking forward to Gabe getting back to his Dad's house, since it's Friday.

After dinner he's getting antsy, wondering when Gabe will come over. The sun's already down, but it's not dark yet, and he asks if he can go check to see if they're home yet.

"Yeah, go ahead, but don't go anywhere else. It's getting dark."

He grabs his jacket and heads out the door.

Jonathan

When I get down to Gabe's house I see their cars are already parked in the driveway. I wonder if they're still eating dinner since Gabe hasn't come over to my house yet.

I knock on the door, and his Mom answers. "Hi, Jonathan, come on in. Gabe's upstairs in his room."

Huh. They've already finished dinner apparently. Why didn't Gabe come over?

I go upstairs, pass by Natalie's room where I see she's laying on her bed reading, and get to Gabe's door. He's also laying on his bed, reading a comic book. Lame.

"Dude!" I say as I come in. "When did you get here?" I take off my jacket and toss it on his chair.

He sits up. "Hey, Jonathan. We've been here since lunch. I guess I got wrapped up in reading this new manga and forgot to come over. How are you?"

That's annoying. How could a comic make him forget to come and play with me? But I don't tell him that. "Good. Glad you're here. Lemme see your manga!" I put a smile on my face.

"Sure," he says, and tosses it over to me.

Natalie

When Jonathan passes by my room I ask Angel what's up with him and Gabe. Dad asked Gabe after we got here if he was going to go play with Jonathan, but he shrugged and said, "Yeah, maybe in a while." But then he never got around to it. I was so interested in my book that I didn't think of it again until now.

But it is kind of weird. Normally Gabe wants to spend all the time he can with his best friend.

Angel says, "*Your brother has been feeling somewhat reluctant to spend time with Jonathan.*"

"Why?" I ask. "Did they get in a fight or something?"

"*No, but Gabe has noticed a few times that Jonathan's interests are different from his.*"

I look closer at Angel. Sometimes I can see he is trying not to tell me something he knows, like he is worried it'll bother me. I thought the whole God thing would've cured him of that.

"Dude, Angel," I say, rolling my eyes at him. "You know I can tell when you're not saying something, right? You need to get over it! After telling me about God you should understand there isn't anything you can't tell me. So what is it?"

Angel laughs and shakes his head. "*I certainly have no secrets from you, do I, my darling?*"

"Well, it's only fair, since I have no secrets from you, with you watching me and in my head every single second. So, spill it."

He laughs even harder. "*Of course, my dear. You are in charge. The situation with your brother and Jonathan is growing somewhat tense, because Gabe is starting to notice more often when Jonathan is unkind. He is usually careful not to show this side of himself to Gabe, because he values their friendship. However, Gabe has noticed recently that Jonathan seems to enjoy harming others if he can. This is troublesome for Gabe.*"

I nod, thinking. "Well, Jonathan has always been mean to Timothy, and I think Gabe knows it, but he usually tries to ignore it or get Jonathan to do something else instead. Has it happened with anyone else?"

Angel looks like he sighs. Sometimes I wonder about that. I know he isn't actually sighing, but I think he does stuff like that to add to the words he says, to make them mean more than words alone would. Well, I guess people do it too, using their hands and face while they're talking. Maybe I'll ask him to tell me more about it another time. But I don't want to get distracted from the thing about Jonathan.

Angel waits a minute, and I know he heard that whole thing in my head, and he smiles and nods, to tell me I'm right and we can discuss it later if I want. But for now he says, "*Yes, there have been other instances. For example, Gabe has witnessed Jonathan taking pleasure in killing insects, which disturbs your*" *brother. A few days ago when they had their overnight, he believed Jonathan may have injured a small child at McDonald's, although he didn't actually see it happen. But he is starting to suspect. Your brother is a good and kind person, like you are, and these incidents are beginning to lessen his desire to spend time in Jonathan's company."*

"Poor Gabe! Jonathan is his very best friend. It would be sad if he didn't want to be friends anymore." I think about this for a while. "I wish Jonathan would be nicer, so Gabe would like being with him better."

Angel shakes his head and smiles. *"Sadly, my dear, Jonathan is who he is. You have seen how disagreeable he can be. It doesn't seem likely that he will change for the better."*

Yeah, he's been mean to me and Timothy for a long time. I hinted to him a couple of months ago that he should act nicer, since his guardian angel might be watching, but he didn't care. Mostly me and Timothy try to stay away from him.

Angel is watching me, calm like always, following along as I think. I pick back up the book I was reading. It's a children's bible. My grandma gave it to me for my birthday. She always likes to take us to church with her when we visit. That's pretty much the only time I've been to church. She talks about God and Jesus a lot too. And even about guardian angels, ever since I found her painting of one at her house in Albuquerque when I was really little. I think she wishes Gabe and me would always go to church and pray and stuff. We've done that stuff with her. I do it to make her happy when we're together. I have never seen any point in praying to God when Angel is always sitting right here.

And now, of course, I'll never have any reason to pray to God. Now that I know he doesn't even exist. Only guardians exist, like Angel.

But, I've started reading the bible. Since Angel told us last week there isn't a God, and religion is something people made up, I've wished there was something we could do to make people stop hurting each other over religion. I've always wanted people not to hurt each other, but the idea that they'd do it over some fake God who has never existed makes me really upset. I want to figure out if there is a way to change it. And I decided the best way to start is to try to understand it better. So I'm reading this children's Bible.

The stories are interesting, I guess, a lot like other myths I've read. Like Greek mythology and stuff.

I'm about to start reading again, but I hear Jonathan and Gabe horsing around in the room next door. They sound like they're having fun, but I wonder if it will last. If Gabe is starting to wish Jonathan was nicer, I don't know how much longer they'll be friends. Poor Gabe.

Well, wait a minute! I'm trying to understand religion more so I can find a way to change things for the better. I wonder if I could do that with Jonathan! Like, could I try to understand him better, make friends with him, and help him be nicer? It would be easier for Gabe to keep his best friend if he wasn't being so mean all the time.

It would be like an experiment! Before I go trying to change something huge like the way people hurt each other over religion, maybe I could see if I can change one person. Just Jonathan. It would be a good start. And it's probably best to start small.

Angel is watching me while all this runs through my head, and he's starting to look a little alarmed. *"Darling,"* he says, *"of course you would like to help Jonathan be a nicer person, for your brother's sake, but I do not know how it would be possible."*

"Well," I say, "can't hurt to try. And I can't really know what to do unless I understand him better."

Angel laughs softly and lifts his hands up. *"Very well, my love."*

So, that's my new experiment. I can't wait to tell Timothy about it when he comes over to play tomorrow. But for now, it's time to start. The first step: trying to understand Jonathan better.

Chapter 20

The Jonathan Project

Jonathan

Gabe and I are in his room, goofing around. It's too dark to play outside, but I won't have to go home for a while. His Dad came in a few minutes ago and told us we should settle down before we break something. So now we're getting ready to play with his Legos. We had started building a big castle a few weeks ago, so we figure we can get back to doing some work on it.

We are pushing some of his clothes and other stuff out the way to make room on his floor for building. "Hi," I hear from the doorway, and I look up. There is Natalie standing there, smiling at me.

What the heck? Gabe's sister never plays with us.

I look at Gabe, who shrugs. "What do you need, Natty?" he asks her.

"Nothing," she says. "I was just wondering what you guys are doing. Can I play with you?"

"Um, yeah, I guess," he says. "Okay with you, Jonathan?"

"Yeah, whatever," I say. I don't really care if she plays with us. As long as her dumb friend isn't around, she can be pretty fun. She used to hang around with us a long time ago. And she's never tattled on me.

She gives me a big bright smile and sits down on the floor next to me. "So, what are you playing with?" she asks.

"Legos, duh," I tell her, pointing to the Legos spread all around us.

"Cool!" she says, like it's the most exciting thing ever. "This castle is so neat! What can I do to help?"

I look over at Gabe again and raise my eyebrows at him. Why is she suddenly being so interested when she never has before?

Gabe always tries to make his little sister happy, though. So he inspects the castle, trying to find something for her to do, and says, "Um, you want to maybe color some flags we can put up on the castle?"

"Sure!" she says, way more enthusiastic than I've ever seen her before.

So before long, while Gabe and I are sorting through his Legos to find all the knights and horses and stuff to set up around the castle, Natalie has some paper and crayons and is starting to draw some flags. I have to admit they look really cool, authentic like some of the banners we saw in the Knight's Tale movie last week. With designs on them like on their shields and stuff. Having her here playing with us isn't too bad.

Natalie's

It will never fail to amaze me to watch my remarkable Seer operate. She has launched into her newest enterprise with steely determination and unbridled optimism. Once she has decided to do something, she cannot be swayed from her purpose.

Her current effort reminds me of the endeavor years ago to make Timothy comfortable, after they first met when they were mere toddlers. Their first encounter made her realize Timothy struggles with social situations, and quickly becomes overwhelmed when his surroundings are challenging. She immediately set out to find a way to bring him peace and happiness. In doing this, she used me efficiently, like a mechanic uses his accustomed tools, to analyze the situation and derive the best results.

She is doing so again. As she interacts with the boys, she is constantly checking with me to see how Jonathan is receiving her attentions, and adjusting her actions to best set him at ease with her presence. She understands that her interest seems unusual for him, so her goal for tonight is simply to play with the boys in a way which will leave Jonathan content to be in her company.

It is working. When she first arrived in Gabe's room, Jonathan was suspicious, wondering about what motive she could possibly have. However, as the evening together progresses, he is simply a child enjoying playtime with other children.

Jonathan is certainly not entirely diabolical. He is, after all, just a human child. His history of tormenting Natalie and her best friend has made me very leery of seeing her in Jonathan's presence, but this evening is unfolding exactly as she had hoped.

Jonathan's Guardian watches the scene with wry acceptance, knowing the girl's intent. The Guardian anticipates the growth in Jonathan's soul which might occur as a result of interacting with the Seer.

I need to remind myself that I should always be guided by my Seer, not by my own desires or instincts. She has directed our activities towards experiences I have been sometimes reluctant to participate in. I have worried that some of her ideas might lead to distressing discoveries, as occurred when I was compelled to explain how human religions are all mythology. But these times have always resulted in growth, and learning, and understanding. For myself as well as for the child. I must follow her lead, do as she wishes, comply with her will. It is not for me to construct her life. I must only accompany her as she walks along the path she chooses.

If Natalie believes she can help Jonathan be a nicer person, then I must try to believe the same.

Stefanie

Brad and I are taking advantage of Jonathan being over at his friend's house to watch some t.v. We record our favorite shows on our VCR each week, then watch them later when we get the chance. We've just finished up the latest episode of Smallville.

Brad checks the time. "I need to go grab Jonathan. It's getting close to bedtime." He leans over and gives me a kiss. "Be right back."

I head into the kitchen to clean up a little. As I'm finishing up, Brad and Jonathan head back in.

"Hey kid," I say, and lean down to give his head a little peck. "Want a bedtime snack?"

"Sure," he says.

I get him some crackers and he sits down at the table. I join him and pop one of his crackers into my mouth. It's nice to want to eat food again, after a few weeks of feeling sick all the time.

"Have fun at Gabe's?" I ask him.

"Yeah," he says, munching on crackers, "Natalie helped us with our Lego castle."

"Really?" I ask. I don't think that happens very much. Natalie has always seemed too, I don't know, dainty and intellectual to enjoy the sort of rough-housing Gabe and Jonathan usually engage in. "Has she done that before?"

"Not really. I thought it'd be annoying to have his little sister with us, but it was fine. She drew some cool flags to put up on the castle. She didn't bother us at all."

Huh. Well, that's nice, I guess. "All right, kid, time to take a bath."

"Awwwww! Do I have to? I didn't even have school today!"

"Oh, okay, I guess you can skip it tonight. Go get ready for bed. I'll be there in a few minutes."

He pushes back his chair and heads down the hallway to his room. Glad he's in a good mood tonight.

Natalie

I think tonight went really well. Jonathan wasn't mean to me at all, and he didn't mind me playing with him and Gabe. I kept checking with Angel to make sure I wasn't doing anything that would bother him. So he was happy the whole time and I think we were all able to have fun together.

That was the plan for starters. I want to spend enough time with him to be able to start suggesting ways for him to be nicer. But I can't do that yet, because he'd be annoyed. And there wasn't anything to suggest tonight, since he didn't do anything bad.

I was also really glad Gabe had a good time. He told me over and over how cool he thought my flags were, and Jonathan even agreed. I'm happy Gabe and his friend still get along, even though Angel told me he's starting to have doubts about Jonathan.

So experiment phase one: success.

Angel laughs at me.

"What?" I ask him. "It went great. It was exactly how I wanted it to happen."

"Yes, my darling, of course. I only laugh because I am so delighted at how well you executed your plan for the evening. I agree. It was a brilliant success. So far."

Well, I guess I should do the experiment properly. I get a fresh notebook out. I don't want to keep notes about this in the same one I use for homework. I open the notebook, think for a minute, then write at the top of the first page, "The Jonathan Project."

Chapter 21
Words

November 24, 2001

Timothy

I'm going over to Natalie's today. Since she's always at her Dad's house on weekends, my Mom has agreed to drive me over there again.

When Mom drops me off, I go up to Natalie's room, while Mom stays downstairs to talk with her parents. Natalie meets me halfway down the stairs. "Hi!" she tells me. "I have a new idea for an experiment to tell you about."

"I do, too," I tell her.

I've been thinking of ways to work on hearing Guardian better. I can detect him if I'm trying to open my mind, and he's trying to talk to me. If both of those things aren't happening at the same time, I can feel his presence when I open my mind, but nothing else. When I can hear him, I am not exactly hearing his words, more like I can almost figure out what he is trying to say.

It isn't very clear or precise, and I'd like to improve on that. I want to be able to hear words.

We get into her room and she closes the door like always, so we can talk privately. We don't want anybody hearing us talk to our guardians. "Tell me about your experiment," she says when she turns around from the door. "Is it about Guardian?"

"Yes," I say. "I keep my mind open a lot of the time, and sometimes I know what he is saying to me, but I can't really hear words. It's more like remembering a dream, not like something real that is happening. So I've been thinking of ways to practice, and hopefully learn how to hear him a lot more clearly."

She is sitting on her desk chair, kicking her legs. "Okay," she says, "what do we do?"

I sit down on her bed and take my notebook out of the bag I brought with me. "Can you get a notebook out too?"

"Sure," she says, and reaches in her desk drawer and gets out a notebook. Then she sits and waits to see what we'll do next.

"All right, here's what I want to do. I want you to write down a word, but don't show me. Then I'm going to try to hear Guardian tell me the word." I look up into the air, wishing I knew better where to look when I'm talking to my guardian. "Guardian, can you check her word, and then try to use energy to tell it to me?"

Natalie looks over to where Angel must be, then tells me, "Yes, Guardian is going to watch what I write and then try to tell it to you. What kind of word should I write?"

"Probably best to stick with a noun," I tell her. We're learning about nouns in school. "It'll be easier if the word is an object, not a description or a feeling or something that isn't real."

She thinks for a second, then writes something down, using her other hand to shield the page from my eyes. Then she looks up at me and waits to see what will happen next.

I close my eyes, and open my mind. It's a weird feeling, but I'm getting used to it. I don't think I could ever explain it to someone else. It feels like I am actually doing something in my brain, like making my mind open up like a cupboard door. I feel Guardian there inside my mind, and wait to see if I can hear anything.

After a couple of minutes I feel like I'm getting something, but I can't tell what exact word it is. It's like I'm getting the idea of something, though, sort of like a dream. What is it? Something big. Like, an animal maybe? I can't tell, so I write down "animal" in my notebook.

"Okay, Natalie, show me what your word was." She holds up her notebook, and I see that she had written "elephant." I hold up my notebook so she can see I wrote "animal."

"That's really good!" she says. "Wow! I think you're getting much better at this! It was an animal, so it counts, right?"

I'm not satisfied. "I didn't hear it though. More like I felt it, and it wasn't precise enough to know exactly what you wrote." I sigh. "Can we try again? Is that okay with Guardian?"

After a couple of seconds, Natalie tells me, "Angel says Guardian will always be willing to try whatever you like." She thinks for a moment, then says, "Timothy, I don't think you ever need to be worried that Guardian would get tired of trying your experiments. Angel is always completely patient with every single thing I ever want to do. I don't think guardians can ever get bored or anything like that." She looks over to where Angel is, then smiles. "Angel says I am precisely correct."

Hmmm. Well, good to know. "All right, then, let's try again. Please write another word on the next line."

We try it over and over, but the same thing keeps happening. I get a sort of impression of something, and write down a word, but it's never exactly the same word. Like, when Natalie writes "airplane", I write "machine." When Natalie writes "house", I write "box". It's never quite right.

After a lot of tries, maybe Guardian wouldn't ever get tired of it, but I'll bet Natalie is. "I tell you what," I tell her, "let's try this experiment a different way. We don't really need to be together to do this. We can do it at night after I go home. How about every night before bedtime, say at 8:00, you write down a word, and tell it to Angel. He can tell Guardian. I'll listen at eight and write down what I think the word is, then we can compare notes at school in the morning. That way we aren't doing the same thing over and over in one day. Maybe practicing a little bit every day is more likely to work."

Natalie says, "Angel, will you remind me every night at eight that it's time to write down a word?" She listens for a second and then nods at me. "Okay, we'll do it."

Natalie

After Timothy's experiment with Guardian, I think he might want to take a break and do something else. But he remembers I had told him I had an experiment too, and asks me, "Now, what was your experiment idea?"

I've been a little worried about telling him about this, since Jonathan is his least favorite person. But what he said about practicing a little bit every day gives me an idea.

"You know how I've been reading the bible, trying to understand religion so I can figure out a way to help people stop hurting each other over it?"

"Yes," he says.

"Well, I'm thinking maybe I should try to do something smaller. Like what you said, about doing your word experiment with Guardian a little bit at a time, rather than all at once. Maybe doing a piece at a time will make it easier."

"Okay," he says, "so what do you want to start with?"

I take the notebook where I had been writing down all the words for his experiment, turn it back to the first page, and hand it to him.

He takes the notebook, reads "The Jonathan Project" at the top, and his forehead wrinkles. He looks up at me like he's about to say something, but instead he looks back down and reads the notes I wrote last night after phase one of my experiment.

When he's finished reading, he doesn't look very happy.

"Sooooo," he says slowly, "you are going to spend more time with Jonathan?"

"Yes," I tell him, "so I can get to know him well enough to understand how to help him change to be a nicer person."

He's frowning. "I don't think he will ever be a nicer person."

"Well," I say, "we can't know for sure. And I think this is a really good place for me to start experimenting, to see whether I can help people behave better. Don't you think? That I should try to figure out how to help just one person?"

He huffs out a big sigh. I can tell he's trying to find a polite way to say what he thinks. Then he throws up his hands and says, "But he's so awful! He's always so mean! What if he hurts you?"

"I don't think he will. I'm always checking with Angel to make sure I know what he's thinking. So I can change what I'm doing if I think the experiment is going the wrong way. I think it can work."

Timothy looks really doubtful. "Does Angel think it can work?"

"Well, not really. Angel thinks Jonathan isn't very likely to change. But I want to give it a try."

Angel is watching us discuss this. Timothy doesn't seem to be any happier. In fact he is starting to seem sad, not like he thinks I'm going to be wasting my time, but like he thinks something even worse will happen. He shuts his mouth tight and I can tell he won't want to talk at all any more. I've seen that expression on his face before, when he gets too emotional to speak. I look over at Angel to find out what Timothy is thinking, since apparently Timothy isn't going to tell me. Angel says, *Timothy is concerned he is also going to have to spend more time with Jonathan, and he knows it would be unlikely to end well for him.*

Oh.

"You don't have to worry, Timothy, I won't spend extra time with Jonathan while you are here. You won't have to be around him."

But this doesn't seem to make Timothy any happier. "What is it, Timmy?" I use the old name I used to call him when we were younger. "Why do you look so sad?" I never want Timothy to be sad.

"I don't know," he mumbles.

"Come on, please tell me," I say. "I want to know what you're thinking." I can ask Angel again but I wish Timothy would share it with me.

"Okay, fine," he says, wiping his nose with his sleeve. "I guess if you are going to be spending all your time experimenting on Jonathan, I won't get to see you as much."

"Oh!" I have to admit I hadn't thought of it that way. "Um, maybe. But I'll still be in class with you, and whenever we're over at my Mom's house I'll see you there. I'll make sure we'll still spend lots of time together."

He still looks very glum. "All right," he says sadly. "I guess it's a good experiment. But I'm going to miss you if you end up spending a lot more time with him instead of me."

Now I feel terrible. I really want to help Jonathan change, but I don't want Timothy to end up feeling lonely because of my experiment. I try to think of a solution.

"Well, maybe once Jonathan starts being nicer, you can hang around with us too?"

Timothy stares at me like I'm insane. Well, maybe not.

"All right," I say, "how about we work extra hard on your experiment to be able to hear Guardian better? If you can start really understanding what he's saying, I can talk to you all the time through Angel and Guardian. It'll be like we're always together!"

"Yeah, okay," he says, but he doesn't sound convinced. He gives a heavy sigh. "Well, tell me more about your plans for the Jonathan Project." I guess he figures he might as well help me plan out the experiment.

That's good. He'll be fine. And I'm going to help Jonathan be better too. Everything will work out great.

I look over at Angel, who shrugs.

Fine. Nobody else is convinced, but I'm going to do this. I'll make it work.

Chapter 22

Take Advantage

Laura

After Timothy runs upstairs with Natalie, I hang around for a while at Ron's house, talking to him and Brenda. I'm very glad to take advantage of the chance to hear all about their desert trip. I spent Thanksgiving dinner with them at Brenda's place, but the kids were around so this is the first time we've really had the chance to talk. It sounds like it was so romantic! I'm very impressed with Ron for setting it all up. He must have planned out every single part of it.

And they are so, so happy now. Like, blissful. They were happy before, but I think neither one of them was completely sure how the other was feeling, so there was always a little bit of tension. That's gone now.

"So, have you started planning a wedding yet?"

Brenda chuckles. "Only a little. When I told my Mom about it, she was so excited. She started talking about having another gigantic wedding and inviting everybody in the world. We were more inclined to have a very small event, maybe down at the courthouse with only the two of us. But now that my Mom is involved, I think we might end up compromising and doing it in Albuquerque, to make her happy. We could do it in her church, that's where we got married the first time. But we'll still keep it really small, just family probably."

"Any thoughts on when?"

"Well, we're considering doing it over spring break next year. It's the last week in March. It'll be nice to take the kids back for a family trip to New Mexico. Show them the sights, where we used to live and stuff."

Ron is sitting there glowing silently. He hasn't said much about it. "So, Ron," I ask him, "Do you have any preferences?"

He grins. "None at all. This is all Brenda. I will go along with absolutely anything she wants to do. Once I got that ring on her finger, my part was done."

We all laugh.

"In the meantime," Brenda says, "is Mike's ship still coming in?"

"Yeah," I say, "as far as I know the schedule is still set for it to get back on December 5. I can't believe it's really happening. After September 11, I was afraid he'd be gone for another year. But they've already been deployed since June, so I guess they figured that's long enough for this time."

Ron asks, "Is Timothy excited to see his Dad again?"

I sigh. "To be honest, not really. I think Timothy likes the house to be quiet, with just the two of us. Or with Natalie over, of course. He and Mike never really seem to be able to see eye to eye."

I've been worried about it. I love Michael so much, and I know he loves Timothy, but he's never been able to feel comfortable with our son. Timothy is so different from what Michael had envisioned having a son would be like. There's no throwing baseballs together or riding bikes or wrestling. Timothy is a cerebral creature, not an athletic one. So when Michael is home, I often feel myself trying to mediate between the two of them, trying to isolate them from each other where possible. It's difficult.

Brenda looks at me sympathetically. She knows exactly what I'm thinking. She and I have talked about this endlessly.

Ron probably regrets bringing it up. "Well," he says somewhat awkwardly, "I'm sure it'll be fine." He shrugs and smiles hopefully.

Brenda and I look at each other and laugh. Oh my gosh. We might love our husbands, but men will never understand things the way women do. Maybe it's because women talk about every little thing in excruciating detail with each other. I doubt men do.

Although, Ron did attend to every excruciating detail of the camping trip. Maybe we're not so different after all.

Stefanie

The kids are out playing in the yard. Brad had to go in to work. The weekend after Thanksgiving is always a really busy time at the store, for some reason. So I have a quiet moment inside by myself.

I pick up the ultrasound picture from my last doctor's appointment. It looks like a peanut. A cute little peanut. Everything seems to be going along fine. I'm wrapping up the first trimester in a few days, and the morning sickness seems to have gone. We won't know the gender for a while. I kind of feel like it's a girl, though. Maybe, I have to admit to myself, I just hope it's a girl. It'd be nice to have one of each. Otherwise I'd be so outnumbered around here. One girl in a house with three guys? Ack!

Well, it's not for a while. I have to try not to get ahead of myself. I have so much to do now. I'm glad I should be finished with school by the time the baby is born. Assuming the due date is accurate.

I'm not going to have much leisure time for the next three weeks. Two weeks before finals, and I still have a couple of projects to work on this weekend. Not to mention preparing for the holidays. Then in January I start my last semester, and my internship. I'm so glad I'm feeling better. Wanting to barf constantly during class made it hard to concentrate, I'll say that much. I hope the rest of my pregnancy is easy enough to not be distracting while I am so busy next semester.

I look out the window at Jonathan and Gabe. They seem to be doing okay, and it's an hour or so before I need to make lunch. So I guess I should take advantage of the opportunity to get a little studying done.

I pull out my textbook and a highlighter, and start reading my assignment.

Brad

"I'm home!"

I kick my shoes off and head into the kitchen. I'm home a little earlier than I expected. The store was quieter than we thought it would be, so I got off by the mid-afternoon.

Stefanie is sitting at the table studying. She looks up and gives me a smile. I see through the window that Jonathan has Gabe over, and they're out playing tetherball in the back.

I come over to Stef and lean down to give her a kiss. "Hi darlin', how you doing?"

"Good," she says. "The boys have been playing out back most of the day, so I've been able to get some studying done."

I sit down at the table across from her. "While they're still out there, there's something I want to ask you. I was talking to my manager at work, and she gave me a really good idea. Or I think it might be a really good idea."

"Oh?" she says, closing her textbook. "What is it?"

"Well, you know how we were wondering how Jonathan is going to react to being a big brother?"

"Yeah," she says, looking perplexed at where I could be going with this.

"So, one of the things I have wondered about is whether he's gotten so used to being an only child that it'll be hard for him to do stuff like share. He's never had to do anything for anyone other than himself."

"Um, yeah," she says, one eyebrow raised. I can tell she wants me to get to the point.

"Well, my manager gave me an idea. A way to help Jonathan learn how to take care of something, maybe get outside himself a little."

She silently looks at me and waves her hand, to tell me to go on.

"How about getting him a dog?"

She sits back, looking somewhat alarmed.

"Before you think you're going to end up having to do a lot to take care of it, I promise you that me and Jonathan can do everything. I know how, I lived in a foster home once with a dog, I learned how to do all the work. All the walks and feedings and baths and whatever. I know you have a ton on your plate, so I'm not planning for this to be a new chore for you. I think it might really help Jonathan get used to helping out, and learning how to take care of something. Before he becomes a big brother."

Stef is silent, a thoughtful look on her face. "Hm. I don't know." She looks out the window at the kids playing in the back. "I think he'd like to have a dog. And yeah, you're right, he could probably use some lessons in responsibility. We've never really required much of him."

I smile at her and grab her hand. I can see her processing this, mulling it over in her mind. I wait.

"Well, maybe?" she says. "Like, what kind of dog? Where would we get it?"

I think she's sold. It should be downhill from here. "I think we should take Jonathan to the pound, and let him pick out whatever rescue dog he wants. That way he'll be really invested in it, and be more inclined to participate in taking care of it."

She squeezes my hand. "Wow, Brad, you've really given this a lot of thought, haven't you? And I think you're right, letting him pick it out would be the way to get Jonathan to feel like it's his responsibility. Maybe you should be the one studying psychology." She jokingly pushes her book across the table at me.

Heh! "Nah, babe, I'm no scholar. You're the brains around this joint."

She chuckles a little, and I cut it off with a kiss. Might as well take advantage of the quiet before the herd of boys comes running back in here.

Chapter 23

Something To Tell You

Ron

Since next weekend is Gabe's birthday, Brenda and I have been talking about what we should do to celebrate. It still feels surprising and wonderful to know that whatever we plan, it will be together. Too many years went by where we had to have separate celebrations with the kids for each holiday. So much wasted time.

But, I am trying to overcome all the regret I've been living with for so long. Being engaged again to Brenda is like a whole new life has been dropped into my lap, and I intend to savor every moment of it.

So after Gabe gets back from playing at Jonathan's house, we talk about a birthday plan while the four of us are eating dinner.

Brenda starts. "So, Gabe, you're going to turn ten years old next Saturday. Double digits! I can hardly believe it!"

Gabe grins. "Um, yeah Mom, I know!"

We all laugh. "Well," Brenda goes on, "we haven't really made a plan for how to celebrate your birthday yet. We thought we should think of something good. Ten is a pretty significant birthday."

Gabe and Natalie immediately turn to each other with wide eyes. Planning a birthday celebration is obviously an important and thrilling task. Natalie gets a very thoughtful look on her face.

Gabe wants some parameters. "Like, what are you thinking we could do?"

Natalie points out to her brother exactly what I have been thinking, "It'll be nice to be able to do something all together. We won't have to do one birthday at Mom's house and another birthday at Dad's house."

Gabe sees the benefit of this. "So," he speculates, "rather than do two little things, maybe we could do one big thing?"

Brenda and I look at each other and grin. She says, "Sure. I don't know whether you'd rather have a regular birthday party, or maybe do something a little more grown up like going out to a fancy dinner? Or maybe we could go somewhere fun during the day?"

Gabe says, "I'd rather go somewhere fun. Like a park or something?"

"Well," I say, hauling out a suggestion I've been eager to make, "Legoland opened a couple of years ago and we've never gotten around to going. Want to give it a try?" I've been wishing to find a time to take the kids, but with only having them a day and a half on weekends there never has seemed to be a good time. That's all changed now.

Gabe explodes out of his seat with a whoop. "Yes!" Natalie claps her hands and yelps, an unusually exuberant display for her. She is clearly caught up in Gabe's excitement.

Gabe asks, "Can we bring Jonathan? Oh man, he'd be so excited to come!"

"Well, sure, sounds fine, if it's okay with his parents." I look over at Natalie, expecting her to chime in with a request to bring Timothy. However, she has a thoughtful expression on her face, and she remains silent. I wonder, as always, what's going on in that head of hers.

Gabe starts heading towards the door. "I have to go tell Jonathan! He's gonna flip!"

"Hang on, kiddo, I'll walk down there with you, so I can ask his parents if it's all right with them."

Surprisingly, Natalie asks, getting up from the table, "Can I walk down there with you too?" That's unexpected - she doesn't normally have any desire to go to Jonathan's house. Huh.

"Sure, kid, get your shoes."

Jonathan

Running down the street to Gabe's house, to tell him my amazing news, I'm surprised to see Gabe and his Dad and sister walking towards me. I run right up to Gabe, and say, "I have something to tell you!"

Hilariously, at the exact same time, he says the exact same thing. "I have something to tell you!" Natalie and her Dad laugh with us.

"Okay," Gabe says, "you go first."

"I'm getting a dog!" I practically scream it out, I'm so excited. I can still hardly believe it. "At dinner Mom and Dad told me they've decided they are going to take me to the dog pound tomorrow to pick out a pet dog!"

"OMG!" Gabe says. "That is so awesome!"

Even Natalie seems happy for me. "A puppy dog?" she says, putting her hands up to her mouth. "That'll be so nice!"

"Yeah," I say, "I get to pick out whatever dog I want! Think I should get a great big dog or a little dog?"

Before Gabe answers, his Dad says, "Can we head on back to your house, Jonathan? I have something to ask your parents."

Oh yeah, they were out here for something, weren't they? "What were you going to tell me, Gabe?"

"For my birthday next weekend, we're going to Legoland, and you can come with us!"

"What?!" I shriek. "Heck yes!" This day keeps getting better and better. "Come on!" I yell to Gabe, and start tearing back down the street in the opposite direction, to get home and ask Mom and Dad. I hear Natalie giggling behind me as Gabe and I run.

Natalie's

It is interesting how the relationship dynamics between the three children seem to be shifting tonight. For the better, possibly. I don't know if it could be attributed to Natalie's decision to intervene in Jonathan's life, as much as it is simply the coincidence of both boys having exciting news to share at the same time.

However, since last night's play session, when Natalie joined the two boys, I have noticed each of them has had a slight adjustment in attitude towards the other. Gabe's concerns about Jonathan's behaviors have receded. And Jonathan's resentment toward Gabe, which had been simmering since Gabe defeated him at a video game, has all but vanished. Their friendship seems restored to what it was previously, one of childish exuberance, nothing more.

Did spending time with Natalie last night contribute to this? It is impossible to tell. It is true there is something about the Seer's mere presence which brings an atmosphere of peace and joy to those around her, even without any conscious effort on her part. This is enhanced when she deliberately attempts to make another person happy. And she has been doing so with Jonathan. She continues to focus on ways to further her current ambition, The Jonathan Project. Only time will tell whether her attempt to improve Jonathan's behavior will succeed.

But I feel more hopeful, watching the children chattering together in Jonathan's living room as their parents discuss the Legoland plan for next weekend. The boys speak excitedly about which rides and other attractions will be available to them. Natalie pays close attention to their conversation, silently participating by smiling and nodding and reacting with pleasure to each of their suggestions. Gabe is accustomed to having Natalie constantly demonstrating her quiet love and approval as she watches him speak. However, Jonathan has not experienced this before, and it is clear he is keenly aware of her smiling upon him as he and Gabe make their plans for the amusement park outing.

She draws me into the interaction, saying silently to me, although to all outward appearances her attention is entirely focused on the boys as they speak, "See, Angel? Jonathan and Gabe are getting along perfectly fine. My plan is working. Admit it!"

I smile and nod at her, mirroring her actions with the boys. The plan does seem to be unfolding exactly as she wishes.

Chapter 24

Shelter

November 25, 2001

Jonathan

I can't sit still in the car as we drive to the animal shelter. Mom and Dad are in the front, still talking to me about how I will have to be responsible for the dog, I'll have to feed it and take it for walks and clean up after it and whatever. Fine! I am super excited about the idea of having a dog of my own, so I'm willing to do anything it needs. This is going to be amazing!

I've always wished to have a pet. I mean, sometimes I find lizards and stuff outside, but those don't last very long and they aren't much fun to play with. They always just try to get away from me. But a dog will stay with me, and do whatever I want it to do.

When we finally park and get out of the car, I can't wait to get inside and see what they have. We have to go by the front desk first and talk to someone, and Mom and Dad fill out some paperwork. I'm dying to get back inside, where I know the animals are waiting. I can smell them, which isn't great but I figure if I only have one I'll make sure to keep it clean so it isn't smelly. I can hear them too, yipping and barking.

Finally, the lady at the front takes us through the door to see the dogs. There are rows of cages, and lots of dogs look up from what they were doing to watch us walk in. Some of them lay their heads back down, but some of them come right up to the door of their cage and stick out their tongues and pant while they watch us.

"Well," Dad says, "what do you think? Take a look and see if any of them seem like they want to come and live with you."

To be honest, it's a lot to take in. All of those big eyes staring at me. The lady says I can come down with her and look closer, so I follow her slowly along the rows of cages. There's a big tan dog who looks sad, and a little dinky dog that yips at me.   There's a couple of cats too. I keep going, looking at each one, wondering which one is my dog.

Down at the end of the row I notice a little dog, a nice dark brown color, very fluffy and cute, watching me with an eager face. It has big yellow-brown eyes, and ears that kind of flop down on the side of its head. It has white paws, and a white patch all the way around its neck. It puts its little white paw up on the bar of the cage and sort of scratches it, like it's trying to get me to play. It gives a funny little bark.

Mom and Dad and the lady watch while I stop in front of this cage. I bend down to get a closer look, and it pokes its foot out through the cage, closer to me, so I touch the paw. It gives another bark. I sit down on the floor next to it and try to reach in to touch its fur.

"Do you like this one, Jonathan?" Mom says, and I nod, still looking into the cage. Then she asks the lady, "What kind of dog is it?"

The lady says, "This is a male puppy, about two or three months old. We believe it is a labrador and border collie mix. He weighs about 13 pounds, but he'll get bigger pretty fast. He'll probably end up weighing about 50 or 60 pounds. He probably won't be available for very long. Young puppies are very popular and usually get snatched up pretty quickly."

She crouches down next to me on the floor. "Would you like to hold him?" she asks me.

"Yes, I would!"

She stands back up. "Okay, follow me. We have a room where you can play with him for a little while, and get to know him." I take my hand back out of the cage, where I was still touching his fur, and stand up. The poor little guy whines when I move away.

We follow her down to another door. She lets us into a room where there are some chairs, and some pet toys, like balls and stuff for them to climb on. "Wait here," she says, "I'll bring him right in."

In a couple of minutes she's back, holding the brown puppy in her arms. She comes over to me, strokes his head a couple of times, then puts him down in my lap, where I'm sitting on one of the chairs.

The dog squirms around in my lap. I pick him up and lift him closer to my face, and he reaches up with his little nose and sniffs me. He looks so happy, and pants with his tongue hanging out while he squiggles. I set him back down on my lap, and he starts sniffing me all over and pressing on me with his little white paws.

Mom and Dad both reach over and pet him too, and he tries to lick their hands. It makes them laugh.

I feel his soft ears and pet his cute little face. When my finger gets close to his mouth, he opens it up and sort of munches me softly. The shelter lady hands me a little toy stick and says, "Here, let him chew on this. He's like a human baby who wants to chew on things." So I put the stick up to his mouth, and he starts chomping on it, holding it down with his paws. After a while he gets quieter, and lays on me, trying to snuggle close to my stomach.

I can't believe how good the puppy feels here in my arms, sitting on me, happy to be with me. He's so warm, and fluffy, and wiggly, and friendly. I get this happy glowing feeling from holding him. It feels so right.

I look up at Mom and Dad, and I can see they know it too. This is our dog.

Gabe

I've been waiting for Jonathan to get back from the pound to pick out his dog. He said as soon as he gets home I should come over to see it. I'm waiting out in the front yard, bouncing a ball, so I can see when their car comes driving up.

When I see them pull into their driveway, I run back into the house and yell, "Dad! I'm going over to Jonathan's!"

Natalie isn't up in her room like usual. I'm surprised to see her standing right next to the front door, already wearing her shoes. "Can I come too?" she asks.

I'm about to ask her why, but she says, "I want to see Jonathan's new puppy. Is that okay?"

"Um, yeah, I guess," I say.

So we walk down there, and by the time we get to his house they are outside in the backyard. I go around the side to get in through the gate, Natalie tagging along with me.

And there is Jonathan, sitting on the ground with the cutest little brown puppy. The dog is sitting on the grass in front of him, reaching its paw up and tapping his knee, its little tongue hanging out. His parents go back out to the front and start carrying some stuff in from the car.

Jonathan looks up and says, "Check out my puppy!" He has a huge smile on his face.

I head over and sit right down on the ground with him. Natalie follows, but she doesn't sit yet, she stands there next to Jonathan, holding her hands together in front of her, staring with huge eyes at the dog.

"That's so cool!" I tell him. "What's its name?"

"I don't know yet," he says, "I haven't named him. I have to think of something just right."

"Can I pet him?" I ask.

"Sure."

So I reach over and put my hand on his fuzzy brown back, and he squiggles backwards to see what's touching him. Then he tumbles over to me and starts sniffing my hand and trying to get up on me. OMG this is the cutest little thing ever.

Natalie is still standing there in a trance, and when she sees the dog trying to get up on me she sort of squeaks. "He's so cute!"

The dog stops what he's doing on my lap when he hears her, and he pads over to her feet and sits right in front of her, looking up. She drops to her knees, and leans over to pick him up. I can tell she is totally in love with this dog already. "Ooooohhh!" she says, holding him in her arms like a baby and petting his fuzzy fur. "You're so cute! You're such a good puppy!"

I laugh at how much she loves the dog. It's cute, yeah, but she clearly thinks this is the most wonderful thing she has ever seen. She holds the puppy up higher towards her face, and leans her head down to touch him. Her hair falls over onto him while he squirms around in delight.

"Huh," Jonathan says. I look over at him, and see he is watching Natalie and his dog bonding. I'm worried for a second he'll be annoyed, but he doesn't seem to be. "Check that out. Their hair is exactly the same color."

I swing my head back around, and sure enough, you can't tell where Natalie's hair ends and the dog's fur begins. "Ha!" I laugh. "What a funny coincidence."

Natalie keeps holding the dog, talking baby talk to him, while he tries to lick her face. Jonathan and I look at each other and laugh. "Hey, come over here," he tells me, "you need to see all this stuff we got for him."

We go over and Jonathan starts showing me the dog supplies. There's a cushion for him to sleep on, and bowls, and food, and something called puppy pads that I guess are sort of like diapers, to put on the floor in case he pees before he learns he's supposed to go outside.

"You can help me take care of him, Gabe," Jonathan offers.

"Sure! I'd love to! Maybe we can teach him tricks and stuff!"

"I want to help too," Natalie says, still cuddling the puppy. He starts trying to chew on her fingers, and it makes her giggle.

"Okay," Jonathan shrugs, "you can help too." He sees the dog chomping her hand, and says, "Here, take this toy for him to chew on. The lady at the shelter told us he's like a baby, so he likes to chew on things." He hands her the little toy, and Natalie holds it up for the dog. He immediately starts gnawing on it.

I'm glad Jonathan doesn't seem annoyed about sharing his puppy, especially with my little sister. She doesn't usually play with us, although the last couple of days she has hung around with us more.

This is going to be fun.

Chapter 25

Puppy

Jonathan's

“*How wonderful, my darling, to be the master of this new little creature. The animal will be utterly yours, dependent on you, will love you no matter what occurs.*”

It is a delight to watch my Guarded interact with the dog. His emotions are unusually benign towards the creature. Generally, when Jonathan encounters animals he speculates about what he can do to them, and often enjoys the thrill of power he experiences while controlling them, sometimes tormenting them. I revel in such times, experiencing the flaring vigor of his blazing soul as he exercises dominion over lesser beings. Surprisingly, he has not yet begun to imagine what he can inflict upon his new little pet. I anticipate it will begin soon, and we will both savor the delights of his mastery.

Jonathan is, of course, sharing his joy with his closest friend Gabe. It is unusual, though, to have the Seer partaking so earnestly. He has previously felt her to be nothing more than the younger sibling of his friend, not a worthy companion in her own right. Furthermore she has been the occasional target of his amusing mischief, whenever the opportunity has presented itself.

But now, she has arrogantly determined that she can influence Jonathan to abstain from activities which she finds distasteful. I am certain this will not succeed. My beloved, with his formidable soul, is too potent to allow himself to be altered by whatever machinations she can contrive. He should not condescend to listen to any suggestions she might make.

However, as she enacts her ludicrous project in an attempt to change him, he seems to already grow accustomed to her presence. The longer he remains in her company, the more his disdain for her diminishes. Her Guardian whispers to her constantly, helping her find ways to soften Jonathan's attitude regarding her. I find myself growing strangely resentful towards the girl, as she uses her unique capabilities to target my own shining boy.

I see nothing I can do to stop her, other than my usual exhortations to my darling to do as he pleases.

However, I have been learning how to intensify my suggestions to my beloved, using the enhanced energy technique which was initially discovered by the Seer and her Guardian. I have been experimenting myself with this concept, occasionally filling my words to Jonathan with more of the energy I use to speak to him. I have felt myself changing, growing stronger, feeling more tangible, the more I use this energy. And my beloved boy has started sensing me more strongly. He does not, of course, have any idea of my existence. But he has started to perceive certain thoughts and memories which I am suggesting. To him, this seems like sudden remembrance, or insight, or inspiration. But it is coming from me. And I revel in my power to influence him ever more strongly.

"My dearest, yes, enjoy your new pet, share the delight with your best friend. You don't need the help of the strange girl, you and your friend can certainly do everything needed to care for the animal."

Ron

I hear the kids and Jonathan's parents in the backyard, so I go around through the gate. They are all out there, watching a cute little puppy cavort on the lawn, chasing tennis balls as the kids throw them around. What a scene!

Brad and Stefanie seem to be enjoying themselves as much as the kids. I head over to them. "Hey," I say, "looks like you picked out a really cute dog."

Brad grins over at me, as Stef kicks a rolling ball back over to Jonathan. "Yep! We let Jon pick out whatever he wanted, and he found this little puppy. The lady at the pound said we were pretty lucky, they don't have young puppies like this very often."

"What kind of dog is it?"

"A labrador/collie mix, I guess. He seems very friendly. The kids have been having a blast with him all afternoon."

Stefanie chimes in, "I sure hope we can housebreak him quickly."

Brad laughs. "No problem, babe, he's obviously really smart. He's already learning to chase the ball and stuff. I'm sure it won't take long."

"Well, kids," I call over to Gabe and Natalie, "you need to say goodbye to the puppy. It's time to head back over to your Mom's place."

Gabe stands up and comes over, saying good-bye to Jonathan. Natalie, however, surprises me by saying, "Awwwww!" That's different. She never complains about anything. She looks at the dog longingly, then over at me like she's going to ask to spend more time here. But then she apparently changes her mind, because she goes over to where Jonathan is petting the dog.

She lightly touches his shoulder. "Can I say goodbye to him?" she asks.

He looks surprised, then nods, rubbing his shoulder where she touched him. Natalie picks up the puppy, and holds him in her arms, snuggling him and rubbing her face into his fur. She apparently adores the little thing.

While she's saying her farewells, I tell Brad and Stefanie, "Okay, we'll be back on Friday, then Saturday is Legoland day! I figure we'll leave pretty early in the morning to get up there by the time they open."

Gabe grins. "Oh yeah! I had almost forgotten!" He calls over to Jonathan, "Hear that Jon? Remember Legoland is next weekend!"

Jonathan nods, somewhat distractedly, still watching Natalie cuddling his puppy. After another smooch to the dog's head, she passes him back over to Jonathan, gently depositing the puppy back into his arms.

"Thank you, Jonathan, for letting me play with your new dog," she quietly says.

He holds the dog the same way she had been. "Sure," he replies.

"Okay kids, let's go," I say. "See you guys next weekend."

The kids follow along after me, Natalie still seeming strangely reluctant. She walks slowly, looking back over her shoulder as we leave the back yard. What's gotten into her? I guess it's the dog - who knew she'd love it so much?

Chapter 26

Progress

Timothy's

Timothy has been waiting all afternoon for the sounds of Natalie and her family returning from her father's house. He is lying on his bed, attempting repeatedly to open his mind to my words. I have continued the attempt to achieve true communication with him, but the effort has been spotty at best.

The only incident in which he clearly understood my message was days ago when Natalie was crying, and I urged him to comfort her. It seems the intense emotional atmosphere of the moment contributed to the effort, and my communication came through to Timothy more clearly than at any other time.

We have attempted repeatedly to experiment with this endeavor. Each time, I use the level of energy which was successful when he heard me suggest that he hold Natalie. Last night as requested, Angel transmitted to me a word which Natalie had written in her notebook. I attempted diligently to convey the word, and Timothy's perception was very close, but not exact. As has happened many times before, what he seems to receive from me is a general impression, rather than a specific message. The contact occurs, but is not perfect.

I know he is disappointed the effort has not been successful as yet. To him, it appears to be taking too long. He has no understanding of the fact that his progress is phenomenal, unprecedented, astonishing. I am unaware of any human who has ever achieved this much in the past, without actually being a Seer. Humans have felt the presence of their Guardians occasionally, have sensed the emotional comfort being relayed in times of stress. But never actual words, never true dialogue. We are not there yet, but I know Timothy will continue trying.

Of course I will assist him in every way I can, eternally patient with his efforts, always loving, infinitely impressed with his incredible intellect and determination. I no longer doubt he will succeed.

Timothy

When I hear Natalie get home, I figure I'll wait a few minutes and then go over there. But instead, I hear her knocking on our front door right away. Good.

I leave my room and have reached the stairs when Mom opens the door. Natalie smiles at my Mom and then meets me on the stairs.

"Hi Timothy," she says, seeming even happier than normal, "how was your day?"

I wait until we are back in my room with the door closed. "It was fine," I say, sighing a little. "No real progress yet."

"Did you get my word?" she asks.

I get my notebook, and show her where I wrote "dog" last night.

Her eyes get wide, and she opens up her notebook and shows me that she had written "puppy".

I nod. "Well, it's closer."

She says, "But Timothy! It's almost exactly right! I think you're really getting there!"

"Maybe," I say. "I still don't feel like I am truly hearing Guardian. I get these feelings, like the way it feels when you are dreaming, and when I hear him it's like when you first wake up and you remember the dream you were having. It slips away unless you try to hold on to it. That's what it's like with Guardian."

We sit down on the floor like usual, with our notebooks, so we can compare notes about our experiments. I know she has stuff to tell me about her experiment, The Jonathan Project, although I can't pretend to be very excited about it.

But instead of showing me her notebook, she is listening to Angel. After a minute she says, "Guardian and Angel heard what you thought about how it is like dreaming when you are hearing Guardian. They think you are right, because the way a guardian normally talks to their human is by using the same part of the human's mind they use for dreaming." She listens again. "Angel says it is called the sub-con-scious," she says, saying it slowly since it isn't a word she is used to.

That's interesting. I've heard of it before. I read a lot of science books, not only the ones for second-graders. The teacher lets me read anything, and my Mom takes me to the library to check stuff out, too. I haven't read very much about the subconscious though. I think about this for a minute, then say, "So, Angel and Guardian, I guess you talk to the part of the mind for dreaming, but I think with a different part, the conscious part."

Natalie listens, then says, "Yes."

"Well," I say slowly, "could that be part of the problem? Like, the message is going to a different part of my brain than what I am using to listen?"

I wait while Natalie watches Angel. "He says it is an interesting theory. However, it seems like when you open your mind, when you're trying to hear Guardian, the part opening is linked to the sub-con-scious part." It's going to take her a couple of tries to be able to say that word.

I look at Natalie, and know she's looking at Angel, and hearing him talk as easily as she can hear me. "So, what part is Natalie using?"

Natalie looks surprised. "Huh," she says. "I have no idea." She looks at Angel and I wait.

"Angel says he doesn't really understand how it works with me. He says I am a 'Seer', and that means I can see him, and hear him. He thinks it means my brain is different from regular people." She shrugs, then giggles. "I guess we always knew that!"

I laugh a little bit with her. Yes, her brain is obviously different. Like mine is different, but not in the same way.

"I'll have to think about this some more," I say. "I'll bet there's ways to experiment with whether I am listening with the right part of my mind. Maybe if I figure it out, I can hear Guardian better."

After a moment, Natalie says, "They say you are correct as always, and they are confident you will be able to think of a good experiment to test this." She smiles at me. "You know how much we all love how smart you are, right Timothy?"

I duck my head and smile. "Yeah, I guess so. Thanks."

Then I sigh. I will need some time to think about the parts of the mind theory. For now though, I guess we should talk about Natalie's experiment.

"So, how is your experiment going, Natalie? The Jonathan Project," I say, and I can't keep my voice even when I say his name. I really really don't like Jonathan and I really wish she wasn't trying to spend more time with him. But I still want to help her with her experiment if I can.

She looks like she gets more happy and excited when I ask her about it. Sigh.

"It's going great so far!" she says. "And something else happened. Jonathan got a dog! That's what I was thinking about last night when I wrote puppy for you. I was thinking of him getting a puppy!"

"Oh," I say. "I hope Jonathan isn't mean to the dog."

Her face falls when I say that, then she listens to Angel, and sighs. "I don't think he will be. I'm going to try to make him nicer, and I hope it means he won't try to hurt the puppy or anyone else. But Angel says he 'shares your concern'," she says, rolling her eyes.

Natalie's

Natalie's assessment of the progress of her current project is correct. It is indeed going well, far better than I could have predicted. Jonathan has responded to her interest swiftly. Her natural empathy and kindness, coupled with her use of me as a tool to understand his nature, have already had an effect. He has spent years viewing her as an annoyance, or as a target for his misbehavior, but not as a friend. Her brother is his friend, and she has been considered nothing more than the little sister who is sometimes present. But he has never before been the beneficiary of her purposeful warmth. Her Seer's nature is difficult to resist.

After only two days of unknowingly being the subject of her experiment, his attitude has already been redirected. He has found her to be more interesting, and more amiable, than he ever imagined. He enjoyed her company, separately from enjoying the companionship of her brother.

Furthermore, the addition of his new little pet has contributed to his adjustment in attitude. As his Guardian has noticed, Jonathan's normal inclination to view a small creature as a target for harm has not been triggered. His positive feelings towards the young animal seem genuine.

Are the two events related? Is his delight in receiving a pet amplified by Natalie's attentions? It seems oddly coincidental that two such moments would occur simultaneously.

But it does appear clear that Natalie's efforts are being met with success. In two days of companionship, Jonathan has made no moves towards cruelty, and in fact has had no thoughts to that end. I have monitored his thoughts carefully in order to report them to Natalie, and detected none of his usual spitefulness. It has been puzzlingly unusual. I had not anticipated her experiment bearing fruit so rapidly.

Even more puzzling, and somewhat more troubling, is the reaction of Jonathan's Guardian. Of course the Guardian is aware of Natalie's project, and has met the concept with a strange disdain. All other Guardians who encounter Natalie are wholly invested in her success. As a Seer she is a compelling and beloved presence for our kind. This Guardian, though, believes it is somehow ... unfair... for the Seer to be directing her abilities in this manner. I have never before encountered a Guardian who feels what can only be described as resentment. But Jonathan's Guardian appears to begrudge Natalie's success in improving the boy's demeanor.

This is perplexing. Guardians always welcome any chance for improvement in their humans. When a human commits troublesome acts, their Guardian may not approve, but will accept the action as a means of augmenting their shared soul. But Jonathan's Guardian appears to have progressed further along that spectrum, and seems to actually approve of Jonathan's cruelty, even crave it.

What can this mean?

Timothy's Guardian follows my line of thoughts, and is also concerned. This is a new development, a change in normal Guardian perspective. We do not know whether this will hinder Jonathan from being able to continue to improve in the way Natalie wishes. However, as a Guardian's exhortations for calm or peace are only very rarely sensed by the human, it is unlikely Jonathan would be able to sense his Guardian's preference for more unpleasant actions.

Would he?

Chapter 27

River

Natalie

I know Timothy doesn't approve of my experiment with Jonathan. I don't want him to be upset with me, but I am positive I can help Jonathan be nicer. I can't stop now, especially when I know it is already working. Jonathan didn't do one bad thing all weekend, and Angel said he wasn't even thinking about mean stuff. He was too busy playing with me and Gabe, and we were all enjoying the new puppy.

I think this will work! And if this works, I know I will be able to help even more people.

So I want to convince Timothy that it is going to be okay.

I show him the notes I wrote in my notebook last night, about the time I spent with Jonathan. When we were playing together with the Legos he felt fine about me being there, and even liked the flags I made for their castle. Then when we were playing in the yard with the puppy all day, I think Jonathan was actually happy I was there. He kept giving me things to use, like toys and balls, to play with the dog.

I think having a puppy will be another thing that will help Jonathan be a nicer person. Angel told me he wasn't thinking about anything mean at all, because he was so happy having a dog. And I love the dog so much. I already miss holding the little thing, he was so cute, and he seemed to love me too. I can't wait until I get to see him again next weekend. I hope Jonathan has thought of a name for him by then.

I definitely want to stick with the experiment. Maybe I'll even try to spend some time with Jonathan and Gabe at school, at recess or lunch. But I have to make sure that Timothy will be all right.

When Timothy finishes reading my notes, he looks up. "Well," he says, "I guess so far it's going all right. But how do you know if Jonathan is really getting nicer, or if he just managed to spend two days without hurting you?"

"Angel is watching, and telling me everything he is thinking. If he started thinking about mean stuff, or was going to do something bad, Angel would tell me first so I could stop it."

Timothy doesn't look convinced. "But how would you stop it? He's bigger than you. And meaner than you could ever be. You might not expect whatever is going to happen, and you wouldn't be able to protect yourself." He seems very anxious about this.

I know I can stop Jonathan if he tries to do something bad, but I have to think about how I know. Timothy watches me while I think. One of the things I love about our friendship is how we are each very patient when the other one is trying to think of how to say something. So he waits for me. I listen to Angel, too.

"Well," I finally say, "I'm not sure how to explain it. But I know I can. I have always been able to help people see things in a different way."

He still doesn't look convinced, so I tell him, "I've done it with you. Especially when we were smaller, if you were upset about something, I could touch you, and be close to you, and it would help you calm down. Do you remember?"

He gets a faraway look in his eyes, then nods. "Yes, I remember." But he still doesn't look happy. "I hope it works on Jonathan too."

Angel whispers to me, "*Your friend is very worried that you are taking the risk of being harmed by Jonathan. However, you are correct that your touch and presence are able to calm others, including Timothy, and now Jonathan. Please reassure Timothy I will be with you, and if Jonathan seems inclined to do something harmful, I will alert you at once so you can change his mind. Or if you can't, you can at least avoid him.*" I know Angel doesn't want Timothy to worry.

So I tell Timothy, "Angel will be with me, and he will be able to warn me if something bad is going to happen. If it is, I will either try to get Jonathan not to do it, or if I can't, I'll leave. I will be safe. Please don't worry about me, Timothy."

He sighs. I can tell he's still worried, but I know I'll be okay. He'll see.

"Well," he says, "what are the next steps in the experiment?" He figures there isn't anything he can do to stop me, so at least he'll help me get organized.

"Thank you, Timothy," I tell him. "Thank you for trusting me. This will work."

He looks sad, but determined to help me. I am so lucky he's my friend.

Timothy's

My sweet boy is trying so hard to achieve communication with me. While talking to the Seer about her project with Jonathan, he tried to concentrate on her experiment. But a part of his mind was still involved with the idea he was developing to further experiment with me.

Now that we are alone, we don't have the benefit of Natalie and Angel to translate for us. Of course I hear everything he is thinking and saying, and I try to transmit feelings of love and unity to him.

We perform our new nightly ritual, in which Natalie writes a word in her notebook at 8 p.m. in her home, and Timothy tries to hear me tell him what it is. The word tonight is "river", inspired by her reading of the children's bible, which she has been studying in an attempt to better understand how religions develop. She is very taken by the fable of the mother of Moses placing her infant into a basket on the river, in the hopes that he would reach safety. I try to transmit the image of the river to Timothy, as he opens his mind to me and I imbue the word with power. He glimpses the image, and writes "water." Again, he is so close, but yet unsatisfied.

"Guardian," he says, "I want to try this a new way. If you are talking to the part of my mind that dreams, I want to try to keep my mind open while I fall asleep. Let's see if I can hear you when I'm almost dreaming."

I send him my feelings of love and approval and willingness, and he is able to sense them dimly. He does not truly appreciate how much progress he has made. His ability to regularly detect my feelings is a great achievement. Yet he does not feel it is tangible enough.

I continue to talk to him, as he lies on his pillow and drifts towards sleep, keeping his mind open as much as possible as drowsiness overtakes him. Just as he is nearly asleep, an incredible thing happens.

We connect. We truly connect. He hears that I am repeating the word "river" to him lovingly, over and over.

It jolts him awake.

"River!" he bursts out, and scrambles to his notebook, crossing out what he had written earlier, and writing the word "river" in the light of the streetlamp outside his window.

"Thank you, Guardian, it worked! Please tell Angel."

He climbs back into bed, and is somehow able to find sleep quickly.

Overwhelmed with joy and love, I transmit the information to Angel, and hear him informing Natalie. They are both filled with a sense of triumph over Timothy's achievement.

She addresses me directly, knowing I will be able to hear her from next door. "Guardian, thank you!" the sweet little Seer tells me. "Timothy wanted this so much. I'm so happy it worked. I'm sure he'll find a way to keep going with it. I think soon you guys will be able to talk all the time. Good night!"

Brenda's

My beloved and her soon-to-be husband are in each other's arms, believing the children are asleep, enjoying their renewed love for each other. As always during these times, his Guardian and I observe quietly, reveling in the glowing souls of our Guarded as they experience their delights. Passion, when imbued with love, can expand the soul more than almost any other human experience.

Natalie breaks into my thoughts, as she has been doing every night since she began including me in her extraordinary group. "Good night, Lady. Good night, Knight." She giggles a little at the homonyms, hearing the word sounds repeat.

She has continued to keep each of the family Guardians in her thoughts. It is amazing how she has united us into a clan of individuals, all perfectly real in her mind, humans and Guardians alike. I do not know if I will ever grow accustomed to the marvelous sensation of belonging it brings to be part of this collective, rather than a solitary Guardian tending to the life of a singular human.

"*Good night, sweet Natalie.*" I know Angel will relay my response.

Chapter 28

Legoland

December 1, 2001

Gabe

"Good morning, ten year old!" I roll over in bed and find Mom sitting there, her hand on my shoulder. "Happy Birthday!" she says.

Oh yeah! Today's my birthday! "Thanks," I say, smiling and rubbing my eyes.

"Okay, get up kiddo, we have to get going soon. We want to be there when Legoland opens."

That's all it takes for any sleepiness to be over. I jump out of bed and rush into the bathroom, hearing her laughing behind me.

When I come out of the bathroom, Natalie is standing there in the hallway, smiling at me, and holding a present in her hands. "Happy Birthday, Gabe," she says and gives me a little one-armed hug, while holding the present in her other hand.

"Thanks, Nat."

She hands it to me, and says, "Open it!" It isn't heavy, and doesn't make any noise when I shake it.

I tear open the paper, and lift open the lid of the box. Inside are a bunch of different banners she's drawn, obviously to add to our Lego castle. It looks like she's used markers for these, not crayons. They're very detailed. She's watching me eagerly. "That's cool, Nat, thanks," I tell her.

"Look," she says, "they're the banners from Knight's Tale."

Oh, wow. I wouldn't have known that. "Thanks! We'll put them on later, with Jonathan, okay?"

She smiles and nods happily. She's not bad for a little sister.

Jonathan

My Dad walks over with me, and watches while we all climb in the car. Natalie is the littlest one so she has to sit in the middle seat. She's still super tiny, like the size of a kindergartner. "Have a great time!" Dad says.

Gabe and I are so excited. I've never been to Legoland either. Some of our friends at school have, though, so we've both heard a lot about what you can do there. I'm excited for the dragon roller coaster. Gabe wants to do the thing where you build little cars out of Legos and race them down ramps. We are talking about everything on the car ride up there. Natalie is listening, looking back and forth between us while we're talking.

While Gabe is talking about what we should do when we first get there, I am only half listening. Part of me is also thinking about Natalie. I used to think she was annoying, but not so much lately. Like, she has been really nice to me, nicer than she used to be, especially since I got my new dog. We had a fun time playing with him last night again, after they got back to their Dad's house.

Then, I suddenly remember the time I pushed her over into the bushes in my yard a couple of months ago. That was hilarious. I haven't done anything lately to pick on her. I'm always thinking of ways to trick people since it's so fun, and she's so tiny that she's an easy target. But she normally avoids me, and I hardly ever get the chance to do anything to her. It's always kind of thrilling to do stuff like that, and it's funny how she never tells on me. She's sitting right next to me, and our legs are touching. I think I could probably do something right now, like pinch her, when Gabe isn't watching. I know she wouldn't say anything.

But as soon as I start thinking about it, she lifts her head up, and silently looks straight into my eyes, and puts her hand right on top of my hand.

Well, that's weird. Why do I get the feeling she knows exactly what I was thinking about?

I look down into her eyes, and she gives me a strange little smile and nods her head at me.

Okay, she is annoying after all. I think I'll go back to ignoring her.

I tell Gabe we can do whatever he wants when we get there, since he's the birthday boy.

Jonathan's

"Yes, my dear, the girl is so peculiar, you will do well to have nothing to do with her. How annoying that she preempted the clever trick you were devising! Focus on your friend, my amazing boy, you will have a lovely time together at the new amusement park. There will be other opportunities for fun pranks."

The Seer is beginning to demonstrate her eerie abilities to others, including to my own beloved. Even her brother has started to notice she has an unusual way of anticipating events. It won't be long before others see it as well.

I anticipate the time when her bizarre behavior begins to make others uneasy, as she has made my dearest Jonathan. Once the people around her begin to sense she is unnatural, she will experience rejection. Hopefully, when that occurs, she will not feel so haughty. Merely being a Seer does not give her the right to try to control the actions of others. My darling boy enjoys his little mischiefs. Who is she to try to change one iota of his marvelous persona?

I yearn for the failure of her offensive experiment. I will continue to encourage my beloved to ignore her efforts. I was pleased that with an increased use of energy, my stronger whispers seemed to penetrate his subconscious mind. I was able to redirect his thoughts away from considering how friendly she is, to whether he would have an enjoyable opportunity to inflict some petty harm upon her.

He should not change for her. He should not change at all. He and his soul should only grow in power and might.

Natalie

When Angel tells me Jonathan is thinking about pinching me, I am able to stop him by looking at him and touching his hand. He didn't do it, but I'm still really disappointed. I was hoping he was over it, and wouldn't want to hurt people any more.

Angel whispers, "*My darling, although Jonathan has shown some improvement, I believe to truly change him will be a much more substantial undertaking. If you wish the experiment to continue, and eventually lead to success, I fear you must have a great deal of patience.*"

Fine. I know this sort of thing takes time. I can keep trying, as long as it takes.

Natalie's

I do not tell her what is truly troubling me. The intervention of Jonathan's Guardian, in bringing to his mind a memory of how he enjoyed inflicting harm upon Natalie, changed the direction of Jonathan's thoughts. His newfound regard for Natalie shifted back to his former view of her as a potential victim. Natalie might be disappointed, but I am genuinely alarmed.

The Guardian seems determined to actively oppose Natalie's efforts. Although I have often witnessed Guardians, including myself, strive for their humans to be safe from harm by others, I have never seen this. The Guardian has begun to not only approve of Jonathan's harmful actions, but actually wants to prevent Jonathan from improving his behavior.

Jonathan and his Guardian appear to be caught in what might be referred to in modern parlance as a feedback loop. Jonathan enjoys the harm he inflicts, and his Guardian revels in the power it brings to him. Then the Guardian whispers encouragement, bringing Jonathan to desire more of the same. The arrangement is not unheard of, as there have obviously always been humans who wished to cause harm to others.

But this Guardian has taken the process a step further. The Guardian covets the intense flare of power in Jonathan's soul which is experienced with each misdeed. And rather than cede to Natalie's efforts to create a more kindly personality in Jonathan, his Guardian intends to oppose her. Natalie's direct intervention, her specific attempt to change Jonathan, is seen as a threat by his Guardian.

Furthermore, the unusual situation caused by the presence of a Seer in Jonathan's life has resulted in knowledge being passed to his Guardian which would not otherwise have been available.

The element which concerns me the most, is what Jonathan's Guardian has learned by observing our group's experiments. All the nearby Guardians were aware when we discovered how to imbue our communications with energy. This Guardian is alone, though, in starting to experiment with it as well. When Jonathan had his sudden memory of pushing Natalie into the bushes, which disrupted his friendlier line of thought, it occurred because his Guardian used additional energy in communicating with him. The Guardian used the energy technique we discovered to deliberately pull the memory from the back to the front of Jonathan's mind. Jonathan is being manipulated by his Guardian into continuing along his dark path of malfeasance. The Guardian is experiencing remarkable success by deploying this method, overheard as Timothy and Natalie conducted their experiment on Guardian communication. Jonathan's Guardian now uses what was learned from Natalie, as a weapon against her. The irony is profound. As is the danger.

How can Natalie succeed in her goal to help Jonathan, against the direct opposition of his Guardian?

I have no idea.

And I am truly concerned for Natalie. Not only will her experiment likely fail, but she has unknowingly encountered a hostile opponent standing in the way of her success.

I do not know what to do. I do not know whether I should tell her.

Gratefully, I hear the shared concern of the other Guardians here with us on our excursion. Lady, Knight, and Gabe's Guardian all observe and share my thoughts.

I will communicate with them, try to find ideas. But perhaps we should do this another time, when Jonathan's Guardian is not present, and cannot hear our plans. Attempting to hide something from another Guardian is another bizarre development.

What have we come to?

Natalie

Angel is still worried about Jonathan thinking about hurting me in the car. But I was able to stop him, like I said I would. I think Angel is way too bothered about this whole thing. "Relax," I tell him in my head, "it's fine."

We're inside Legoland now, and it is pretty fun. I'm trying to stay with Gabe and Jonathan, but I think they keep forgetting about me, they're having so much fun together. That's fine. I want Gabe to enjoy his birthday as much as he can. So a lot of the time I'm staying back with Mom and Dad.

They are having fun too. It's nice to see them holding hands sometimes. I'm so glad everything is working out for them. It'll work out for Jonathan too. Everyone will see.

We went on some rides, and now we are in the building with a bunch of tables and Legos, where you can build whatever you want with the Legos. There are ramps to race the cars you build, so Gabe and Jonathan are building cars, racing them down the ramps, then grabbing them at the bottom and rushing back to the table to modify their creations. I'm working on a car of my own. I don't really care if it wins races, but I do want it to be pretty. So I'm building it as carefully as I can, until I think I have it just right.

When I'm sure it is perfect, I take it over to the ramp to get ready to race it. Gabe and Jonathan come right up behind me. I guess they are ready to race again too. When we are about to start the race, Jonathan suddenly pushes his car over into my car's lane, so when the gate goes down his car crashes into mine and it breaks into pieces. It happened too fast for Angel to get the chance to warn me so I could stop it.

Jonathan looks at me with glee on his face, like he can't wait to see me get upset about my car being broken. I sigh, and shake my head sadly at him. I'm upset, but not about the car. I'm sad my plan isn't working as well as I had hoped. Jonathan sees I'm not going to cry or tattle, so he shrugs and grabs his car, going back to the table to build it over again. Gabe picks up the pieces of my car and hands them back to me, saying, "Sorry, Nat, but you can build it again. Accidents happen." He goes to join Jonathan.

I don't know, maybe Angel is right. Maybe this experiment won't work after all. I guess sometimes scientists do experiments that fail, even if most of our experiments have led to great discoveries.

Angel smiles sadly along with me, following my thoughts. Oh well. I shrug like Jonathan did, and go sit with Mom and Dad to wait for the boys to be done.

Jonathan's

"Yes, my darling boy! We have caused the Seer to doubt whether she can succeed in her preposterous mission. We must continue showing her that you are not going to change. You are perfect the way you are."

Chapter 29

Brainy

December 2, 2001

Timothy

I'm hearing Guardian better every day. Last night I got Natalie's word right away, but it's probably because it was so obvious. The word was "Legoland", and I know that's where they went yesterday. I'll have to ask her to start giving me harder words.

Ever since I figured out how to open my mind right when I'm falling asleep so Guardian's messages can come to me pretty clearly, I've been experimenting with it. There's a feeling you get when your mind is almost dreaming but before you're asleep, and I'm starting to be able to create the feeling even when I'm not sleeping. I have to make my mind go very quiet, and relax myself as much as I can. When the dreamy feeling comes, if I open my mind then, I can tell what Guardian is saying. It isn't easy to do, but I'm getting better at it. And I can't hear Guardian as well as I know Natalie can hear Angel, but I can definitely get his messages. Maybe not word by word, but I can sense his meaning. It's not perfect, but it has really progressed a lot.

Guardian is happy about it too. That's getting better too - my ability to sense his feelings. It's starting to be almost constant. I can usually feel him near me, and can tell what he's feeling. You'd think it would feel strange, but it doesn't. More like it's comforting. I like having him there.

I wonder what he looks like. I haven't thought about this before, since I've been focusing so hard on hearing him, but I wish I could see him too. I know it's not possible, but at least I'd like to get a description. I suppose all the guardians look like Angel does, but I guess I could ask Natalie to have Angel describe him for me. Maybe if I can picture Guardian in my mind, I'll be able to communicate with him better.

When I see Natalie later, I'll remember to ask.

I get back to reading my book. Mom brought me to the library yesterday to find books about how the mind works. I want to learn more about the subconscious. I wasn't able to find anything for someone my age, which isn't surprising. So I got a few books that are probably for older kids, maybe even for college students. I have to admit this stuff is hard to read, but I'm trying to find parts I can understand.

Guardian is near me, and I feel his support, and it helps me concentrate.

Laura

I'm getting nervous. Michael will be here in a few days, after another long deployment. It's been six months. I feel pretty lucky it didn't turn out to be longer. After September 11, when our military got involved in all sorts of new conflicts, I was afraid his deployment would be extended a lot longer. But as far as I can tell, he'll still be back on December 5.

I'm spending the weekend getting the house clean. Timothy is up in his room reading. I couldn't believe the stack of textbooks he got about brain development on our last trip to the library. I doubt he's going to be able to understand much of what he's reading, but he's giving it a try. He's determined. He goes through phases, where he is intensely interested in something and I end up helping him find books he uses to try to figure it out. A while ago it was physics, when he wanted to try to learn about how the Twin Towers fell in New York after the planes hit them. Now apparently it's neuroscience. What a kid.

I've tried to explain to him that some fields of study, especially in the sciences, will probably require years of coursework before he can really start understanding some of this stuff. Also, he'll be able to major in whatever he wants in college to get really detailed about what he's learning. But he's not willing to wait so long. He wants to learn now.

I wonder what Michael is going to think about all this. He's always found Timothy a little hard to relate to. Is seeing his seven-year-old with his nose buried in a college textbook going to make him proud of how smart he is? Or freak him out about how weird he is? Maybe a little of both.

It's always both with Timothy. Smart and weird. My wonderful little brainy weirdo, I think, smiling as I scrub the bathtub.

Natalie

It won't be dinnertime for a couple of hours, but we came back to Mom's a little early so she can get some stuff done at home. That means I have time to go to Timothy's. I'm glad. I have a lot to talk to him about.

When I get there he's reading about brain stuff. I sit on the floor and look through his books. This stuff is way over my head. Ha! Stuff about brains is over my head - that's a funny pun. I don't tell Timothy though, I don't think he'd appreciate it. He's not a big fan of puns. Angel laughs a little. At least he enjoys my jokes.

I pick up another one of Timothy's library books. "Isn't this for, like, high school students? Or even college?" I ask him.

"Yeah," he says, shrugging. "I can't understand very much, but I really wanted to try to learn more about the subconscious. I've been using it a lot, you know, to hear Guardian more and more."

"Are you hearing him all the time now?" I ask, excited. I really want him to have what I have with Angel.

"No," he says, "but when I focus I can usually hear him now. It's a lot of effort though. I'm still doing the thing where I open my mind like before, but now I also try to make my mind feel like it's almost dreaming. It works best when I'm about to go to sleep at night, or when I first wake up. I can hear him pretty clearly then. During the rest of the time, it's a lot harder, but if I concentrate I can still do it."

I show him my notebook. He gets his out, and we look at "Legoland" written in both books. He smiles. "It was too easy, Natalie, I knew that was where you went yesterday. Was it fun?"

I'm not sure he really is very interested in hearing about how fun Legoland was, but he does try to be polite. "Yes," I tell him, "but I'm not sure The Jonathan Project is going very well."

He scrunches up his forehead. "Why not? He didn't hurt you, did he?"

"Well, no, but he thought about it. And he wrecked my Lego model car on purpose. For some reason it seems like he wanted to start being mean again. He was doing so well, then he changed back to the way he used to be. I don't know why."

"Natalie, I think you're the only one who ever thought this would work. Maybe it just can't. Are you going to keep trying?"

I huff out my air. "I'm not sure. I am starting to think it won't work, but I don't want to give up yet. If I can't help one kid be nicer, how can I help everyone else? I feel like this is a test and I'm worried I'm going to flunk." I cross my arms and lean back against the side of his bed.

He actually reaches out and pats my shoulder. "Natalie, if there is anybody in the world who can do it, it's you. If you want to keep trying, you should. But please be careful."

"Yeah, I will. Both, I mean. I will keep trying, and I will be careful."

Angel says, "*He is right, beloved. If there is any way to accomplish your goal, you are the person who will find it. But he is also right to caution you. There is risk involved in being together with a person like Jonathan.*"

"Well, Angel, that's what you're here for, right? To help me be careful. I trust you to help me."

Natalie's

My concern has only grown as I have considered the situation. Natalie has no idea she is facing not simply a misbehaving child, but his Guardian who is increasingly hostile to her.

Jonathan's Guardian has continued to use our discovery about additional energy in his communication to Jonathan, and it appears to be transformative. As it has transformed each of us. However, our transformations have been temporary, causing us to have more powerful communications while directing the additional energy at each other, and for a short time following each event.

With Jonathan's Guardian, the transformation appears more profound. The desire to encourage Jonathan's misdeeds has grown over time. His Guardian had long since stopped wishing for Jonathan to be kinder, because there is so much burning growth in his soul with each incident of cruelty. But just as the energy experiment caused me to feel an increase in strength, it has strengthened the resolve of Jonathan's Guardian. His Guardian begins to feel a ruthless desire to participate in Jonathan's wrongdoing, not exclusively for the enhanced growth of Jonathan's soul, but to satisfy a growing sadistic yearning to witness the suffering of others. This trait has blossomed enormously since we discovered how to enhance our communications with energy. The use of the technique is transforming Jonathan's Guardian into something none of us has ever seen before, something which has grown far beyond the function of a supportive and nurturing caretaker of a human soul. This Guardian wants to taste pain.

It is terrifying.

Timothy's

I share Angel's alarm regarding the development of Jonathan's Guardian. Jonathan has long been an antagonist for Timothy, frequently teasing and annoying my beloved. However, until recently this has not amounted to much more than typical childhood bullying.

I think about the day, some weeks ago, when Timothy and Natalie asked Angel and myself to speak with Jonathan's Guardian, to request that Jonathan be encouraged to be kinder. It was the first day Angel and I started communicating directly with each other, at the behest of the Seer. Even then, we could not envision a way to make the request, particularly as Jonathan's Guardian already disdained any concept of trying to improve Jonathan's behavior.

But things have grown much more complicated, making the situation impossible to resolve. The Seer is committed to an endeavor to help Jonathan improve himself, and his Guardian actively opposes this project. Furthermore, the Guardian has begun using our energy technique, which we painstakingly discovered through experimentation directed by my beloved Timothy. No other Guardians have presumed to indulge in such a thing, even though they are aware of our efforts. Jonathan's Guardian, though, has begun using this energy technique to not only enhance the whispered suggestions to Jonathan, but to grow into a more powerful entity.

I agree with Angel, it is terrifying. Neither of us has any experience with this type of metamorphosis in a Guardian. The other Guardians in the family, Knight and Lady and Gabe's, gravely listen to our concerns. We share a common intent to discuss the issue with each other later, after our humans are asleep and do not require our attention. Such a conversation was inadvisable while the family was still at the house of Natalie's father, because Jonathan's Guardian would have been able to hear the discussion, being in a nearby house. Our discussion might not be heard from that distance tonight, but of course the next time Jonathan is near the children, presumably tomorrow at school, his Guardian will know all once again. It is unclear what to do about any aspect of this situation. But we must consider it together.

More remarkable developments. A group of Guardians scheduling a meeting, so to speak. A Guardian council.

How things have changed.

Chapter 30

Appearance

Natalie's

While Guardian and I are pondering the growing problem regarding Jonathan and his Guardian, of course we are also attending to the conversation between the children.

Natalie has resolved to continue her efforts with Jonathan, but no longer wishes to discuss it tonight. She will let the problem rest in the back of her mind overnight, and hope to have gained insight in her dreams by the morning. This is another aspect of the subconscious mind which Timothy is attempting to educate himself regarding, and that he has begun actively using in his contact with Guardian.

She wishes to redirect the conversation to that contact. "Tell me more about how it's going with Guardian. Like, how much are you hearing him?"

"I'm hearing him a lot more, like I said. I also feel his feelings all the time now." He pauses for a moment. "There is something else I want to know, that I think might help."

Eagerly, Natalie asks, "What?"

"Well," Timothy replies, "you've told me what Angel looks like. But I don't know what Guardian looks like. I wish I could picture him when he's talking to me. I think it would help me hear him better. I've been imagining him looking like an angel, but I want to know all the details. Angel, can you describe Guardian for me?"

177

How strange, that this question, regarding the appearance of Guardians, is one which I used to dread. I knew it would arise someday, and I worried it would be difficult to answer in a way the children could understand. However, in light of the looming difficulty with Jonathan and his Guardian, the question of appearance seems simplistic.

I smile at Natalie, and she waits expectantly for my answer. *"My children, although this might come as some surprise to you, this is not a question with a simple answer."*

Natalie raises her eyebrows and tilts her head. "It seems simple enough. Look at Guardian and tell me what you see."

This makes me chuckle. *"If only it were that easy, my darling. First I must explain something to you about Guardians, about how we are made."*

She looks at me quizzically, and repeats this to Timothy. He is equally puzzled. Neither of them can imagine how this could possibly be so complicated.

I look to Guardian, who merely waits for me to continue. Sometimes it seems Guardian finds it amusing to watch me put in the position of having to answer the children's more challenging questions. I think he's enjoying this.

"You know I have told you in the past that Guardians are made of what your scientists might refer to as dark matter."

Natalie repeats this, and they both nod their heads.

"And also, you know that this type of matter does not interact with your physical world in any way."

Again, they nod.

"Because of this, as strange as this may sound to you, Guardians do not actually have a physical appearance."

As I anticipated, Natalie scoffs at this obvious misstatement after she repeats it to Timothy. "What? Yes you do. I'm looking at you right now."

"Yes my darling, but what you are seeing is not my true form. I have created this image for you to see, forming myself into the shape of the angel which you expected when you were extremely young."

The children stare at each other, then Natalie looks back over at me. They are both silent for a long moment. "This isn't what you really look like?" she asks, perturbed, indicating with her hands the apparition of an angel which she clearly sees before her.

"It is what I look like, for you. I fabricated this shape for your benefit. As soon as you were born, I knew you could see me, so I tried to make a nice shape

for you to look at. At first, I was merely a friendly face for you to see. I assumed this angel form somewhat later, after you saw the guardian angel painting in your grandmother's house." I smile at her expression of astonishment, and add, *"For a brief time, I even looked like the little Beanie Baby angel bear you used to carry around with you all the time."*

Her eyes light up. "Little Angel! I remember him! I used to love that bear."

"I know, my darling, and I had altered my appearance to be similar to it. After you saw the painting, I shifted again to more closely resemble the angel depicted there."

Timothy is growing increasingly astonished as he listens to Natalie speaking, first relaying my comments, then adding her side of the conversation. "So," he says, "guardians can look like anything they want?"

"Essentially. Guardians can form themselves into any shape which seems most helpful. They often assume a human form, because it helps the Guardian feel closer to their own human."

Natalie says, "I feel like this is the craziest thing you've ever told us, and that includes you telling us there isn't even any God!"

I laugh. I am pleased this discussion is happening. One more question answered, one more topic out of the way.

Timothy repeats his original question. "So, what does Guardian look like?"

I smile. *"This is the reason I felt I must explain the situation before answering your question. Guardian has no actual appearance at all. He has never formed himself into any shape."*

Timothy wrinkles his forehead. "So does that mean he's invisible?"

Natalie is not convinced. "No," she objects, "I know you can see him, Angel. I see you looking over at him while he's talking to you."

"Yes, my darling, you are very perceptive. I can direct my gaze to where Guardian is located. However, I do not see any shape there." I pause for a moment, considering. *"There is something, though, it is not as if he is entirely invisible. When a Guardian has never assumed a specific form, their presence can be seen by other Guardians as a faint trace of matter in the air."*

Now Timothy is all business. "Please describe it exactly. Is it like a cloud?"

I laugh a little, as Guardian enjoys watching me try to describe him. *"Yes, you might say perhaps it looks a bit like a cloud. Or, possibly more like a faint wisp of steam."*

"Okay," says Timothy, and draws his notebook over to himself, prepared to take notes. The little scientist at work. "How big is the wisp of steam? Exactly, please."

Guardian is the one laughing now. I try to view him analytically. The laughter makes no difference in his form, any more than his other emotions would change his shape. "*I will attempt to describe it as precisely as I am able. The wisp is no more than 12 inches in diameter. It is approximately spherical. There is no color. It is neither dark nor light. There truly is almost no physical form at all.*"

Timothy notates his book. "Well, thanks, I guess that sounds about as accurate as possible." He sighs. "I wish he looked like something, though. I really wanted to be able to imagine him while he talked."

"*My dearest Timothy, Guardian would be delighted to assume any form you prefer. As I have crafted this appearance for Natalie's benefit, so Guardian can shape himself into whatever you think would be best. In fact, Guardian has been considering, since you began speaking with him, whether he should assume some kind of physical manifestation.*"

Timothy's eyes grow large. "Oh!" he says. "Uh, wow, that's something to think about."

"*Guardian wishes to know if you would like for him to appear human. He can create a shape as vague or as detailed as you would like. If you prefer, while you are considering whether you would like something more specific, he can assume a humanoid shape, then wait for further instructions.*"

Timothy quirks his head to the side. "Um, yeah, I guess that would be good, if you wouldn't mind, Guardian."

Natalie laughs. "Honestly, Timothy, you have to agree, right? This is the craziest thing yet!"

Chapter 31

Guardian Council

Gabe's

It is nearly midnight. My beloved is sleeping soundly, dreaming of amusement parks. His parents have retired for the night, and after reading together companionably in bed for a time, have also fallen asleep. Next door, Timothy and his mother slumber as well.

Only the Seer is still awake, reading in her darkened room. She does not have a lamp turned on in her room, not wishing for her parents to realize she is still awake. So she has parted the curtains in her window, allowing the light from the streetlamp outside to enter. The light would normally be too dim for human eyes to use for reading. However, Natalie appears to have unusual abilities beyond her status as a Seer. One of these abilities is that she can see her book despite the lack of sufficient lighting. Another is that she does not appear to require as much sleep as ordinary humans. It is quite typical for her to linger far into the night, reading her books, long after her parents believe her to be asleep.

She continues to be fascinated by the stories in the children's bible she has been reading. She has progressed well into the New Testament, and has just completed a tale about Jesus casting out demons. It is remarkable to observe her young mind as she tries to make sense of the biblical stories, particularly in light of her recently acquired knowledge that the concept of deities is an invention of humanity. She tries to come to terms with each story in the bible, and has begun categorizing them as either tales of basic human lives, or as involving the presence of Guardians. An entire philosophy is developing in her mind as she accomplishes this task.

She has not yet discussed this to any great extent with her Guardian, who of course observes as she consumes the literature. She wishes, as is typical when she reads, to complete the text, then consult with Angel to assist her understanding of what she has read.

Shortly after midnight she finally senses the need for sleep, so she closes the bible and her eyes. Soon she is dreaming as well.

Angel waits for a time to be certain she will not awaken, then he turns his attention to our group. We have all been waiting. We have all seen the transformation in Jonathan's Guardian, and we all share a concern for the well-being of the children. For all four of the children, not only Gabe and Natalie and Timothy. What can the situation mean for Jonathan himself? Although the problems are centered upon him, he is also a human child, worthy of the love and protection of Guardians. The fact that his own Guardian has strayed from the usual role of loving observer puts him at risk as well.

Each of the other Guardians in the group have become accustomed to actually speaking with each other, having been encouraged to do so by Natalie's schemes. I have observed this development with fondness, and not a little amazement. But as Gabe has been less involved with the events necessitating the communication, I have not directly participated until tonight. It is important that I share this discussion with the other Guardians, as my beloved's dearest friend is likely to be greatly impacted as these events unfold.

Therefore, I bring myself to address the group, speaking to them directly rather than simply knowing they will be aware of my thoughts. I wish to participate in this group as one of them, not simply as an observer. *"I believe I have spent more time in the company of Jonathan and his Guardian than have any of you, simply because my Guarded and the boy spend so much of their time together,"* I begin. *"I have watched his Guardian achieve the current condition which is so concerning to us all. I believe I can share information in this regard which may be important."* I find, once I begin, it is not difficult to communicate in this direct fashion.

Angel smiles at me. *"Yes, Gabe's Guardian, please continue. You are, indeed, the most closely involved with Jonathan and his Guardian of any here."* His use of the moniker to address me emphasizes the fact that I am the only

Guardian here who has not received a name. Named Guardians! How odd is this situation.

And how odd to be speaking directly with others of my kind. I acclimate quickly, though, and continue. *"As soon as Angel and Guardian commenced their experiment regarding whether they could communicate over a distance, all Guardians nearby were aware of what was happening. It seemed to be a fascinating development involving the Seer, but not pertinent to any of the rest of us. However, Jonathan's Guardian seemed to become almost obsessed with the concept."*

Angel looks to Guardian, and they share a memory of the night in which they learned to "yell" at each other. A flash of mutual amusement passes between them. Again, seeing Guardians find amusement outside of that generated by their Guarded is unusual. The entire situation is unprecedented.

Guardian watches, waiting for me to continue. Of course, he is not in the same house with the rest of us, but next door, near Timothy. This makes no difference in our ability to communicate with each other. I notice Guardian's appearance is shifting. He is one of the less common Guardians who has never made any effort to form an appearance, but after the conversation with Timothy earlier this evening, he has begun to shift his form into one with a more human-like shape. All of the Guardians in our group have such a shape, but of course Angel's appearance is a far more substantial manifestation than any of us have ever witnessed before. His angel form is incredibly tangible and detailed, created for the benefit of the Seer.

I re-focus on the information I am relaying. *"I believe the fact that Timothy and Natalie had also been discussing an effort to alter Jonathan's behavior the same day impacted his Guardian's view of the discovery made through the communication experiment. When Jonathan's Guardian felt the rush of energy generated by Angel and Guardian, it immediately added to the existing perception of Jonathan being at a disadvantage. Jonathan's Guardian feels it is most unfair for the Seer and her friend to be using their Guardians as tools to modify Jonathan's behavior. Jonathan's Guardian has grown to resent the Seer, not merely because she has used Angel's knowledge to avoid Jonathan's bullying, but because she has begun to utilize the knowledge in a way which targets Jonathan directly."*

The other Guardians listen carefully to my description. All have already surmised this, but my perspective is helping to clarify the situation.

"With the opinion that the Seer has an unfair advantage over Jonathan already in place, the new ability of Angel and Guardian to communicate with a strangely powerful method seemed alarming, even threatening. Jonathan's Guardian did not wish for this ability to be held exclusively by Guardians who appear opposed to Jonathan. Therefore, very quickly Jonathan's Guardian began experimenting with the use of power which had been demonstrated by Angel and Guardian."

Angel and Guardian regard each other again, ruefully. They have known for quite some time that the experiments being performed by the children could lead to discoveries which may have unintended consequences. However, they had only imagined such consequences impacting their own Guarded. They did not anticipate another Guardian using their acquired knowledge in a menacing way.

I continue describing how Jonathan's Guardian used the information they had unwittingly provided. *"It began slowly, with the faintest glimmer of additional energy being used while whispering to Jonathan. It soon became evident this was an effective way of transmitting thoughts to Jonathan. Of course the child has no awareness that the thoughts are coming from his Guardian. He has no inkling of the existence of a Guardian. When his Guardian uses energy, which is occurring ever more powerfully, and with increasing frequency, Jonathan will sometimes perceive what seems to be a sudden memory, a flash of insight, or an unexpected idea. But with the additional use of power to transmit the thoughts, his Guardian has grown increasingly able to direct Jonathan's actions. His Guardian craves the pain which Jonathan has sometimes enjoyed inflicting on vulnerable creatures. We have all observed the way such actions cause Jonathan's soul to brighten. His Guardian lusts after this, desiring more frequent incidents, more opportunities to revel in the glowing soul. The use of extra energy in the whispered suggestions to commit such acts has been quite effective."*

The group of Guardians listens soberly to my description, with increasing dismay.

"Two events have happened in the last few days which have interfered with this process. First, Jonathan received a new pet dog, and rather than immediately designing ways to torment the creature as his Guardian anticipated, Jonathan has felt true affection for the animal. Second, the Seer launched her project to modify Jonathan's behavior. Her attempt has met with more success

than his Guardian would like. As a result his Guardian has put ever more effort into his attempt to sway Jonathan back to the path of cruelty. The use of power to communicate ideas to Jonathan has grown enormously, and the boy has found it impossible to resist what he perceives as wicked urges."

This has been tragic to behold. I am filled with grief as I continue. *"My beloved Gabe, who is at heart a very kind and loving child, was already beginning to grow disturbed over Jonathan's occasional malicious behavior. This was terribly disheartening to him, as he and Jonathan have been the dearest of friends for many years. Gabe genuinely likes Jonathan, and greatly enjoys his company. He does not wish to see his friendship end, but he has been increasingly disturbed by what he is witnessing. After the Seer began her project and Jonathan improved, Gabe was so pleased and happily renewed his friendship with the other boy. But for the last day or two, he has grown to regret it, as Jonathan seems unable to stop himself from committing unpleasant acts. Gabe witnessed a number of minor incidents directed against Natalie. Jonathan even targeted Gabe himself on a few occasions, which was a great surprise to Gabe, who had never before experienced such abuse. Those incidents were minor, and Gabe has chosen to overlook them for now. But if they continue, I believe Gabe will eventually need to terminate the friendship. This will be a terrible loss for him."*

The other Guardians all share my grief. *"What's more,"* I go on, *"Jonathan is detecting the change himself. He had felt more kindly disposed towards both Natalie and his new dog, and was enjoying those feelings. Now that his Guardian has been forcing his hand, causing Jonathan to increase the frequency of the cruel tricks, the boy is beginning to feel self-loathing. He has always enjoyed such incidents, but he recently has felt out of control, and does not like to feel he cannot stop himself. He has always before conducted himself with exquisite care, to ensure he is not detected. He senses that if he continues at the current rate, before long his parents or others will witness his wrongdoing, and he will be in trouble. This has never occurred before, and he does not wish for it to happen. However, when his Guardian directs a powerful blast of energy into a suggestion to do harm to another, Jonathan feels compelled to do it."*

Brenda's Guardian, Lady, experiences a rush of compassion for Jonathan. *"The poor child. It is not only Natalie and Gabe who may be harmed. Jonathan is being forced by his Guardian to become the worst sort of human. This is tragic."*

Timothy's Guardian is less sympathetic. *"Jonathan has been cruel to Timothy for many years, long before we discovered how to use energy to communicate. This path was laid by Jonathan, and his Guardian began by only encouraging him in what he most loved to do. I do not see Jonathan as the victim here."*

"Regardless of how this began, we all agree the current situation is untenable," Angel breaks in. *"Jonathan's Guardian is causing him to be crueler than he naturally would be. Gabe is at risk of losing his best friend. And my Seer is planning to continue to insert herself into a potentially dangerous situation, without being aware of the truths involved. I have hesitated to describe the problem to her. I neither wish for fear to hold her back from her purpose, nor for her to be harmed by it if she proceeds. This is the reason I asked you all to meet with me tonight. I need guidance about what to tell my beloved child."*

Of all of us, of course, Angel is the only one for whom the situation presents options. We can observe, and encourage, and attempt to influence our own Guarded through our unheard whispers. Angel is the only one who can hold actual conversations with his Guarded; in fact she frequently demands it. Timothy's Guardian is in a unique position, having begun to communicate in a very rudimentary fashion with the boy, but their only true conversations occur through Angel and Natalie.

Angel is the one who must reach a decision, must formulate a plan. We all sympathize with his plight, but none of us has any better idea for how to proceed.

Timothy's Guardian reminds Angel, *"Even if your decision tonight is to withhold information from Natalie, I have watched over and over again as she and Timothy have pulled information from you which you had not planned to impart. Their desire for knowledge is insatiable, and I feel quite certain they will learn what is happening, whether you currently wish to share it or not."*

Angel agrees, uneasy but resigned. *"You are correct. Many times I have resolved not to broach certain topics, but the Seer always manages to acquire the information she desires."*

Knight contributes for the first time this evening. *"If we are to assume that Natalie will learn the truth of how Jonathan's Guardian has evolved, perhaps the only question is whether Angel should tell her immediately, or wait until she asks. It has been my observation that she and Timothy always find a way to ask the right questions at the right time. Their acquisition of knowledge seems to help them learn and grow. I believe learning about Jonathan's Guardian will be useful, when the time is right. May I suggest, Angel, that you simply wait for the topic to arise during one of your conversations with the children?"*

Angel regards each of us, and finds us all in agreement. *"Very well. You are correct. The two children have been incredibly perceptive and capable in their questioning. I am sure this conversation will occur soon. Jonathan and his Guardian appear to be spiraling towards ever more dire actions, which will lead to more questions. I will wait."*

Lady adds, *"In the meantime, I suggest that each of us keep the others informed immediately as to any developments. We are all involved now, and all wish to assist. And we all know now how to communicate across any distance. We should each relay every detail as this unfolds."*

We all agree. We will wait, and watch, and share. I believe I will be the most involved, as my beloved is with Jonathan with the most frequency. I will observe him and his Guardian carefully, and share information with the others. With the group. The most unusual group of Guardians, to my knowledge, in history.

Chapter 32

Back Home

December 5, 2001

Natalie

Timothy is unhappy. I feel the sadness and worry rolling off of him, even while he is focusing on our science lesson in class. This is usually his favorite part of the week, but he is too worried to enjoy it today. Today is the day his Dad's ship gets home. He's been gone for six months. I wish Timothy was excited, but he's mostly worried that with his Dad home things around his house won't be so peaceful any more. When it is only Timothy and his Mom, things seem very simple. Timothy and I spend a lot of time together, and his Mom is very nice and helps us with our experiments and stuff. But when his Dad is home, I don't go over there as much. I know Timothy loves his Dad, but he never feels like his Dad is very happy with him. His Dad always wants to do stuff that Timothy doesn't really like, sports and riding bikes and stuff. Timothy is not athletic at all. So he's nervous about this starting when he gets home today.

But the other thing bothering him is even worse. The Jonathan Project really seems to be an epic fail. For a while I could tell Jonathan was getting nicer, and we were able to play together, and even have fun together. But then it was like Jonathan missed being awful, and he has gotten even worse. He was mean to me all weekend, and even mean to Gabe. When I tried to touch his hand, or

188

smile at him, or even a couple of times asked him to stop what he was doing, he laughed and ignored me. Angel hasn't been very much help. When we first started the project, Angel was able to tell me what Jonathan was thinking, if he started planning to do something mean, so I could stop it. But Angel says it is happening all the time now, so I should just expect it. Angel isn't happy about me still trying.

But I really don't want to give up. I don't know why Jonathan has gotten so terrible again. Today I tried to go over and talk to him and Gabe at lunch, for a couple of minutes while Timothy was finishing his sandwich. I thought it would be all right to go say Hi for a minute. I didn't think it would bother Timothy. But then Jonathan ended up following me back over and telling Timothy that he's a weirdo, which made me feel worse than ever. I don't know what to do.

Angel watches me, listening to me think, his eyes looking very sad. I think to him, "Is Guardian doing everything he can to help? Timothy feels so sad, so can Guardian try to share happier feelings?"

Angel says, "*Of course, my dearest, Guardian has been constantly communicating to Timothy, and the feeling of calm he is receiving from this is probably the only thing keeping him from becoming overwhelmed and needing to leave the classroom.*"

Oh. Last year Timothy used to do that a lot, when he got too upset in class. He's gotten special permission to go to the office and calm down when he needs to. But he hasn't had to do it in second grade so far, and I'm extra sad to hear he is close to needing to again.

I reach over and touch his shoulder. He looks at me, and I nod at him, telling him with my eyes that we are all here with him, helping him. Me and Angel and Guardian. Timothy nods back. He knows. He still feels unhappy though.

Laura

There he is. I see Michael coming towards me, after waiting here with all the other families at the Navy pier. I'd walk towards him, but it's too crowded, so all I can do is smile and wave as he makes his way through all the other people. When he gets to me, he drops his bag and pulls me in for a hug. Ah, this feels so good. I've missed being in his arms so much. He holds me for a long time, all the other people and activity melting away. He clutches me tightly, almost desperately.

When he finally releases me, I reach up for a kiss, but after a brief peck he leans down to pick up his bag. "It's good to see you, Laura," he says, his voice filled with an unusual strain.

I look at him more carefully. He appears very tired. His hair is clipped as short as it always is while on board, and he's clean shaven, but somehow he looks, I don't know, haggard. He even seems thinner. Wow. I know this deployment has been awful. His ship was actually involved in Operation Enduring Freedom, the military action that happened after the September 11 attacks. I don't know any of the details, since I don't think he's allowed to talk about it, and he certainly hasn't put anything in his infrequent letters. But I can see it has really taken its toll on him. My heart melts with compassion for him.

"Come on, Mike, let's go home. You look like you could use a good rest. You get two weeks of leave now, right?"

He nods. "Yeah. Let's go."

Michael's

The relief felt by my beloved at returning to his home is profound. This has been an extremely difficult six months for him to endure. While halfway through their scheduled deployment, when he and his shipmates learned there had been an attack against the United States, he began feeling an increased sense of stress and tension. The ship quickly received orders to take part in the military's plan for retaliation, and the crew participated in launching missiles against the opponent mere weeks after the September 11 attacks.

Although Michael and his shipmates were jubilant at participating in the successful missile strikes, leading to the defeat of the enemy, it began to haunt his dreams. In his conscious mind, the missile attacks were obvious and necessary steps which must be taken. But his subconscious mind brought him images in dreams of the missiles landing, tearing through buildings and people, killing not only combatants but civilians and bystanders. He has suffered from many sleepless nights, awakening with a jolt from nightmares relentlessly replaying these images again and again in his sleeping mind. His health has begun to suffer as a result of the fatigue. He has experienced headaches, listlessness, lack of appetite.

My concern for my dearest is intense, but I have been able to do nothing to alleviate his troubles. While dreaming his imagination creates ever more horrible scenes to view, and I cannot penetrate his mind no matter how I try. While awake, he sometimes has flashes of the dreams, and tries to carry on with his duties woodenly, ignoring his mental and physical symptoms. My whispers accomplish nothing.

We have both longed for the deployment to be finished, for the period of rest which he will be allowed upon returning home. It is my fervent hope that being with his family again will bring the peace he needs to recover.

Laura

We're laying in bed, after. As always when his ship gets back, the first thing Michael wants to do is have sex, and I am eager as well. I miss him so much when he's gone. Being with him again reminds me of how much my body needed it. It was particularly intense this time, brief and fierce.

He immediately falls asleep afterwards, holding me. I'm curled up next to him, my head laying on his chest, feeling his heartbeat. I am not sleepy, but I don't get up or move, because I don't want to disturb his sleep. He really seems to need it. I'm content to lie here with him. I don't need to be anywhere else for a couple of hours.

He is definitely thinner, I can tell. His ribs seem closer to the surface of his skin. I wonder if they aren't feeding him well enough. I'll take care of that. I start thinking about making a cake to go with the dinner I already have stewing in the crockpot. Chocolate or lemon? Probably lemon, I think he'd like it better.

He suddenly twitches under my head, and I feel his heart rate change from the slow steady thud of sleep, starting to speed up, until it is racing frantically. What is wrong? He's still asleep, he must be dreaming. I wonder if I should wake him up.

But I don't need to. He twitches more, then suddenly bolts upright with a shout, knocking me off his chest. I reach out to him, touch his back. "Honey?"

He looks over at me, confused for a moment, then when he realizes where he is, he exhales shakily and lays back down. He draws me back to him, holding me tightly. I relax back into his arms.

"Sorry," he breathes. "Bad dream."

"What was it about?" I ask.

"Nothing. I've been having bad dreams lately." He clearly doesn't want to talk about it.

I listen to his heart slow down again, but he can't fall back to sleep. He sits back up. "I'm gonna take a shower."

I watch as he heads to the bathroom, seeing his unusually slender form. He's been on deployments before, but this one seems to have really taken a toll.

Now that he's back home, I'll just have to love on him extra hard. I'll take care of him.

Chapter 33

Reunion

Timothy's

Timothy is anxious as he rides home in his mother's car. This has been a difficult few days for him. As anticipated, Jonathan's Guardian has continued to provoke cruel acts, and Timothy has been the unfortunate recipient on several occasions. Jonathan has taunted him, has called him names, and has even thrown small objects at him. Timothy as always tries to ignore it, but it is increasingly difficult.

The Seer is dismayed, attempting repeatedly and unsuccessfully to intervene. Her Jonathan Project is clearly failing, and she begins to wonder what is actually going on. She is far too perceptive to overlook the fact that the escalation in Jonathan's behavior is unusual even for him.

The conversation which Angel anticipates will be coming soon.

In the meantime, Timothy is trying hard to focus on his reunion with his father. Natalie has discussed this extensively with him, knowing that in the past the two have had problems connecting. She has even tutored him in how best to greet his father, playacting the scene together so Timothy will feel comfortable. Timothy intends to fulfill her instructions precisely, and is running over it in his mind.

I whisper to him, imbuing my words with energy, as I always do now. He is not making an effort to open his mind or create the dreamlike state which would be required to actually perceive my words. He is too focused on remembering Natalie's instructions. But he feels the support and love I am sending to him, and it helps him to face the upcoming event calmly.

When we arrive home, Timothy's mother tells him his father is very tired from his deployment, and would appreciate a nice peaceful evening. Timothy does not recognize the subtle hint, that she hopes he will be able to avoid becoming overwhelmed with the new situation. She remembers all too well prior times when Timothy's reaction to his newly arrived father was very negative, even hysterical. But Timothy simply nods, and his mother hopes for the best.

As we enter the front door, Timothy sees his father waiting in the living room. As rehearsed with Natalie, Timothy greets his father. "Hi Dad, welcome home," he says, and proceeds to approach his father, reaching out to give him a brief hug. This is precisely as Natalie had scripted the scene for him, and he carries out her instructions exactly.

His father is surprised and delighted, and returns the embrace. "Hey, kid, good to see you," he says. "I think you've grown taller. How are you doing? How is school going?"

"I'm fine," Timothy says, feeling relieved that the initial contact has proceeded as planned. "School is fine. I like second grade."

"Glad to hear it," Michael responds.

There is a silence, as neither can find anything else to add. "Okay," Timothy says, "I'm going to go do my homework." He takes his backpack and climbs the stairs.

His parents regard each other with some amazement. "That went well," Laura chuckles.

Michael's Guardian watches the exchange, pleased the child did not reject contact as has occurred in the past. His Guardian is concerned about Michael's emotional well-being, in the wake of his long deployment. I see the Guardian's memories of the last difficult six months, and understand better the problems Michael has been facing. I am all the more pleased that Natalie has helped Timothy prepare to accept his father's presence once again.

Timothy settles in on the floor of his bedroom and pulls out his homework, resigned to an evening without seeing Natalie. Again, this is as they discussed. Natalie felt it would be best to allow Timothy's family to have the night to themselves, and Timothy reluctantly agreed.

Natalie

"How's it going over there?" I ask Angel.

"*Very well, darling. Timothy remembered everything you practiced with him, and he greeted and hugged his father exactly as you planned. Both of his parents are very pleased, and Timothy is calm. He has finished his homework and is reading one of the books about the mind he checked out from the library.*"

"Okay," I sigh. "Have Guardian tell him I say Hi when he gets the chance." I know it was my idea not to see Timothy tonight, but it's hard, knowing how bothered Timothy has been about Jonathan the last couple of days.

"*Very well,*" Angel says. "*You will also be pleased to know Timothy is not thinking about Jonathan at the moment. He is very engrossed in his book.*"

"Thanks." It's nice how sometimes I don't have to ask Angel what I want to know, he just tells me.

I've finished my homework too, so I pick up the children's bible again. I'm done reading it, but I want to look through the pictures and stories. There's boring parts, and confusing parts, but I think since this version was written for children it's mostly simple enough to understand. I guess I need to read the real grownups bible someday, to get the whole story.

Some of the stories are really nice, but a lot are awful. So much of it is people being really mean to each other, not only during wars, but other times as well. The way it is written, people are always saying God is the reason for stuff, but I know better. A whole lot of it has to be people making stuff up for their own reasons, like to get power over others. A lot of the stories have people talking to angels, or even demons, and I figure those must be times people were hearing their guardians talking to them. There are prophets who say they talk to God, or know what God wants, and I'm pretty sure some of them were hearing their guardians too.

Angel watches me, waiting to see if I want to ask any questions. I have a lot of questions, but I don't really even know where to start. I wish Timothy was reading the bible too, because I know he'd be able to find all the right questions to ask. But he's too busy reading his books about science and stuff like that. He finds it way more interesting than a bunch of old stories.

"This was all a long time ago, right? Who wrote this, anyway?" I ask.

"*Yes, darling, the stories were written thousands of years ago. It is reasonable to surmise that the tales were told orally for a long time before they were recorded in writing. Many different people must have written the stories down, as I am aware that there were several conflicting versions of each story in circulation, which were eventually compiled into the collection which passes for today's bible."*

"Do you think any of it really happened?" I ask. "Well, actually, you have been around guarding other people for a long time, right? Were you here that long ago? Did you ever see any of this stuff yourself?"

"I believe much of the background information is true. Many of the cultures and civilizations referenced did actually exist, and you can study the archeological evidence which has been found regarding those regions. It is more difficult to know if any of the tales of most individuals in the stories really happened. Except for some documented historical figures, such as the Pharaohs and Roman officials, modern historians do not have records of the people named. As for your second question, no, I did not personally witness any events which seem to be the basis of the stories you have read. Although, over time stories can change in the telling, so it is hard to know for certain."

Maybe I need to read some history books, to try to figure out how much of this could have been real. I wonder if there are books for kids about archeology and stuff. Maybe I'll try to go along with Timothy to the library next time.

I'm thinking of more questions to ask Angel, but he says *"It is eight o'clock, darling, time for your word."*

I grab my notebook and turn to the page where I write the words for Timothy. On the next line, I write "Navy". I figure it's a good one for the day his Dad gets home. It's time for me to get ready for bed, so I go into the bathroom to brush my teeth and stuff. When I come back, I ask Angel, "Well?"

"He heard the word very quickly, my sweet girl, as he has almost every night lately. I also asked Guardian to pass along your greeting, while Timothy's mind was receptive, and he heard that you told him Hi. He told Guardian to tell you Hi as well, and that he will see you in the morning."

That's good. I'm glad Timothy is hearing Guardian, and I'm glad it went okay for him when his Dad got home. I'd be glad about everything if it wasn't for Jonathan.

Chapter 34

Tomorrow

December 7, 2001

Brad

Thank God it's Friday.

This has felt like a very long week. Between trying to house train the new dog, and Jonathan moping around all week about Gabe not being at his Dad's house, Stef and I have been pretty stressed out. Especially Stef, with finals going on, and being pregnant, and everything. And besides, Jonathan has really been a pill. I'm worried that maybe getting him a pet wasn't the best idea, but we're committed now.

So I'm glad his friend will be back over here for the weekend. Hopefully that will put him in a better mood, and they can play together with the puppy, maybe help with the training.

We're finishing dinner, and Jonathan says, "I want to go to Gabe's house. I'm sure he's back by now."

Stefanie says, "It's already getting dark, honey, you probably need to wait until tomorrow."

Jonathan scowls, and I can tell he's getting ready to argue, but the doorbell rings. He jumps up and runs to answer the door, with me following along behind. It's Ron and his kids. Well, that's a relief. I didn't want to have an argument with Jonathan. Stef really doesn't need that.

"Hey," Ron says. "I hope it isn't too late, but the kids really wanted to come over and see the puppy."

"Great!" I say. "Come on in."

The dog has chased after Jonathan to the door, and as soon as the kids get in, he rushes over to Natalie and starts trying to jump up on her. He only comes up to her knees, normally, but when he jumps he gets high enough to practically knock her over.

It doesn't seem to bother her though. She kneels down and rubs his head, while he pants and excitedly wags his tail. She looks over to Jonathan and asks, "Have you named him yet?"

"Yeah," Jonathan tells her, "I've decided to call him Socks. Because he has..."

"Little white paws!" she finishes for him. "It's such a perfect name, Jonathan!"

He smiles at the praise, clearly pleased she likes the name. She smiles happily back at him.

Gabe asks, "Does he know any tricks yet?"

I laugh. "We're still working on getting him not to pee on the carpet."

Natalie

I'm glad we went to visit Jonathan and Socks. I think the puppy loves me as much as I love him. And Jonathan managed not to be mean the whole time we were there. It wasn't very long, and Dad waited and talked to Jonathan's parents while we played with the dog.

It does bother me that Angel said Jonathan was thinking of whether he could do something mean to me, but with all the grownups in the room he couldn't think of a way to do it without getting caught.

I don't know why Jonathan is thinking about mean stuff again. He seems to go back and forth, between being mean and being okay, and it's confusing.

After getting ready for bed, I'm in my room with Angel reading. He tells me when it's time to write a word, so I get out my notebook and write "tomorrow". Timothy told me I should start writing more challenging words, so I've been trying to avoid easy things like objects. He's coming over here tomorrow, so I used the word to also be a message to him about our plans. Hopefully he'll think that's clever.

In a couple of minutes Angel says, *"Timothy got your word, and your message, and told Guardian to tell you he'll see you tomorrow."*

Michael's

My beloved and his wife are taking their son to play at the home of his friend, the Seer. Her parents have an unusual arrangement, living in one home during the week, and another home on weekends. I believe this is a lingering byproduct of their former separation, and they will be changing their residential situation at some point. For now, apparently a routine has developed in which Timothy goes to play with Natalie at her father's home on Saturdays.

When Michael returned from deployment a few days ago, I was genuinely startled to discover the changes which have occurred regarding his son. Timothy has been made aware by the Seer that he has a Guardian of his own. This alone would be astounding, but the child has managed to find a way to communicate with his Guardian. I have never seen such a thing in my existence. Furthermore, the Guardians of the Seer and others in her family have begun directly communicating with each other, and have implemented a way to do so at a much greater distance than usual. When I first discovered these changes I was flabbergasted, but have been trying to adjust to the new reality. Guardians chatting with each other, like humans!

In the meantime, my focus continues to be my own beloved, naturally. It has been disappointing to both of us that his return home has not brought with it the peace he needs to truly rest. He and his wife are happy to be together again, and even their child has been far more receptive to his father than in the past. But Michael's nightmares will not leave him alone. His soul is clouded, darkened by his internal struggle. Every night, he continues to awaken suddenly from horrible dreams of violence and death. He has frequently disturbed his wife by crying out as he jerks awake. It is distressing to both of them.

It has only been a few days. Perhaps with time his mind will be able to heal itself. I try to help. Constantly, I whisper to him, trying to help him find peace, find calm in the love of his family, find security in his home. It is the most I can do. And I can hope.

Timothy

When Natalie and I get up into her room the first thing we do, like always, is compare our notebooks. As I knew, she had written "tomorrow".

"That was a neat trick, Natalie, using the word as a message. Thanks."

She smiles. "I thought so! I'm glad you noticed."

"I've been thinking we probably don't need to do the 8 o'clock experiment any more. I get it every time now."

Her forehead wrinkles. "Really? Okay, I guess, if you don't want to, but I think it's kind of fun."

"We can keep doing it if you don't mind. I like the practice, and it's nice to hear from you before bedtime. I just didn't want to keep making you do it if it's getting boring for you."

"No! Let's keep doing it. Maybe I can try more than one word? Since you're getting so good at it, do you think you should move up to whole sentences?"

Oh! That's a good idea. "Yes, good plan. I want to be able to really communicate with Guardian, so let's give it a try. So, starting tonight, write a whole sentence and we'll see how that goes."

She smiles. I'm glad she's happy to keep doing it.

I hear Gabe and Jonathan out playing in the back yard. That's the only problem with coming here to play with Natalie on Saturdays. I usually end up seeing Jonathan too. It used to be that we would mostly ignore each other while we are here, but he's been going out of his way at school this week to come over and say something mean to me, so I'm afraid it will happen today.

"Natalie, can I ask you a favor?"

She looks surprised. "Sure."

"I know Angel is telling you lately what Jonathan is thinking about, for the Jonathan Project. Will you give me some warning if he's about to do something mean to me?"

Her smile vanishes. "Of course. I'm so sorry about what's happening with Jonathan lately. I don't know why he's being extra mean. It's the exact opposite of what I wanted to happen."

I don't even ask her if she's ready to give up yet. I know she's not. She's quiet for a minute, listening to Angel, I suppose.

"I had an idea about something to do today," she says. She picks up the children's bible. "I've finished reading this, and I was talking to Angel about whether any of it is true. He told me he doesn't know if any of the stories about the people in it really happened, but the places it happened in really existed, and there have been some discoveries by archeologists about them. So, I think I want to see if I can find some books about it, and try to figure out more about the places where the bible stories happened."

"Yeah, sounds really interesting. I'd like to know more about the archeology."

"How about we ask if my Mom or Dad can take us to the library? We could look for books there. Maybe you could find more books about the brain too."

I always love going to the library, so this sounds like a terrific plan. "Yeah, I'd like to do that. I'm still working on the brain books I got out last time, but I'll help you look for archeology books."

"Great!" she says, and jumps up to head downstairs. When we get down there, her Mom is in the kitchen.

"Mom," she says, "can we ask you a favor?"

Her Mom puts down the cloth she's holding. "Sure," she says.

"Timothy and I would like to go to the library. Could you drive us over there?"

Right then, Gabe and Jonathan come in from the backyard. Natalie's Mom says, "Yes, we can go to the library, that sounds nice. Boys, would you like to come?"

Oh drat. Well, they wouldn't care about books, would they?

But no, Jonathan immediately says, "Sure, let's go to the library, Gabe!"

Gabe looks confused, but shrugs. "Um, okay."

Natalie looks over at me. This isn't what she had planned for either. But she gets a thoughtful look on her face, and I know she is figuring out what to do.

"I have an idea, Jonathan," she says to him in a very friendly voice. "Maybe they have some books there about training dogs. You and Gabe said you want to teach Socks some tricks, right?"

Jonathan looks surprised. "Yeah, that's not a bad plan. I was going to try to use their computer to play games, but I guess they have books too." He and Gabe look at each other and start laughing. Apparently it was meant to be a joke. I don't usually get it when people are joking, but Natalie laughs with them. I'm not sure if she really thinks it's funny, or if it's just part of the Jonathan Project, and she's trying to make him happy. Probably that.

When we are going out to the car, Natalie has even figured out what to do about where everyone should sit. "I'm the smallest, so I can sit in the middle again between Gabe and Jonathan. Timothy can have shotgun!"

She's so nice to me. I know she did it so I didn't have to sit in the back seat with Jonathan. I'm so lucky she's my friend. I feel Guardian agreeing with me, while we all get in the car.

Chapter 35

Library

Brenda

A trip to the library wasn't on the schedule for today, but if the kids all want to go I am fully supportive. Even Gabe and Jonathan are enthused about books? Odd but good.

Maybe while they're looking for their dog training books or whatever I can glance through some wedding magazines. I know it's a second wedding, so it won't be as big a deal as our first, but I'd still like to do some planning. I wonder if I can find some suggestions about good second wedding dresses. A big floofy white one doesn't really seem appropriate this time around.

When we arrive the kids all take off into the back, so I figure I'll let them do whatever they want for a while. I wonder how long a library can possibly hold their attention? I imagine Natalie and Timothy would stay here all day if they could, since they're both such little bookworms. But Gabe and Jonathan? Unlikely.

So I find a couple of bridal magazines and relax in one of the comfortable chairs in the reading area. I find myself lost in thought, ideas about our upcoming wedding swirling around through my head.

It's so strange, how I both can't believe we're getting married again, and how it is the most obvious and inevitable thing possible. Even though it was years and years, the period during which Ron and I were separated seems like a distant memory now. Like a bad dream, and I have finally awakened to the truth that we love each other, and are meant to be together. Every minute with him seems so natural, and so profoundly wonderful.

I flip the page, and see a dress I like. Hmm, this one has possibilities. Sort of a dark cream color, not white, and no lace or flounces. Very simple and elegant. I think Ron would like it.

"Stop it!" a kid shrieks from the back of the library. Startled, I look up from the magazine. There are more shrieks, from more kids, and a crashing sound of something falling over. As I'm getting up, hoping it isn't my kids but with a sinking feeling that it probably is, a librarian is already running past me towards the sounds of the ruckus. I follow along behind her.

We turn the corner to an aisle of bookshelves at the same time, and find Gabe and Jonathan rolling around on the ground next to a toppled shelf with books scattered everywhere, yelling and pummeling each other. Natalie is trying desperately to pull them apart, and Timothy is standing to the side white as a sheet. I am horrified.

The librarian and I rush to put an end to it. I push Natalie out of the way so we can grab the boys. I manage to get hold of Gabe's arm and jerk him up and away from Jonathan. The librarian is holding Jonathan.

Gabe immediately gets control over himself, trying to slow his breathing. I release his arm. He goes straight over to Natalie. "Are you okay?" he asks. She nods, her eyes as wide as saucers, her hands over her mouth. She is clearly stricken with as much horror as I am about the scene. Timothy rigidly stares silently down at his feet.

Jonathan can't calm himself down. He is yelling wordlessly and struggling with the librarian, an older lady. Another staffer comes running up, a young man who takes over, wrapping his arms around Jonathan from the back. The elder librarian steps away, thoroughly flustered.

Jonathan fights against the arms holding him tightly and yells, "Let me go!"

The young man says, "I will if you calm down, man, okay? Just calm down."

Natalie, probably inadvisably, steps forward, and places her hand on Jonathan's shoulder, above where the staffer is holding him in place. "It's okay, Jonathan, it's going to be okay," she murmurs quietly to him.

The fight seems to go out of him. He goes limp in the staffer's arms, and after a second to make sure he's really done fighting, the young man releases him. Jonathan sinks to the ground and buries his face in his hands, breathing heavily.

Natalie crouches next to him, and puts her arm around his shoulders. Gabe tries to go over there too, but I hold him back. I've seen Natalie calm Timothy down a million times, she can probably do it with Jonathan too.

She silently stays with him for a minute, and he visibly relaxes. After a moment he lifts his face from his hands, looks into her eyes, and shakily says, "I'm sorry."

Wait, Jonathan is apologizing to Natalie? Not Gabe? What is going on here?

She nods. "It's okay, Jonathan. I think it's time to go home, all right?"

He nods sullenly, and gets up after her. She looks over at me. "Yes, let's go," I say to the kids.

I turn to the librarian, thoroughly mortified. "I am so sorry. Do you need me to help clean this up?" There is a small shelf lying on its side, and books are scattered everywhere. The staffer goes over to pull the shelf upright.

She says, "No, I think it's best if you go ahead and take them home." She clearly wants us gone as much as I want to leave. Thank goodness, I need to end this horrifying incident and get to the bottom of what happened.

"Okay, thank you. And again, I am so sorry. Come on, kids."

Jonathan and Gabe silently follow along after me, Gabe's mouth set in a furious line, and Jonathan crossing his arms over his chest. Natalie takes Timothy's hand. He has been frozen like a statue this whole time. "Come on, Timothy, let's go," she gently tells him, and he comes along robotically. As Natalie passes the librarian and the staffer, she stops and apologizes, and thanks them as well.

I have Jonathan sit in front, figuring he and Gabe should be separated from each other. Nobody complains about the seating. All the kids simply climb into the car without comment. I can tell they are all still reeling emotionally about whatever just happened. The car ride home is tense and completely silent. I don't want to start interrogating them while I'm driving, for fear of starting anything up again.

When I pull into the driveway, Ron is in the front yard mowing. He comes over with a smile on his face, but as he sees the car full of grim expressions he stops and raises his eyebrows. I get out first, and whisper to him, "Gabe and Jonathan got into a fight. I think it would be best for Jonathan to go home. Can you take him?"

"Um, yeah," he says, clearly as shocked as I am about the boys fighting.

The kids have climbed out. Natalie tells Jonathan, "It'll be okay, Jonathan. I think you should go home and rest."

He nods, clearly very unhappy, and follows along behind Ron, staring at the ground.

The kids are behaving differently than ever before. I have to find out what happened.

Gabe

I can't believe any of this is happening. What the hell is wrong with Jonathan?

Mom tells us to come inside, and sits all three of us down at the kitchen table. "All right," she says, "who wants to tell me what happened?"

Natalie and Timothy look at each other but stay quiet. Mom looks at me.

Okay, fine, I'll tell her. "Jonathan took away the book Timothy was reading. When Natalie tried to get him to give it back, he punched her." I feel my throat closing up, I'm so mad about it. I can't talk any more.

I am never going to get the image out of my head, my supposed best friend hauling off and smacking my tiny little sister right in the face. It was the most awful thing I've ever seen. And when he did it, he had this terrible expression on his face, like punching her was the most exciting thing he'd ever done. When she fell over backwards and crashed into the bookcase, he started going after her like he wanted to hit her again. That's when I jumped on him.

Brenda

What? I look at Natalie, and realize for the first time that a light bruise is developing along her jaw. "Oh my God," I say, "are you okay, Natalie?"

"Yes," she says, rubbing her face. "I'm fine." She seems very subdued, almost in shock.

Well at least there's something I can do about this part. I get up and go to the freezer to prepare an ice pack. "Here," I tell her, "hold this up to your face, right here."

She sighs, but does what I tell her. Timothy is staring at her with wide eyes. I look back over to Gabe. "Why were you and Jonathan fighting?" I ask him.

"He punched my sister, Mom," he says in an incredulous tone, like he can't believe I even had to ask. His face crumples, and I can see that the realization of the situation is starting to sink in. "I guess I lost it. I pushed him to get him away from her, then he started hitting me too."

I look at him more carefully. I can't see any bruises or anything. "Are you hurt?'

"No," he says in a low voice.

I look back over at Natalie. "Is that what happened?" I ask her.

"Yes," she says, her face the picture of worry and regret. Timothy nods as well.

I sigh. I can't imagine what got into Jonathan. I've never seen him misbehave this badly before. I guess there have been times when Timothy and Natalie have complained that Jonathan was teasing them, but it never seemed at all serious.

Ron comes back in the front door, and joins us at the table. He sees Natalie with an ice pack on her face, and is alarmed. "So what happened?" he asks. "Jonathan didn't say a word. I had to tell his Dad that apparently he and Gabe had a fight, but I wasn't there so I don't know anything else about it. I told him I'd call after I find out what's going on."

I sigh and shake my head. "Well, the kids say Jonathan punched Natalie after she tried to make him give a book back to Timothy." The kids are all sitting silently, listening to my recitation of the event. They don't protest that I'm getting anything wrong. "So Gabe pushed Jonathan away from her, and that started a fight. They knocked over a shelf, books were everywhere, they were punching each other. The librarians and I had to break it up. It was awful."

Ron's eyes are practically bugging out of his head. "Are you all right, Natalie?" he asks. "Can I see?"

She puts the ice pack down. "I think I'm finished with this, Mom."

Ron looks at her face and sees the blossoming bruise. He strokes her hair lightly, and gives her a kiss on top of her head. I can see the shock in his eyes being replaced with anger. Somebody hurt his little girl. He looks over at Gabe, and they lock eyes, and something unspoken passes between them. I think they are sharing the anger at the idea of Natalie being harmed, and Ron is giving Gabe silent approval for trying to protect his sister. Each gives the other a subtle nod. It's strangely manly, this soundless exchange. Gabe suddenly seems very grown up to me.

We all sit quietly for another minute. Then Natalie asks, "Can Timothy and I go upstairs now?"

It occurs to me that nobody has checked to see how Timothy is doing. Nobody except Natalie, that is. He hasn't said a single word. "Timothy, how are you feeling?" I ask him. "Are you all right? Do you feel like you want to go home?"

"No," he says. "I want to stay here with Natalie."

Of course he does. "Okay, you kids all go on upstairs." It's late morning, and I know after the shock wears off everyone is going to be getting hungry. "I'll let you know when lunch is ready."

The three of them trudge up the stairs. After all the yelling in the library, their silence is a profound contrast.

Ron and I stare at each other, sitting together at the table.

"I guess I should call Brad," he says.

"No," I say, "I'll do it. I'm the one who was there."

Chapter 36

Brawl

Stefanie

The ring of the phone startles me, even though I am waiting for it. Brad and I have no idea what's going on. Ron dropped off Jonathan and said he didn't know anything other than the kids got in a fight, and he'd call when he learns more. Jonathan ran straight back into his room without saying anything at all. I followed after him, thinking he'd want to talk, but he clearly doesn't. He is laying face down on his bed, his head buried in his arms. I don't think he's crying, but he is obviously very upset. So I want to hear from Gabe's parents about what happened before I try to talk to Jonathan.

"Hello?"

"Hi, Stefanie, this is Brenda."

Ah. Makes sense. Ron said he'd call, but I know he wasn't even there when it happened. "Hi, Brenda. Can you tell me anything more?"

I hear her exhale, then inhale. "Yeah. I brought Gabe and Jonathan to the library with Timothy and Natalie. They were in the back of the library, and I heard them yelling. So I went running back there, and saw Gabe and Jonathan fighting. The librarian and I pulled them apart."

I ask, "You mean, physically fighting? Not just yelling at each other?"

She sighs again. "No, they were physically fighting. On the ground, hitting each other, knocking over books. It was bad." I can tell she really regrets having to tell me this.

"Do you know what started it?" I ask her.

"Yes." She pauses, and I get the uncomfortable feeling that even worse news is coming, because she is hesitating before sharing it. Oh no.

Finally she continues. "Apparently Jonathan took away a book Timothy was reading. Natalie tried to get him to give it back, but instead Jonathan punched her in the face."

I gasp. "What?"

"I know," Brenda says. "I can hardly believe it either. But Natalie has a bruise on her face. She and Gabe and Timothy all say the same thing. Apparently Gabe pushed Jonathan away from Natalie, and that's when the two of them started fighting. After we broke it up and everyone calmed down, the kids all cooperated with coming home. None of them have wanted to talk at all since then. I pretty much had to drag it out of them."

A hot rush of emotion is climbing my throat and burning in my cheeks. I don't know what to say.

I think she can tell I'm having a hard time speaking. She adds, "I think we are going to head on back over to my house for the rest of the weekend. The kids will have a couple of days to cool off before they see each other again at school."

"Okay," I say, embarrassed at how puny my voice sounds. "I'm ... I'm sorry about all of this."

"It's all right, Stefanie, kids fight sometimes. I think they'll probably all get over it and be fine by Monday."

Jonathan's

Perhaps I pressed him too hard.

I have been utilizing increasing power in my voice for weeks now, encouraging my beloved to behave in ways which will empower his soul. It is what I am here for, after all, to guard his soul, to help it grow. I have learned that the actions which most expand the power of his soul are ones in which he exercises dominion over others. The more brutal his action, the better, and the brighter glows his soul. Therefore, I have been constantly encouraging him to do so. Even when he seems hesitant or reluctant, when I whisper in his ear, ever more loudly, that he should do it, he capitulates ever more frequently. I am pleased that I seem to be redirecting his priorities towards actions which will cause intense growth in our soul.

I have noticed sometimes after such events, he seems disturbed. Then, I do my best to comfort him, reassure him that it is best to do what he wishes, and he should always discount the insignificant feelings of others, in favor of taking actions which bring him pleasure. And I remind him that cruelty always brings us pleasure. There is nothing more important to me.

Today's incident at the library began well enough, with the four children searching for books. Jonathan and the siblings were looking for dog training books, as they had discussed, and I whispered to him that this was a good plan, as he should be able to entirely control his pet, and these books and the other children may assist him in learning how to do so. The other child, Timothy, who has so often been the foil for my beloved's clever tricks, was not participating in the group event, and was instead searching for history books.

When Jonathan noticed this, I encouraged him to correct Timothy by confiscating his book. Timothy should join the group, I whispered, should support Jonathan in his task. He should not be allowed to disregard the group activity being conducted to benefit Jonathan.

When Jonathan took the action I suggested, the Seer interfered. Of course she did. She has constantly been at odds with my goals for Jonathan, especially since she launched her aggravating project. Her suggestions to him are in opposition to mine. My poor darling has felt conflicted over and over again, with my instructions washing over him as irresistible urges, but then Natalie's advice dampening his desires. I have had to generate more and more energy in my communications, to attempt to override the girl's irritating insertion of her wishes into Jonathan's decisions.

When Jonathan seized the book from the other boy, Timothy shouted, "Stop it!" Natalie stepped over, and gently placing her hand upon Jonathan's, quietly said, "Jonathan, can you please give Timothy his book back?"

As soon as she acted, I used more power than ever before to counteract her suggestion. *"My dearest,"* I whispered, or more accurately thundered, *"care not for the insipid suggestions of this bizarre girl. She has prevented you from pursuing your desires too many times. You must stop her!"*

Jonathan experienced my admonishment as an overwhelming burst of rage, combined with a desperate lust to commit violence against the girl. His mind was flooded with the certain knowledge that it was her standing in the way of what he wanted, her blocking his will, and she must pay for it. His fist clenched and flew out before her Guardian had any chance to warn her, and the violent contact with her face was enormously satisfying. As Jonathan watched her fly backwards and crash into the shelf, her tiny body knocking it to the ground in a cascade of books, I experienced a phenomenal rush of pleasure, as our shared soul blazed ferociously.

"More! Again!" I shouted to him, uncaring of anything else, eager for the moment to continue, wanting to prolong the almost orgasmic sense of fulfillment flooding through me.

Jonathan's self-will was subsumed within my own, his thoughts in abeyance as he had no choice but to carry out my suggestions. The moment was perfect, the best of my long existence. My beloved was following my instructions, feeding glory into our soul, obeying my desires as much as his own. He moved forward to continue his assault on the annoying Seer.

Then her wretched brother came flying into the action, and the moment was ruined. Jonathan's mind was too overwhelmed to make any conscious decisions, and he unthinkingly brawled with the boy who has been his best friend for years.

After the adults intervened, and Natalie again inserted her officious wishes into the situation, Jonathan became calm, and strangely quiet.

I now fear that I went too far. Jonathan has never been so confused, so distressed. His thoughts are tangled, incoherent. Worst of all, he feels a sense of self-loathing, as though his righteous actions were somehow wrong. He feels an awful guilt as he remembers how much he enjoyed striking Natalie. And his soul is alarmingly dimming.

I must try to correct his impressions of the event. He must realize that only his needs, his soul - our soul - should be of concern to him. I am whispering to him, but I am not using additional power. I worry my use of such for the last several weeks may have been too much for his young mind to absorb. Perhaps we both need a hiatus from my program of encouraging more frequent soul-enhancing actions.

I am sure if I let him rest from the additional power, things will quickly revert to normal.

I am eager to resume the use of power. But not yet. Not quite yet.

Brad

I'm sitting next to Stefanie and listening as she talks to Brenda. When she hangs up, we are both stunned. I ask her to repeat for me what Brenda told her, not sure I understood what the phone call was about. But no, I heard it right. Stef tells me Jonathan punched Natalie when she tried to get him to give the other kid his book back. Then I guess Gabe jumped on him and they had a fight that Brenda had to break up. It sounds terrible.

Stef's face is red, and big fat tears are starting to leak out of her eyes. It's bad, but is it really that bad? Kids fight, like Brenda said. I'm about to tell her it isn't the end of the world, no need to cry. But then she says, "I think this is my fault. I've known Jonathan was being mean to Natalie sometimes, and to her other friend, and I've tried to ignore it. I figured I should let the kids sort out their own problems. But I should have disciplined him more! If I had, this wouldn't have happened!" She is starting to sob.

And now I get it. She's blaming herself, thinking she's a bad mom. But she's wrong. She's the best mom ever. She's always so loving and patient and organized. Jonathan couldn't hope to have a better mom. She doesn't realize how perfect she is. I see why she's upset. She's worried she isn't any good. And since she's having another baby she's probably worried about that as well.

I pull her into my arms. I'm not worried about Jonathan. He's eight years old. I had some fights when I was a kid. Well, a lot of fights. I spent the last years of my childhood shuffling between foster homes, or even sometimes just couch-surfing wherever I could. It's something that I don't talk about, not even with Stef. She knew it back when we were in high school, but even then I tried to keep it to myself. She grew up very differently, quietly, just her and her Mom, so she has no concept of how rough things can get.

I've been completely committed to letting Jonathan have the sort of childhood I didn't, and we've done a good job, I think, even though neither of us have parents around who can help us. I think we're figuring it out, especially Stef. She's amazing. And Jonathan is just being a boy. So I am completely distressed to see Stef being so hard on herself.

"Shhh, Stef, darlin', shhh." I put my hand on her head, stroking her hair. "Honey, you're the best mom I've ever seen. You take care of Jonathan so perfectly. I'm always amazed at how on top of everything you always are."

She sniffles, and I think the tears are slowing down. Hopefully I'm getting through. "Please don't blame yourself for him acting like a boy. Fighting is normal. Believe me, I did it myself, and I think I turned out okay."

She nods a little against my chest, then leans back to wipe her face. "You think so? You think this is regular boy stuff?" She didn't have any siblings, so she probably doesn't even realize this.

"Definitely," I tell her. "This is completely normal. But you're right, we should discipline him for fighting. He needs to learn. How about I go talk to him, and I'll revoke some privileges or something. That should teach him a lesson."

"Okay," she sighs shakily.

When I'm sure she is calmer, I get up and go down the hallway to Jonathan's room. I don't think he's moved since he got home. He's laying flat on his bed, face down, head in his arms. Is he asleep?

I sit on his bed and touch his shoulder. "Jonathan, we need to talk," I say.

"Fine," he says sullenly. So he isn't sleeping. Probably waiting to see how much trouble he's in.

He doesn't move, though. "Turn over, kid," I tell him. "I want you to explain what happened."

He doesn't turn over immediately, but before I ask him again he sighs heavily and rolls over. He doesn't sit up though. He stares at me from his pillow.

"So?" I ask him. "Tell me about the library." This should be good. I figure he'll make up some wild story to try to get out of being in trouble. Probably blame it on someone else.

Surprisingly, though, he tells me the same thing Brenda said. Taking a deep breath first, in a monotone he says, "I took Timothy's book away. Natalie told me to give it back. I hit her. Then Gabe pushed me, and we started fighting. The grownups made us stop."

Oh. I was prepared to have to confront him with the fact I know all of this stuff, but here he is admitting the whole thing. And he seems really weird. Like, his emotions are completely flat. He doesn't even seem worried about being in trouble. Maybe he's in shock about Gabe fighting him?

"Well," I say, hesitating, not sure how to approach this. "Can you tell me why?"

"I don't ... I don't know," he says, and suddenly his deadpan facade crumbles. His face screws up, not so much like he is going to cry, but like he is disgusted.

With himself. "I couldn't stop myself, Dad. All of a sudden, all I wanted was to hit her." He sits up and clenches his fist, holding it to his forehead, grimacing.

Wow, he is way more upset about this than I expected. I don't know what to do next. This is actually kind of alarming. Before I can pull myself together, he goes on. "And the worst part, Dad, was I liked it. I liked hitting her. It felt good." His voice breaks. "I must be some kind of monster."

"No! No, Jonathan, of course you're not a monster. You're only a boy who's starting to grow up, and sometimes when that happens you get feelings you can't control." Maybe he's starting puberty early? I mean, that brings all sorts of urges. I remember feeling violent sometimes. Not til a little older, though. He looks at me, like he is afraid to feel relieved.

"Honestly, kid, nothing you did was so unusual. It was bad, yes. You should never give in to the urge to be violent. But you have to understand, urges like that don't make you a monster. They make you human. You just have to learn to control yourself better."

He does look like he is feeling calmer. I hope I'm getting through to him.

"You understand, of course, there has to be a consequence for what you did."

He hangs his head, but he almost looks relieved. Like he's happy to have a normal consequence to having misbehaved normally. Instead of having me agree that he's some sort of monster. "Okay," he says.

"All right," I say. "No t.v. for a week. That way you'll be able to spend time thinking about how to make sure you control yourself better next time something like this happens."

He nods, not arguing at all about losing his t.v. privileges. "Dad," he says, then hesitates.

"Yeah?"

"Do you think I should, I guess, go over there? I'm worried Gabe hates me now."

Oh yeah, I should have thought of this. Of course it would be bothering him too.

"I don't think Gabe hates you. But I think it would be a good idea to let everyone calm down first. Besides, Gabe and his family are going back over to his Mom's house. You can talk to him when you see him at school on Monday."

He looks crushed. But now I've taken away his t.v., he can't use it to make himself feel better. I know. "Why don't you go play with Socks? He's been out in the backyard waiting for you."

A wave of obvious relief washes across his face. He wipes his eyes on his sleeve.

"Come here, kid, let me give you a hug." I give him a tight squeeze. "You know your Mom and I love you even when you do something wrong, right? But we want to help you learn to be better."

He allows me to hug him, but gets away as soon as he can. He never has liked hugging. He gets up and heads outside.

I follow him down the hall and watch as he passes Stef, who has obviously been standing there listening to our conversation. She pats him on the shoulder.

When we get back out to the family room and look out the window, he is with the dog, but not chasing around and roughhousing like usual. He is sitting on the ground, holding the puppy in his arms, perfectly still, his face buried in the dog's fur. The puppy is sniffing around and wagging his tail. But Jonathan isn't moving.

Chapter 37

Aaron

Natalie's

The horror of the moment in the library will be etched in my memory forever. The worst of it was not even being unable to stop my beloved from being assaulted and injured by the terrible boy. It was watching his Guardian goading him into it. It was as though the needs of the child mattered not at all to his Guardian. The Guardian greedily manipulated the boy, increasing the use of power tenfold to create an irresistible compulsion to attack Natalie. It happened so suddenly I was helpless to do anything to stop it. I had barely started to warn her before she had already been struck and was falling backwards onto the bookshelf.

Even more horrifying, the resulting blaze in Jonathan's soul created such hunger in his Guardian, that they both wanted only to continue the attack. More precisely, the Guardian wanted it, craved it, lusted after it. And when the Guardian shouted the command, *"More! Again!"* Jonathan immediately complied. It was as though Jonathan himself lost all agency, and was acting in the moment only as a tool of his Guardian. He was literally helpless to stop himself, even if he had wanted to.

This is unprecedented. A Guardian has forced a terrible act to be committed by the human being Guarded. I know of no prior time when a Guardian was the one who initiated the action of a human. This is not Guarding. This is using. This is depraved. This is evil.

How can it be stopped?

At least Jonathan's Guardian has chosen to stop using the additional power for now, as it has become obvious that Jonathan's mind is beginning to fracture under the constant assault he is unknowingly enduring from his Guardian's use of power against him.

The Guardian has completely lost the way of Guarding. The well-being of Jonathan has ceased to be considered in any way. It is only the increasing brilliance of Jonathan's soul which is being prioritized, and the sick pleasure the Guardian has begun to personally feel as Jonathan is forced to commit ever more heinous acts.

This is dangerous. For Jonathan. For all humans around him. And particularly for Natalie, who has incurred the wrath of Jonathan's Guardian, and has begun to be singled out for his increasing abuse.

I must warn her. I would not wait any longer even if she did not broach the topic, but she already has. She asked me silently on the car ride back from the library what was really going on with Jonathan. I told her I would explain what I could, but I felt it would be best to do so while Timothy was also involved in the discussion. So she has been waiting for the opportunity to be alone with him, so they can ask their questions. She understands that first her parents must be satisfied in receiving answers to their own questions.

When her mother gives her the ice pack for her face, Natalie does not disclose that she has other bruises on her body, caused by her collision with the bookshelf. I ask her if she shouldn't also mention this to her mother, and she dismisses the suggestion as ridiculous. She is happy to allow her mother to continue with the misapprehension that the bookshelf had been knocked over by the boys, not by Natalie's own tiny body.

She is confident her bruises will heal quickly, and is happy she suffered no injury so severe that she cannot conceal it from her mother. Only the bruise on her face was detected.

Natalie does not understand, yet, that the speedy healing she relies on is unusual. She assumes all people's injuries mend themselves as quickly as hers do. She does not know this is incorrect. I have long surmised her unusual abilities include certain physical attributes which she does not yet know are exceptional. But those are not of concern at the current time. My priority must be to warn her about the danger posed by Jonathan and his Guardian. Even with her accelerated healing abilities, she is at substantial risk.

When we reach her room, and she has closed the door, she first turns to her friend. "Timothy, I asked Angel what is really going on with Jonathan. I've thought for a while this is way worse than the way he normally acts. We know he can be a bully, but I can tell something else is happening. It was super obvious today. So Angel told me in the car over here he would explain, but he wanted you to be a part of the conversation too. That's why I've been waiting to talk to him more about it."

Timothy somberly nods. "Thank you for waiting, Natalie. I've been thinking the same thing. Something has gotten into Jonathan I don't understand. Angel, do you know what it is?"

"Yes, my dearest children, I do comprehend much more than you about why Jonathan has been behaving in such a way. I have wanted to tell you, but I thought it would be best to observe events as they unfolded, to wait until you asked for more information."

Natalie receives this information with some surprise and quizzically relays it to Timothy. He, as always, comprehends a great deal about what was said. He asks, "So, Angel, you've known for a while too that something else is wrong, but you decided to wait to say anything? Why?"

Ah, he immediately jumps to the heart of the matter.

"The situation is very complicated, and I asked for guidance from the other Guardians surrounding us. All of them have given input about how to proceed. Not only Timothy's Guardian, but also those of Natalie's parents and brother. Knight, and Lady, and Gabe's Guardian. We have all conferred about what to do regarding Jonathan and his Guardian, who is also a part of this."

Natalie is amazed as she repeats this to Timothy. "So," she comments, "you've all been talking about this? All of our Guardians?"

"Yes, my dear, as it involves all of our Guarded, we wished to come together to try to assess the situation. It involves Jonathan's Guardian. Gabe's Guardian has been able to share information about how Jonathan's Guardian has been interacting with him. Guardian has also been closely involved."

Natalie tries to repeat all of this, but she frowns. "Hold on," she says. "This is too confusing, you saying 'Guardian' over and over. Guardian is Timothy's. We should have names for everyone, like for Knight and Lady, so it's easier to know who we're talking about. Don't you think?" she asks me.

I smile at the dear child. *"Of course, darling, if it will make it easier for you to follow our conversation, you should assign names. Gabe's Guardian is listening, as are Guardian, Knight and Lady. Gabe's Guardian would be perfectly happy to have a name assigned by you."*

She thinks for a moment. "You know how you said guardians can be any shape? What shape is Gabe's guardian?"

My little Seer is so endearing, wanting the tangible description in order to best create a moniker for her brother's Guardian. *"Gabe's Guardian has assumed the form of a young man, more or less,"* I tell her. Like most Guardians who have assumed a human form, it is a general outline, without a great deal of detail. The purpose of the form is not for the human's benefit since it will never be seen, but for the Guardian to feel more at one with the human they are Guarding. Details are not needed for this purpose.

Natalie nods, and closes her eyes, and begins to consider what name to assign to the Guardian of her beloved brother. Especially after today, she appreciates how protective Gabe can be, and how much he supports her. As when she named Knight and Lady, she considers her recent reading. At the time, she had been reading tales of medieval history. More recently, she has finished reading the children's bible. She considers stories of brothers in that book, and her mind settles on one. She opens her eyes. "Gabe's Guardian," she says, addressing the Guardian directly, "there is a story in the bible of Aaron, who was a good helper to his brother Moses. The story I was reading said the name Aaron means 'strong'. I think Gabe is strong, and he is a good helper. Does Aaron seem like an okay name for you?"

Gabe's Guardian is overwhelmed with emotion at being included in the group of named Guardians. What is more, he is profoundly moved by Natalie's careful consideration of a name to give to him. I tell her, *"Gabe's Guardian would be very grateful to be known as Aaron, and believes it is the perfect name. He thanks you for choosing a name for him so carefully."*

Natalie smiles. "Okay, now that's done, please tell us what's going on with Jonathan."

I am pleased to know I will not have the time to do so at this moment. Jonathan is nearby with his Guardian, who although focused on Jonathan at the moment, is also aware as always of our conversation taking place in the house down the street. As when the other Guardians and I discussed the situation previously, I would prefer to have this conversation at a sufficient distance to not be overheard. Therefore, I need only hesitate a moment before answering Natalie, knowing her mother is about to interrupt.

"Kids, come on downstairs," Brenda calls. "It's lunchtime."

Natalie and Timothy glance at each other. Natalie sighs and looks over at me. I smile placidly at her. She knows we will resume when she and Timothy are alone again. She does not yet know there will be a further delay, because her parents have decided to return to her mother's house right after lunch, rather than remaining for the rest of the weekend. They have discussed the situation regarding the children, and feel having some distance between Gabe and Jonathan for a couple of days would benefit them.

As the children sit down to their sandwiches, Ron explains this to the children. "Kids, it turns out we're going back to the other house after lunch. We called Timothy's parents, and they are out for the rest of the day, so Timothy can still hang out with us until they get back."

Gabe is somewhat relieved, because he had been worried he would need to see Jonathan again today or tomorrow, and did not know what to say or do. Gabe is extremely conflicted about Jonathan, but mostly he is very angry with him for harming Natalie. Gabe's Guardian, or Aaron as I should now call him, has of course been whispering to Gabe, trying to bring him calmness and clarity.

Timothy and Natalie wish they could resume their conversation sooner, but are glad to know they can do so as soon as we all arrive back at Brenda's house. The brief delay will harm no-one.

I continue to monitor the activity at Jonathan's house, and am pleased his Guardian has reverted to a normal volume in communicating to the child. Jonathan is very shaken by the manipulation he has been experiencing, feeling something is fundamentally wrong with him which is causing him to be cruel to Natalie and others. Before his Guardian began using power to control him, Jonathan enjoyed his petty injuries to smaller children and creatures, and thrived with the unheard positive reinforcement provided by his Guardian. But now that his Guardian has discovered a way to actually control Jonathan's actions, forcing him to commit increasingly violent and harmful acts, Jonathan senses the loss of control over himself. The feeling of powerlessness over his own actions is deeply disturbing to him. The ability to time his antics to avoid detection was an important part of what appealed to him so much about his cruel games. But lately he finds himself impulsively acting without caution, and he simply feels powerless to stop himself. The game no longer feels fun to him. It makes him feel desperate and unhappy.

Furthermore, he has grown to value and enjoy Natalie's company since she launched her effort to help him. As a result, he does not wish to harm her. The fact that he has continuously felt the desire to do so, against his own will, is creating unhealthy confusion and turmoil in his mind. He does not realize he has been torn between her wishes and those of his Guardian.

I do not know how this can end well for him.

Chapter 38

Demon

Gabe's

I am now Aaron. Named for the brother of the famous prophet Moses, as my own beloved is the brother of the Seer. The parallels are meaningful, and it is deeply impressive how Natalie derived this name. I am forever grateful, and forever changed. I am Aaron.

As we travel back to Brenda's home, the children are all quiet in the back seat. The adults discuss plans for the rest of the weekend, since they have altered course and will be returning early to this residence.

Gabe is deep in thought, wondering about what happened with Jonathan. All of the children, Gabe included, have noticed recently that Jonathan's negative behavior has escalated. Gabe hasn't any idea why, but he knows it is unacceptable. The fact that Natalie was victimized by Jonathan has deeply soured Gabe against his friend.

At the age of 10, Gabe is entering the pre-adolescent phase of his life, and has begun maturing emotionally. Jonathan, although younger than Gabe, has been able to maintain their close friendship with his exciting personality and daring. However, it is not unlikely that Gabe would soon be moving on to friendships with peers closer to his own age, even without the current trouble involving Jonathan and his Guardian. I do not know how it will impact Jonathan if Gabe begins distancing himself. However, I would prefer this to occur for Gabe's benefit. A kinder group of friends, or even simply a group of friends closer to his own age, would be more appropriate for Gabe as he approaches adolescence.

When we arrive home, Gabe quickly notifies his parents he is going to go and play with some of the other boys who live in the complex, and who he saw playing a ball game in the nearby field as his father parked the car. I am very pleased about this development. He has sometimes enjoyed the company of these slightly older boys, but does not often have the chance to play with them while spending weekends at his father's house. These children seem like appropriate companions to my beloved.

We will remain in close enough proximity for me to also participate in the conversation taking place between the Seer and the other Guardians.

In the meantime, I whisper encouragingly to my dearest one. *"What a lovely opportunity to spend time with these other boys, my dear. You shall have an enjoyable time this afternoon, an unexpected pleasure. Perhaps the events of today will work out for the best."*

Timothy's

When Natalie and Timothy arrive home, the adults are unsurprised to see them immediately run up the stairs and close the door to Natalie's room. This is normal.

Natalie immediately begins. "Okay, Angel, what's happening with Jonathan?"

Angel regards each of us to ensure we are all prepared to participate as needed in the conversation. Of course we are. Even the others, whose Guarded are involved in separate activities, have no trouble both monitoring the actions of their own humans, while attending carefully to this very important discussion.

"Children," he begins, *"you will recall the day, about two months ago, when you conducted the experiment to determine whether Guardians can communicate over longer distances."*

Timothy and Natalie glance at each other, surprised at this unexpected statement. What could this possibly have to do with Jonathan, they both wonder. Neither of them speaks, but Timothy nods.

"Do you remember I told you that when Guardian and I began 'yelling' at each other, every other Guardian in the region was able to hear this?"

"Yeeeessss," Natalie says, slowly, already starting to put the pieces together. Timothy frowns and waits.

"One of the Guardians who heard it, of course, was Jonathan's, because they were in a house nearby when the experiment was conducted."

Natalie suddenly realizes although she knew about the other Guardians hearing the disturbance, she had never thought to inquire about whether this had any repercussions. Frankly, neither did Angel or myself, at least initially. We knew the activities of the Seer were always observed with interest, but we did not anticipate any other Guardian would be motivated to do anything other than watch from a distance. Even with Jonathan's Guardian, who we noticed was greatly fascinated with the discoveries we made during the night of experimentation, we assumed it would end with fascination only. Not with implementation.

Soon, however, we saw what was happening. We watched Jonathan's Guardian learn by observing our communications with each other, and with our humans. And we beheld when the learning was put into action, and Jonathan's Guardian began manipulating him deliberately, using the power technique we had unintentionally demonstrated.

"When we participated in the experiment, we did not know Jonathan's Guardian would take what we had learned and begin to use it himself."

After listening to Natalie repeat this to him, Timothy asks, "Do you mean Jonathan's Guardian is talking to you too?"

"I am afraid not. He is talking to Jonathan."

"What?" Timothy is bewildered. "Do you mean Jonathan can hear his Guardian, like I can hear mine?" Timothy and I have continued to progress in our communication. Timothy practices almost constantly the method of opening his mind, and when he is not focusing on other things like studying or reading, he also attempts to induce the dreamlike state in which he can hear much of what I am telling him. It does not flow as smoothly as the communication the Seer has with Angel, but the progress we have made in mere weeks is astonishing.

"No," Angel says, filled with consternation and grief over the situation, and over having to explain this to our beloved children. *"Jonathan does not know of the existence of his Guardian, and has never thought of making any of the efforts Timothy uses to make his mind receptive to the communication of his."*

Angel pauses while Natalie relays this information. The children wait, confused, for further explanation.

"I have explained in the past that what humans normally perceive from their Guardians is a very occasional burst of emotion, such as when the human is experiencing a stressful time, and the Guardian can transmit a sense of peace or calm to help the human."

The children listen, trying to understand.

"What Jonathan is hearing, then, is not words, nor any message. He does not know what is happening. What he experiences when his Guardian uses power to speak to him is an enhanced emotional state."

"But," Natalie bursts out, "why is he getting meaner? Why isn't it helping Jonathan be calmer and more peaceful, like you say happens when most people hear their Guardians?"

"Because, sadly, that is not the message Jonathan's Guardian is sending to Jonathan." The children are growing frustrated, unable to comprehend where this is heading.

Angel goes on, *"I must remind you of another aspect of what you have learned about Guardians. I have explained that the Guardian is here to share the soul with the human, and to help the soul grow. Sometimes the soul can grow even when the actions taken by a human are bad, or cruel, or violent. Remember this?"*

"Yes," Timothy says after Natalie relays the words, his brow furrowed as he tries to piece together what is being said. "And you said even if the Guardian doesn't really like what the human is doing, at least they are happy the soul is growing because of it, right?"

"You remember correctly, my dear. Now we can return to the situation with Jonathan's Guardian. For years now, Jonathan's Guardian has ob-served when Jonathan is cruel to you, or to others, his soul grows brighter and stronger. His Guardian has begun not merely accepting this behavior, but actually desiring it."

Natalie feels a growing sense of horror as she repeats this to Timothy. "Are you saying," she whispers, suddenly comprehending how all of this links together, "that is what his Guardian is using power to tell him? To be mean?"

"Tragically, yes. Jonathan's Guardian is already very unusual, in wishing for his human to be cruel to others, because of how much it strengthens his soul. This is rare, but not unheard of. What is different now is Jonathan's Guardian has discovered that by using the power technique learned through

our unplanned demonstration, Jonathan can actually perceive his Guardian's desire for cruelty."

My Timothy wishes to clarify, to understand precisely what this means. "So, do you mean Jonathan's Guardian is using power to tell Jonathan to do bad stuff? And that is what Jonathan is hearing?" Angel nods, and Natalie sees Timothy's statement is accurate.

"Can't Jonathan ignore him?" Natalie asks desperately. "I know that Jonathan was starting to get nicer, I really think that is what he wants to do. So can't he try not to listen to his Guardian?"

"He does not have the ability to do that. First, he has no idea he has a Guardian, so he cannot distinguish between what he senses from his Guardian and thoughts he is creating himself. Second, he isn't hearing the messages from his Guardian as though they are spoken words. He perceives them as raw emotion, almost always negative emotion. His Guardian encourages him to commit violence, and Jonathan believes it is an urge coming from within himself."

Again, Timothy wants to clarify. "So, what happened today at the library, was because of Jonathan's Guardian?"

"Yes," Angel confirms sadly. *"Jonathan's Guardian used power to instruct him to take the book away from you, Timothy. Jonathan did so. Then, when Natalie tried to convince Jonathan to give it back, his Guardian used much more power than ever before to tell Jonathan he had to stop Natalie. The power created an overwhelming emotion in Jonathan which he had no way to control."*

The children listen with wide eyes, aghast at what they are hearing. Natalie is extremely distressed even as she continuously repeats the words for Timothy.

Angel goes on, wanting the children to understand what happened. *"Jonathan experienced this message from his Guardian as sudden rage, and an irresistible urge to commit violence. When he struck Natalie, he was not in control of himself. His Guardian was essentially controlling him."*

Natalie remembers some of the stories she has recently read in the bible. "You mean, like, he was possessed? Like with a demon?"

"Yes, my dear," Angel says, brokenhearted at the pain this knowledge is inflicting on his beloved, but committed to ensuring she understands the danger she is in. *"That is a very good analogy. This is very much like a story in which a human is being controlled by an evil spirit."*

She covers her face with her hands, distraught. She is shattered to think the boy she has tried to help, to befriend, is being victimized by his own Guardian. She does not assign blame to Jonathan. She never has. She has only ever wanted to help him. Now, she sees the problem is far more serious than she had realized. Jonathan is helplessly in the control of a powerful and evil entity. And she has a sudden flash of inspiration.

With a wry smile, a strangely adult expression of humor in the face of adversity, she says, "Well, I know what to call Jonathan's Guardian now, so he has a name too."

Timothy has been staring at the carpet as his mind processes everything he is learning. He looks up at her. "What will you call him?"

Her face filled with an expression of deep resolve, she says, "Demon. His name is Demon."

Chapter 39

He Deserves To Know

Ron

I should have seen this coming. I think I was so wrapped up in my own head, in my plans with Brenda, in my joy that she has taken me back, I was ignoring what was going on with Gabe. I've seen Jonathan pull some stunts over the years, but I never really thought it was serious enough to pay much attention. Besides, Gabe is a big kid, and older than Jonathan, so I knew he could hold his own. Natalie seemed to have realized a long time ago she should stay away from him, so I was never worried about her.

But then recently she has started hanging around with Jonathan too. I figure probably because he has a cute little puppy now, and it has drawn her to him. I should have given this more thought. I should have realized with Jonathan's history of pranks, Natalie would end up on the receiving end if she was spending time with him.

But not this. I never imagined he would punch her in the face. Little Natalie, my tiny daughter, the kindest and gentlest person I have ever known. How could anybody ever want to do her harm?

And how could I have allowed it to happen?

I hated myself for so many years, for what I did to Brenda, that this feels almost familiar. Jonathan might have been the one who threw the punch, but I am her father. I should have found a way to protect her. I failed.

The only thing I can think to do at the moment is separate the kids. It's a good thing, it turns out, we have a second house to retreat to. We've spent months dithering about which one we should land in, and going back and forth because we couldn't reach a decision. So for today I'm glad we could simply pack ourselves in the car and drive over here.

I'm still fuming, though, ever since I realized what happened. Thank God Gabe was there. As upset as I am about Natalie being hurt, I am incredibly proud of Gabe for doing his best to protect her. He did the job of a man, my job. I'm so grateful to him.

I don't know what will happen next, but I know I have to pay more attention. I have to make sure the kids are all right.

They seem fine for now. Gabe is off playing ball with some kids who live here, and Natalie of course is up in her room playing with Timothy. They don't seem any the worse for wear, thank goodness.

Natalie's

It is an eerily appropriate name. Demon. For it is truly what Jonathan's Guardian has become. A malevolent spirit, controlling Jonathan for his own sinister purposes. Demon has told himself all along that he is doing it for the benefit of Jonathan's soul, is simply helping Jonathan to develop and grow strong. But the purpose has been buried under the greed for more which Demon feels when Jonathan's soul is blazing with misdeeds. Jonathan is no longer being Guarded. He is Demon's pawn.

The conversation pauses while the children absorb what they have learned, and while the Guardians contemplate the new name for Jonathan's Guardian. Demon. All accept it as perfectly descriptive.

After a minute or two, Natalie asks, "So, what can we do about it?"

I raise my hands to demonstrate helplessness. *"I do not know, darling. I only wanted to make sure you are aware of the situation. It is dangerous, and you must be careful."*

Timothy has been mulling over all of the events of the day in his mind, and he chimes in after hearing his friend repeat my warning. "Natalie, he's right. You said you would be safe, but that was before, when you thought it was just Jonathan being mean. Now we know his Guardian has turned evil and is controlling him, I think the Jonathan Project is too dangerous now. You won't be able to change Jonathan. You'll end up getting hurt even worse."

Natalie asks, "Is there any way for you Guardians to tell Demon to stop it?"

"No, my dear, it would be ineffective. Remember, whenever any of us are near Demon, he knows what we are thinking and doing. He already knows we wish for him to change his ways, and return to simply being a Guardian. He does not care at all what we think. None of us can invent any plans for changing the situation, I'm afraid. I believe Timothy is right, and the only safe thing for you is to stay away from Jonathan."

Of course Natalie finds this completely unacceptable. "No!" she insists. "I can't leave Jonathan alone when I know Demon is using him to hurt people! It's hurting Jonathan too. I could feel it today. Even though part of him liked what was happening, he also felt terrible about it. He's scared. He knows something is wrong, but he doesn't know what it is.   I have to find a way to help him."

I am stymied. I have no useful suggestions to make. I have always known that I must be guided by my Seer, but I can see no safe path forward for her. I cannot imagine how she, merely a child, can formulate any plan which will help Jonathan without hurting her. Demon is the most important factor. There is no conceivable way she can oppose a Guardian who has become evil.

Natalie

I don't care what Angel says, I am not going to give up on Jonathan. Now I know what's going on, I know he needs my help more than ever. Not only to make him nicer. But to actually save him.

I think about my poor brother. Gabe has been feeling a little sad lately, since Demon has started making Jonathan so mean. He's even been mean to Gabe sometimes, but Gabe has tried to continue being his friend. I think if Gabe knew what was really going on, he'd want to help too.

Well, that's it, isn't it! I have to tell Gabe. Gabe is big, and strong, and he loves me and loves Jonathan. Gabe is the one who can help with Jonathan.

I still don't know how, but at least I know the next thing I have to do.

I have to tell my brother about guardians.

Gabe's

As my beloved enjoys playing a game of ball with the neighborhood boys, I listen attentively to the discussion between the Seer and the other Guardians.

Her sorrow at learning about how Demon is afflicting Jonathan is profound. As is her determination to find a way to help.

"Angel," she announces, "I know what I have to do. I'm going to tell Gabe about guardians, and about what Demon is doing. I know he'll be able to help."

I am thunderstruck. I know Timothy has long been aware of Angel, and has recently become aware of his own Guardian. He and Guardian have even devised a way to communicate with each other.

But I never extrapolated their situation to my own. I never thought my own beloved would someday learn of my existence.

And now the Seer has announced it is going to happen tonight. Gabe will be told about me.

I feel myself explode in joy at the thought, then immediately feel deep concern. Natalie has been put into danger by incurring the enmity of Demon. By drawing her brother into the situation, he might face similar risk. I know by spending time around Jonathan he already has experienced some of his friend's pranks. But if Demon decides Gabe is a threat, I fear the situation may escalate.

Angel hears my concerns, and decides he must relay them to Natalie. *"My darling,"* he says, *"I understand your motivation in wishing to recruit your brother to help Jonathan. But you should consider carefully before you do this. Demon has specifically directed Jonathan's actions against you, because Demon feels threatened by you. He does not want to allow you to change Jonathan. If you draw Gabe into this, if Gabe is aware of Guardians and aware of Demon, it is possible he will be targeted as well. I know you would not wish to bring harm to your brother."*

Natalie hadn't thought of it this way. Her forehead wrinkles with concern. She turns to her best friend for guidance. Timothy worries more for Natalie's well-being than Gabe's, but he still wishes no harm to come to his friend's brother. "I think," he begins, then hesitates slightly, "I think Gabe should know. If there was something going terribly wrong with you, Natalie, I would want to know about it. Jonathan is his best friend. I think he'd want to know."

Natalie looks relieved, to hear Timothy affirm her belief. She looks to Angel for his opinion.

Angel reluctantly agrees. *"Yes, darling, Timothy is correct that Gabe has the right to know his friend is in distress. Gabe has wondered what is wrong. He will want to know the truth. However, the news about Guardians may be difficult for him to believe. I suggest you proceed carefully."*

Natalie nods, determined to make this work. "Yes. He deserves to know. I'll figure out a way to tell him. I think I'll do it tonight. You probably won't be here any more, Timothy, but can you keep your mind open so Guardian can try to tell you if anything happens you should know about?"

"Yes," Timothy says. He is still very worried about Natalie. "Natty," he says, using a rare nickname, "after you tell him, if Gabe decides you should stay away from Jonathan, will you listen to him?"

She pauses for a moment, considering this. She knows how worried Timothy is, Angel is. She does not wish to cause worry. "Okay," she says, reluctantly. "If Gabe knows what's going on and wants us to stay away from Jonathan, I will." She hesitates for a moment, then feels she must add, "Well, at least until I come up with a better plan."

Timothy accepts this answer for now. He understands Natalie will not readily give up on the plan to help Jonathan. In the meantime, his scientific side emerges. "Okay, Natalie, you need to have a plan for how to tell Gabe. Do you remember the first experiment we did on Angel?"

She considers. "You mean the one with the dice and stuff?"

"Yes," he says. "Remember I said we would need ways to prove it if we ever wanted to tell someone about Angel?"

"Oh!" she says, realizing where he is leading. "You're right. I'll need to prove it to Gabe, or else he'll never believe me. All right, what do you think I should do?"

They revert to a place where they are comfortable, approaching this as though they are planning a new experiment. Timothy offers a number of suggestions, and Natalie takes some notes about what she should say to her brother when she introduces this topic later.

I can hardly believe Gabe is going to learn about me tonight. I must prepare myself, and must try to prepare him. My whispers to him will be of acceptance, openness, discovery. He will be learning shocking news on many levels. I hope he is glad this decision has been made for him. I hope he does not come to regret learning about me.

Chapter 40
Dice

Gabe

It's been a strange day. Horrible earlier, then really nice this afternoon. I'm glad I got to play with the kids around here. Being with them always feels, I don't know, easier somehow than being with Jonathan. Jonathan is a challenge. It's exciting to be with him but I always feel like I have to stay on my toes with him. This afternoon I was playing soccer and stuff. Simple, basic games. It was refreshing, after Jonathan went so crazy this morning at the library.

I still can't believe any of it happened. I wasn't surprised when he yanked Timothy's book away, but I can not wrap my head around him hitting Natalie. Why on earth did he do that? I even understand him fighting me, since I did push him, after all. But hitting my little sister? What the heck?

Almost like she heard me thinking about her, Natalie pushes open the door to my room and pokes her head inside. Mom already said goodnight to us, but since it's Saturday she lets us stay up later than usual as long as we are doing quiet stuff in our rooms.

"Hey, Nat," I say. "Did you run out of books to read or something?"

She giggles. "No, there's always more books. I was wondering if I could come in for a while?"

"Sure." I put down my Gameboy and scooch over on my bed to make room for her.

She climbs up and snuggles against me. "Hey," I say, remembering, "let me see your face." She lifts her little pointy chin so I can see the bruise Jonathan left there. "It doesn't look too bad," I tell her. "I'm really sorry he did that."

She shrugs. "It's fine." She waits a moment. I can tell she wants to say something else, and wonder why she can't just spit it out. She moves away from me, and sits cross-legged on the end of my bed, facing me.

She squints like she's trying to remember something, then finally says, "Gabe? I know you've been wondering what's wrong with Jonathan. Well, I think I know."

"Oh really? More than just he's being a big jerk?"

"Yeah. I know why."

"Okay. Why?"

"First, I have to tell you something else. Something that is going to sound very weird to you."

What?

"What?"

"It's about..." she hesitates again, "... about guardian angels."

Um, okay. "What, are you reading a story about it?"

"No," she says, "it isn't from a book. It's real. I have to tell you about real guardian angels."

Oh man. My sister has such an imagination. I don't know why she has decided to drag me into one of her pretend games, but I suppose I'll do it to make her happy. Maybe it's because Timothy went home and so she needs somebody else to play with.

Sure, I'll play along with it. She had a rough morning. I don't mind being nice to her.

"Okay, guardian angels. What about them?"

She looks at me with a little smirk, like she can tell I think this is a silly game. "They're real, Gabe."

"Sure," I say. I wonder how long it's going to take to play this game. "Real. Okay, now do we pretend we can see them?"

She laughs softly and shakes her head. "I know you think this is a game, Gabe. It's not. I actually mean it. Guardian angels are real."

"We're not playing something?" If not, I wonder when I can get back to my Gameboy, where I can actually play something.

"No," she says, "it is not like a game on your Gameboy."

She always does that. She has this weird knack for saying exactly what I'm thinking. I suppose it's because she is super observant. She is always quietly watching everything going on.

"Yes," she says, "I know what you're thinking."

What? "Are you trying to spook me out, sis?"

"No. I don't want you to be scared. But I do need to make you understand. It might seem spooky, but please listen. I can explain this."

This doesn't feel like a game anymore.

"No," she repeats, "it's not a game."

Okay now she is being spooky.

"I'm sorry, Gabe, I really don't want you to be spooked out. Everything is going to be fine. But you need to hear me out. Please."

"Okay, I'll listen. What is going on?"

She inhales, pauses, then says, "Everybody has a guardian angel. Every single person. Their angel watches everything they do, all the time. Their angel loves them and wants to help their souls grow."

"Well, that's nice, I guess. Although I hope they don't watch EVERYTHING!"

She giggles. "They do, but they try to be polite if you want some privacy in the bathroom or something."

I still can't tell if she's making this up to play a game, or if she's trying to be serious about believing in guardian angels.

"Gabe, I am being serious. I told you, it's not a game."

"How on earth do you keep doing that?" It's like she's answering questions I'm not saying out loud. It's a little creepy.

She leans forward, and looks at me straight in the eyes, like she wants me to pay very close attention to what she is saying. "It's because I can talk to my guardian angel."

Natalie's

It is going well so far. Her brother is dubious, of course, but she repeatedly demonstrates she knows what he is thinking, as I constantly whisper to her the thoughts going through his mind. This is her strategy, to show him that she is able to use her Guardian's knowledge. She and Timothy planned this out, and she considers this to be phase one of this experiment. The experiment to see if she can convince Gabe of the truth.

"Okay," Gabe says, "how do you learn how to talk to your guardian angel?"

"He still suspects you are playing a pretend game."

"It's not a pretend game, Gabe," she says. "I can talk to my Angel. But I didn't learn how, I was born this way."

She thinks for a moment, recalling the past. "I don't know whether you'll remember this, but I used to have an imaginary friend. I used to call him Angel, or Big Angel. Do you remember that at all?"

"He does remember it, a little. He was also quite young."

"Maybe," Gabe says slowly. "I think it used to be your little Beanie bear, though, right?"

She smiles radiantly at him. "Yes! Except it wasn't actually the Beanie bear, I loved that because it looked like my Angel."

"Well," Gabe says, "I do remember you talking about 'Angel' all the time. I thought you grew out of it."

She looks at him seriously. "I stopped talking about it, when I realized nobody else could see my Angel, and I didn't want people to start laughing at me. But I didn't grow out of it. Angel has always been with me."

"He doesn't think you are playing a game anymore, but he's confused about why you imagine you are seeing an angel."

"I'm not imagining it, Gabe. I can prove it to you."

"Really?" Gabe asks. "How could you prove it?"

"Angel can tell me anything you are thinking. He's been telling me this whole time."

"He realizes you have been repeating his thoughts during this conversation."

"I've been saying what you're thinking already, but that's probably not clear enough for you to believe. Let's try it a different way, okay Gabe?"

"Um, okay."

"His perception is shifting. He is starting to feel a little scared, sensing there is something supernatural occurring. This is not something he has ever seriously thought about before."

"Gabe, you really don't have to be scared. I know this is different from anything you've thought about before, but it's something I have lived with my entire life. So have you, but you haven't known about it until now. You'll be fine." She leans over and touches his hand, and smiles at him encouragingly.

"He grows more curious, wanting to understand what you mean."

"Okay," she says, "let's try an experiment. Why don't you think of a number. Angel can tell me what you are thinking."

Gabe's eyebrows go up, but he is willing to try.

"He is thinking of the number eleven."

"Eleven," she tells him. "Try again."

"He is surprised, but thinks perhaps it was a fluke. Now he is thinking of the number four hundred and fifty six."

"Four hundred and fifty six," she says. "Try again. This time think of any random thing you want, not a number."

"He is feeling slightly frightened, realizing this is really happening. But he feels a dawning wonder as well."

"It's okay, Gabe, it isn't scary, really. I'm just trying to show you. It's actually really cool. Come on, think of something random. Angel will tell me."

"He is remembering a moment during today's soccer game with the neighborhood boys. A boy named Jacob kicked the ball to another boy named Bob. The ball bounced off of Bob's head, but it was an accident, because he wasn't actually watching. He was distracted by a sports car driving past. The entire group laughed uproariously, calling out 'Accidental header!'"

Natalie chuckles at the story. "That sounds like it was funny, Gabe, when Bob made an accidental header because he was watching a sports car when Jacob kicked the ball to him." She smiles at him.

Gabe's mouth falls open.

"He sees."

"This is really real?" Gabe asks.

"It really is. I have more ways to prove it. Want to see more?"

"He would."

"Um, yes?" Gabe says.

"Okay," Natalie says, businesslike, continuing with her prepared demonstration. She reaches into her pocket and pulls out two dice. "Here, take these." She glances around the room and finds an empty cup. "Shake the dice in the cup, then put it upside down on the desk. So neither of us can see what they say. Angel can still see, and he'll tell me."

"He grows more fascinated with what you are teaching him, and he is feeling excited to learn more. His sense of fear is turning into amazement."

"It's cool, Gabe, isn't it? See? Nothing to be afraid of. It's actually really wonderful." She has planned it this way, to share the wonder, the discovery, long before she mentions the dark truth about Demon. She wants Gabe's introduction to the concept of Guardians to be very positive.

Gabe shakes the dice in the cup, flipping it over so the dice are concealed within. He looks at Natalie expectantly, but not really believing this is going to work.

"He doubts this will work. The dice show three and five on the top sides."

"This really does work, Gabe. The dice are three and five. Check it and see," Natalie smiles at him.

Gabe removes the cup, sees the three and five on the dice, and his immediate reaction is to laugh in wonder. "No way!"

"Now he is enjoying himself, and feels delight at what seems increasingly real to him."

Natalie grins at him. "Do it again!"

He shakes the cup and sets it down.

"Two and four."

"Two and four," she says.

He lifts the cup and whoops.

"Shh!" Natalie cautions him. "Don't get Mom in here, she'll make us go to bed!"

"Ooops," he says, then grinning hugely, shakes the cup again.

"One and three."

"One and three."

He checks, and is delighted. Although he realizes this isn't a game, it feels like a game to him.

"Okay, Natalie, this is awesome, you're right. But how is it working? Like, is there actually some angel there telling you the answers?"

"Yes," she confirms, "that's exactly what's happening. I can see my guardian angel, and he talks to me all the time. He tells me whatever I want to know."

"And you've always seen an angel? Even when you were little?"

"Yes, Angel has always been here with me. Every minute, since I was born. It's not only me, though. Everyone has a guardian angel. But I'm the only one who can see mine."

"Really? Do you know why?"

"Why I can see Angel? He tells me I have a special gift, something nobody else has. That's why I can see him."

"He begins to wonder about whether he has a guardian angel too."

"You have one too, Gabe. Your guardian angel loves you as much as mine loves me. You can't see yours, but he's there, loving you, right now."

"Can you see my angel?"

"No, I can only see my own. But he tells me about what the other ones are saying all the time."

"This still seems unreal to him, but magical. He wants to believe it."

"It is like magic, I know. But it's real. You can believe you really have a guardian angel."

"Too bad I can't talk to mine," Gabe muses. "That'd be a pretty cool dice trick to show my friends."

Natalie smiles. "It's a cool trick, I know. But I did it so you'd believe me. It was Timothy's idea."

Gabe is surprised. "Timothy? He knows about your angel?"

"Yeah," Natalie says, "Timothy has known for a long time."

"I'll bet Timothy wishes he could talk to his, too."

Natalie considers what to say next. "Well, actually, Timothy has been working on it." She waits to see Gabe's reaction.

"What do you mean? I thought you said you had a special gift and nobody else can do it."

"Well, that's true. I'm the only one who can do it easily. I see Angel as well as anything else. But Timothy is working on a way to hear his. It's really hard, and it takes a lot of practice, but he's starting to get it."

Gabe is astonished. "Seriously?"

Natalie has an idea. She says, out loud to me so her brother can hear, "Angel, can you ask Guardian to have Timothy wave at us out his window?"

She crosses to Gabe's window and holds back the curtain. Timothy's window is visible across the way. "Watch Gabe, this will probably take a minute, for Timothy to get the message. It's a lot harder for him."

Gabe crosses the room to join Natalie in peering out the window.

"This seems increasingly strange to him, but also wonderful. He is excited to be learning about this new aspect of your world."

After a few seconds go by, the curtains on Timothy's window are moved aside, and he is seen by the children, standing there, wearing his pajamas, and waving at them.

Natalie grins and waves back at him. Gabe stares open-mouthed. Timothy moves away from his window and the curtain drops back into place.

Chapter 41

We'll Figure It Out

Gabe's

It is such a momentous occasion. I whisper to him constantly, affirming the message of the Seer, filling my words with love and support. I still seem like an abstract concept to him. His statement that he would like to speak to me is only motivated by the image of himself amazing other children with similar tricks to what Natalie has shown him. He hasn't had time to contemplate the idea of my existence more deeply.

The demonstration with Timothy has astonished him. Natalie being able to relay Gabe's thoughts, and the numbers on the hidden dice, were amazing enough. But Timothy clearly receiving a message in the next house over has cemented in Gabe's mind the fact that Natalie's claim about guardian angels must actually be real.

"It's real. I can't believe it. But it has to be real, Natalie," he says, incapable of any speech more profound.

She impulsively hugs him. "I knew you'd believe me!" she says joyfully. "I'm so glad you know!"

He hugs her back. "Yeah," he says, still more stunned than anything else, unable to process this information further.

She sits back on his bed, and he follows her, not knowing if she has more information to share.

"My darling, you have learned so much already. I am here, always, to help you understand everything. It brings me much joy for you to have obtained this knowledge. I feel closer to you than ever before."

Gabe still has the dice clutched in his hand. He idly shakes them, then suddenly remembers he is holding them. He stares down into his hand.

"Do you need more demonstrations?" Natalie asks him. "I think you already believe me, but we could try the dice again, or other stuff, if you want more proof."

"No," he says. "I mean, maybe we can do the dice again later for fun, but I believe you. You don't need to prove anything else." They sit silently for a minute as he contemplates the things she has told him. He thinks about Timothy being aware of the guardian angels.

Then he remembers how this conversation began. "Hey - I just remembered you told me about this because of Jonathan. You said you know what's wrong. I guess it's because your guardian angel told you? What did he say?"

Natalie worries about introducing the topic of Demon's malfeasance so early in Gabe's introduction to the concept of Guardians. She fears her brother will be frightened. However, she feels that she must explain.

"Yes, Angel told me what's wrong with Jonathan. I guess I have to explain more to you about what guardian angels are here for, so you can understand. Okay?"

He is perplexed. "Well, all right."

She asks, "Do you remember what I said about what they are here to do?"

"Um... watching us?"

"Yes, but not only that. It's the reason they are watching us. It's to help our souls grow."

He hadn't really paid attention to that part of her statement earlier, being more focused on the slightly amusing image of being constantly observed. "Sooooo...." he prompts, not sure what she means.

Angel whispers to her, *"He doesn't understand what you mean, darling, perhaps you can clarify that we share a soul with our humans."*

She nods in response to what Angel has told her. "Okay, let me back up. Each human has a soul, right? Like Grandma has told us. Well, not exactly like that, but we do have a soul." She waits for him to acknowledge this much.

"Sure, I guess," he says. The concept of the soul, indeed all of his grandmother's religious teachings, have never much interested him.

"Well," the Seer continues, "the reason we have a soul is because our guardian angel brings it to us when we are born. We basically share it with them. And while we are alive, it grows, and everything we do changes it. Our guardian angel wants us to grow the soul to be strong and beautiful, because after we die they get it back to keep forever."

Angel nods, "*You are explaining this very well, my dear.*"

Gabe struggles with this esoteric concept, but he basically understands what she is attempting to relate. "So it's all about us having a soul?"

"Yes," she confirms, "and us growing the soul. It's what they're interested in. The way what we do changes the soul. Do you get it?"

He snorts. "Well, no, honestly, but I hear what you're saying. Are you getting to the part about Jonathan?"

She meets his eyes, sadly. He senses there is something making her reluctant to go forward. "Um, is something wrong with Jonathan's soul? Is that what's going on?"

She brightens. "You're so smart, Gabe." He smiles and ducks his head.

"Yeah," she goes on, "that's sort of what's happening. See, when a guardian angel sees their human do something that grows the soul, they try to encourage their human to do more of it. Not everything that grows a soul is good. Sometimes even mean stuff can help a soul grow. Like the kind of mean tricks Jonathan plays on people."

Gabe's brow furrows. He knows what she means, having observed Jonathan for years inflicting petty injuries on others, aware Natalie has often seen this behavior. He did not give these incidents much thought, not believing they were consequential in any way. Angel describes his unfolding thought process to Natalie, and she waits while he remembers Jonathan's history.

"Yes," she says, "when he was doing stuff like hurting lizards or pushing toddlers, even though that stuff is mean, it did help his soul grow." She waits again, wanting him to be able to process each concept before she carries on.

He nods, ready for her to continue.

"So the problem is Jonathan's guardian angel likes it when he does stuff like that, because it makes his soul keep getting stronger. And now, his guardian angel is trying so hard to make Jonathan do it more, Jonathan is starting to lose control of himself, and doing it when he doesn't even want to."

This is too much for Gabe to understand. "What? I thought people can't talk to their angels. This doesn't make any sense."

"Well," Natalie says, not wanting to get into describing the entire process of communication between Guardians, "his guardian angel has learned a way to tell Jonathan what to do. Jonathan doesn't have any idea it is happening, he thinks the thoughts are popping into his head, and he hates it because he thinks it means he is a terrible person. He doesn't know the thoughts are coming from his guardian angel. But he can't control himself when he gets these thoughts."

Suddenly Gabe pictures the moment when Jonathan, shockingly, struck Natalie at the library. He begins to understand.

"Yes," Natalie tells him somberly, after Angel relays to her what Gabe is thinking, "when he hit me today that is exactly what happened. It makes sense when you think about it. He didn't seem like himself, did he? It seemed like he wasn't in control, right?"

"Yeaaahhh," Gabe says slowly. "Yeah, I haven't been able to figure it out. It was so weird. It was like he wasn't thinking at all. I couldn't imagine why he did it. So, he wasn't deciding to do it? His guardian angel was making him do it?"

"Yes," Natalie tells him sadly.

Gabe's perception shifts. "So, guardian angels aren't good? Like, they aren't here to help us? They're evil?" His alarm fills me with dismay. "That's really scary, Natalie."

She grabs his hand. "No, Gabe, they're not evil! Only one is. Only Jonathan's guardian. Angel tells me he has never heard of another guardian doing what Jonathan's is. It's not normal at all. All of the other ones are good, and loving, and they really are here to help." I notice she has stopped using the term "guardian angel" and has reverted to simply "guardian". I know she had started with the more commonly used term to assist Gabe in understanding. He does not notice the change.

Gabe is perturbed. He has learned too much to absorb.

"That's the only reason I told you, Gabe. Because Jonathan's guardian is such a problem. All the other guardians don't know what to do about it. They are all super worried. They don't know how to help."

"Well I sure don't know what to do!" Gabe bursts out. "You can't possibly think I would have any answers!" His emotions are in turmoil. It all seems overwhelming. This evening he has been perplexed, amazed, frightened, and now alarmed and even somewhat angry. He feels too much is expected of him.

"No," she says, her face crumpling with distress. "I didn't expect you to. I just thought, well, Jonathan is your best friend. I figured you would want to know what's wrong. Timothy thought so. That you deserve to know."

Gabe's sense of outrage instantly deflates. He realizes now her purpose. She wants her brother to understand that she is trying to help his best friend, and she wants him to be a part of the process. She doesn't want him to be excluded from knowing the truth.

"Oh. Yeah, you're right. I guess it's good to know." He sighs and shakes his head. "Thanks for telling me, Nat. You're a good sister. Very weird, but a good sister."

She throws her arms around him. "I love you Gabe! And I just want to help Jonathan. I don't know how we are going to do it, but I think we'll figure it out."

Chapter 42

New Awareness

Laura

I'm glad Ron and Brenda were able to keep Timothy all day, even after they came home early from Ron's house. I had plans, and I'm really happy they worked out. Brenda assured me when she called that the tiff in the library with Jonathan didn't seem to disturb Timothy too much, and he wanted to keep playing with Natalie, so we didn't need to come home. He seemed fine when I picked him up after we got back.

And we ended up having such a nice day. Poor Michael has not been himself since he got home from deployment. He has nightmares constantly. I don't think he has had a single peaceful night of sleep. Every night at least once he jerks awake, often sitting bolt upright, sometimes yelling. A couple of times he has even actually jumped out of bed and stood there with his fists up like he is ready to fight somebody. Then he comes fully awake, and collapses back in bed, mumbling "sorry" to me for waking me up. It's been really hard. He says he doesn't remember the dreams in the morning, but I think he must remember at least something. I think he doesn't want to talk about it.

So today I wanted to try something new, something to help bring some peace to his mind. Brenda has described how wonderful their trip to the desert was last month, and how peaceful it was to be outdoors for a day. I thought maybe Michael could use something like that. A way for nature to bring him some healing.

We didn't go all the way out to the desert, but there's a nature park near here called Mission Trails, and we headed out there and hiked around for a couple of hours. It was a nice day, with cool weather perfect for walking outdoors. I packed up a lunch, and we enjoyed it sitting on some big chunks of granite up on the hill we had climbed. I'm not usually much for hiking, so it was a little hard for me, but it was wonderful to see Mike actually relax. He sat with his eyes closed for a while after finishing his sandwich, absorbing the sunlight, feeling the breeze and listening to the birds chirping. I think it was really good for him.

I'm glad he and Timothy have been fine with each other since he got home. They haven't interacted much. To be honest, I think they are each too wrapped up in their own heads. But they are coexisting peacefully, and that's about the best I can hope for.

When I go into Timothy's room to kiss him goodnight, he is stepping back from his window. "What were you doing, sweetie?" I ask him.

"Waving goodnight to Natalie and Gabe," he says, climbing into bed.

"Oh, okay, how nice." I smooth the covers over him and kiss his forehead. "Are you going to play with them again tomorrow?"

"Yes," he says. "Goodnight, Mom."

I chuckle. I guess I'm dismissed. I kind of miss when he used to like me to read him bedtime stories. Hardly any point now, since he devours books like he's starving. "Don't stay up too late reading," I say, stroking his hair. "Goodnight, kiddo."

Timothy

Even though I was keeping my mind open, waiting to hear anything about how Natalie was doing, I was surprised when Guardian told me to go wave out the window. I was really glad about it. It means Gabe understands about Guardians, and Natalie's plan is working. I'm looking forward to hearing tomorrow about how the experiment went.

I hope that Gabe knowing is going to help Natalie stay safer. I don't want to see Jonathan hurting her again. And I have a feeling he will keep doing it, because Demon is so mad at her. If she keeps trying to help Jonathan, Demon is going to try even harder to stop her. It's dangerous, and I want Gabe to understand that part. Hopefully I'll get the chance to talk to him tomorrow, too. I don't usually talk to Gabe very much. I don't usually talk to anyone except Natalie, really. But now that he knows what's going on I think I will.

I want to make sure Gabe will keep trying to protect Natalie. I'm unhappy with myself for not doing it today. I froze like a statue, which is what I normally do when I get stressed out. It was very unhelpful in the situation. I don't want to be useless if Natalie needs me. I want to help, like the time when she was crying and Guardian made me see what to do.

"Guardian," I whisper to him, "can you please help me know what to do next time? If Natalie needs me again, I want to make sure to do whatever I can. I don't want to be useless."

I feel him agreeing. I don't really need to hear his exact words most of the time. I can usually tell how he feels now, as long as I keep my mind open and still. It's hard, because my mind is never normally still. I'm usually thinking about a lot of things, so I have to make myself stop to hear him. But I've been practicing all the time, and it's getting easier to do. So it has been getting easier to hear Guardian.

It makes me feel really good, knowing I have Guardian here with me and helping me. I can tell it makes him feel good too.

I lay in bed with my book. I was going to be reading books about history tonight, to try to prove some bible stories for Natalie, but we didn't get the chance to check out any books from the library today. We had to go after the fight. So I'll re-read one of these books about the subconscious again. I can get more books another time.

Gabe

I wake up early for some reason, with a feeling something has changed. It's not even really light outside yet. I have to think about what day it is to try to figure out what feels different. It's Sunday. Why am I in my room at Mom's house instead of at Dad's house?

Oh. Yeah. That. It all comes rushing back to me. The fight with Jonathan, coming home early, playing soccer, then the super weird conversation with Natalie.

I do believe her, that's for sure. There's no way she was tricking me. And I don't think she would ever want to trick me anyway. She's too nice for that. I don't think I've ever seen her playing any tricks. She was telling me the truth.

It explains a lot. I've always noticed that Natalie knows more about what's going on than I do. It often seems like she knows stuff is going to happen before it does. I never expected her to tell me it's because her guardian angel is telling her things, though.

I keep feeling like I should be completely creeped out by everything she told me. Especially the part about Jonathan's guardian angel making him do bad things. Even the part about everyone having one, always watching. I mean, I guess it means there is one here watching me right now. That seems weird. But it doesn't feel scary for some reason. I feel okay with it.

Well, I don't hear anybody else up yet, but I'm wide awake. I guess I'll wait before I get up. I grab my Gameboy and start playing where I left off when Natalie came in last night.

Gabe's

It is staggering to hear my beloved contemplate my presence. It still seems very intangible to him. But I know he is sensing my affirmations, my whispers of love and support and togetherness. He might normally feel alarmed by the information he learned, but doesn't realize his sense of acceptance is due in large part to my diligent efforts in transmitting calm and contentment to him.

It is also because he learned this lesson from the Seer. In addition to being his beloved little sister, her empathic abilities helped him adjust to the new reality without panic. By coordinating with Angel, she was able to instruct Gabe in the perfect way to guide him towards acceptance without fear.

It was marvelous to behold.

Natalie

I open my eyes and look for Angel. He is smiling at me, sitting at the foot of my bed like always. But I know today is different. Today Gabe knows, too.

"How is Gabe?" I ask Angel.

"He is very well, my dear. Your explanation last night was flawless. He never really had the chance to grow frightened over the strange new information he was receiving. Everything you said was perfect for him. Today he accepts

the truth of everything you told him. He has been awake for some time, playing with his Gameboy and contemplating the nature of Guardians."

He's already awake? I jump up and get dressed in a hurry. I want to see for myself how he's doing. He must have more questions. Also, I know Timothy will want to hear about everything. Maybe Gabe can hang around with us for a while today, so we can all talk together.

When I open my door, Gabe is heading out of his room too. "I heard you get up," he says. Then he gets a gleam in his eyes, and with a big smile, says, "What am I thinking?" He waits eagerly.

I laugh and wait for Angel to tell me. It's about the Gameboy game he was just playing. "Um, apparently about Mario throwing Koopa shells at Bowser?"

"Ha! Yes!" he laughs. I am very happy that he is enjoying this so much. It will make everything else so much easier.

"Timothy is coming over after breakfast," I tell him. "Can all three of us talk for a while? Before you go play with your other friends?"

"Well, duh, yes, obviously."

Angel tells me, *"Gabe is extremely eager to talk to Timothy too. His new awareness has sparked a great deal of curiosity about everything having to do with Guardians."*

I smile and hold Gabe's hand. "Let's go eat breakfast."

We head downstairs, and find Mom and Dad in the kitchen already. Soon, we are eating cereal. Gabe, like always, splashes a bunch of milk on his Cheerios and slurps it enthusiastically with a spoon. It makes me giggle while I am eating my cereal dry. We always laugh about which way is better, but today we are going to have much more interesting things to talk about.

Chapter 43

We Can Do It

Timothy

When I get to Natalie's door, she opens it before I have a chance to knock. Gabe is standing right behind her. "Hey Timothy! Gabe and I are going outside to play. Want to come?"

This is unusual. Normally we play in our bedrooms, but I guess maybe we're going outside so Gabe will be comfortable? I know he always likes to play outside with Jonathan back at their Dad's house.

Natalie nods at me, so I know I'm right. I know Angel always tells her anything I'm thinking that she'd want to know about. She says, "I thought we could hang out here in the courtyard and talk for a while?"

Gabe is trying to make eye contact with me. That is also unusual. I look at the ground while we are following Natalie. She is heading towards the chairs set up around the grill in the courtyard. Maybe later there will be people out here grilling lunch or dinner, or other children playing, but it is too early now. I know that she wants to have a conversation without other people around to overhear.

When we get to the chairs, Gabe is still staring at me. I keep looking at the ground. I like Gabe, he has always been very decent to me, but I can't look into his eyes. Natalie touches his hand, and quietly tells him, "So you know, Gabe, Timothy doesn't like making eye contact. It's not about you, he just doesn't like to do it." Obviously Angel told her what was happening. I'm glad she came out and told him so that he knows. It's already feeling better for Gabe to know about everything.

"Oh, okay," he says, and shrugs. So he looks at Natalie. She smiles at both of us. She doesn't seem to feel awkward at all, even though this is basically the first time the three of us have tried to really talk about anything important. She's probably happy to have us together. "So," she tells me, "everything worked out fine last night. I told Gabe everything and he believes me."

"Did you have him think of numbers? How about the dice, did you use them?" I ask her.

Gabe laughs. "Yes, and it was so cool. She said it was your idea. Good thinking!"

I nod.

Gabe adds, "It was really you waving at us that made it seem completely real. I'm not sure I was really believing it until then. So, Natalie says you've figured out how to talk to your guardian angel?"

"Yes," I tell him. "If I keep my mind open and clear, then I can feel what Guardian is saying. Not always, but more and more. So I heard him tell me to wave at you through the window. I'm glad it helped."

"Did you know about Jonathan?" he asks.

"Yes. Angel told us yesterday, after the library. Natalie decided to tell you about it. Angel thought it might be too hard for you to know. But I said that I would want to know if something was wrong with Natalie, so you should know about Jonathan."

Natalie is watching, her head turning back and forth to see us while we are talking. I can tell that she is super happy about this. I've never had a real conversation with Gabe before. I'm still looking at the ground, but this isn't too hard. It's sure easier to talk to Gabe than it would be if Jonathan was with him.

"Thank you, Timothy. About saying I deserve to know. Jonathan is my best friend, even if he's been doing awful things. I'm glad I'm in on this."

Natalie says, "I've been trying to help him, Gabe. I thought I could help him be nicer if I spent more time with him. That was before we knew about Demon."

"What?" Gabe yelps. "There's a demon now?"

"No!" she tells him, "No, not a real one. It's what I am calling Jonathan's guardian. When Angel told me about how he has started to control Jonathan, it reminded me of the bible stories where demons were possessing people. Do you remember hearing about those?"

"Uh, not really. I don't really pay attention when Grandma takes us to church."

"Well, it's not that important. But sometimes in the bible it talks about this happening. So I decided to name his guardian Demon."

"Wait, you can name them? Don't they have their own names?"

"No," she says. "Guardians don't usually need names. I've started naming them so when Angel is talking about them I know which one he means."

His eyebrows go up. "Huh. Soooo... you named yours Angel?"

"Yes, when I was really little, after I got that Beanie bear."

"What about Timothy's guardian angel?"

She smiles. "No, Timothy is the one who named Guardian. Angel doesn't call them guardian angels, he calls them guardians. So after Timothy found out about his, he named him Guardian."

Gabe is quiet for a moment, and Natalie waits because she knows that he is thinking about all this. Angel is probably telling her everything. Gabe says, "What about mine? I have one too, right? Does he have a name?"

Natalie smiles at him and touches his hand. "I gave him a name yesterday. I hope it's okay with you."

"Um, yeah, sure. What is it?"

"I named him after another bible story. Aaron. He was the brother of Moses, and he helped Moses a lot. The bible Grandma gave me says that the name Aaron means strong. It reminds me of you, because you are strong and helpful." She looks at him to see what he thinks.

"His name is Aaron now?" he asks.

"Yes," she says. "But I'll bet he'd be okay if you wanted to name him something else. I don't think guardians really care about names."

"No," he says, shrugging. "I guess Aaron is fine. Thanks for naming him, sis."

It's hard to be patient while they talk about stuff I already know about, but I guess I'm used to it. School feels like this a lot. As soon as I get the chance, I ask, "Gabe?"

He looks over at me, looking surprised that I said his name. "Yeah?"

"What do you want to do about Jonathan?" I'm hoping that he says he thinks we should all stay away from him.

But that's not what he wants. "I don't know," he says, looking sad. "Natalie said that we're going to figure out a way to help him."

I was afraid of this. Natalie only wants to help other people. She doesn't care enough about what is safest for her. I have to tell him. "Gabe, you should know that helping him is dangerous. Demon made Jonathan hit her. You know, you saw it happen. Jonathan might be mean, but he wouldn't have done that if Demon wasn't controlling him. I think if Natalie keeps trying to help him, he is going to hurt her even worse."

Gabe's eyes go wide, then he scowls. He looks over at Natalie, but before he can say anything she says, "It'll be okay, Gabe. Angel is here to help, and you can help too. I will be fine."

"No," I say, and she looks at me, probably surprised since I never disagree with her. I try to look right at Gabe while I'm speaking, so he understands how serious this is. I can't look right in his eyes, but I look at the curly hair over his forehead. That's close enough. "Natalie said before, when she first started to try to help Jonathan be nicer, that she'd be fine because Angel could warn her if anything was going to happen. That didn't work yesterday. She still got hit. I don't believe it is safe to keep trying."

Natalie gets that stubborn look on her face, and I know nothing I say is going to talk her out of this. I wonder if Gabe can convince her. I hope he agrees with me.

"Nat, I can't let you get hurt again," he says, and I think maybe he's on my side. But then he continues, "but I can't let Jonathan be in trouble without trying to help him too. I have no idea what to do. But I can't just leave him alone."

"I have been thinking a lot about what to do," she tells us both, very seriously. "I think the answer has to start with telling him. Like I told you, Gabe. I think the only way to solve a problem is to at least know about it. Jonathan doesn't know. Maybe if he does, at least he might understand that he isn't a bad person. I know what has been happening has been bothering him a lot, because he thinks the bad ideas he is getting are from him. Maybe if he knows they aren't his ideas, he'll be able to try to act nicer, even if Demon is telling him to be bad."

She looks sideways, and I know she's listening to Angel. Then she shakes her head. I'll bet Angel tried to tell her it won't work.

Gabe says, "He won't believe you."

"I know," she says, "I sort of told him a couple of months ago and he didn't believe it. But I didn't really try to make him believe. I only mentioned that his guardian angel wouldn't like to see him being mean to people." She stops for a minute and then laughs at what she just said. "Boy, I was wrong about that, wasn't I?"

I say, "Well, the experiment worked with Gabe last night. We can plan out an experiment for telling Jonathan. He'd probably believe the dice demonstration, and you knowing what he's thinking."

Natalie lights up. "So you're going to help?" she asks me.

"Of course, Natalie, I will always help you, even if I don't agree with you. But since I think it is dangerous, I want to be with you. I don't know if I can do anything to protect you, but I have to be there to try."

"Oh, Timothy," she says, then she is speechless for a minute. She knows that I will usually do everything I can to stay away from Jonathan, because he has always been so awful to me. I can see from her expression how much this means to her. I feel Guardian's approval too.

"Me too," says Gabe. "If you are going to be around Jonathan at all, ever, I will be there too. Promise me that you will make sure not to be there without me."

I can tell she is feeling very emotional, and she reaches out and takes both of our hands. "Thank you. Thank you both. We can do it. We'll figure it out together."

Chapter 44

Jungle Gym

Jonathan's

My beloved is sitting in his spot in the school play yard, on top of the domed jungle gym. As always on school mornings, he waits here for his friend Gabe. He is nervous, because the last time he saw Gabe was Saturday morning after their altercation.

I mourn for his unsettled emotions, but I do not try to command him to feel otherwise. I have paused my use of energy in my communications to him. Since Saturday morning, I have reverted to my former method, simply whispering to him, knowing that he does not perceive my messages. It is unsatisfactory, after the delight of witnessing him follow my instructions, even unknowingly.

However, his mind has been in such turmoil that I have resolved to refrain from utilizing my new power over him. Up until Saturday, each time he surrendered his will to mine, his soul blazed ever more brilliantly, deliciously. But suddenly, in the wake of the regret which washed over him due to the unwelcome intervention of the Seer and her brother, his soul began dimming, most alarmingly.

I wish to allow him time to return to a state of normalcy before reasserting my influence. I know the moment will come. I already feel his natural personality beginning to re-emerge.

He watches the drive in front of the school, and tenses when he sees his friend arrive. He worries that Gabe will not wish to speak to him. However, Gabe immediately begins walking toward Jonathan.

And what is this? The Seer and her friend, rather than departing to their own classroom as usual, accompany Gabe as he walks in this direction. They are filled with a sense of grim purpose. I perceive at once their intent.

Preposterous. They have determined that they are going to inform Jonathan of my existence. And even more ridiculous, they have assigned a name to me. How presumptuous.

Demon. The Seer has the arrogance to label me with such an insulting moniker. I have no need of a name. I am Jonathan's. I reject her attempt to impose such an epithet upon me.

"My darling, be pleased that your friend wishes to continue your relationship. But pay no attention to the rantings of the strange girl and her weakling friend. You do not need anything from her. You should simply ignore her. Perhaps you can tell her to go away."

As tempting as it is to command him to do this, I refrain. I won't use my power unless I need to. I see his soul glowing brighter already, regaining its former strength. I shall be judicious in my use of power to control him. I must find that delicate balance between dominance and destruction.

Jonathan

Phew. I thought Gabe would totally ignore me from now on. But here he comes. I don't know why Natalie and Timothy are coming too. That's a bummer. But at least Gabe is coming over here. I wait for him to get here.

"Hi," I tell him, when he gets to the monkey bars and starts climbing up to me. Natalie and Timothy don't climb up, they stand down there staring at me. Sometimes I like Natalie okay, but when she's with Timothy they seem like a couple of weirdos.

Gabe looks at me with a funny expression on his face. "Are you okay?" he asks me.

"Yeah," I say. "Um, sorry about fighting you. Are we cool?"

He looks down at Natalie for some reason. "Yeah, but, uh, we have something to tell you. Can you come down?"

"Pfsh. No. I like it up here." I wish Natalie and Timothy would go away. Instead, they look at each other, and then good grief here they are climbing up on the jungle gym too. Timothy looks like some kind of awkward spider. He's clearly never done this before. I laugh at how ridiculous he looks. He stops before he gets up to the top with the rest of us.

"Don't hurt yourself, Timothy," I say, then look over at Gabe so we can share a laugh about how goofy Timothy looks. But Gabe isn't laughing. He looks super serious instead. Huh.

I roll my eyes and look at Natalie. "Aren't you guys worried you're going to be late to class?"

Timothy balances uncomfortably on the bars below us, and pushes his jacket sleeve up so he can see the big dorky watch he has on his skinny arm. A second-grader wearing a watch. What a nerd.

"No," he says. "We still have almost 20 minutes before the final bell rings. That's enough time."

"Sheesh. Enough time for what?"

Timothy and Gabe both look at Natalie. Apparently she's the one who has something to tell me. Good grief. So much for playing with Gabe before class.

"Fine," I say. "What? Just spit it out."

Natalie's expression isn't what I would expect, in response to me being kind of rude to her. She looks like she really cares about me, and really wants to help me. Her big dark green eyes look into mine, very serious. Her dark brown bangs are getting long enough again to fall into them. I don't know what to expect, but I feel like I want to hear what she has to say.

"Jonathan," she starts, "I know you've been having trouble lately. I know that you have felt like you can't stop yourself from being mean to people, like what happened in the library. I know what is causing your problem."

What? I start to tell her my only problem is that she is crazy, but I hesitate for some reason. Actually, she isn't wrong. She has really described what's happening. After the library I felt completely awful, because I hadn't actually wanted to do what I did, and afterwards it didn't make me feel good at all like that stuff usually does. I felt like I had lost control of myself.

She is weirdly waiting, like she is following along with my thoughts. Gabe and Timothy wait too, watching her.

"Okay, fine," I say. "What do you think is causing my 'problem'?" I use my fingers to make air quotes.

"This will sound weird to you, but please listen. If you give me a chance I can prove what I am about to tell you."

What the heck. I put my hands up, shake my head, and open my eyes and mouth, to tell her to just say it. Whatever it is.

"Do you remember a couple of months ago, when you pushed me into the flowers? The day of your lizard funeral?"

I glance at Gabe, and it seems like he isn't surprised or mad to hear this. "Um, yeah, I guess."

"Do you remember what I said?"

"Not really." I do though. She said some weird nonsense about having a guardian angel.

"Yes, you do remember. I said you have a guardian angel, and he wouldn't like to see you doing mean stuff like that."

I look over at Gabe, worried he'll believe what she's saying, about me pushing her. I don't want him to think even worse of me than he did after the library. But he is watching her, like he's not surprised at all by what she said. I suppose not, he did say that they had something to tell me. Holy cow is this all some big plan?

"Okay, fine, I remember that part. I remember thinking you were crazy. You aren't doing anything to convince me otherwise now."

She smiles and shakes her head. "Well, I was telling you the truth. You do have a guardian angel."

I roll my eyes. OMG, why can't she let this go? I look at Gabe, and he nods his head at me. "She's right," he says. "She's shown me proof. We all have guardian angels." Even Gabe really believes this? Can it be true?

I suddenly feel boiling angry, out of nowhere. "Oh, shut up. You're all crazy. Go away and stop bothering me."

Timothy and Gabe look at Natalie, and she nods at them.

Ugh. "Seriously. Get out of here, you weirdos. You too Gabe. You're as bad as them!"

Instead of leaving, Natalie reaches out and touches my hand, using her other hand to help her balance on the bars. "You're only feeling mad because your guardian is making you. He doesn't want you to know about him."

I jerk my hand away. I don't know why. I've started to like it lately when Natalie touches me, but this time it was almost like it burned me. Not like physical pain, but I suddenly had to get away from her. So weird.

I stare at her, but don't know what to say. She's freaking me out. I want to believe she's crazy, but here is Gabe nodding his head, agreeing with her. And I realize she's right, I do keep getting feelings out of nowhere. Like when I wanted to hit her at the library. And when I got mad just now, and when her hand felt like it was burning me.

I start to feel scared, on top of mad, and most of all confused.

"It's okay, Jonathan, I know it's scary and confusing, but I can explain." She looks at me with her big sincere eyes, so full of concern that it almost hurts. "Your guardian angel started liking it when you were being mean, so he started wanting you to do it more. He has learned a way to make you do stuff. Stuff that you don't actually want to do. But I think you knowing about it will help you control yourself better."

Then the rage boils up in me again. Exactly like in the library. It's like I fall off a cliff into an ocean, an ocean of anger, and I'm drowning in it. I scream, "Shut up! Shut up! Shut up!" as loud as I can, and reach over to push her. But Gabe is ready, I think that's what he's been waiting for, and he yanks my arm back before I can touch her. That's when I go crazy. I'm not in control any more.

Gabe

I see it when Demon takes control again, now that I know what I'm looking for. It's like what happened in the library. Jonathan's face goes all red and dark, and his lips peel back in a snarl like an aggressive dog. He screams for her to shut up, and I start reaching out as he is moving to push her. I'm able to grab his arm to stop him from getting to her.

And he loses it. He starts kicking and punching and pushing me. There's no way I can keep my balance, and I fall straight through the bars of the jungle gym onto the ground below. I'm all twisted sideways when I fall, so I can't land properly like I normally would. I feel my ankle crumple under me when I hit the ground, there's a gross sounding crack, and a terrible pain shoots up my leg. I fall over and grab my ankle, yelling. But I don't have time to worry about this, even though the pain is making me feel faint and sick. I try to stand back up, but my ankle won't hold my weight and I fall back down.

He's up there with Natalie, moving towards her, that evil expression on his face. She holds her hands up, and says, "Jonathan, wait! It's going to be okay! I am trying to help you!"

That makes it worse. He starts shrieking like a banshee, not words, just screaming, as he grabs her hands. Timothy is trying to climb up to them, but he is obviously no good at climbing and he isn't going to reach them in time to do anything about it.

I try to hobble over to the side to start climbing too. I know I won't get there before he hurts her.

Chapter 45

Fury

Natalie's

My worst fear manifests. The child is utterly under the dominion of Demon, and is wrestling with Natalie on top of the bars, high above the ground. If she falls she could be seriously injured. Her brother already has been hurt as he fell. Aaron tries to find words to help him, but the situation is so out of control that it appears to be beyond any of our ability to help.

As soon as Demon sensed Jonathan begin to accept Natalie's words, he was consumed with fury. He will never permit Natalie to bring such knowledge to Jonathan, because that would diminish Demon's control over his Guarded. Demon renewed his use of power instantly, increased a thousandfold, flooding Jonathan with a blinding rage, using Jonathan as a tool to stop Natalie from continuing. Gabe intervened, only to be hurled to the ground, where we all heard his bone break with a sickening snap.

Despite this, her brother is trying to get back up to Jonathan, to protect his sister, but it is clearly futile. Jonathan has seized Natalie's arms and is shaking her, trying to dislodge her from the bars of the jungle gym. Her long hair flies about her head as she attempts to resist him. "Jonathan, no, stop!" she cries, but it is no use. Jonathan is not hearing anything but Demon's deafening commands. In a moment, Natalie will inevitably lose this battle and suffer dire harm.

Her peril focuses the attention of all. Each of the Guardians in our family have been closely following these events. Even Knight and Lady are fully present here while the children's parents are heading to their places of employment. I cannot help Natalie physically defeat Jonathan. There is only one thing I can do.

I generate all of the dark energy which I can command, and using every bit of power I have ever known, I bellow, "*STOP!*" at Demon. Immediately, Guardian and Aaron follow my lead, and do the same. In a split second, Knight and Lady have added their voices.

Five Guardians, all screaming STOP at Demon, has an impact. When I experienced this the first time Guardian yelled at me, the effect felt almost physical. Amplified five times, it appears to be literally physical. Demon's appearance, in fact his entire being, wavers, fractures. He is distracted from his commands to Jonathan, and stops shouting at the boy.

The five of us continue, incessantly shouting with all of the energy we can muster, to prevent Demon from renewing his assault. He is stymied, outraged, filled with fury, but unable to take any action under the combined power of our voices.

Jonathan, however, is already too lost in the commands he had received to reverse course. He falters briefly when Demon falls silent, confused, but the anger that had already been set into motion by Demon persists. He continues grappling with Natalie, even as she pleads with him to listen. She slips further, one of her legs losing its place on the bar beneath her, and she is an instant from falling.

Timothy, still too far away on the jungle gym to reach Natalie, adds his voice to the chaos. "Stop!" he screams, and with his mind he reaches out to Jonathan. He uses the method which he had tried and discarded weeks ago, before he learned that to hear Guardian he must passively open his mind to the contact.

This reaching is aggressive, purposeful, dominant, violent. Timothy deliberately thrusts his consciousness forward, seeking Jonathan's, attempting to overpower the other boy's mind.

Driven by the panic he is feeling for Natalie's safety, and enhanced by the power flowing through Guardian as we all shout at Demon, it works. His mind touches Jonathan's. Overwhelmed by Timothy's mental and verbal scream to stop, Jonathan freezes. He becomes silent. His face goes slack. Suddenly, his eyes roll back into his head, and he goes utterly limp. His hands fall from Natalie's arms, and he slips backwards through the bars of the jungle gym, plummeting headfirst to the ground.

Natalie manages to grasp the bars before falling with him, and shrieks to her brother, "Catch him!"

Gabe, with an unnatural boost of energy given to him by Aaron as he continues to draw on excessive power, lunges across the sand beneath the jungle gym, with outstretched arms. As Jonathan's limp body is about to crash to the ground, Gabe reaches his arms beneath him to soften the blow. They collapse together in a heap.

I stop shouting at Demon, as do the others. The silence seems deafening. Gabe extricates himself from beneath Jonathan's still form. Jonathan is not moving.

Natalie and Timothy clamber down from the jungle gym and approach the boys on the ground.

The entire incident, from the moment Jonathan began shouting, has only occupied a minute or two of time. The attention of the teachers, in the usual morning uproar as the students arrive for class, has been attracted by the altercation at the playground, and some of the adults begin to move forward to intervene.

I look more carefully at Jonathan. I see him breathing raggedly, but he is unconscious. He did not suffer a head injury as he fell, because Gabe was able to prevent that. It is unclear why he is not awake. I look to see Demon's reaction to these events, and wonder if Demon feels any remorse at having caused this disaster. Perhaps instead Demon is too angry for remorse?

I am puzzled, though, as I look in Jonathan's direction. I do not see Demon. Natalie is kneeling at Gabe's side, grieved at the injury he has suffered, her hand on his shoulder as he clutches his ankle. Timothy, surprisingly, is the one trying to help Jonathan. He is kneeling next to Jonathan, pressing a hand to his chest to check his breathing, peering closely at his face to see if he is awake.

But Demon is somehow not next to Jonathan. I glance at the others, and see that they have made the same realization. Each of us scans the area, listening, without success. Jonathan's Guardian is nowhere nearby. Jonathan, of all the humans on the playground, for that matter on the planet, is alone.

I have never heard of this phenomenon. A Guardian is, necessarily, always together with their Guarded. They are tied to the soul which lies within. This is impossible.

Chapter 46

What Have We Done?

Timothy

He's breathing, but not awake. I am afraid I hurt him, by grabbing his mind that way. I had told Angel I would never do that again, after the first time I tried it, but there wasn't anything else I could do. I had to stop Jonathan. He was going to hurt Natalie.

I didn't really even think about it. I reached out and grabbed his mind, to make him stop. It worked. He stopped. But I did not expect him to faint, or fall. I do not understand what happened.

I know that later Natalie and I will be able to ask Angel about it.

But for now, there is a big ruckus on the playground. Teachers are running over to us, and kids are running behind them to see what is going on. Natalie is sitting with Gabe, who is holding his ankle, and looking kind of pale and green. I can tell he is in a lot of pain, from the expression on his face.

Natalie looks like she feels terrible. She's worried about Gabe, but even more worried about Jonathan. I can tell she's trying to listen to Angel, but I don't think it is really making her feel any better. I wonder what he's telling her.

The vice principal gets here first, and sees us all on the ground under the jungle gym. "What happened?" she asks.

I look at Natalie, but she's too worried to say anything. Gabe is in too much pain. And obviously Jonathan isn't going to answer. It has to be me.

I don't think anybody but us even knows what happened. That's probably good. "Jonathan and Gabe fell off the jungle gym," I tell her. She doesn't need to know about the whole Demon thing, or the fight. It wouldn't help anything. "Gabe's ankle is injured. Jonathan is breathing but unconscious." I am simply telling her the facts. Somehow it feels easier to do this than I would have expected. It makes me feel more grown up than I ever have before.

She pulls out her walkie-talkie and tells the office that two children are injured and they should call for an ambulance. Uh, yeah, I guess that has to happen now. Then she and a couple of other teachers duck under the bars of the jungle gym to get to Gabe and Jonathan. Some of the other teachers can't, because they would be too big to fit through the bars. The bell rings, so they start telling the crowd of kids that is gathering to get to class.

Natalie and I are shooed away from Gabe and Jonathan. Natalie doesn't want to leave Gabe, but I take her hand and pull her away. I know Gabe is going to be okay, because the adults can take care of him.

So we slip back out through the bars of the jungle gym and go stand next to the swings. "What happened?" I ask her quietly, when I know nobody is listening to us. We keep watching as more people come over. The school nurse is under the bars opening Jonathan's eyelids and shining a light into his eyes. Another teacher is helping Gabe scoot back through the bars so he is out from under the jungle gym.

She stares at everything happening while she talks. "Angel said that he and Guardian and Aaron, and even Lady and Knight, yelled as loud as they could at Demon to stop. So he had to stop yelling at Jonathan." She finally looks away from the jungle gym to look at me. "He said you are the one who stopped Jonathan? How?"

"I grabbed his mind. You remember when I first started trying to talk to Guardian, I was doing it wrong? Angel said it wasn't a nice way to do it. But you were about to fall and Jonathan wasn't stopping. So I had to do it. It worked, but I think it made Jonathan pass out. I'm afraid that I hurt him."

Her eyebrows go up and her forehead wrinkles. "Angel said it isn't a head injury. He doesn't know what's wrong." She looks down at her hands. "There's something else."

"What?"

"Angel says that he can't find Demon."

"What do you mean?"

"Like, apparently Jonathan's guardian isn't here any more. He didn't just stop making Jonathan attack me. He left."

"Why? Because they were all yelling at him?"

"He says they don't know. They've never heard of a guardian leaving their human before, ever. They don't know where he went. They don't know what is happening, with Demon or with Jonathan."

She and I look at each other. I even look into her eyes. We are both feeling the same thing. This isn't only confusing. It's scary. We don't know what is happening, or what will happen next.

What have we done?

Gabe

I'm super worried about Jonathan. They won't let me see him. The nurse and teachers are all crowded around him when the ambulance arrives. It drives right up over the curb onto the playground, and parks next to the jungle gym.

One of the teachers waits with me while the paramedics go take care of Jonathan. Obviously I can wait, even though my ankle feels like it is literally killing me. But why hasn't Jonathan woken up yet? I know he didn't hit his head. I made sure of it. I have no idea how I was able to jump over there in time, but somehow I made it, and he crashed into me, before we both hit the ground. I'm pretty sure he was already passed out when he fell.

The paramedics put a neck brace on Jonathan, and very carefully lift him out of the jungle gym. One of them brings over a stretcher and they load him onto it. He still isn't moving. I am starting to have an anxiety attack about him. "Can I talk to my sister?" I ask the teacher. She was watching Jonathan too. She looks down at me, and sees how worried I am, and she pats me on the shoulder.

"Of course," she tells me, "you wait here." She gets up and walks over to where Natalie and Timothy are waiting, staring at us, their eyes huge. She leads them back over to me. "You'll be okay here with your sister, Gabe, I think? I want to go see if I can help with Jonathan. You stay right here. Don't try to move."

"Yeah, okay," I say, relieved that she's going to leave us alone for a minute. I am dying to hear Natalie explain what's going on.

She knows what I want and starts right away, before I have to ask any questions. She knows we probably only have a minute to talk. Quietly, she says, "Angel and the other guardians all yelled at Demon so loud that he had to stop telling Jonathan what to do. But when Jonathan kept pushing me, Timothy used a method he learned to get into his mind to stop him. I know it sounds weird, but I'll have to explain it later."

I know my mouth is hanging open. "Uh, okay." She can tell that next I want to know what is wrong with Jonathan.

"Angel doesn't know why Jonathan is unconscious. He says you didn't let him hit his head, so it isn't that." I see tears come into her eyes. "Thank you, Gabe. Thank you for catching him. It could have been so much worse if he'd landed on his head. Thank you."

"I don't know how I did it," I confess to her. "It's like I was moving faster than possible. It was very weird."

She gets a thoughtful look on her face. "That might be something Angel can explain later. We'll talk about everything when we all get home. You'll know everything we know, okay?"

I nod. "Yeah, that's good." I still feel grateful she has been including me in everything, although this is some freaky stuff going on. I'd rather know than not know.

The teacher comes back over to me, together with one of the paramedics. In the few seconds we have left before they get here, Natalie leans close to me and whispers, "One other thing. Demon is missing. Angel has no idea why."

I lean back and stare at her. "Well, good," I say. "We got rid of him."

She shakes her head. "It's not that easy. You can't get rid of guardians. This is super weird, and Angel is freaked out by it. He doesn't understand where Demon is, or what's wrong with Jonathan. Something very strange is happening."

Strange? Like this wasn't all totally strange? How can it be even more strange? I stare at her, as the paramedic kneels down next to me. "You hurt your ankle?" he says. "Let me check it out."

Chapter 47

Nurse's Office

Natalie's

The paramedic states that although Gabe will need x-rays to confirm, it appears that his ankle is broken. However, because an unconscious child is a more dire emergency, the ambulance must immediately depart to take Jonathan to the hospital at once. The paramedic believes that Gabe's condition is stable enough to wait for his parents to arrive to take him to urgent care. The school nurse sends an aide back to the office to bring out a wheelchair.

Natalie and Timothy are allowed to remain with Gabe in the nurse's office while they wait for Brenda to arrive. Lady had whispered to Brenda that there is a problem with the children, so she already felt an instinct that she was needed at school even before the call came from the school nurse. She will be arriving shortly.

Gabe has been placed on a cot with his leg elevated, and an ice pack surrounding the broken ankle. There is nothing further that the school nurse is equipped to do for him. Timothy and Natalie sit silently in chairs by his bedside. Natalie is holding Gabe's hand.

The children are surrounded by adults and therefore do not feel free to discuss the situation between themselves. However, Natalie continues to question me silently. I continue to have no satisfactory answers. But I continuously speak, keeping her updated about every piece of information available to me.

"The ambulance carrying Jonathan has gone beyond the distance at which I can detect his presence. He continued to be unconscious up to that point. I fear that I will know nothing else until he is closer once again. And no, I never did begin hearing Demon again."

She returns her gaze to Gabe, who has closed his eyes but is grimacing. His injury is extremely uncomfortable, but he bears it stoically for Natalie's sake. He is more worried about Jonathan than he is about himself. Natalie is terribly worried about them both.

At least I can try to set her mind at ease regarding Gabe. *"Your brother will recover, my dear. His injury is serious, but a broken bone is easily mended by modern physicians. I suspect he will need nothing more than a cast for several weeks."*

"Can you tell what is broken?" she asks, her natural curiosity sparked by my statement.

"Yes, darling, I can see the injury to his bone. It is a bone called the tibia, and there is a small fracture directly above his ankle, caused when he fell and landed unevenly on that foot. It is a common injury which doctors are quite familiar with. He will be well cared for."

She does not wish to disturb Gabe with this information, so she stares at his ankle, wrapped in ice, trying to picture the injury.

I now have more information to impart. *"Your mother is nearly here, dearest. She intends to take Gabe to the urgent care which is next to the hospital emergency room where Jonathan is being taken. This is fortunate, because Lady and Aaron will then be in proximity to Jonathan, and will be able to monitor his situation. We will know more soon."*

Brenda

My heart is pounding, even though I know from what the school nurse said on the phone that Gabe will be fine. She said he fell from the jungle gym and either sprained or broke his ankle. She believes it is probably broken, and suggested I plan to take him straight to urgent care. I want to be practical and calmly take care of business, but my child is hurt, and that is a terrible thing to know. Anxiety fills me.

As soon as I get to the school, I head straight to the office front desk. They immediately usher me to the nurse's office. Natalie is waiting for me at the door.

"Gabe is going to be fine, Mom," she reassures me, taking my hand and looking earnestly up at me. "His ankle is broken but the doctors will be able to fix it right up."

I feel better somehow, despite the fact that she is a seven-year-old, not a doctor. Her assessment seems quite authoritative. "Thank you, sweetie." She leads me over to the cot where he is laying, pale, with his foot elevated.

He smiles gamely at me. "Hey Mom," he says. "Sorry for being a klutz."

Being with my kids helps me calm down. I feel my heart return to a normal rate. "Well, kiddo," I tell him, reaching down to brush my hand against his hair, "I'm sure you'll be fine. We need to go to urgent care and get you checked out."

"Yeah, I know," he says, trying to sit up. Natalie rushes to his side to help him.

"What happened?" I ask them.

They glance at each other. Surprisingly, Timothy, who I had barely noticed sitting there, speaks up. "Jonathan and Gabe were horsing around on the jungle gym, and they both fell off. Jonathan had to get taken to the hospital in an ambulance. He was unconscious, but it wasn't a head injury. They don't know what is wrong with him."

Gabe's jaw tightens with worry at the mention of his friend's injury. "Oh, Gabe," I say, reaching out for his hand. "I'm sure he'll be fine. We'll probably hear something very soon."

It occurs to me to wonder why they were "horsing around" on the jungle gym. Were they actually fighting again? They hadn't seen each other since the library incident. But Gabe is clearly in pain and deeply worried. Now is not the time to ask questions about this.

The nurse brings over the wheelchair. "Here," she says to Gabe, "let's get you in this, and I'll bring you out to the car."

While she is helping him to get settled in the wheelchair, I look over at Natalie. She is as worried as Gabe. "Okay, sweetie, I'm going to take Gabe to the doctor. You should go on back to class. By the time school is over Gabe will be all fixed up and waiting for you at home. Okay?"

"Okay," she agrees, then whispers something in Gabe's ear before the nurse starts wheeling him out. He looks at her and nods.

Chapter 48

Hospital

Stefanie

It's like a nightmare. Like a flashback to the night my Mom died. I'm here in the same waiting room, sitting on the same uncomfortable chairs, clutching Brad's hand, feeling the same panic about a loved one who mysteriously won't wake up. We went back briefly and saw Jonathan and talked to the doctor, before they wheeled him off to get an MRI. He was lying there completely still.

The doctor says there is no apparent physical injury, so they need to get a scan of his head and neck to see if there is something injured inside. They don't have any explanation yet for why he is unconscious.

When the school called to tell me he had fallen at the playground, and that an ambulance was taking him straight to the hospital, I had to call Brad at work. We both got here at the same time. I haven't been able to stop crying the whole time. Tears are still streaming out of my eyes, but at least I'm not sobbing any more. My heart is clenched into a knot. Brad is silent and pale, his jaw rigid with anxiety.

Finally, the nurse calls us back. We hurry to the ER cubicle where Jonathan has been wheeled on his gurney. He is still lying completely motionless. I stand next to him, smoothing his hair back from his forehead.

After another eternity, the doctor comes in. "We've gotten the MRI scan results, and there does not appear to be any brain injury. There is also no visible injury to the spine. We've run some blood work and are waiting for those results. His heart rate and breathing are normal. I'm afraid we have no answer to why he is unconscious."

I start sobbing again. Brad tightens his arms around me.

The doctor continues, "We are going to admit him for observation. At this time there isn't anything to do but monitor him. A nurse is going to come in to set up an i.v. glucose drip so he remains hydrated. We'll have our on-call pediatrician come to examine him as soon as we get him upstairs into a room. An infectious disease specialist will come by too, to ask some questions. Wait here while we get a room assigned."

This is terrifying. I'm glad there isn't a brain or spine injury, but what is happening? Brad and I hold each other and wait.

Brenda's

"Yes, my darling, your children are safe, Gabe's injury is treatable, he will be feeling better soon. You are doing well to take care of the youngsters. Everything will be fine."

As Brenda's car approaches the urgent care facility, I am able to detect Jonathan in the nearby emergency room. He is still unconscious. The doctors have detected no physical explanation for this. There is still, bafflingly, no sign of Demon. Jonathan's soul is quiescent, barely glowing. I report this information to our group. I hear Angel relaying the news to Natalie.

It takes some time to care for Gabe's injury. The x-rays confirm the break to his tibia directly above the ankle, as Angel had described to Natalie. No surgery or other intervention is required, but the ankle must be kept motionless during healing. As Angel predicted, the doctor places a plaster cast on Gabe's lower leg and foot. Pain medication is prescribed to keep Gabe comfortable during the first days of healing. Follow-up appointments are scheduled. The doctor and Brenda discuss whether Gabe will need a walking cast, but because there are only a few more days of school before the winter recess, Brenda decides that Gabe can stay home to heal rather than return to school for the rest of the week.

Brenda keeps Ron constantly updated regarding each development through text messages. She assures him several times that he does not need to leave work, that everything is under control and Gabe is fine.

And I, of course, keep Angel updated, so the Seer will be aware of everything as the situation unfolds.

A nurse brings a pair of crutches to Gabe, and gives him some instructions about how to use them. He is to avoid placing any weight on his foot for now.

Throughout the entire process, while Brenda is focused on Gabe's well-being, Gabe is worried about Jonathan. He is so distracted by this worry that he barely registers the discussion about him taking the rest of the week off of school.

After some three hours have passed, Gabe is discharged to return home. As his mother guides him out the door of the urgent care facility, helping him to navigate the new reality of using crutches to walk, he hesitates.

"Mom?"

"Yes, honey? Are you okay?"

"Um, yeah, but I think Jonathan is at the hospital next door. I'm pretty sure that's where the ambulance was taking him."

"Oh, I see." She waits, to see what it is he wants to do.

He leans on his crutches, looking at the strange sight of his toes poking out of a cast, then looks up at her. "Could we, like, go over there? Try to find out how he is?"

"Are you sure you're okay? Don't you want to go home and lie down?"

"No, Mom, all I can think about is Jonathan. I want to see my friend." Tears well up in his eyes. Compassion for his anguish floods her heart.

"Yes, of course, we can go over. I don't know if we'll be able to find anything out, but we'll try."

Natalie's

Natalie is paying no attention at all to the classroom instruction this morning. She is focused exclusively on the information I am providing her about Gabe and Jonathan. How fortunate that they are being cared for in adjoining facilities, so Lady and Aaron can monitor Jonathan's situation as well. They also constantly scan the area, trying without success to find any sign of Jonathan's Guardian.

There is more to relate regarding Gabe than Jonathan. I provide her with far more detail than I normally would about each aspect of Gabe's treatment, to keep her mind occupied and calm, knowing that tangible steps are being taken to correct Gabe's injury.

Her anxiety for Jonathan is fierce. But there is very little to report. All I can do is repeat the negative test results as they are conducted by the doctors. Jonathan's unconscious state is not caused by any injury or illness which can be detected.

As the morning class concludes and the students are dismissed for lunch, Gabe's treatment is finished. I tell Natalie, *"The doctor has finished Gabe's treatment for today and has discharged him. However, rather than going straight home, your mother has agreed to take Gabe next door to the hospital to inquire about Jonathan's status. They will not learn anything more than you know, but Gabe will feel better."*

As Natalie and Timothy sit at the table outside with their sack lunches, she repeats this information to him.

"Still no sign of Demon?" he asks.

"No," she sighs. "Aaron and Lady keep searching for him, but it's like he has vanished."

He turns all of the information she has repeated to him over in his mind. Demon is missing, and there is no medical explanation for Jonathan's condition. "Doesn't it have to be connected?" he asks. He is looking at Natalie, but his question is meant for me. "It can't be a coincidence that Jonathan is unconscious for no reason right when his guardian goes missing."

The boy must be correct. As he so often has, he penetrates to the heart of the matter. *"I believe Timothy is correct,"* I tell Natalie. *"There is no way to know for sure, but we know that humans must be accompanied by a Guardian. I agree there is some correlation between the two events. Sadly, we still have no concept of where Demon has gone."*

Chapter 49

Wake Up

Gabe's

My beloved struggles with his pain, and the new strange experience of walking with crutches, as he and his mother approach the front entrance of the hospital. Gabe's mother inquires at the front desk after a patient, and gives Jonathan's name. After checking the computer the attendant informs them that Jonathan has been admitted and gives them a room number.

Gabe and his mother look at each other, not sure what to do next with this information. The attendant says, "The elevators are right over there," indicating the correct direction.

"Okay, thanks," Gabe says, taking control and swinging with his crutches towards the elevators.

Brenda cautions him in the elevator, "Honey, I don't know if we're going to see him. He might not be allowed to have visitors."

"Whatever," Gabe says. "Even if I don't get to see him I have to know how he is."

When they exit the elevator on the correct floor, they look around to orient themselves and locate the correct room number. As they approach, they see Jonathan's father exit the room. He walks along the corridor towards them, but doesn't see them until they are right next to him and Gabe blurts out, "How's Jonathan?"

Brad looks up. "Oh! Hi," he says. He looks haggard with worry and exhaustion.

Brenda says, "Sorry to disturb you, but we were over at the urgent care and Gabe really wanted to come and check on Jonathan."

Brad looks at Gabe and registers the crutches and cast for the first time. "Oh, yeah, they said you had fallen too. You okay?"

"I'm fine," Gabe says somewhat impatiently. "How is Jonathan?"

Brad scratches his chin, and rubs his hand across his head. "Um, they don't know. He won't wake up. They don't know why. All the test results are negative."

Gabe's chin quivers. "Can... can I see him? Just for a minute? Please?"

"Um, yeah, I guess. Wait a sec, okay, while I check with Stefanie."

"My darling, your friend is being treated by the doctors as best they can. You will see, he has no injury. Be calm, my dear, you will see him soon," I whisper to my dearest boy.

Brad goes back into the room and quietly tells Stefanie that Jonathan's friend is here to visit. Stefanie nods, wipes her eyes, and stands up from her son's bedside.

Brad goes back to the door and beckons to Brenda and Gabe. They enter, somewhat apprehensively, not knowing what they are going to see.

Gabe goes at once to Jonathan. He is lying utterly still, wearing a hospital gown, tucked under a blanket. His face is peaceful, but somehow empty. There is an i.v. attached to the back of his hand, but otherwise there are no medical interventions apparent.

His Guardian is nowhere to be seen.

Gabe's face wrinkles with distress. He leans on his crutches and touches the back of Jonathan's hand, the one without the i.v. needle. He stands silent vigil by his side.

Natalie's

"My dear, Gabe has arrived in Jonathan's room and is visiting at his bedside. Jonathan is completely still. Gabe is very distressed to see his friend in this state, but is relieved to at least know what is happening.

The children have finished their lunch, and are sitting side by side waiting the few more minutes until the bell rings signaling the end of their lunch period. Natalie had no appetite and barely ate a bite of her food.

She relays the information to Timothy. Timothy wishes to know more about the situation in Jonathan's hospital room. I oblige, wishing to bring comfort to the children in any way I can. *"Jonathan's parents are also present in the room. They are quietly talking to Natalie's mother, telling her what the doctors have told them. Gabe is standing quietly next to Jonathan's bed. Gabe is leaning on his crutches, and touching Jonathan's hand. Jonathan has not moved."*

Timothy's expression shifts, to the intensely focused one which I have often observed when he is formulating an experiment. Natalie senses this as well, and eagerly waits to see what he will say.

"I want to do an experiment," Timothy says. "Aaron and Lady will need to help."

I relay this information to Gabe and Brenda's Guardians.

"Yes, Timothy, they are willing to assist in any way you request."

"Our hypothesis is that what is wrong with Jonathan is his guardian is missing, right?"

Natalie nods.

"Well, there are some other guardians there. I know it isn't his guardian, and they aren't sharing his soul, but maybe if the other guardians try to talk to Jonathan, it will help him? Like, can you ask Aaron and Lady to say something to Jonathan? See if anything happens?"

Guardians never speak to humans who are not their own. There would be no cause to do so. Only our own humans, the ones who hold our souls, receive our communications. The presence of our Seer has created the only known exceptions to this rule, as her desire to engage in dialogue has caused all of the Guardians in our family to converse with each other and even with other humans.

I cannot imagine this experiment succeeding, but unquestionably we will always oblige Timothy's wishes.

"Of course, Timothy." I relay Timothy's request to the other Guardians, and wait for their report.

"They both did as you asked, Timothy, and whispered words of encouragement and healing to Jonathan. It had no apparent effect. He remains still."

"Okay, next step of the experiment. Please ask them to use energy to talk to him. Just a tiny bit, a little more than they normally use when talking to their humans."

This piques my interest. We have been guided by this child before into important discoveries. Will this lead to more?

"*Very well, Timothy. Aaron and Lady have begun to whisper to Jonathan, again words of encouragement and healing, but they have elevated their use of energy in speaking to him.*"

"Have them use a little more if that doesn't work."

"*Very well. They will increase their efforts.*"

Gabe

I've been standing here with Jonathan for a few minutes. Our parents are all talking quietly on the other side of the room, leaving us alone. I'm glad about that. I just want to be with him. I'm telling him silently how sorry I am he got hurt, and how much I want him to wake up.

Suddenly, his hand moves underneath mine. "Jonathan?" I ask. The adults look over, but seeing he is still laying there, they go back to their conversation.

But I can tell something is happening. I don't know how, but I feel it. I grab his hand, and start squeezing it tighter. I feel an energy in the air. I don't know how the adults aren't noticing anything, but that's fine, I don't really want them to.

I lean down closer to Jonathan, squeezing his hand. Come on, come on, I think to him. You can wake up.

And he does. His eyes open. He looks right at me.

Brenda's

Gabe's Guardian and I have incrementally increased our use of energy in whispering to Jonathan, as directed by Timothy. "*Sweet child, come back to us, dear, you can reawaken if you choose. Nothing is preventing you.*"

Gabe, newly aware of the presence of his Guardian, and having been touched by the energy being blasted by all of us earlier at the playground, starts to have a vague sense of our efforts. It is not nearly as pronounced as Timothy's ability to sense Guardian, but Gabe begins to feel the energy flowing towards his friend.

Gabe adds his efforts, silently exhorting his friend to awaken.

Aaron and I increase our attempt again, delicately adding to our use of energy. This time, the profound silence within Jonathan's mind is pierced, and he first shifts slightly, then opens his eyes.

Gabe gasps, and the parents look up from their conversation. "Jonathan?" his mother exclaims, rushing to the bed. His father ducks into the hallway to summon a nurse.

Jonathan is gazing directly into Gabe's eyes. Gabe asks him, "Jon? Are you okay?"

It takes a moment for Jonathan to respond. His mind is clouded, fuzzy. His soul, normally so vibrant, barely glimmers. "Hey," he says to Gabe, finding it more difficult than normal to use his vocal chords. The word comes out in a whisper.

I immediately report the success of Timothy's experiment to Angel. Natalie is overjoyed at the news.

As the room fills with medical personnel, Brenda pulls Gabe aside. She whispers to Brad, "We're gonna get going. Please call and let us know how Jonathan is doing later." He nods, hands to his mouth and staring at his son, overwhelmed with emotion.

Natalie's

The report from Lady is both joyous and puzzling. As Jonathan awakens, he is able to speak, and respond to the questions of the doctors. He has no apparent physical or mental symptoms resulting from his period of unconsciousness.

However, the Guardians can sense that his mind seems very different from before. To the doctors he appears weak, and they suggest to his parents that he simply needs more time to recover. But it is not his body which is weak. It is his soul. His spirit. He regards the room, and the people within it, with an uncharacteristic passivity. The spark within, the dominant personality, the eagerness to experience life, all have dwindled. Jonathan is there, but it is as though he is only a shadow of himself. He is awake, but detached. He seems empty.

Timothy's hypothesis must be correct. It is the absence of his Guardian which is causing Jonathan's condition. The efforts of Lady and Aaron were able to awaken him, but not restore him. Clearly, Jonathan needs Demon to return. He is not himself without his Guardian.

However, Demon continues to be utterly absent. The other Guardians and I continue searching, stretching our perception to our extreme limits, to no avail. Although Jonathan's soul is still present, and therefore his Guardian must be somewhere, he is nowhere that we can discover.

Chapter 50

Energy

Gabe

Mom has me all set up on the couch, with my leg up on a pillow, a tray of food next to me, the t.v. remote in my hand, and my crutches leaning nearby. I can finally relax, now that I know Jonathan is awake. I have to wait for Natalie to get home so I can talk to her about everything. I still don't understand anything that happened.

The door opens, and Natalie runs in, followed by Timothy and his Mom. My Mom comes around the corner from the kitchen, and Timothy's Mom goes in there with her to talk.

Natalie and Timothy sit on the floor right next to the couch. "How's your ankle?" she asks.

"Fine," I tell her, impatient to get to the important stuff. "They gave me some pain medicine, I don't even feel it right now. Do you know that Jonathan is awake?"

"Yes," she says, and huffs with relief. "Angel told me everything." She has lowered her voice to barely above a whisper, worried the adults might overhear. But they are talking about everything in the kitchen, I don't think they're paying any attention to us.

"Good," I say, "now you can tell me what's really going on. I was there but I don't think I saw what was actually happening."

"Angel says you are very perceptive. There was more going on. When you got to the hospital, we were at lunch, so we were able to talk to Angel about what was happening. We think Timothy is the one who figured out what was wrong with Jonathan."

"What was it?" I ask. I'd be surprised, but I'm starting to realize that Timothy knows a lot more than I've ever given him credit for.

Timothy says, also very quietly, "I hypothesized that the problem was that Demon is missing. Since every human has a guardian watching over their soul, I thought Jonathan might be unconscious because his wasn't there. So I asked Angel to have your guardian, and your Mom's, talk straight to Jonathan. I thought any guardian would be better than no guardian. It didn't work at first, but when I asked them to use more and more energy to talk to him, it finally woke him up."

"What energy?" I ask.

Natalie says, "We haven't really told you all the details about everything yet. We were focused on getting ready to talk to Jonathan, so we didn't really explain it all. But the guardians didn't ever used to talk to each other. I got them to start doing it, then Timothy asked them to try to talk louder so they could hear each other farther apart than normal. They had to use more energy to do that."

I'm not sure I'm following, but I say, "Um, all right."

She goes on, "That ended up being the whole problem with Jonathan. Demon heard the other guardians using energy to talk to each other, and he started doing it with Jonathan, and that's how he learned how to control Jonathan. The more energy he used the less control Jonathan had over what he was doing."

I think I'm catching on to what she is saying.

"So when all the guardians yelled at Demon today, that's what they were doing. Using all the energy they could. Something about it made Demon go away." She looks over to the side, and I'm starting to realize it means she is listening to Angel.

"But then it helped Jonathan at the hospital?" I ask.

"Yes," Timothy says. "The use of energy was bad when Demon did it, but all the other times it's been good. It's the way I have started being able to hear Guardian. So when they used energy to talk to Jonathan, he was able to wake up. Not too much like Demon was doing, since they didn't want to hurt him. They found the right amount."

I remember something Natalie said earlier, before we went to the office. "Timothy, what did you do on the playground? Natalie said you did something else to make Jonathan stop pushing her?"

Timothy nods seriously. "Yes. When I am listening to Guardian, I do it by making my mind quiet and open. But the first time I tried, I did it by trying to reach out and grab him with my mind. It gave me a headache, and Angel said I shouldn't do it that way again. I guess sometimes bad people do it to hurt others. I said I wasn't going to do it any more, but I did it today to Jonathan. That's when he fainted." His forehead wrinkles, and he suddenly seems more emotional than he usually is. "I'm afraid what I did hurt him.

Natalie shakes her head. "No, Timothy, Angel says he doesn't think that's what it was. He says he thinks Jonathan was already hurt by what Demon was doing, and what you did just made Jonathan stop feeling so angry. The problem is that Demon is missing, not what you did. You actually saved me. Then Gabe saved Jonathan from getting hurt when he fell."

We are all quiet for a minute, thinking about the way everything turned out. Our Moms are still in the kitchen, talking. I hear my Mom describing what happened at the hospital today with Jonathan.

I remember something else. "Did you say before that Angel might be able to explain why I was able to catch Jonathan? I really still don't know how it worked. I didn't think there was any way I would get there in time, but then somehow I did."

She looks to the side again. "Angel says because so much energy was flowing, while all five guardians were yelling at Demon, some of that energy must have given you some extra ability. He doesn't understand it either, but he figures the energy gave you whatever you needed to do it."

Timothy looks at the ceiling, obviously thinking. "There's still a lot we don't understand, isn't there? I think I need to take some notes about all of this.

Natalie smiles. "I'll go get a notebook."

Chapter 51

Where Is Demon?

Natalie's

The school week has ended, and the family has returned to Ron's house. Gabe and Jonathan each spent the week at home, convalescing.

Jonathan was in the hospital for one night for observation, but the doctor discharged him in the morning when there was no evidence of any physical impairment. They advised his parents that the incident would be labeled "idiopathic", simply meaning unexplained. They scheduled a series of follow-up appointments, but otherwise had no additional treatment suggestions.

Gabe impatiently endured his exile to the couch. The first two nights he slept downstairs, but then insisted that with his crutches he could easily make it to his room. Now, with several days of practice, he is swinging around, proficient in the use of the crutches, almost reveling in the feeling of walking with them. He has spent the last two afternoons with the boys in the neighborhood, regaling them with tales of his adventures, although leaving out any mention of guardians. He will continue to keep Natalie's secret.

As soon as we arrive at Ron's house, Gabe says, "I want to go see Jonathan."

"Me, too," Natalie immediately adds.

"Okay," their mother tells them. "I'll walk down there with you, I want to see how everyone is doing."

"Me, too," Ron copies Natalie with a grin.

The four of them walk to Jonathan's house, surprisingly not needing to walk slower than usual to match Gabe's pace. He has become quite skilled with the crutches.

Brad answers the door. "Hey," he says with a smile, "come on in."

The adults gather in the living room, and converse about the drama which unfolded earlier in the week. They are all relieved to be past the worst of it, and pleased that both boys are clearly recovering from their ordeal. I hear Jonathan's parents relate that their son is fine now, but he has been very quiet since returning from the hospital. They do not feel any particular sense of alarm about this.

The children join Jonathan, who is in the back yard with his dog. The dog's ears perk up as he hears them arrive, and he leaps up and runs to Natalie the moment he sees her, panting and frantically wagging his tail.

She smiles joyfully at the little creature and drops to her knees to embrace him. "Hi Socks! How are you?"

Gabe approaches Jonathan, who is sitting on the ground where he had been holding the dog. Jonathan watches him come near, but makes no other move. Gabe knows he could not rise easily from the ground if he were to sit there, so he stands before Jonathan, leaning on his crutches. "How are you Jon? I saw you in the hospital. Do you remember?"

"Yes," Jonathan says, quietly. Then makes no further remark.

"Are you okay now?" Gabe tries again.

"Yes," Jonathan repeats.

Natalie looks up at Jonathan quizzically. Rather than questioning Jonathan directly, she silently asks me, "Is he okay?"

"*I can not tell, my darling. Physically he is healthy, even mentally he seems normal. But as you see, he is far more quiet and passive than ever before. I do not know whether this will remain the case.*"

"He's missing Demon, isn't he?" she thinks to me.

"*Yes, clearly that is so, even though he does not know it. His excitement in life, his spark, so to speak, appear to be missing.*"

She frowns and regards Jonathan, absently petting the dog in her lap. She begins to contemplate whether there is anything she can do to help him. She feels guilty about the situation. She knows it has been decisions made by her which led to this outcome. She and Timothy created the experiment which invented the method of using energy, which was then commandeered by

Demon, leading to Jonathan's downfall. She always is motivated by the desire to help others, but she feels she has instead harmed Jonathan.

"My dearest, it was not you who caused this. The situation unfolded as it did without any ill intent on your part. Do not let this discourage you from your curiosity, and from your efforts to learn."

Gabe continues his efforts to talk with Jonathan, but is met with only more brief answers. He begins to feel frustrated.

Jonathan's demeanor is distant, meek, and disengaged. His soul is so quiet and dim, it resembles that of a newborn baby, a tiny burning ember, new to existence, barely beginning to form. It bears little resemblance to the blazing monolith which his soul had become under Demon's influence.

The child has profoundly changed. I would find it to be an improvement, as he appears to pose no threat to my beloved in this condition, except that it also seems tragic. Without even knowing it, he is lost.

As is his Guardian. Jonathan needs him. He is incomplete without him.

I continue to search fruitlessly for any sign of his Guardian. I and the other Guardians in our family have begun using additional energy not exclusively to communicate with each other, but to also expand our area of perception, to broaden our horizons. But there is no trace. It is unfathomable. We are all baffled. We all share the same question.

Where is Demon?

www.ingramcontent.com/pod-product-compliance
Lightning Source LLC
Chambersburg PA
CBHW021040310726

48969CB00006B/1744